THE WOLVES OF MIDWINTER

Anne Rice is the author of over thirty internationally best-selling books including The Vampire Chronicles (from *Interview with the Vampire* to *Blood Canticle*), the Mayfair Witches sequence, The Songs of the Seraphim and now The Wolf Gift Chronicles, the first of which was *The Wolf Gift*. She lives in Palm Desert, California.

Interview with the Vampire
The Feast of All Saints
Cry to Heaven
The Vampire Lestat
The Queen of the Damned
The Mummy
The Witching Hour
The Tale of the Body Thief
Lasher
Taltos
Memnoch the Devil
Servant of the Bones
Violin
Pandora
The Vampire Armand
Vittorio, The Vampire
Merrick
Blood and Gold
Blackwood Farm
Blood Canticle
Christ the Lord: Out of Egypt
Christ the Lord: Road to Cana
Called Out of Darkness
Angel Time
Of Love and Evil
The Wolf Gift

THE WOLVES OF MIDWINTER

The Wolf Gift Chronicles

ANNE RICE

Chatto & Windus

LONDON

Published by Chatto & Windus 2013

First published in the United States by Alfred A. Knopf in 2013

2 4 6 8 10 9 7 5 3 1

Copyright © Anne O'Brien Rice 2013

Anne O'Brien Rice has asserted her right under the Copyright, Designs
and Patents Act 1988 to be identified as the author of this work

First published in Great Britain in 2013 by
Chatto & Windus

Random House, 20 Vauxhall Bridge Road,
London SW1V 2SA
www.rbooks.co.uk

Addresses for companies within The Random House Group Limited can be found at:
www.randomhouse.co.uk/offices.htm

The Random House Group Limited Reg. No. 954009

A CIP catalogue record for this book
is available from the British Library

Hardback ISBN 9780701188252
Trade Paperback ISBN 9780701188269

The Random House Group Limited supports the Forest Stewardship Council® (FSC®), the leading
international forest-certification organisation. Our books carrying the FSC label are printed on FSC®-
certified paper. FSC is the only forest-certification scheme supported by the leading environmental
organisations, including Greenpeace. Our paper procurement policy can be found at:
www.randomhouse.co.uk/environment

MIX
Paper from
responsible sources
FSC® C016897

Printed and bound by CPI Group (UK) Ltd, Croydon, CR0 4YY

Dedicated

to

Victoria Wilson

Nancy Rice Diamond

Millie Ball

and

Father Joseph Cocucci

What can I give Him,
Poor as I am?
If I were a shepherd
I would bring a lamb,
If I were a wise man
I would do my part,
Yet what I can I give Him,
Give my heart.

—From "In the Bleak Mid-Winter,"
  by Christina Rossetti (1872)

The Story So Far

Reuben Golding, a young San Francisco reporter, finds his life changed forever by a visit to Nideck Point, an enormous mansion on the Mendocino coast, where he is bitten by a mysterious animal after the murder of the beautiful owner, Marchent Nideck. Reuben, grieving for Marchent, soon discovers he has inherited the house and also he has become a form of werewolf.

Fully conscious in his lupine form, Reuben is drawn to protect innocent victims of violence against evil attackers. Soon hunted by the police far and wide as the California Man Wolf—a popular superhero—he finds love with Laura, a woman who accepts him in wolfen form. They make their home at Nideck Point where an old portrait of "distinguished gentlemen" on the library wall seems somehow connected to the Wolf Gift that Reuben has been given.

Sinister scientists appear who seek to gain control over Reuben, pressing Reuben's suspicious parents, Dr. Grace Golding and her husband, poet and professor Phil Golding, with urgent claims of concern for their "disturbed" son. Reuben's brother, Father Jim Golding, having learned Reuben's secret in the Confessional from Reuben, is powerless to do anything about what he knows.

Meanwhile Reuben, the inexperienced superhero, blunders in bringing yet another innocent into his realm when he accidentally bites Stuart McIntyre, the teen victim of a murderous gay bashing.

Reuben and Stuart are soon cornered at Nideck Point by the scientists who would take them prisoner, only to have the plot foiled by the surprise appearance of another Man Wolf before astonished law officers, paramedics, family members, and the newly arrived "distinguished gentlemen" from the library portrait.

The Story So Far

Nideck Point becomes the haven of Reuben, Stuart, Laura, and the Distinguished Gentlemen, with elders Felix and Margon offering answers to all Reuben's questions about his new nature, the defeated scientists, and the origin of the ancient tribe of Morphenkinder to which Reuben and Stuart now belong.

The Wolves of
Midwinter

I

IT WAS THE BEGINNING of December, deeply cold and gray, with the rain pounding as always, but the oak fires had never burned brighter in the vast rooms of Nideck Point.* The distinguished gentlemen, who had now become in Reuben's argot the "Distinguished Gentlemen," were already talking of Yuletide, of old and venerable traditions, of recipes for mead, and food for a banquet, and ordering fresh green garland by the mile to adorn the doorways, the mantelpieces, and the stairway railings of the old house.

It would be a Christmas like no other for Reuben, spending it here in this house with Felix Nideck, Margon, and Stuart, and all those he loved. These people were his new family. This was the secretive yet cheerful and embracing world of the Morphenkinder to which Reuben belonged now, more surely than to the world of his human family.

A charming Swiss housekeeper, Lisa by name, had joined the household only a couple of days ago. A stately woman with a slight German accent, and a very well-bred manner, she had already become the mistress of Nideck Point, seeing to countless little details that gave everyone more comfort. She actually wore a uniform of sorts, consisting of soft flowing dresses in black silk or wool that fell well below the knee, and wore her blond hair in what used to be called a French twist, and smiled effortlessly.

The others, Heddy, the English maid, and Jean Pierre, Margon's valet, had apparently been expecting her and they deferred to her, the three of them often whispering together almost furtively in German as they went about their work.

* The name Nideck is pronounced with a long *i* to sound like "Nigh-deck" or "Neideck."

Each afternoon, Lisa turned on the "Three O'Clock Lights," as she called them, saying it was Herr Felix's wish that they never be forgotten, and so the main rooms were always cheerful as the winter darkness closed in, and she saw to the fires that had become indispensable for Reuben's peace of mind.

Back in San Francisco, the little gas fires of Reuben's home had been pleasant, yes, a luxury certainly and often entirely neglected. But here the great blazing hearths were a part of life, and Reuben depended on them, on their warmth, on their fragrance, on their eerie and flickering brilliance, as if this were not a house at all, Nideck Point, but the heart of a great forest that was the world with its eternally encroaching darkness.

Jean Pierre and Heddy had become more confident since Lisa's arrival in offering Reuben and Stuart every comfort imaginable, and bringing coffee or tea unbidden and slipping into rooms to make beds the instant that the groggy sleepers had left them.

This was home, taking shape ever more completely around Reuben, including its mysteries.

And Reuben really didn't want to answer the frequent phone messages from San Francisco, from his mother and father, or from his old girlfriend, Celeste, who had in the last few days been calling him regularly.

The mere sound of her voice, calling him Sunshine Boy, set him on edge. His mother would call him Baby Boy or Little Boy once in a while. He could handle this. But Celeste now used her old title of Sunshine Boy exclusively for him whenever she talked to him. Every message was to Sunshine Boy, and she had a way of saying it that struck him as increasingly sarcastic or demeaning.

Last time they'd spoken face-to-face, right after Thanksgiving, she had laid into him as usual, for dropping his old life and moving to this remote corner of Mendocino County, where apparently he could "do nothing," and "become nothing" and live on his looks and the "flattery of all these new friends of yours."

"I'm not doing nothing," he'd protested mildly, to which she'd said, "Even Sunshine Boys have to make something of themselves."

Of course there was no way under heaven that he could ever tell Celeste what had really happened to his world, and though he told himself she had the best of intentions for her endless and carping concerns, he sometimes wondered how that was possible. Why had he ever loved Celeste, or thought that he loved her? And more significantly, perhaps, why had she ever loved him? It seemed impossible they'd been engaged for a year before his life was turned upside down, and he wished for nothing more right now than that she would leave him alone, forget him, enjoy her new relationship with his best friend Mort, and make poor Mort her "work in progress." Mort loved Celeste, and Celeste did seem to love him. So why wasn't all this over?

He was missing Laura painfully, Laura, with whom he'd shared everything, and since she'd left Nideck Point to go back home, to think over her crucial decision, he had had no word from her.

On impulse he drove south to seek her out at her home on the edge of Muir Woods.

All the way, he meditated on the many things that had been happening. He wanted to listen to music, to daydream, to enjoy the drive, rain or no rain, but matters closed in on him though not unhappily.

It was afternoon and the sky was leaden and gleaming and the rain never let up. But he was used to this now and had come to see it as part of the winter charm of his new existence.

He'd spent the morning in the town of Nideck with Felix, as Felix made arrangements to have the entire main street decorated for Christmas with greenery and lights. Every tree would be wrapped and twinkling, and Felix would finance the lighting and trimming of every storefront, as long as the owners went along with it, which they very cheerfully did. He wrote a check to the innkeeper for special decorations in the main room, and conferred with a number of residents eager to decorate their houses as well.

More merchants had been found for the old empty stores on the main street—a dealer in special soaps and shampoos, a vintage-clothing merchant, and a specialist in laces, both antique and modern. Felix had bought the one and only old motion-picture theater, and was having it renovated but for what he was not certain.

Reuben had to smile at all of this ultra-gentrification. But Felix had not neglected more practical aspects of Nideck. He'd been in contact with two retired contractors who wanted to open a variety hardware store and fix-it shop, and several people were interested in the idea of a café and newsstand. Nideck had some 300 people, and 142 households. It couldn't support the businesses that were coming in, but Felix could, and would until the place became a quaint and charming and popular destination. He had already sold off four lots to people who would be building appropriately designed homes within walking distance of downtown.

The elderly mayor, Johnny Cronin, was in ecstasy. Felix had offered him some sort of financial grant to quit his "miserable job" sixty miles away in an insurance office.

It was agreed there would be a Sunday Christmas festival soon to which handicraft people of all sorts would be invited, ads would be taken in the various local papers, and Felix and the mayor were still talking over a late lunch in the main dining room of the Inn when Reuben decided he had to break away.

Even if Laura was not ready to discuss her decision one way or the other, he had to see her, had to steal whatever embrace he could from her. Hell, if she wasn't home, he would be happy just to sit in her little living room for a while, or maybe stretch out and nap on her bed.

Maybe it wasn't fair to her for him to do this, but maybe again it was. He loved her, loved her more than he had ever loved any girlfriend or lover before her. He couldn't stand being without her, and maybe he ought to say so. Why shouldn't he say so? What could he lose? He wouldn't make or break her decision for her by what he did. And he had to stop being fearful as to what he would think or feel about whatever she chose to do.

It was just getting dark when he pulled into her drive.

Another urgent message came in on his iPhone from Celeste. He ignored it.

The little steep-roofed house in the woods was warmly lighted against the great dark gulf of the forest, and he could smell the oak fire. It struck him suddenly that he should have brought a little gift with him, flowers perhaps, or even maybe . . . a ring. He hadn't thought of this before, and he was suddenly crushed.

And what if she had company, a man of whom he knew nothing? What if she didn't come to the door?

Well, she did come to the door. She opened it for him.

And the moment he set eyes on her he wanted to make love to her, and nothing else. She was in faded jeans and an old gray sweater that made her eyes look all the more smoky and dark, and she wore no makeup, looking quietly splendid, with her hair free on her shoulders.

"Come here to me, you monster," she said at once, in a low teasing voice, hugging him tightly, kissing him all over his face and neck. "Look at this dark hair, hmmm, and these blue eyes. I was beginning to think I dreamed every minute of you."

He held her so tightly he must have been hurting her. He wanted a moment of nothing but holding her.

She drew him towards the back bedroom. She was rosy-cheeked and radiant, her hair beautifully mussed and fuller than he'd remembered, certainly more blond than he'd remembered, full of sunlight, it seemed to him, and her expression struck him as sly and deliciously intimate.

There was a comforting blaze in the black-iron Franklin stove. And a couple of little glass-shade lamps lighted on either side of the oak bed with its soft lumpy faded quilts and lace-trimmed pillows.

She pulled the covers down and helped him take off his shirt and jacket and pants. The air was warm and dry and sweet, as it always was in her house, her little lair.

He was weak with relief, but that lasted only a few seconds, and then he was kissing her as if they'd never been separated. Not too fast, not too fast, he kept telling himself, but it didn't do any good. This was hotter, all this, more exuberant and divinely rough.

They lay together after, dozing, as the rain trickled down the panes. He woke with a start, and turned to see her with her eyes open looking at the ceiling. The only light came from the kitchen. And food was cooking there. He could smell it. Roast chicken and red wine. He knew that fragrance well enough and he was suddenly too hungry to think of anything else.

They had dinner together at the round oak table, Reuben in a terry-cloth robe she'd found for him, and Laura in one of those lovely white flannel gowns she so loved. This one was trimmed with a bit of blue embroidery and blue ribbon on the collar and cuffs and placket, and it had blue buttons, a flattering complement to her dazzled, confidential smile, and her glowing skin.

They said nothing as they ate the meal, Reuben devouring everything as always, and Laura to his surprise actually eating her food rather than pushing it around on her plate.

A stillness fell over them when they'd finished. The fire was snapping and rustling in the living room fireplace. And the whole little house seemed safe and strong against the rain that hammered on the roof and the panes. What had it been like to grow up under this roof? He couldn't imagine. Morphenkind or not, he realized, the great woods still represented for him a wilderness.

This was something he loved, that they did not make small talk, that they could go hours without talking, that they talked without talking, but what were they saying to one another, without words, just now?

She sat motionless in the oak chair with only her left hand on the table, her right hand in her lap. It seemed she'd been watching him as he cleaned the plate, and he sensed it now and sensed something particularly enticing about her, about the fullness of her lips and the mass of her hair that framed her face.

Then it came over him, came over him like a chill stealing over his face and neck. Why in the world hadn't he realized immediately.

"You've done it," he whispered. "You've taken the Chrism."

She didn't answer. It was as if he hadn't spoken at all.

Her eyes were darker, yes, and her hair was fuller, much fuller, and even her grayish-blond eyebrows had darkened, so that she looked like a sister of herself, almost identical yet wholly different, with even a darker glow to her cheeks.

Dear God, he whispered without words. And then his heart began tripping and he felt he was going to be sick. This is how he'd looked to others in those days before the transformation had come on him, when those around him knew something had "happened" to him and he'd felt so completely remote, and without fear.

Was she that remote from him now, as he'd been from all his family? No, that couldn't be. This was Laura, Laura who'd just welcomed him, Laura who'd just taken him into her bed. He blushed. Why had he not known?

Nothing changed in her expression, nothing at all. That's how it had been with him. He'd stared like that, knowing others wanted something from him, but unable to give it. But then, in his arms, she'd been soft and melting as always, giving, trusting, close.

"Felix didn't tell you?" she asked. Even her voice seemed different, now that he knew. Just a richer timbre to it, and he could have sworn that the bones of her face were slightly larger, but that might have been his fear.

He couldn't get the words out. He didn't know what the words were. A flash of the heat of their lovemaking came back to him, and he felt an immediate arousal. He wanted her again, and yet he felt, what, sick? Was he sick with fear? He hated himself.

"How do you feel?" he managed. "Are you feeling bad at all, I mean are there any bad side effects?"

"I was a little sick in the beginning," she said.

"And you were alone and no one—?"

"Thibault's been here every night," she said. "Sometimes Sergei. Sometimes Felix."

"Those devils," he whispered.

"Reuben, don't," she said in the most simple and sincere way. "You mustn't for a moment think that anything bad has happened. You mustn't."

"I know," he murmured. He felt a throbbing in his face and in his hands. Of all places, his hands. The blood was rushing in his veins. "But were you ever in any kind of danger?"

"No, none," she said. "That simply doesn't happen. They explained all that. Not when the Chrism's passed and there are no real injuries to the person. Those who die, die when their injuries can't be overtaken by the Chrism."

"I figured as much," he said. "But we don't have a rule book to consult when we begin to worry, do we?"

She didn't answer.

"When did you decide?"

"I decided almost immediately," she said. "I couldn't resist it. It was pointless to tell myself I was pondering it, giving it the consideration it deserved." Her voice grew warmer and so did her expression. This was Laura, his Laura. "I wanted it, and I told Felix and I told Thibault."

He studied her, ignoring the impulse to take her to the bed again. Her skin looked moist, youthful, and though she'd never looked old, she'd been powerfully enhanced, there was no doubt of it. He could hardly bear to look at her lips and not kiss them.

"I went to the cemetery," she said. "I talked to my father." She looked off, obviously not finding this easy. "Well, talked as if I could talk to my father," she said. "They're all buried there, you know, my sister, my mother, my father. I talked to them. Talked to them about all of it. But I'd made the decision before I ever left Nideck Point. I knew I was going to do it."

"All this time, I was figuring you'd refuse, you'd say no."

"Why?" she asked gently. "Why would you think such a thing?"

"I don't know," he said. "Because you had lost so much and you might want so much more. Because you'd lost children, and you might want a child again, not a Morphenkind child, whatever that would be, but a child. Or because you believed in life, and thought life itself is worth what we give up for it."

"It is worth dying for?" she asked.

He didn't answer.

"You speak like you have regrets," she said. "But I guess that's bound to happen."

"I don't have regrets," he said. "I don't know what I feel, but I could imagine your saying no. I could imagine your wanting another chance at a family, a husband, a lover, and children."

"Reuben, what you have never grasped . . . what you seem absolutely unable to grasp . . . is that this means we don't die." She said it without drama, but it was cutting to him and he knew it was true.

"All my family have died," she said, her voice low and a little scolding. "All my family! My father, my mother, yes, in due course; but my sister, murdered in a liquor store robbery, and my children gone, dead, taken in the most cruel ways. Oh, I've never spoken of these things to you before, really; I shouldn't now. I hate when people tout their suffering and their losses." Her face hardened suddenly. Then a faraway look took hold of her as if she'd been drawn back into the worst pain.

"I know what you're saying," he said. "I don't know about death. Not anything. Until the night Marchent was killed, I only knew one person ever that had died, Celeste's brother. Oh, my grandparents, yes, they're dead, but they were so old. And then Marchent. I knew Marchent for less than twenty-four hours, and it was such a shock. I was numb. It wasn't death, it was catastrophe."

"Don't be in a hurry to know all about it," she said, a little defeated.

"Shouldn't I?" He thought of the people whose lives he'd taken, the bad guys the Man Wolf had ripped right out of life, thoughtlessly. And it came down on him hard that very soon Laura too would have that brute power, to kill as he'd killed, while she herself would be invulnerable.

There were no words now for him.

Images were crowding his mind, filling him with an ominous sadness, and a near despair. He pictured her in a country cemetery talking with the dead. He thought of those pictures of her children that he'd glimpsed. He thought of his family, always there, and then he thought of his own power, of that limitless strength he enjoyed as he mounted the rooftops, as the voices summoned him out of humanity and into the single-minded Man Wolf who would kill without regret or compassion.

"But you haven't fully changed yet, have you? Not yet?"

"No, not yet," she said. "Only the small changes so far," she said. She looked off without moving her head. "I can hear the forest," she said with a faint smile. "I can hear the rain in ways I never heard it before. I know things. I knew when you were approaching. I look at the flowers, and I swear I can see them grow, see them blossoming, see them dying."

He didn't speak. It was beautiful what she was saying and yet it was frightening him. Even the soft secretive look on her face frightened him. She was staring off. "There's a Norse god, isn't there, Reuben, who can hear the grass grow?"

"Heimdall," he said. "The keeper of the gate. He can hear the grass grow and see for a hundred leagues in the day or in the night."

She laughed. "Yes. I see the stars themselves through the fog, through the cloud cover; I see the sky no one else can see from this magical forest."

He should have said, *Just wait, just wait until the full change comes on you,* but his voice had died in him.

"I hear the deer in the forest," she said. "I can hear them now. I can almost . . . pick up the scent. It's faint. I don't want to imagine things."

"They're there. Two, out there, just beyond the clearing," he said.

She was watching him again, watching him in that impassive fashion, and he couldn't bear to look her in the eyes. He thought about the deer, such tender, exquisite creatures, but if he didn't stop thinking about them, he would want to kill both of them and devour them. How would she feel when that happened to her, when all she could think of was sinking her fangs into the neck of the deer and tearing out its heart while the heart was still beating?

He was aware that she was moving, coming around the table towards him. The soft clean scent of her skin caught him by surprise as the forest in his mind receded, dimmed. She settled in the empty chair to his right and then she reached out and put her hand on the side of his face.

Slowly he looked into her eyes.

"You're afraid," she said.

He nodded. "I am."

"You're being truthful about it."

"Is that a good thing?"

"I love you so much," she said. "So much. It's better that than saying all the correct things, that you realize now we'll be together in this, that you will never lose me now as you might have, that I'll soon be invulnerable to the same things that can't hurt you."

"That's what I should say, what I should think."

"Perhaps. But you don't tell lies, Reuben, except when you have to, and you don't like secrets, and they cause you pain."

"They do. And we are both a secret now, Laura, a very big secret. We are a dangerous secret."

"Look at me."

"I'm trying to do that."

"Just tell me all of it, let it flow."

"You know what it's about," he said. "When I came here, that first night, when I was wandering out there in the grass, the Man Wolf, and I saw you, you were like some tender, innocent being, something purely human and feminine and marvelously vulnerable, standing there on the porch and you were so . . ."

"Unafraid."

"Yes, but fragile, intensely fragile, and even as I fell in love with you, I was so afraid for you, that you'd open your door like that, to something like me. You didn't know what I was, not really. You had no idea. You thought I was a simple Man of the Wild, you know you did, something out of the heart of the forest that didn't belong in the cities of men, remember that? You made a myth of me. I wanted to enfold you, protect you, save you from yourself, save you from myself!—from your recklessness, I mean your inviting me in as you did."

She seemed to be weighing something. She started to speak but didn't.

"I wanted to just take away all your pain," he said. "And the more I learned of your pain the more I wanted to annihilate it. But of course I couldn't do that. I could only compromise you, bring you halfway into this secret with me."

"I wanted to come," she said. "I wanted you. I wanted the secret, didn't I?"

"But I was no primal beast of the woods," he said, "I was no innocent hairy man of myth, I was Reuben Golding, the hunter, the killer, the Man Wolf."

"I know," she said. "And I loved you every step of the way to the knowledge of what you are, didn't I?"

"Yes." He sighed. "So what am I afraid of?"

"That you won't love the Morphenkind that I become," she said simply. "So you won't love me when I'm as powerful as you are."

He couldn't reply.

He sucked in his breath. "And Felix, and Thibault, do they know how to control when the full change happens?"

"No. They said it would be soon." She waited, and when he said nothing, she went on. "You're scared you won't love me anymore, that I won't be that tender, vulnerable pink thing that you found in this house."

He hated himself for not answering.

"You can't be happy for me, you can't be happy that I will share this with you, can you?"

"I'm trying," he said. "I really am, I'm trying."

"From the very first moment you loved me you were miserable that you couldn't share it with me, you know you were," she said. "We talked about it, and it was there when we didn't talk about it—the fact that I could die, and you couldn't give this gift to me for fear of killing me, the fact that I might never share it with you. We talked of that. We did."

"I know that, Laura. You've every right to be furious with me. To be disappointed. God knows, I disappoint people."

"No, you don't," she said. "Don't say those things. If you're talking about your mother and that dreadful Celeste, well, good, you disappoint them for being far more sensitive than they can guess, for not buying into their ruthless world with its greedy ambition and nauseating self-sacrifice. So what! Disappoint them."

"Hmmm," he whispered. "I've never heard you talk like that before."

"Well, I'm not Little Red Riding Hood anymore, now am I?" She laughed. "Seriously. They don't know who you are. But I do and your father does, and so does Felix, and you're not disappointing me. You love me. You love who I was and you're afraid of losing that person. That's not disappointing."

"I think it should be."

"It was all theoretical to you," she said. "That you might share the gift with me, that I might die if you didn't. It was theoretical to you that you had it. It all happened too quickly for you."

"That's the truth," he said.

"Look, I don't expect anything of you that you can't give," she said. "Only allow me this. Allow me to be part of all of you, even if you and I can't be lovers anymore. Allow that, that I'll be part of you and Felix and Thibault and . . ."

"Of course, yes. Do you think they would ever allow me to drive you away? Do you think for a minute I'd do that? Laura!"

"Reuben, there isn't a man alive who doesn't feel possessive of the woman he loves, who doesn't want to control his access to her and her access to him and his world."

"Laura, I know all that—."

"Reuben, you have to be feeling something about the fact that they gave me the Chrism, whether you wanted them to do it or not, that they made their decision about me and with me essentially without seeing me as part of you. And I made my decision the same way."

"As it should be, for the love of—."

He stopped.

"I don't like what I'm finding out about myself," he said. "But this is life and death, and it's your choice. And do you think I could endure it if they'd left it up to me, if they'd treated you as if you were my possession?"

"No, I don't," she said. "But we can't always reason with our feelings."

"Well, I love you," he said. "And I will accept this. I will. I will love you as much after as I love you now. My feelings might not listen to reason. But I'm giving them a direct order."

She laughed. And he did in spite of himself.

"Now, tell me. Why are you here alone now, when the change might come at any time?"

"I'm not alone," she said. "Thibault's here. He's been here since before dark. He's out there, waiting for you to leave. He'll be with me every night until it's resolved."

"Well, then why don't you come home now?" he demanded.

She didn't answer. She was looking off again as if listening to the sounds of the forest. "Come back with me now. Let's pack up and get out of here."

"You're being very brave," she said quietly. "But I want to see this through here. And you know that's better for both of us."

He couldn't deny it. He couldn't deny that he was terrified that the transformation might come on right now as they sat there. The mere thought of it was more than he could bear.

"You're in safe hands with Thibault," he said.

"Of course," she said.

"If it was that Frank, I'd kill him with my bare claws."

She smiled, but didn't protest.

He was being ridiculous, wasn't he? After all, hadn't Thibault—whenever he'd received the gift—been invigorated by it? What was the practical difference between the two men? One looked like an elderly scholar and the other like a Don Juan. But they were both full-blooded Morphenkinder, weren't they? Yet Thibault conveyed the grace of age, and Frank was forever in his prime. And it struck him suddenly with full force that she would look as beautiful as she was now forever; and he himself, *he himself,* would never grow older, or look older or seem older—never become the wise and venerable man that his father was, never ever age beyond this moment. He might as well have been the youth on Keats's Grecian urn.

How could he have failed to realize these things, and what they must mean to her, and should mean to him? How had he not been transformed by that awareness, that secret knowledge? It was theoretical to him, she was right.

She *knew.* She'd always known what the full import of it all was. She'd tried to get him to realize it, and when he did let it penetrate now, he felt even more ashamed than ever of fearing the change in her.

He stood up and walked to the back bedroom. He felt dazed, almost sleepy. The rain was heavy now, pounding the old roof above. He felt an eagerness to get on the road, to be plowing north through the darkness.

"If Thibault weren't here, I wouldn't think of leaving," he said. He pulled on his clothes, hastily buttoning his shirt, and slipping on his coat.

Then he turned to her and the tears rose in his eyes.

"You will come home just as soon as you can," he said.

She put her arms around him and he held her as tightly as he dared, rubbing his face in her hair, kissing her over and over again on her soft cheek. "I love you, Laura," he said. "I love you with all my heart, Laura. I love you with all my soul. I'm young and foolish and I don't understand all of it, but I love you, and I want you to come home. I don't know what I have to offer you that the others can't offer, and they're stronger, finer, infinitely more experienced—."

"Stop." She put her fingers against his lips. "You are my love," she whispered. "My only love."

He went out the back door and down the steps in the rain. The forest was an invisible wall of darkness; only the wet grass showed in the lights from the house. And the rain stung him and he hated it.

"Reuben," she called out. She stood on the porch as she had that first night. The Old West–style kerosene lantern was there on the bench but it was not lighted, and he could not make out the features of her face.

"What is it?"

She came down the steps, into the rain.

He couldn't resist taking her in his arms again.

"Reuben, that night. You have to understand. I didn't care what happened to me. I didn't care at all."

"I know."

"I didn't care whether I lived or died. Not at all." The rain was flooding down on her hair, on her upturned face.

"I know."

"I don't know that you can know," she said. "Reuben, nothing paranormal, psychic, supernatural has ever happened to me. Nothing. Never have I had a presentiment, or a foreboding dream. Never has the spirit of my father or my sister, or my husband or my children come to me, Reuben. Never has there been a comforting moment when I felt their presence. Never did I have an inkling that they were alive somewhere. Never has there been the slightest breach of the rules of the natural world. That's where I lived until you came, in the natural world."

"I do understand," he said.

"You were some kind of miracle, something monstrous yet fabulous, and the radio and the TV and the newspapers had been chattering about you, this Man Wolf thing, this incredible being, this hallucination, this spectacular chimera, I don't know how to describe it—and there you were—there you were—and you were absolutely real, and I saw you and I touched you. And I didn't care! I wasn't going to turn away. I didn't care."

"I understand. I know. I knew it at the time."

"Reuben, I want to live now. I want to be alive. I want to be alive with every fiber of my being, don't you see, and for you and me, this is being alive."

He was about to pick her up, to carry her back into the house, but she stepped away and put her hands up. Her nightgown was soaked and cleaving to her breasts, and her hair was dark around her face. He was chilled to the bone and it didn't matter.

"No," she said, stepping back, yet holding firmly to his lapels. "Listen to what I'm saying. I don't believe in anything, Reuben. I don't believe I'll ever see my father again, or my kids, or my sister. I think they are just gone. But I want to be alive. And this thing means we don't die."

"I do understand," he said.

"I care now, don't you see?"

"Yes," he answered. "And I want to understand more, Laura. And I will understand more. I promise you. I will."

"Go now, please," she said. "And I'll be home soon."

He passed Thibault on the way to his car. Thibault, portly and dignified, in a shining black raincoat standing under the great Douglas fir, with an umbrella, a big black umbrella, and maybe Thibault gave him a nod, he didn't know. He just got in his car and headed north.

2

IT WAS TEN O'CLOCK when he reached home, and the house was cheerful, with a lot of the sweet-smelling evergreen garland already around the fireplaces, and the fires going as always, and a scattering of cheerful lamps lighted throughout the main rooms.

Felix was at the dining table, in fast conversation with Margon and Stuart about the plans for Yuletide, a map or diagram spread before them on butcher paper, and a couple of yellow notepads laid out with pens. The gentlemen were in their pajamas and Old World satin-lapel robes, while Stuart wore his usual dark sweatshirt and jeans. He looked like a wholesome American teenager who had wandered into a Claude Rains movie.

Reuben smiled to himself over that little bit of musing. It was wonderful to see them all so animated, so happy in the light of the fire, and to smell the tea and the cakes, and all the fragrances he now associated with home—wax, and polish, and the oak logs burning on the hearth, and of course the fresh smell of the rain that always worked its way into this big house, this house with its damp dark corners that surrounded so many yet never really embraced anyone.

The old French valet Jean Pierre took Reuben's wet raincoat, and immediately set a cup of tea for him at the table.

Reuben sat quiet, drinking the tea, distracted, thinking of Laura, half listening and nodding to all the Christmas plans, vaguely aware that Felix was stimulated about all this, uncommonly happy.

"So you're home, Reuben," said Felix cheerfully, "and just in time to hear our grand designs, and to approve, and give us your permission and your blessing." He had his usual radiance, dark eyes crinkled with good humor, his deep voice running on with easy enthusiasm.

"Home but dead tired," Reuben confessed, "though I know I can't sleep. Maybe this is my night to become a lone wolf and the scourge of Mendocino County."

"No, no, no," whispered Margon. "We're all doing so well, cooperating with one another, aren't we?"

"Being obedient to you, you mean," said Stuart. "Maybe Reuben and I should go off together tonight and, you know, get in real trouble like the little wolves that we are."

He made a fist and slammed Margon a little too hard on the arm.

"Did I ever explain to you boys," asked Margon, "that this house has a dungeon?"

"Oh, complete with chains, no doubt," said Stuart.

"Amazingly complete," said Margon, narrowing his eyes as he gazed at Stuart. "And proverbially dark and damp and dismal. But that never stopped some of the expiring inmates from carving grim poetry into the walls. Would you like to spend some time there?"

"As long as I can have my blankie and my laptop," said Stuart, "and meals on schedule. I might get some rest down there."

Another mocking growl came from Margon and he shook his head. " 'They flee from me that sometime did me seek,' " he whispered.

"Oh not another secret poetic communication," said Stuart. "I can't stand it. The poetry's getting so thick in here I can't breathe."

"Gentlemen, gentlemen," said Felix. "Let's keep it brisk and light and in keeping with the season."

He looked intently at Reuben. "Speaking of dungeons, I want to show you the statues for the crèche. This will be a splendid Yuletide, young master of the house, if you'll allow it."

He went on quickly explaining. December sixteenth, two Sundays before Christmas, was the perfect day for the Christmas festival in Nideck, and the banquet here at the house, for all the people of the county. The booths and shops in the "village," as Felix more often than not called it, would close at dark, and everyone would come up to Nideck Point for the evening festivities. Of course the families must come, Reuben's and Stuart's, and whatever old friends either wanted to include. This was the time to remember everybody. And Father Jim must bring the "unfortunates" from his church in San Francisco, and buses could be provided for that.

Of course the sheriff would be invited, and all the law enforcement officers who had so recently been crawling over the property on the night the mysterious Man Wolf had perpetrated his murderous attack on the two Russian doctors in the front room. And the reporters, they'd all be invited too.

They'd have huge tents on the terrace, tables and chairs, oil heaters, and twinkling lights beyond imagining.

"Picture the entire oak forest," said Felix, gesturing to the woods beyond the dining room window, "completely festooned in lights, tree limbs positively dressed in lights, and the paths strewn with thick mulch, and strolling mummers and carolers roaming about, but naturally the boys' choir and the orchestra will be on the front terrace along with the crèche and the bulk of the tables and chairs. Oh, this will be too splendid." He pointed to the rough diagram he'd drawn on the butcher paper. "Of course the banquet proper will be served in this room, continuously from dark until ten p.m. But there'll be stations properly positioned at all key points for the mulled wine, the mead, the drinks, food, whatever people want, and then all the house flung wide open so every soul in the neighborhood can see the public rooms and bedrooms of mysterious Nideck Point once and for all. No secrets anymore as to the 'old place' where the Man Wolf recently ran rampant. No, we'll show the world. 'Welcome, judges, congressmen, police officers, teachers, bankers . . . good people of Northern California! It was through that front room that the notorious Man Wolf rampaged, and out that library window that he vaulted into the night.' Say the word, young master. Shall all this be done?"

"He means to feed the entire coast," said Margon solemnly, "from south San Francisco to the Oregon border."

"Felix, this is your house," said Reuben. "It sounds marvelous!" And really it did. It also sounded impossible. He had to laugh.

A fleeting memory came back to Reuben of Marchent describing so happily how "Uncle Felix" had loved to entertain, and he was almost tempted to share it with Felix.

"I know this is soon after my niece's death," said Felix, his voice reflecting a sudden shift in mood. "I'm well aware of that. But I cannot see our being dark for this, our first Christmas. My beloved Marchent would never have wanted that."

"People in California don't mourn, Felix," said Reuben. "Not that I've ever seen anyway. And I can't imagine Marchent being disturbed by this either."

"I think she'd heartily approve of the whole thing," said Margon. "And there's a great wisdom to letting the press troop through this house at their leisure as well."

"Oh, I'm not doing it merely for that," said Felix. "I want a great celebration, a fete. This house must have new life in it. It must be a shining lamp once again."

"But surely this crèche—you're talking about Jesus and Mary and Joseph, right?—but you don't believe in the Christian God, do you?" asked Stuart.

"No, certainly not," said Felix, "but this is the way these people in this time celebrate Midwinter."

"But isn't it all a lie?" Stuart demanded. "I mean aren't we supposed to free ourselves from lies and superstition? Isn't that the obligation of intelligent beings? And that is what we are."

"No, it's not all lies," said Felix. He lowered his voice for emphasis, as if gently imploring Stuart to consider things differently. "Traditions are seldom lies; traditions reflect people's deepest beliefs and customs. They have their own truth, don't they, by their very nature?"

Stuart was staring askance at him with skeptical blue eyes, his freckles and boyish face as usual making him look like a rebellious cherub.

"I think the Christmas myth is eloquent," Felix continued. "Always has been. Think of it. The Christ Child was from the first a brilliant symbol of the eternal return. And that's what we've always celebrated at Midwinter." His voice was reverent. "The glorious birth of the god on the darkest night of the year—that's the essence of it."

"Hmmm," said Stuart with a little mockery. "Well, you do make it sound like more than Christmas wreaths in malls and canned carols in department stores."

"It's always been more than that," said Margon. "Even the most commercial trappings of the malls today reflect the old pagan ways and the Christian ways woven together."

"There's something nauseatingly optimistic about you guys," said Stuart seriously.

"Why," asked Margon. "Because we don't mope about lamenting our monstrous secrets? Why should we? We live in two worlds. We always have."

Stuart was puzzled, frustrated, but in general coming around.

"Maybe I don't want to live in that old world anymore," said Stuart. "Maybe I keep thinking I can leave it behind."

"You don't mean that," said Margon. "You're not thinking."

"I'm all for it," Reuben said. "It's usually made me sad in the past, carols, hymns, the crib, the whole thing, because I never much believed in anything, but when you describe it that way, well, I can live with it. And people will love it, won't they?—I mean all this. I've never been to a Christmas celebration quite like what you're planning. In fact, I seldom go to Christmas celebrations of any kind."

"Yes, they will love it," said Margon. "They always have. Felix has a way of making them love it, and making them want to come back year after year."

"It will all be done right," Felix said. "I have just enough time, just enough, and money will be no obstacle this first year. Let the better planning come next year. Why, maybe this year, I'll try more than one orchestra. We should have a small one out there in the oaks. And of course a string quartet in here in the corner of this room. And if I can get a fix on how many children are coming . . ."

"Okay, noblesse oblige, I get it," said Stuart, "but my mind's on being a Morphenkind, not serving eggnog to my old friends. I mean what has all this to do with being a Morphenkind?"

"Well, I'll tell you right now what it has to do with it," said Margon sharply, eyes flashing fiercely on Stuart. "This fete will be two Sundays before Christmas Eve, as Felix has explained. And it will satisfy the desires of your respective families as to all holiday commemoration. It will do more than that. It will give them something splendid to remember. And then on December twenty-fourth, there must be no one here but us, so that we can celebrate the Yule as we've always done."

"Now this sounds interesting," said Stuart. "But what exactly do we do?"

"There's time to show you," said Felix. "If you walk northeast of the house for approximately ten minutes you'll come to an old clearing. It's surrounded by large stones, very large stones, in fact. There's a little creek running beside it, off and on."

"I know that place," Reuben said. "It's like a rude citadel. Laura and I found it. We didn't want to climb over the boulders at first, but we found a way inside. We were so curious about it." A flash of memory: the sun slicing through the canopy of branches, the great floor of rotted leaves, and saplings rising from old tree stumps, and the hunkering and uneven gray boulders covered in lichen. They had found a flute there, a little wooden flute, a lovely thing. He didn't know what had become of it. Surely Laura had it. She'd washed it in the creek and played more than a few notes on it. He heard the sound suddenly, faint, mournful, as Felix went on.

"Well, that is where we celebrated our rites for years," Felix explained, his voice as always patient and reassuring as he looked from Stuart to Reuben. "There are no remains now of our old bonfires. But that is where we gather, to make our circle, to drink our mead, and to dance."

" 'And the hairy ones shall dance,' " said Margon wistfully.

"I know that phrase," Stuart said. "Where does it come from? Sounds deliciously creepy. Love it."

"Title of a short story," said Reuben, "and haunting words."

"Go further back," said Felix, smiling. "Page through the old Douay-Rheims Bible."

"Right," said Reuben. "Of course." Reuben quoted from memory, " 'But wild beasts shall rest there, and their houses shall be filled with serpents, and ostriches shall dwell there, and the hairy ones shall dance there: And owls shall answer one another there, in the houses thereof, and sirens in the temples of pleasure.' "

A little approving laugh came from Felix, and Margon gave a small laugh as well.

"Oh, you so love it when the genius here recognizes some arcane quote or word, don't you?" said Stuart. "The literary prodigy strikes again! Reuben, the star of the Morphenkindergarten class."

"Take a lesson from him, Stuart," said Margon. "He reads, he remembers, he understands. He stores up the poetry of the ages. He thinks. He meditates. He advances!"

"Oh, come on," said Stuart. "Reuben's not a real guy. He came off the cover of *Gentlemen's Quarterly.*"

"Sigh," said Reuben. "I should have left you out there in the wilds of Santa Rosa after you mauled your stepfather."

"No, you shouldn't have," said Stuart, "but you know I'm kidding, man. Come on. Seriously, what's your secret for remembering things like that? You have a card catalog in your head?"

"I have a computer in my head, just like you do," said Reuben. "My dad's a poet. And he used to read Isaiah out loud to me when I was a kid."

"Isaiah!" said Stuart in a deep voice. "No Maurice Sendak or Winnie the Pooh? But then of course you were destined to grow up to be a Man Wolf, so the usual rules didn't apply."

Reuben smiled and shook his head. Margon gave a low growl of disapproval.

"Morphenkindergarten," said Margon. "I think I rather like that."

Felix was paying not the slightest attention. He was looking again at his Christmas diagrams and lists.

Reuben was beginning to see this festival, and he warmed to it the way he'd warmed to this house as soon as he'd come to know it.

"Isaiah!" Stuart continued to scoff. "And you godless immortals dance in a circle because Isaiah said to do it?"

"Don't make a fool of yourself," cautioned Margon. He was annoyed. "You're missing the point entirely. We were dancing in our circle at Midwinter before Isaiah came into the world. And on that night, we will mourn Marrok, who's no longer with us—one of our own whom we've lately lost—and we will welcome you—formally—you and Reuben and Laura into the company."

"Wait a minute," said Stuart, jolting Reuben out of his reverie. "Then Laura's decided? She's going to be with us!" He was elated. "Reuben, why didn't you tell us?"

"Enough for now," said Felix gently. He rose to his feet. "Reuben, you come with me. As master of the house, you need to see a few more of the cellar chambers belowstairs."

"If they're dungeons, I wanna see them!" Stuart said.

"Sit down," said Margon in a low ominous voice. "Now pay attention. We have more work to do on these plans."

3

TIRED AS HE WAS, Reuben was game for a trip to the cellars, and followed Felix willingly down the steps. They passed quickly through the old furnace room and into the first of the many passages that made up a labyrinth before the final tunnel to the outside world.

In the last week electricians had been rewiring these low-roofed hallways, and some of the mysterious chambers, but much remained to be done and Felix explained that some of the rooms could never be opened for electrical light.

There were oil lamps and flashlights in cabinets here and there, between locked doors, and Reuben realized as he followed Felix under the dim overhead bulbs that he had no idea as to the extent of the construction under the house. These crudely plastered walls glistened with moisture in places, and as he followed Felix now into completely foreign territory, he glimpsed at least ten doors on either side of the cramped hall.

Felix had a large flashlight in hand, and stopped before a door with a combination lock.

"What is it? What's troubling you?" Felix asked. He laid a firm hand on Reuben's shoulder. "You came in miserable. What's happened?"

"Well, nothing's happened," said Reuben, partly relieved to be talking about it, and partly ashamed. "It's just that Laura has decided, as I'm sure you know. And I didn't know. I was with Laura this afternoon. I miss her and I don't understand how I can want her to come home so much and be so afraid of what's happening to her. I wanted to carry her back here by force and I wanted to flee."

"You really don't understand?" Felix asked. His dark eyes were filled with a protective concern. "It's easy enough for me to understand," he said. "And you mustn't condemn yourself for it, not at all."

"You're always kind, Felix, always kind," Reuben said, "and there are so many questions on the tip of my tongue about who you are and what you know. . . ."

"I realize that," said Felix. "But in a very real way, who we are now is what counts. Listen, I've loved you as if you were a son to me from the first moment I met you. And if I thought it would help to tell you all the stories of my life, I'd do it. But it won't help at all. This you must live through on your own."

"Why am I not happy for her," Reuben asked, "happy to share this power, these secrets, what's wrong with me? From the first moment I knew I loved her, I wanted to give her the Chrism. I didn't even know the name of it. But I knew that if it could be passed, given, and I wanted to . . ."

"Of course you did," said Felix. "But she's not simply a person in your mind, she's a lover." He hesitated. "A woman." He turned to the small combination lock and, shifting the flashlight under his arm, worked the dial quickly. "You're possessive of her, you have to be," Felix went on. He cracked the door but didn't enter. "And now she's one of us, and it's out of your hands."

"That's exactly what she said," Reuben answered. "And I know I should be happy that it's out of my hands, that she's been accepted without conditions, that she's seen as whole and entire and her own person. . . ."

"Yes, of course you should, but she's your spouse!"

Reuben didn't respond. He was seeing Laura again, by the creek, holding that small wooden flute, and then playing it, tentatively, making that melody that rose mournfully, as if it were a little prayer.

"I know this," said Felix. "You have an exceptional capacity to love. I've seen it, felt it, knew it when we first talked to each other in the lawyer's office. You love your family. You love Stuart. And you love Laura deeply, and if for any reason you cannot bear to be around her anymore, well, you will deal with it with love."

Reuben wasn't so sure of that, and suddenly the difficulties, the potential for difficulties, overwhelmed him. He thought of Thibault under the tree outside of her house, waiting there so quietly in the darkness, and a raging jealousy took hold of him, jealousy that Thibault had given her the Chrism, jealousy that Thibault, who'd warmed to her from the beginning, might be far closer to her now than Reuben was. . . .

"Come," said Felix. "I want you to see the statues."

The flashlight threw a large yellow beam before them as they entered a cold white-tiled room. Even the ceiling was tiled. And at once Reuben's eyes made out a great cluster of white-marble crèche figures, finely carved, robust, and baroque in proportions and costume, as rich as any Italian statues he had ever seen. Surely these had come from some sixteenth-century palazzo or church across the sea.

They took his breath away. Felix held the flashlight as Reuben examined them, wiping the dust from the Virgin's downcast eyes, her cheek. Not even in the famous Villa Borghese had he ever seen anything more plastic or lifelike rendered in stone. The tall figure of the bearded Joseph loomed over him, or was it one of the shepherds? Well, here was the lamb, and the ox, yes, finely detailed, and there suddenly as Felix moved the flashlight were revealed the opulent and splendid Three Kings.

"Felix, these are treasures," he whispered. How pathetic had been Reuben's imaginings of a Christmas crib.

"Well, they haven't been on the terrace at Yuletide for almost a hundred years. My beloved Marchent never laid eyes on them. Her father detested such entertainments, and I spent too many winters in other parts of the world. It wore me out, pretending to be my own mortal descendant. But they'll be displayed this Yuletide, and with all the proper accoutrements. I have carpenters all ready to build a stable enclosure. Oh, you'll see." He sighed.

He let the flashlight pass over the huge figure of the richly adorned camel, and the donkey with his large tender eyes . . . so like the eyes of the beasts that Reuben had encountered, the soft open unquestioning eyes of the animals he'd killed. A shock passed through him as he looked at it, thinking of Laura again, and the scent of the deer outside her house.

He reached out to touch the Virgin's perfect fingers. Then the light settled on the Christ Child, a smiling and beaming figure with flowing hair and bright joyful eyes, lying on the bed of marble hay with his arms outstretched.

He felt a pain looking at this, a terrible pain. There had been a time long, long ago when some belief in these things had galvanized him, hadn't there? When as a little boy he'd looked at such a figure and felt the deep consummate recognition that it meant unconditional love.

"Such a story," Felix said in a low whisper, "that the Maker of the Universe would descend to us in this humble form, come all the way down and down and down from the far reaches of his creation to be born amongst us. Was there ever a more beautiful symbol for our desperate hope at Midwinter that the world will be born anew?"

Reuben couldn't speak. For so long, he'd bought all the flippant dismissals . . . a pagan feast with a Christian story grafted to it. Was it not something for the devout and the godless to both reject? No wonder Stuart was so suspicious. The world today was suspicious of such things.

How many times had he sat there silently in church watching his beloved brother, Jim, celebrate the Mass and thought, *Meaningless, all of it, meaningless.* He'd long to be released from the church into the bright, open world again, to be looking simply at a starry sky or listening to the sound of the birds that sing even in the darkness, to be alone with his deepest convictions, simple as they were.

But some other deeper and finer feeling was dawning in him now, that it was not all "either-or." A magnificent possibility was occurring to him, that disparate things might in some way be united in ways we had to come to understand.

He wished he could talk to Jim just now, but then Jim would come to this Christmas fete and they would stand before this crèche, and they could talk together as they always had. And Stuart, Stuart would come to understand, to see.

He felt a great relief that Felix was here, with his resolve and his vision, to make something like this grand Yuletide party truly work.

"Margon's not tired of Stuart, is he?" he asked suddenly. "He understands, doesn't he, that Stuart is just so damned exuberant!"

"Are you serious?" Felix laughed softly. "Margon loves Stuart." He dropped his voice to a confidential whisper. "You must be a very sound sleeper, Reuben Golding. Why, it's Zeus carrying off Ganymede just about every night."

Reuben laughed in spite of himself. Actually he was not much of a sound sleeper, or certainly not every night.

"And we'll have the finest musicians," Felix resumed as if talking to himself. "I've already made calls to San Francisco, and found inns along the coast where they can be put up. Operatic voices, that's what I want for the adult choir. And I'll bring the boys' choir from Europe if I have to. I have a young conductor who understands. I want the old carols, the traditional carols, the ones that capture something of the irresistible depth of it all."

Reuben was quiet. He was looking at Felix, stealing a long slow look at him as Felix looked lovingly on this family of marble sentinels. And Reuben was thinking, Everlasting life, and I do not begin to know. . . . But he knew that he loved Felix, that Felix was the light shining on his path now, that Felix was the teacher in this new school in which he found himself.

"Long ago," Felix said, "I had a splendid home in Europe—." He went quiet, and his usually cheerful and animated face was shadowy and almost grim. "You know what kills us, don't you, Reuben? Not wounds, or pestilence, but immortality itself." He paused. "You are living in a blessed time now, Reuben, and you will be until all those you love here are gone, until your generation is in the earth. Then immortality will begin for you. And someday centuries from now, you will remember this Yuletide and your beloved family—and all of us together in this house." He drew himself up, impatiently, before Reuben had a chance to respond, and he gestured for them to leave.

"Is this the easiest time, Felix?" he asked.

"No. Not always. Not everyone has the remarkable family you

have." He paused. "You've confided in your brother, Jim, haven't you? I mean he knows what you are and what we are."

"In Confession, Felix," said Reuben. "Yes, I thought I'd told you. Perhaps I didn't. But it was in Confession and my brother is the kind of Catholic priest who will die before he breaks the seal of the Confessional. But yes, he knows."

"I sensed as much from the very start," Felix said. "The others sensed it, of course. We know when people know. You will find this out in time. I think it's rather marvelous that you had such an opportunity." He was musing. "My life was so very different. But this is not the time for that tale."

"You must trust, all of you," said Reuben, "that Jim would never—."

"Dear boy, do you think any of us would ever harm your brother?"

When they reached the stairs, he put his arm around Reuben again, and paused, his head down.

"What is it, Felix?" Reuben asked. He wanted somehow to tell Felix how much he cared for him, reciprocate the warm words Felix had spoken to him.

"You mustn't fear what's to come with Laura," Felix said. "Nothing is forever with us; it only seems so. And when it stops seeming so, well, that is when we begin to die." He frowned. "I didn't mean to say that. I meant to say . . ."

"I know," said Reuben. "You meant one thing and something else came out."

Felix nodded.

Reuben looked into his eyes. "I think I know what you're saying. You're saying 'treasure the pain.'"

"Yes, why maybe that is what I'm saying," said Felix. "Treasure the pain; treasure what you have with her, including the fear. Treasure what you may have, including the failure. Treasure it because if we don't live this life, if we don't live it to the fullest year after year and century after century, well, then, we die."

Reuben nodded.

"That's why the statues are still there, in the cellar, after all these years. That's why I brought them here from my homeland. That's why I built this house. That's why I am back under this roof, and you and Laura are an essential flame! You and Laura and the promise of what you are. Hmmm. I don't have your gift for words, Reuben. I make it sound as if I need you to love one another. That's not right. That's not what I meant to say at all. I come to warm my hands at a blaze and to marvel at it. That's all."

Reuben smiled. "I love you, Felix," he said. There was not a lot of emotion in his voice or in his eyes, only a deep and comfortable conviction, and the conviction that he was understood, and that no more words really were necessary.

Their eyes met, and neither needed to say a word.

They went on up the stairs.

In the dining room, Margon and Stuart were still at work. Stuart was going on about the stupidity and vapidity of rituals, and Margon was protesting softly that Stuart was being an incorrigible nuisance on purpose, as if he were arguing with his mother or his old teachers at school. Stuart was laughing impishly and Margon was smiling in spite of himself.

Sergei wandered in, the great blond-haired giant with the blazing blue eyes. His clothes were streaked with rain and dirt, his hair full of dust and bits of broken leaf. He looked ruddy and dazed. A curious silent exchange passed between Sergei and Felix, and a strange prickling feeling came over Reuben. Sergei had been out hunting; Sergei had been the Man Wolf tonight; the blood was pounding in him. And Reuben's blood knew it and Felix knew it. Stuart too sensed it, eyeing him with fascination and resentment, it seemed, and then glancing at Margon.

But Margon and Felix simply went back to work.

Sergei drifted off to the kitchen.

And Reuben went up to get snug with his laptop by the fire and research Christmas customs and the pagan customs of Midwinter, and maybe begin an essay for the *Observer*. Billie, his editor, was calling just about every second day. She wanted more material from him. So did the readers, she said. And he liked the idea of penetrating the different attitudes, positive and negative, towards Christmas, of probing why we were so ambivalent about it, why the ancient traditions often disturbed us as much as the spending and shopping, and how we might start thinking about Christmas in a fresh and committed way. It felt good to think of something other than the old cynical cliches.

Something occurred to him. He realized he was trying to figure a way to express what he was learning now without revealing the secret of how he was learning it, and how learning itself for him had so totally changed. "This is the way it will be," he whispered. "I'll pour out what I know, yes, but there will always be a holding back." Even so, he wanted to get busy. Christmas customs, Christmas spirit, echoes of Midwinter, yes.

4

Two a.m.

The house slept.

Reuben came down the stairs in his slippers and heavy wool robe.

Jean Pierre, who often took the night shift, was sleeping on his folded arms at the kitchen counter.

The fire in the library was not quite out.

Reuben stirred it, brought it back to life, and took a book from the shelves and did something he had always wanted to do. He curled up in the window seat against the cold window, comfortable enough on the velvet cushions, with a throw pillow between him and the damp chill panes.

The rain was flooding down the glass only inches from his eyes.

The lamp on the desk was sufficient for him to read a little. And a little, in this dim uncommitted light, was all he wanted to read.

It was a book on the ancient Near East. It seemed to Reuben he cared passionately about it, about the whole question of where some momentous anthropological development had occurred, but he lost the thread almost at once. He put his head back against the wood paneling and he stared through narrow eyes at the small dancing flames on the hearth.

Some errant wind blasted the panes. The rain hit the glass like so many tiny pellets. And then there came that sighing of the house that Reuben heard so often when he was alone like this and perfectly still.

He felt safe and happy, and eager to see Laura, eager to do his best. His family would love the open house on the sixteenth, simply love it. Grace and Phil had never been more than casual entertainers of their closest friends. Jim would think it wonderful, and they would talk. Yes, Jim and Reuben had to talk. It wasn't merely that Jim was the only one of them who knew Reuben, knew his secrets, knew everything. It was that he was worried about Jim, worried about what the burden of the secrets was doing to him. What in God's name was Jim suffering, a priest bound by the oath of the Confessional, knowing such secrets which he could not mention to another living being? He missed Jim terribly. He wished he could call Jim now.

Reuben began to doze. He shook himself awake and pulled the soft shapeless collar of his robe close around his neck. He had a sudden "awareness" that somebody was close to him, somebody, and it was as if he'd been talking to that person, but now he was violently awake and certain this could not possibly be so.

He looked up and to his left. He expected the darkness of the night to be sealed up against the window as all the outside lights had long ago gone off.

But he saw a figure standing there, looking down at him, and he realized he was looking at Marchent Nideck, and that she was peering at him from only inches beyond the glass.

Marchent. Marchent, who had been savagely murdered in this house.

His terror was total. Yet he didn't move. He felt the terror, like something breaking out all over his skin. He continued to stare at her, resisting with all his might the urge to move away.

Her pale eyes were slightly narrow, rimmed in red, and fixing him as if she were speaking to him, imploring him in some desperate way. Her lips were slightly parted, very fresh and soft and natural. And her cheeks were reddened as if from the cold.

The sound of Reuben's heart was deafening in his ears, and so powerful in his arteries that he felt he couldn't breathe.

She wore the negligee she'd worn the night she was killed. Pearls, white silk, and the lace, how beautiful was the lace, so thick, heavy, ornate. But it was streaked with blood, caked with blood. One of her hands gripped the lace at the throat—and there was the bracelet on that wrist, the thin delicate pearl chain she'd worn that day—and with the other hand she reached towards him as if her fingers might penetrate the glass.

He shot away, and found himself standing on the carpet staring at her. He had never known panic like this in all his life.

She continued to stare at him, her eyes all the more desperate, her hair mussed but untouched by the rain. All of her was untouched by the rain. There was a glistening quality to her. Then the figure simply vanished as if it had never been there.

He stood still, staring at the darkened glass, trying to find her face again, her eyes, her shape, anything of her, but there was nothing, and he had never felt so utterly alone in his life.

His skin was electrified still, though he had begun to sweat. And very slowly he looked down at his hands to see they were covered in hair. His fingernails were elongated. And touching his face and hands, he felt the hair there as well.

He'd begun to change, the fear had done that to him! But the transformation had been suspended, waiting, waiting perhaps for his personal signal as to whether it should resume. Terror had done that.

He looked at the palms of his hands, unable to move.

There were distinct sounds behind him—a familiar tread on the boards.

Slowly he turned to see Felix there, in rumpled clothes, his dark hair tousled from bed.

"What's the matter?" Felix asked. "What's happened?"

Felix drew closer.

Reuben couldn't speak. The long wolf hair was not receding. And neither was his fear. Maybe "fear" wasn't the word for this because he'd never feared anything natural in this way in his life.

"What's happened?" Felix asked again, drawing closer. He was so concerned, so obviously protective.

"Marchent," Reuben whispered. "I saw her, out there."

Now came the prickling sensations again. He looked down to see his fingers emerging from the disappearing hair.

He could feel the hair receding on his scalp and on his chest.

The expression on Felix's face startled him. Never had Felix seemed so vulnerable, so almost hurt.

"Marchent?" Felix said. His eyes narrowed. This was acutely painful for him. And there wasn't the slightest doubt that he believed what Reuben was telling him.

Reuben explained quickly. He went over everything that happened. He was heading for the coat closet near the butler's pantry as he spoke, Felix tagging after him. He put on his heavy coat, and picked up the flashlight.

"But what are you doing?" Felix asked.

"I have to go outside. I have to look for her."

The rain was light, little more than a drizzle. He hurried down the front steps and walked around the side of the house till he was standing beneath the large library window. He had never been on this exact spot before. He'd seldom even driven his car along the gravel drive here to the back of the property. The whole foundation was elevated of course, and there was no ledge on which Marchent, a living breathing Marchent, could have been standing.

The window was bright with the lamplight above him, and the oak forest stretching out to his right beyond the gravel drive was impenetrably dark, and filled with the sounds of the dripping rain, the rain forever working its way through leaves and branches.

He saw the tall slim figure of Felix looking out through the window, but Felix did not appear to see him down there looking up. Felix appeared to be looking off into the blackness.

Reuben stood very still, letting the light drizzle dampen his hair and his face, and then he turned and, bracing himself, he looked off into the oak forest. He could see almost nothing.

A terrible pessimism came over him, an anxiety bordering on panic. Could he feel her presence? No, he couldn't. And that she might, in some spiritual form, some personal form, be lost in that darkness terrified him.

Slowly he made his way back to the front door, looking off into the night all around him. How vast and foreboding it seemed, and how distant and hideously impersonal the roar of the ocean he couldn't see.

Only the house was visible, the house with its grand designs, and lighted windows, the house like a bulwark against chaos.

Felix was waiting in the open door, and helped him with his coat.

He sank down in the chair by the library fire, in the big wing chair that Felix usually claimed early every evening.

"But I did see her," Reuben said. "She was there, vivid, in her negligee, the one she wore the night she was killed. There was blood on it, all over it." It tormented him suddenly to relive it. He felt for a second time the same alarm he'd experienced when he first looked up at her face. "She was . . . unhappy. She was . . . asking me for something, wanting something."

Felix stood there quietly with his arms folded. But he made no effort to disguise the pain he was feeling.

"The rain," said Reuben, "it had no effect on her, on the apparition, whatever it was. She was shining, no, glistening. Felix, she was looking in, wanting something. She was like Peter Quint in *The Turn of the Screw*. She was looking for someone or something."

Silence.

"What did you feel when you saw her?" Felix asked.

"Terror," said Reuben. "And I think she knew it. I think she might have been disappointed."

Again, Felix was silent. Then after a moment, he spoke up again, his voice very polite, and calm.

"Why did you feel terror," he asked.

"Because it was . . . Marchent," Reuben said, trying not to stammer. "And it had to mean that Marchent is existing somewhere. It had to mean that Marchent is conscious somewhere, and not in some lovely hereafter, but here. Doesn't it have to mean that?"

Shame. The old shame. He'd met her, loved her, and failed utterly to stop her murder. Yet from her he had inherited this house.

"I don't know what it means," said Felix. "I have never been a seer of spirits. Spirits come to those who can see them."

"You do believe me."

"Of course I do," he said. "It wasn't some shadowy shape as you're describing it—."

"Utterly clear." Again his words came in a rush. "I saw the pearls on her negligee. The lace. I saw this old heavy lace, kind of dagged lace along her collar, beautiful lace. And her bracelet, the pearl chain she'd been wearing, when I was with her, this thin little bracelet with silver links and little pearls."

"I gave her that bracelet," Felix said. It was more a sigh than words.

"I saw her hand. She reached, as if she were going to reach through the glass." Again there came the prickling on his skin but he fought it. "Let me ask you something," he continued. "Was she buried here, in some family cemetery or something? Have you been to the grave? I'm ashamed to say I didn't even think of going there."

"Well, you couldn't have attended any funeral, could you," said Felix. "You were in the hospital. But I didn't think there was a funeral. I thought her remains were sent to South America. To tell you the truth, I don't honestly know if that's true."

"Could it be that she's not where she wants to be?"

"I can't imagine it mattering to Marchent," said Felix. His voice was unnaturally a monotone. "Not at all, but what do I know about it?"

"Something's wrong, Felix, very wrong, or she wouldn't have come. Look, I've never seen a ghost before, never even had a presentiment or a psychic dream." He thought of Laura saying those very words, more or less, that very evening. "But I know ghost lore. My father claims to have seen ghosts. He doesn't like to talk about it over a crowded dinner table because people laugh at him. But his grandparents were Irish, and he's seen more than one ghost. If ghosts look at you, if they know you're there, well, they want something."

"Ah, the Celts and their ghosts," said Felix, but it was not meant flippantly. He was suffering and the words were like an aside. "They have the gift. I'm not surprised Phil has it. But you can't talk to Phil about these things."

"I know that," said Reuben. "And yet he's the very person who might know something."

"And the very person who might sense more than you want him to sense, if you begin to tell him about all the things that puzzle you, all the things that have happened to you under this roof."

"I know, Felix, don't worry. I know."

He was struck by the somber, bruised expression on Felix's face. Felix seemed to be flinching under the onslaught of his own thoughts.

Reuben was ashamed suddenly. He'd been elated by this vision, horrific as it was. He'd been energized by it, and he hadn't thought for one second about Felix, and what Felix must surely be experiencing just now.

Felix had brought up Marchent; he had known and loved Marchent in ways that Reuben could scarce imagine, and he, Reuben, was going on and on about this, the apparition having been his, his brilliant and unique possession, and he was suddenly ashamed of himself. "I don't know what I'm talking about, do I?" he asked. "But I know I saw her."

"She died violently," Felix said in that same low and raw voice. He swallowed, and held the backs of his arms with his hands, a gesture Reuben had never seen in him before. "Sometimes when people die like that, they can't move on."

Neither of them spoke for a long moment, and then Felix moved away, his back to Reuben, nearer to the window.

Finally in a raw voice he spoke.

"Oh, why didn't I come back sooner? Why didn't I contact her? What was I thinking, to let her go on year after year . . . ?"

"Please, Felix, don't blame yourself. You weren't responsible for what happened."

"I abandoned her to time, the way I always abandon them . . . ," Felix said.

Slowly he came back to the warmth of the fire. He sat on the ottoman of the club chair across from Reuben.

"Can you tell me again how it all happened?" he asked.

"Yes, she looked right at me," Reuben said, trying not to give way again to a gush of excited words. "She was right on the other side of the glass. I have no idea how long she'd been there, watching me. I never sat in the window seat before. I always meant to do it, you know, curl up on that red velvet cushion, but I never did it."

"She did that all the time when she was growing up," said Felix.

"That was her place. I'd be working in here for hours, and she'd be in that window seat reading. She kept a little stack of books right there, hidden behind the drapery."

"Where? On the left side? Did she sit with her back to the left side of the window?"

"She did, as a matter of fact. The left-hand corner was her corner. I used to tease her about straining her eyes as the sun went down. She'd read there until there was almost no light at all. Even in the coldest winter she liked to read there. She'd come down here in her robe with her heavy socks on and curl up there. And she didn't want a floor lamp. She said she could see well enough by the light from the desk. She liked it that way."

"That's just what I did," Reuben said in a small voice.

There was a silence. The fire had died to embers.

Finally Reuben stood up. "I'm exhausted. I feel like I've been running for miles. All my muscles are aching. I've never felt such a need for sleep."

Felix rose slowly, reluctantly.

"Well, tomorrow," he said, "I'll make some calls. I'll talk to her man friend in Buenos Aires. It ought to be easy enough to confirm that she was buried as she wanted to be."

He and Felix moved towards the stairs together.

"There's something I have to ask," said Reuben as they went up. "Whatever made you come down when you did? Did you hear a noise, or sense something?"

"I don't know," said Felix. "I woke up. I experienced a kind of frisson, as the French call it. Something was wrong. And then of course I saw you, and I saw that the wolf hair was rising on you. We do signal each other in some impalpable way when we go into the change, you're aware of that."

They paused in the dark upstairs hallway before Felix's door.

"You aren't uneasy being alone now, are you?" Felix asked.

"No. Not at all," said Reuben. "It wasn't that kind of fear. I wasn't afraid of her or that she'd harm me. It was something else altogether."

Felix didn't move or reach for the doorknob. Then he said, "I wish I'd seen her."

Reuben nodded. Of course Felix wished for that. Of course Felix wondered why she would come to Reuben. How could he not wonder about that?

"But ghosts come to those who can see them, don't they?" Reuben asked. "That's what you said. Seems my dad said the same thing once, when my mother was scoffing at the very idea."

"Yes, they do," said Felix.

"Felix, we have to consider, don't we, that she wants this house restored to you?"

"Do we have to consider that?" Felix asked in a dejected voice. He seemed broken, his usual spirit utterly gone. "Why should she want me to have anything, Reuben, after the way I abandoned her?" he asked.

Reuben didn't speak. He thought of her vividly, of her face, of the anguished expression, of the way that she had reached towards the window. He shuddered. He murmured, "She's in pain."

He looked at Felix again, vaguely aware that the expression on Felix's face reminded him horribly of Marchent.

5

THE PHONE WOKE HIM EARLY; when he saw Celeste's name flashing on the screen, he didn't pick up. In a half sleep he heard her leaving her message. ". . . and I suppose this is good news for somebody," she was saying, her voice uncharacteristically flat, "but not for me. I talked to Grace about it, and well, I'm considering Grace's feelings too. Anyway, I need to see you, because I can't make a decision here without you."

What in the world could she be talking about? He had little interest and little patience. And the strangest most unexpected feeling came over him: he could not remember why he had ever claimed to love Celeste. How had he ever become engaged to her? Why had he ever spent so much time in the company of someone who personally disliked him so much? She had made him so unhappy for so long that the mere sound of her voice now irritated him and bruised him a little, when in fact his mind ought to be on other things.

Probably Celeste needed permission to marry his best friend, Mort. That was it. That had to be it. It was only two months since he and Celeste had broken their engagement and she was feeling uneasy about the haste. Of course she'd consulted Grace because she loved Grace. Mort and Celeste were regulars in the house on Russian Hill. They'd been dining there three times a week. Mort had always loved Phil. Phil loved to talk about poetry with Mort, and Reuben wondered how that would set with Celeste these days, since she had always thought Phil such a pathetic person.

As he showered, he reflected that the two people he really wanted to see today were his father, and his brother, Jim.

Wasn't there some way to broach the subject of ghosts with Phil without confiding in Phil about what happened?

Phil had seen spirits, yes, and Phil would have some old folklore wisdom on the matter, undoubtedly, but there was a wall now between Reuben and all those who didn't share the truths of Nideck Point, and he could not breach that wall.

As for Jim, he feared Jim's suspicion of ghosts and spirits would be predictable. No, Jim didn't believe in the devil, and maybe Jim didn't believe in God. But he was a priest and he often said the things he thought a priest had to say. Reuben realized that he hadn't really confided in Jim since the Distinguished Gentlemen had come into his life, and he was ashamed. If he had had to it do over again, Reuben never would have confided in Jim about the Wolf Gift. It had been so unfair.

After he'd dressed and had his coffee, he called the only person in the world with whom he could share the haunting and that was Laura.

"Look, don't drive all the way down here," Laura immediately offered. "Let's meet someplace away from the coast. It's raining in the wine country but probably not as hard."

He was all for it.

It was noon when he reached the plaza in Sonoma, and he saw Laura's Jeep outside the café. The sun was out, though the pavements were wet, and the center of town was busy as always in spite of the damp chill in the air. He loved Sonoma, and he loved its town plaza. It seemed to him that nothing bad could ever happen in such a gentle, pleasant little California town, and he hoped for a few minutes to browse the shops after lunch.

As soon as he saw Laura waiting for him at the table, he was struck again by the changes in her. Yes, the darkening blue eyes, and the luxuriant blond hair, and something beyond that, a kind of secretive vitality that seemed to infect her expression and even her smile.

After he'd ordered the largest sandwich the place had to offer, along with soup and salad, he began to talk.

Slowly, he poured out the story of the haunting, lingering on every single detail. He wanted Laura to have the entire picture, the sense of the house in its stillness and above all, the vivid intensity of Marchent's appearance, and the eloquence of Marchent's gestures and troubled face.

The crowded café was noisy around them but not so that he had to talk in anything but a confidential voice. Finally he'd reported everything, including his conversation with Felix, and he fell on his soup in his usual wolfish fashion, forgetting manners entirely and drinking all of it straight out of the bowl. Sweet fresh vegetables, thick broth.

"Well, do you believe me?" he asked. "Do you believe that I actually saw this thing?" He wiped his mouth with the napkin and started in on the salad. "I'm telling you, this was no dream."

"Yes, I think you saw her," she said. "And obviously Felix didn't think you imagined this either. I guess what frightens me is you might see her again."

He nodded. "But do you believe she's existing somewhere, I mean the real and true Marchent. Do you believe she's in some sort of purgatorial state?"

"I don't know," she said frankly. "You've heard the word 'earthbound,' haven't you? You know the theories, don't you, that some ghosts are earthbound spirits, people who have died and simply cannot move on. I don't know if any of it's true. I've never believed in it much. But the dead person remains out of confusion or some emotional attachment when it should be moving into the light."

He shuddered. He had heard those theories. He had heard his father talking of "the earthbound dead." Phil spoke of the earthbound dead as suffering in a kind of purgatory created for themselves.

Vague thoughts came back to him of Hamlet's ghost and its horrifying descriptions of the fires of torment in which it existed. There were literary critics who thought the ghost of Hamlet's father was actually from hell. But these thoughts were absurd. Reuben didn't believe in purgatory. He didn't believe in hell. Actually, he had always found talk of hell highly offensive. He'd always sensed that those who did believe in hell had little or no empathy for those they assumed to be suffering there. Indeed, quite the opposite. Hellfire believers seem to delight in the idea that most of the human race would end up in just such a horrible place.

"But what does earthbound mean, exactly?" he asked. "Where is

Marchent now at this very moment? What is she feeling?" To his mild amazement, Laura was actually eating her food. Quickly cutting several pieces of veal European style, she devoured them and moved on through the plate of scaloppine without stopping for breath. When the waitress set down the roast beef sandwich, naturally he snapped back to the task at hand.

"I don't know," said Laura. "These souls, assuming they exist at all, are trapped, clinging to what they can see and hear of us and our world."

"That makes perfect sense," he whispered. Again, he shuddered. He couldn't help it.

"This is what I would do, if I were you," she said suddenly, blotting her lips, and swallowing half the iced cola in her glass. "I'd be open, willing, eager to discover what the ghost wants. I mean, if this is the personality of Marchent Nideck, if there is something coherent and real and feeling there, well, be open to it. Now I know this is easy for me to say in a cheerful little crowded café in broad daylight, and of course, I haven't seen this, but that is what I'd try to do."

He nodded. "I'm not afraid of her," he said. "I'm afraid that she's miserable, that she, Marchent, does exist somewhere and it's not a good place. I want to comfort her, do what I can to give her whatever she wants."

"Of course."

"Do you think it's conceivable that she's troubled about the house, about the fact that Felix is back now, yet I own the house? Marchent didn't know Felix was alive when she gave me the house."

"I doubt it has anything to do with that," said Laura. "Felix is rich. If he wanted Nideck Point, he'd offer to buy it from you. He isn't living there as your guest because he lacks the means." She went on eating as she spoke, easily cleaning her plate. "Felix owns all the property bordering on Nideck Point. I heard him talking about it to Galton and the other handymen. It's no secret. He was discussing it casually with them, hiring them to do other work. The Hamilton place to the north has belonged to him for the last five years. And the Drexel place to the east was bought by him long before that. Galton's men are working on those houses now. Felix owns the land south of Nideck Point, all the way from the coast inland to the town of Nideck. There are old homes throughout these areas, homes like Galton's home, but Felix stands ready to buy each and every one of them whenever the owners want to sell."

"Then he did plan to come back," said Reuben. "He planned to come back all the time. And he does want the house. He has to want it."

"No, Reuben, you've got it wrong," she said. "Yes, he planned some-day to return. But not while Marchent was connected to the property. After she'd moved to South America, his agents made repeated offers under various names to purchase the house, but Marchent always refused. Felix told me this himself, just in conversation. Nothing secre-tive about it. He was waiting her out. Then events caught him com-pletely unawares."

"The point is he wants it now," said Reuben. "Of course he wants it. He built it himself."

"But he's not in any hurry," she said.

"I'll give it to him. It never cost me one silver dime."

"But do you think this ghost knows all these things?" Laura asked. "Does this ghost care?"

"No," he said. He shook his head. He thought of Marchent's con-torted face, thought of her hand extended, as if to reach through the glass. "Maybe I'm on the wrong track. Maybe it's the Christmas plans that are disturbing her spirit—plans for a party so soon after her death. But maybe that's not it at all."

Again, he had a strong sense of Marchent, as if the apparition had involved a new and eerie intimacy, and the misery he'd felt seemed infinitely more deeply rooted in the Marchent he knew.

"No, the party plans wouldn't offend her. That wouldn't be enough to bring her back from wherever she is, make her visit you in this way."

Reuben's mind drifted. He fell silent. He realized nothing more could be known until this spirit appeared to him again.

"Ghosts often come at Midwinter, don't they?" Laura asked. "I mean, think of all the Christmas ghost stories in the English language. That's always been a matter of tradition, that ghosts walk at this time of the year; they're strong at this time, as though the veil between the living and dead becomes fragile."

"Yes, Phil always said the same thing," Reuben said. "That's why Dickens's *Christmas Carol* has such a strong hold on us. It's all that old lore about spirits coming through at this time of year."

"Come back to me," said Laura taking his hand. "Don't think about this any more now." She motioned for the check. "There's a little bed-and-breakfast near here." She smiled at him, the most incandescent and gently knowing smile. "It's always fun, isn't it, a different bed, different rafters overhead."

"Let's go," he said.

Two blocks away in a charming Craftsman cottage nestled in a garden, they made love in an old brass bed below a close sloping ceiling. Yellow flowers in the wallpaper. Candle on the old cast-iron mantel. Rose petals on the sheet.

Laura was rough, urgent, inflaming him with her hunger.

Suddenly she stopped and drew back.

"Can you bring it on now?" she whispered. "Please, do it. Be the Man Wolf for me."

The room was shadowy, quiet, white shutters closed against the fading afternoon light.

Before he could reply, the metamorphosis had begun.

He found himself standing by the bed, his body yielding up the wolfen coat, the claws, the rippling, elongating tendons of his arms and legs. It was as if he could hear his mane growing, hear the silken hair covering his face. He looked about him with new eyes at the quaint, fragile furnishings of the room.

"And this is what you want, madam?" he asked in the usual low, baritone voice of the Man Wolf, so much darker, richer than his own normal voice. "We are risking discovery, are we, for this?"

She smiled.

She was studying him as never before. She ran her hands over the fur on his forehead, her fingers gripping the long rougher hair of his head.

He drew her towards him and then down on the bare boards. She pushed and pulled as if she wanted to provoke him, beating against his chest with her fists even as she kissed him, pressing her tongue to his fang teeth.

6

It was late afternoon when Reuben returned from Sonoma. The rain was thin but steady and the light almost as dim as twilight.

When he caught sight of the house he felt an immediate relief. Workers had finished lining every single window on the façade with tiny bright yellow Christmas lights in perfectly neat lines, and the front door was framed with thick evergreen garland wound with lights as well.

How cheerful and comforting it looked. The workmen were just finishing, and the trucks pulled off the terrace right after he pulled up. Only one truck remained for the crew that was working on the guesthouse on the lower slope, and it would soon be gone as well.

The main rooms were also extremely cheerful, with the usual fires going, and a great undecorated Christmas tree stood to the right of the conservatory doors. More thick and beautiful green garland had been added to the fireplaces and their mantelpieces. And the delicious fragrance of the evergreens everywhere was sweet.

But the house was empty, and that was odd. Reuben had not been alone in this house since the Distinguished Gentlemen had arrived. Notes on the kitchen counter told Reuben that Felix had taken Lisa down the coast for shopping; Heddy was napping; and Jean Pierre had taken Stuart and Margon to the town of Napa for dinner.

Strange as this was, Reuben didn't mind it. He was deep in his thoughts of Marchent. He'd been thinking of Marchent on the long drive back from Sonoma, and it only now came to him, as he put on a pot of coffee, that his afternoon with Laura had been blissful—the lunch, the bed-and-breakfast lovemaking—because he had not been afraid anymore of the changes in her.

He took a quick shower, putting on his blue blazer and gray wool pants as he often did for dinner, and was on his way down the hall towards the stairs when he heard the low, faint sound of a radio coming from somewhere on the west side of the house, his side of the house.

It took him only a moment in the hallway to locate the origin of the sound. It was Marchent's old room.

The hallway was grim and shadowy as always, as it had no windows, and only a few scattered wall sconces with parchment shades and small bulbs. And he could see a seam of light under her door.

There came that eerie throbbing terror again, only slowly. He felt the transformation coming but did all in his power to stop it as he stood there, shaken, and not certain what to do.

A dozen explanations might account for the light and the radio. Felix might have left on both after searching for something in Marchent's closet or desk.

Reuben was unable to move. He fought the prickling in his face and hands, but he couldn't entirely stifle it. His hands were now what somebody might call hirsute and a quick examination of his face told him it was the same. So be it. But of what use was this subtle enhancement against the possibility of a ghost?

The radio was playing an old dreamy melodic song from the nineties. He knew that song, knew that slow hypnotic beat and that deep female voice. "Take Me As I Am"—that was it. Mary Fahl with the October Project. He'd danced to that song with his high school girlfriend, Charlotte. It had been an old song by then. This was too palpable, too real.

Suddenly, he was so angry with his own panic that he knocked on the door.

The knob slowly turned and the door opened, and he saw the darkened figure of Marchent looking at him, the lamp behind her only partially illuminating the room.

He stood stock-still staring at the dark figure, and slowly her features became visible, the familiar angles of her face and her large unhappy and imploring eyes.

She wore the same bloodstained negligee and he could see the light glinting on countless tiny pearls.

He tried to speak, but the muscles of his face and jaw were petrified, as were his arms and his legs.

They weren't two feet apart.

His heart seemed about to explode.

He felt himself backing away from the figure, and then the entire scene went dark. He was standing in the silent empty hallway, trembling, sweating, and the door to Marchent's room was closed.

In a fury, he opened the door and walked into the darkened room. Groping for the wall button he found it and snapped on a collection of scattered small lamps.

The sweat broke out all over his chest and arms. His fingers were slippery with it. The wolf change had stopped. The wolf hair was gone now. But he still felt the pringling and the tremors in his hands and feet. And he forced himself to take several slow breaths.

No sound of a radio, no sight of a radio even, and all the room as he remembered it from the last time he'd inspected it before Felix and Margon and the others had ever come.

The windows were done in elaborate white-lace-ruffled curtains, and so was the canopy of the heavy brass four-poster bed. An old-fashioned dressing table in the far-north corner had been fitted with a skirt in the same starched white-lace ruffles. The bedspread was pink chintz and the overstuffed love seat by the fire was covered in the same fabric. There was a desk, ultra-feminine like all the rest, with Queen Anne legs, and white bookshelves half filled with a few hardcover books.

The closet door was ajar. Nothing inside but a half-dozen padded clothes hangers. Pretty. Some were covered in toile, others in pastel silk. Perfumed. Just there on the closet bar, empty hangers—a symbol for him suddenly of loss, of the horrid reality of Marchent having vanished into death.

Dust on the shelves above. Dust on the hardwood floor. Nothing to be found, nothing to which a vagrant spirit might have sadly attached itself—if that's what vagrant spirits did.

"Marchent," he whispered. He put his hand to his forehead, then took out his handkerchief and wiped the sweat from it. "Marchent, please," he whispered again. He couldn't remember from the lore he'd heard all his life whether a ghost could read your mind. "Marchent, help me," he offered, but his whisper sounded huge in the empty room, and as unnerving to him suddenly as everything else.

The bathroom was empty and immaculate, with empty cabinets. No radio to be seen. Smell of bleach.

How pretty the wallpaper was, an old toile pattern with pastoral figures, in blue and white. This was like the pattern on the padded hangers.

He imagined her bathing in the long oval claw-foot tub, and a wave of her intimate presence caught him off guard, fragments of their moments in each other's arms on that ghastly night, fragments of her warm face against his, and her soft soothing voice.

He turned and inspected the scene before him, and then slowly he made his way to the bed. It wasn't a high bed at all, and he sat down on the side of it, facing the windows, and he closed his eyes.

"Marchent, help me," he said under his breath. "Help me. What is it, Marchent?" If he'd ever known sorrow like this before, he couldn't remember it. His soul was shaken. And suddenly he began to cry. The whole world seemed empty to him, devoid of any hope, of any possibility of dreams. "I'm so sorry about what happened," he said thickly. "Marchent, I came as soon as I heard you scream. I swear to God, I did, but they were too much for me, the two of them, and besides, I was just too late."

He bowed his head. "Tell me what it is you want of me, please," he said. He was crying just like a child now. He thought of Felix downstairs in the library last night, asking himself why he had never come home during all those years, feeling such awful regret. He thought of Felix in the hallway last night saying so dejectedly, "Why should she want me to have anything . . . after the way I abandoned her?"

He took out his handkerchief and wiped his nose and mouth.

"I can't answer for Felix," he said. "I don't know why he did what he did. Or if I do, I can't say. But I can tell you that I love you. I would have given my life to stop them from hurting you. I would have done that without a thought."

A kind of relief coursed through him, but he felt it was cheap and undeserved. The finality of her death deserved better. The finality of her death left him crushed. Yet he had, in a rush, said so many things that he'd been longing to say and that felt good, though perhaps it didn't matter to her at all. He had no idea whether or not Marchent really existed in any realm where she might see him or hear him, or what the apparition at the door had been.

"But all this is true, Marchent," he said. "And you left me the gift of this house, and I did nothing to deserve it, nothing, and I'm alive here, and I don't know what's happened to you, to you, Marchent—I don't understand."

He didn't have any more words to speak out loud. In his heart, he said, *I loved you so much.*

He thought of how unhappy he'd been when he met her. He thought of how desperately he'd wanted to be free not only of his loving family but of his miserable connection with Celeste. Celeste had not loved him. She had not even liked him. And he had not liked her either. That was the truth. It had all been vanity, he thought suddenly, her wanting the "handsome boyfriend" as she called him so often to others in that high mocking tone, and him believing he ought to want such a smart and adorable woman whom his mother liked so much. The truth was Celeste had made him miserable, and as for his family, well, he'd needed to escape them for a while if he was ever to find what it was that he wanted to do.

"And now thanks to you," he whispered, "I live in this world."

And remembering suddenly her love for Felix, her grief for him, her weary conviction that he was dead and gone, he knew a pain that he could hardly bear. What right had he to the Felix for whom she'd mourned? The injustice of it, the horror of it, paralyzed him.

For a long moment he sat there shivering, shivering as if he were cold when he wasn't cold, his eyes closed, wondering at all of it, and very far now from the terror and the shock he'd felt only moments ago. There were worse things in this world than fear.

A sound came from the bed, the sound of the springs and the mattress creaking, and he felt the mattress shifting just to his right.

The blood drained out of his face, and his heart began to skip.

She was sitting next to him! He knew it. He felt her hand suddenly on his hand, supple flesh this, and the pressure of her breasts against his arm.

Slowly he opened his eyes, and looked into hers.

"Oh God in heaven," he whispered. He couldn't stop the words from coming though they were slurred and low. "God in heaven," he said as he forced himself to look at her, truly look at her, at her pale pink lips and the fine pen-stroke lines of her face. Her blond hair was glistening in the light. The silk of the white negligee, right against his arm, was rising and falling with her breath. He could feel her breath. She drew even closer, her cold hand covering his right hand as it tightened its grip, and her other hand closing on his left shoulder.

He looked right into her soft moist eyes. He made himself do it. But his right hand moved away from hers in a sudden jerking motion that he couldn't control, and with it he made the Sign of the Cross. It had been like a spasm and he was suddenly red with shame.

A little sigh came from her. Her eyebrows puckered and the sigh became a moan.

"I'm so sorry!" he said. "Tell me. . . ." He was stammering, clenching his teeth in his panic. "Tell me . . . what can I do?"

The expression on her face was one of unutterable torment. Slowly she lowered her gaze and looked away, her bobbed hair falling down over her cheek. He wanted to touch her hair, touch her skin, touch all of her. Then her eyes veered back to him, full to the brim with misery, and it seemed she was about to speak; she was struggling desperately to speak.

At once the vision brightened as if it were filling with light and then it dissolved.

It was gone as if it had never been. And he was alone on the bed, alone in her room, alone in the house. The minutes ticked as he sat there, unable to move.

She wasn't coming back, he knew it. Whatever in God's name she was now—ghost, spirit, earthbound—she'd taxed herself to the limit of her powers, and she wasn't coming back. And he was sweating again, his heart thudding in his ears. The palms of his hands and the soles of his feet burned. He could feel the wolf hair under his skin like myriad needles. It was torture to hold it back.

Without resolving to do it, he got up and hurried down the stairs and out the back door.

The cold darkness was descending, the molten clouds lowering, and the woods turning into shadow all around. The invisible rain sighed like a living thing in the trees.

He got in his Porsche and he drove. He didn't know where he was headed, only that he had to be away from Nideck Point, away from fear, from helplessness, from grief. Grief is like a fist against your throat, he thought. Grief strangles you. Grief was more awful than anything he'd ever known.

He kept to the back roads, vaguely aware that he was moving inland and the forest was on either side of him wherever he went. He wasn't thinking, so much as feeling, stifling the powerful transformation, again and again feeling the tiny needlelike growth of the hair all over him as he forced it back. He was listening for the voices, voices from the Garden of Pain, listening, listening for the inevitable sound of someone crying out frantically, someone who could speak, someone who was yet alive, someone who was crying for him though he or she couldn't know it, someone he could reach.

Pain somewhere, like a scent on the wind. A little child threatening, kicking, sobbing.

He pulled off the road and into a grove of trees and, folding his arms defensively over his chest, he listened as the voices came clear. Again the wolf hair pushed at him like needles. His skin was alive with it. His scalp was tingling and his hands were shuddering as he struggled to hold it back.

"And where would you be without me?" the man snarled. "You think they wouldn't put you in jail? Sure, they'd put you in jail."

"I hate you," sobbed the child. "You're hurting me. You always hurt me. I wanna go home."

And the man's voice rolled over her voice, in guttural curses and threats—ah, the grim, predictable sound of evil, the greed of utter selfishness! Give me the scent!

He felt himself breaking through his clothes, every inch of his scalp and face burning as the hair broke out, his claws extended, his thick hairy feet pushing out of the shoes. He tore off his jacket, shredding the shirt and pants with his claws. The mane came down to his shoulders. *Who I truly am, what I truly am.* How quickly the fur covered all of him, and how powerful he felt to be alone with it, alone and hunting as he had hunted on those first thrilling nights before the elder Morphenkinder had come, when he'd been on the very edge of all that he could comprehend, imagine, define—reaching for this luscious power.

He took to the forest in full wolf coat, running on all fours towards the child, his muscles singing, his eyes finding the jagged and broken ways through the forest without a single mishap. *And I belong to this, I am this.*

They were in an old decrepit trailer home half concealed by a thicket of broken oaks and giant firs. Small ghostly windows flashing with bluish television light gleamed before him in a cramped wet yard of butane tanks, trash cans, and old tires, with a rusted and dented truck parked to one side.

He hovered, uncertain, determined not to blunder as he'd done in the past. But he was ravenously hungry for the evil man only inches away from his grasp. Television voices chattered inside. The child was choking now and the man was beating her. He heard the thwack of the leather belt. The scent of the child rose sweet and penetrating. And there came the rank foul smell of the man, in wave after wave, the stench mingling with the man's voice and the reek of the dried sweat in his filthy clothing.

The rage rose in his throat as he let out a long, low growl.

The door came off too easily when he yanked it, and he threw it aside. A rush of hot fetid air assaulted his nostrils. Into the small narrow space, he forced himself like a giant, head bowed under the low ceiling, the whole trailer rocking under his weight, the jabbering television crashing to the floor as he caught the scrawny screaming red-faced bully by his flannel shirt and drew him back and out into the clattering cans and breaking bottles of the yard.

How calm Reuben was as he picked the man up—*Bless us, O Lord, for these are Thy gifts!*—how very natural he felt. The man kicked at him and pounded at him, face savage with terror, like the terror Reuben had felt when Marchent embraced him, and then slowly and deliberately Reuben bit into the man's throat. *Feed the beast in me!*

Oh, too rich, this, too rich in salt and rupturing blood and relentless heartbeat, too sweet the very viscid life of the evil one, too beyond what memory could ever record. It had been too long since he'd hunted alone, feasting on his chosen victim, his chosen prey, his chosen enemies.

He swallowed great mouthfuls of the man's flesh, his tongue sweeping the man's throat and the side of his face.

He liked the bones of the jaw, liked biting into them, liked feeling his teeth hook onto the jawbone as he bit down on what was left of the man's face.

There was no sound in the whole world now except the sound of his chewing and swallowing this warm, bloody flesh.

Only the leftover rain sang in the gleaming forest around him as if it were now bereft of all the small eyes that had seen this unholy Eucharist and fled. He abandoned himself to the meal, devouring the man's entire head, his shoulders, and his arms. Now the rib cage was his, and he went on delighting in the crackling sound of thin hollow bones, until suddenly he could eat no more.

He licked his paws, licked the pads of his palms, wiped at his face, and licked his paw again as he cleaned himself with it as a cat might have done. What was left of the man, a pelvis and two legs? He hurled the remains deep into the forest, hearing a soft shuffling collection of sounds as they fell to the earth.

Then he thought the better of this. He moved swiftly through the trees until he'd recovered the body, or what was left of it, and he carried it with him farther away from the trailer until he came to a small muddy clearing by a little stream. There he dug quickly down into the damp earth, and buried the corpse there, covering it as best he could. Here the world might never find it.

Then he started to wash his paws in the stream, splashing the icy water over his hairy face, but he heard the child calling him. Her voice was a shrill piping sound: "Man Wolf, Man Wolf." She called it over and over again.

"Man Wolf!" he whispered.

He hurried back to find her, near hysterical, in the door of the trailer.

Painfully thin, a child of seven or eight at most, with tangled blond hair, she begged him not to leave her. She wore jeans and a filthy T-shirt. She was turning blue from the cold. Her little face was streaked with tears and dirt.

"I prayed for you to come!" she sobbed. "I prayed for you to save me and you did."

"Yes, darling dear," he said, in his low gruff wolfish voice. "I came."

"He stole me from my mommy," she sobbed. She held out her wrists, scarred from the ropes with which he'd tied her. "He said my mommy was dead. I know she's not."

"He's gone now, precious darling," he said. "He'll never hurt you again. Now stay here until I find a blanket in there to cover you. And I'll take you to where you'll be safe." He stroked her little head as gently as he could. How impossibly frail she seemed, yet so unaccountably strong.

There was an army blanket on the stale bed inside the trailer.

He wrapped her in this tightly, as if she were a newborn, her large eyes settling on him with total trust. Then he took her up with his left arm, and plunged fast through the trees.

How long they traveled, he didn't know. It was thrilling to him to have her safe in his arms. She was silent, folded against him, a treasure.

On he moved until he saw the lights of a town.

"They'll shoot you!" she cried out when she saw the lights. "Man Wolf," she pleaded. "They will!"

"Would I let anyone harm you?" he asked. "Be quiet, little darling."

She snuggled against him.

On the edges of the town, he crept slowly, safe in the underbrush and the scattered trees, until he saw a brick church with its back to the forest. There were lights in a small rectory-style building beside it, and an old metal swing set in a paved yard. The big rectangular wood-framed sign on the road said in giant black movable letters: GOOD SHEPHERD CHURCH. PASTOR CORRIE GEORGE. SERVICE: SUNDAY AT NOON. There was a phone number in squarish numerals.

He cradled the child in both arms as he approached the window, comforting her because she was afraid again. "Man Wolf, don't let them see you," she cried.

Inside the rectory, he could see a heavyset woman, alone, at a brown kitchen table, in dark blue pants and a simple blouse, with a paperback book propped up to read as she ate her lonely meal. Her wavy gray hair was cropped short, and she had a simple no-nonsense face. For a long moment, he watched her as the scent of her came to him, clean and good. He had no doubt of it.

He set the child down, carefully removing the bloodstained blanket, and gestured to the kitchen door. "Do you know your name, darling?" he asked.

"Susie," she said. "Susie Blakely. And I live in Eureka. I know my phone number too."

He nodded. "You go to that lady, Susie, and you bring her to me. Go on."

"No, Man Wolf, go, please!" she said. "She'll call the police and they'll kill you."

But when he wouldn't go, she turned and did as she was told.

When the woman came out, Reuben stood there gazing at her, wondering what it was she really saw in the dim light of the window—this tall hairy monster that he was, more beast than man, but with a man's bestial face. The rain was just a mist now. He scarcely felt it. The woman was fearless.

"Well, it *is* you!" she said. An agreeable voice. And the little child beside her, clinging to her, pointed and nodded.

"Help her," Reuben said to the woman, conscious of how deep and rough his voice sounded. "The man's gone who was hurting her. They'll never find him. Not hair nor hide of him. Help her. She's been through terrible things, but she knows her name and where she belongs."

"I know who she is," the woman said under her breath. She came a little closer to him, looking up at him with small, pale eyes. "She's the Blakely kid. She's been missing since summer."

"You'll see to it then——."

"You have to get out of here," she said with a wagging finger as though talking to a giant child. "They'll kill you if they see you. These woods were crawling with every harebrained backwoods gun-toting crazy in the country after you last appeared. People came from out of state to hunt you. Get the hell out of here."

He started to laugh, ruefully aware of how very strange that must have seemed to both of them, this hulking dark-haired beast chuckling under his breath like a man.

"Please go, Man Wolf," said the little girl, her pale cheeks coloring. "I won't tell anybody I saw you. I'll tell them I ran away. Go, please, run."

"You tell them what you have to tell them," he said. "You tell what sets you free."

He turned to go.

"You saved my life, Man Wolf!" she cried.

He turned back to her. For a long moment he gazed at her, her strong upturned face, the quiet steady fire in her eyes. "You're going to be all right, Susie," he said. "I love you, darling dear."

And then he was gone.

Racing into the rich, fragrant thickness of the forest, the bloody blanket thrown over his shoulder, tunneling at incalculable speed through the brambles and the broken branches, and the crackling wet leaves, his soul soaring as he put the miles between himself and the little church.

An hour and a half later, he fell down exhausted on his bed. He was sure that he'd slipped in without anyone being aware. He felt guilty, guilty for going out without the permission of Felix or Margon and doing the very thing that the Distinguished Gentlemen didn't want for him and Stuart to do. But he felt exultant, and he felt exhausted. And guilty or not, for the moment, he didn't care. And he was almost asleep when he heard a mournful howling somewhere outside in the night.

Perhaps he was already dreaming but then he heard the howling again.

To all the world, it might have been the howling of a wolf, but he knew otherwise. He could hear the Morphenkind in the howling, and it had a deep plaintive note to it that no animal could make.

He sat up. He couldn't conceivably figure which of the Morphenkinder was making such a sound or why.

It came again, a long, low howl that made the hair come again to the backs of his hands and his arms.

Wolves in the wild howl to signal one another, do they not? But we are not really wolves, are we? We are something neither human nor animal. And who among us would make such a strange, sad sound?

He lay back on the pillow, forcing the hair all over his body to recede, and leave him alone.

It came again, almost sorrowful, this howling—full of pain and pleading, it seemed.

He was more than half asleep, and tumbling into dreams, when he heard it for the last time.

A dream came to him. It was confused even in the dreaming. Marchent was there, in a house in the forest, an old house full of people and lighted rooms, and figures coming and going. Marchent cried and cried as she talked to the people around her. She cried and cried and he couldn't bear the agonized sound of her voice, the sight of her upturned face as she gestured and argued with these people. The people did not appear to hear her, to heed her, or to answer. He couldn't clearly see the people. He couldn't clearly see anything. At one point Marchent rose and ran out of the house and, in her bare feet and torn clothes, she ran through the cold wet forest. The bristling saplings scraped her bare legs. There were indistinct figures in the darkness around her, shadowy figures that appeared to reach out for her as she ran. He couldn't stand the sight of it. He was terrified as he ran after her. The scene shifted. She sat on the side of Felix's bed, the bed they'd shared, and she was crying again and he said things to her, but what they were, he didn't know—it was all happening so swiftly, so confusedly—and she said, "I know, I know, but I don't know how!" And he felt he couldn't stand the pain of it.

He woke in the icy-gray morning light. The dream fell apart as if it were made of melting frost on the panes. The image of the little girl came back to him, little Susie Blakely, and with it the miserable realization that he was going to have to answer to the Distinguished Gentlemen for doing what he had done. Was it on the news already? "Man Wolf Strikes Again." He roused himself uneasily and was thinking about Marchent as he stepped into the shower.

7

HE DIDN'T CHECK his phone until he was on his way down the stairs.
He had text messages from his mother, his father, and his brother all
saying essentially "Call Celeste."

What in the world could she possibly want?

An amazing sound greeted him when he headed for the kitchen,
that of Felix and Margon obviously arguing. They were speaking that
ancient tongue of theirs, and the argument was heated.

Reuben hesitated in the kitchen door long enough to confirm that
they were really going at it, with Margon actually red in the face as he
thundered under his breath at a plainly infuriated Felix.

Frightening. He had no idea what it meant, but he turned around
and left. He'd never been able to bear it when Phil and Grace actually
fought or, frankly, when any two people had a violent argument in his
presence.

He went into the library, sat down at the desk, and punched in
Celeste's number, thinking angrily that she was the very last person
in the world whose voice he wanted to hear. Maybe if he hadn't been
so damned afraid of arguments and raised voices, he would have rid
himself of Celeste a long time ago and once and for all.

When the call went straight to voice mail, he said, "Reuben here.
You want to talk?" and clicked off.

He looked up to see Felix standing there with a mug of coffee in his
hand. Felix looked completely calm and collected now.

"For you," he said, setting down the coffee. "Did you call your old
ladylove?"

"Good heavens, she's even reached out to you? What's happening?"

"It's important," said Felix. "Critically important."

"Someone's died?"

"Exactly the opposite," said Felix. He winked, and seemed unable to suppress a smile.

He was formally dressed as always, in a tailored wool coat and wool pants, with his dark hair neatly combed, as though ready for whatever the day would bring.

"This isn't what you and Margon were arguing about, was it?" Reuben asked tentatively.

"Oh, no, not at all. Put that out of your mind. Let me deal with the inimitable Margon. Call Celeste, please."

The phone rang and Reuben answered at once. As soon as Celeste spoke his name, he realized she'd been crying.

"What's happened?" he asked, making it as sympathetic and kind as he could. "Celeste, tell me!"

"Well, you might have answered your phone, you know, Sunshine Boy," she said. "I've been calling you for days."

More and more people said this to him, and more and more he had to make guilty excuses, which just now he did not wish to do.

"I'm sorry, Celeste, what is it?"

"Well, in a way the crisis is over because I've made up my mind."

"As to what especially?"

"As to marrying Mort," she said. "Because no matter what you do, Sunshine Boy, in the ivory tower in which you live, your mother's going to take the baby. That has pretty much settled it, that and my refusal to abort my firstborn even if it is the son of an airhead ne'er-do-well."

He was too shocked to say a word. Something kindled in him, something so near to pure happiness he scarcely knew what it was, but he didn't dare to hope, not yet.

She went on talking.

"I thought I was out of the woods. That's why I didn't even bother to tell you. Well, that was a false alarm. I wasn't out of the woods. Fact is, I'm four months along now. And it *is* a boy, and he's perfectly healthy." She went on talking, about the wedding, and about how Mort was fine with it all, and how Grace was already applying to take off a year from the hospital to take care of the child. Grace was the most wonderful woman in the entire world to stop everything to do this, and Grace a brilliant surgeon, and Reuben would never really know how lucky he was to have a mother like Grace. Reuben didn't appreciate anything, in fact, and he never had. That's how he could ignore people's phone messages and e-mails, and isolate himself in Northern California in a "mansion" as if the real world didn't exist. . . . "You're the most selfish, spoiled person I ever knew," she said, her voice rising, "and frankly, you make me sick, the way everything just falls into your lap, the way this mansion up there just fell into your lap, the way no matter what happens somebody does your dirty work and cleans up your messes. . . ."

The torrent continued.

He realized he was staring at Felix, and Felix was looking at him with the usual protective affection as he waited without apology to hear what Reuben had to say.

"Celeste, I had no idea," he said, breaking in on her suddenly.

"Well, of course not," she said. "Neither did I. I was on the pill, for God's sake. I thought I might be, right before you first went up there, and then as I said, I thought I wasn't. And then, well, I had the sonogram yesterday. I wouldn't have an abortion now even if you tried to push me into it. This baby's coming into the world. Truth is, Sunshine Boy, I don't much want to talk to you." She rang off.

He put down the phone. He was staring at nothing, and thinking over a multitude of things, and that happiness was blazing now, making him positively giddy, and then he heard Felix's voice, gentle and confiding.

"Reuben, don't you see? This is the only normal human child you will have."

He looked up at Felix. He was smiling foolishly, he knew it. He was almost laughing for pure happiness. But he was speechless.

The phone was ringing again, but he scarcely heard it. Images were cascading through his mind. And out of the chaos of his conflicting emotions a resolve had formed.

Felix answered the phone and held the receiver out to him. "Your mother."

"Darling, I hope you're happy with this. Listen, I've told her we'll take care of everything. We'll take the baby. I'll take the baby. I'll care for this baby."

"Mom, I want my son," he said. "I'm happy, Mom. I'm so happy, really, I can't figure quite what to say. I tried to tell Celeste, but she wouldn't listen. She didn't want to listen. Mom, I am so happy. Dear God, I am so happy."

Celeste's stinging words were coming back to him, confusing him. What in the world had she meant by all that invective? It just didn't matter, really. What mattered was the baby.

"I knew you would be, Reuben," Grace was saying. "I knew you wouldn't let us down. She had the appointment for the abortion when she told me! But I said, 'Celeste, you can't do this, please.' She didn't want to do it, Reuben. She wouldn't have told anyone if she'd really wanted the abortion. We would never have known. She gave in right away. Look, Reuben, she's just angry right now."

"But Mom, I mean, I just don't understand Celeste," he said. "Let's just do whatever we can to make her happy."

"Well, we will, Reuben. But having a baby's painful. She's already requested a leave from the district attorney's office and she's talking about relocating in Southern California after this is over. Mort's applying to UC Riverside for a job. And it looks good. And I'm talking about giving her whatever she needs to get settled there and start over again. You know, a house, a condo, whatever we can do. She'll land on her feet, Reuben. But she's mad. So let her be mad. And let's be happy."

"Mom, you're not taking off from work for a year," Reuben said. "You don't have to." He looked up at Felix. Felix nodded. "This boy is going to grow up here with his father. You're not giving up your career for him, Mom. He's coming here to live, and I'll be bringing him down every weekend to see you, you understand? Why, the room right next to mine, it's Laura's office, but we'll turn that into a nursery. There are plenty of rooms for Laura's office. Laura's going to be excited when I tell her this."

His mother was crying. Phil came on the line and said, "Congratulations, son. I'm so happy for you. When you hold your firstborn in your arms, well, Reuben, that's when you understand your own life for the first time. I know that sounds trite, but it's true. You wait and see."

"Thanks, Dad," said Reuben. He was surprised at how glad he was to hear his father's voice.

They went round and round for several minutes, and then Grace said she had to get off and call Jim. Jim was scared to death that Celeste would change her mind and call the abortion clinic again and she had to let Jim know everything was all right. Celeste was coming for lunch, and if Reuben called the florist on Columbus Avenue they could have flowers here by one o'clock. Would Reuben please do that?

Yes, he would do that, he said, he would do that right now.

"Look, Mom, I'm going to pay for everything," Reuben said. "I'll call Simon Oliver myself. Let me do this. Let me make the arrangements."

"No, no, I'll handle it," said Grace. "Reuben, you're our only child, really. Jim's never going to be anything but a Catholic priest. He'll never marry, or have children. I resigned myself to that a long time ago. And when we go, what's ours is yours. It's six of one, half dozen of another who pays Celeste on all this."

Finally she rang off.

He called the florist immediately. "Just something big and beautiful and cheerful," he told the guy. "Like this lady loves roses of all colors, but what have you got to make it look like spring?" He was looking at the gray light coming in the windows.

At last, he was able to pick up the mug of coffee, take a deep drink of it, and sit back in the chair and think. He really had no idea how Laura would take it, but she'd know as surely as he knew that what Felix had just said was true.

Fate had given him an extraordinary gift.

This was the only natural child to which he'd ever be a father in this world. It frightened him suddenly to realize this had almost not happened. But it had happened. He was going to be a father. He was going to "give" Grace and Phil a grandson and he would be a wholly human grandson who could grow up before their eyes. He didn't know what the world had in store for him on that score, but this changed everything. He was grateful, grateful to whom he wasn't sure—to God, to fate, to fortune—to Grace, who'd swayed Celeste, and to Celeste, who was giving him his baby, and to Celeste that she existed and to the Fates that he'd had what he had with her. And then the words ran out.

Felix stood with his back to the fire watching him. He was smiling, but his eyes were glazed and faintly red and he looked terribly sad, suddenly, his smile what people call philosophical.

"I'm happy for you," he whispered. "So happy for you. I cannot say."

"Good Lord," Reuben said. "I'd give her everything I had in this world for that child. And she hates me."

"She doesn't hate you, son," said Felix mildly. "She simply doesn't love you, and never did, and she feels quite guilty and uncomfortable about it."

"You think so?"

"Of course," he said. "I knew the first time I encountered her and heard her endless speeches about your 'charmed life' and 'irresponsible behavior' and all her advice on how you ought to plan your entire existence."

"Everybody knew it," said Reuben. "Everybody. I was the only one who didn't know it. But why were we ever engaged then?"

"Hard to say," Felix answered. "But she does not want a child now and so she will sign the baby over to you, and I'd act on that promptly if I were you. And she will happily marry your best friend, Mort, of whom she is not mortally resentful apparently, and may perhaps have a child with him later on. She's a practical woman, and she's beautiful, and she's very smart."

"Yes to all of that," said Reuben.

His mind was running with the most unexpected thoughts, thoughts of baby clothes, and cribs and nannies, and picture books, and soft fleeting images of a little boy seated in the window seat against the diamond-paned glass and him, Reuben, reading to that child from a book. Why, all Reuben's favorite children's books were still in the attic on Russian Hill, weren't they, the lavishly illustrated *Treasure*

Island and *Kidnapped,* and the venerable old poetry books from which Phil so loved to read.

Some hazy sense of the future emerged in which a boy was striding through the front door with a backpack full of textbooks, and then it seemed he was grown into a man. And the future shifted, clouded, became a fog in which Reuben would have to leave the warm circle of his family, and his son—have to, have to flee—unable any longer to disguise the fact that he wasn't growing older, that nothing was changing in him—but then this boy, this young man, this son, would be with them, with Grace and Phil, and Jim, and with Celeste, too, and Mort perhaps, a part of them, after Reuben was gone.

He looked at the windows, and suddenly this little world he'd constructed collapsed. In his memory, he saw Marchent beyond the glass, and he was shuddering once again.

It seemed a long time passed in which Reuben sat there in silence, and Felix stood quietly by the fire.

"My boy," said Felix softly. "I hate to intrude on your happiness just now, but I was wondering. Would you come along with me, perhaps, to the Nideck Cemetery? I thought you might want to come. I talked to our attorney this morning, you know, Arthur Hammermill. And well, it seems Marchent was indeed buried there."

"Oh yes, I do want to go with you," said Reuben. "But there's something I must tell you first. I saw her again. It was last night."

And slowly, methodically, he relived the chilling details.

8

THEY HEADED FOR the Nideck Cemetery under a leaden sky, the rain reduced to a drizzle in the surrounding forest. Felix was at the wheel of his heavy Mercedes sedan.

Arthur Hammermill had seen to Marchent's interment in the family mausoleum, Felix explained, according to clear instructions in Marchent's will. Hammermill himself attended a small ceremony for which a few residents of Nideck had gathered, including the Galtons and their cousins, though there had been no public announcement at all. As for the murderous brothers, they had been cremated, based on their own instructions to "friends."

"I'm ashamed that I never thought to visit her grave," said Reuben. "I'm ashamed. There can't be the slightest doubt that whatever is causing her to haunt, she's unhappy."

Felix never once took his eyes off the road.

"I didn't visit the grave myself," said Felix in a tormented voice. "I had some convenient notion that she'd been buried in South America. But that is no excuse." His voice went dry as if he were on the verge of breaking down. "And she was the very last of my own blood descendants."

Reuben looked at him, wanting so badly to ask how this had played out.

"The very last of those related to me by blood in this world, as far as I know. Since every other scion of my family has long ago withered or vanished. And I didn't visit her grave, no, I did not. And that is why we are doing it now, isn't it? Both of us are visiting her grave."

The cemetery was behind the town, and occupied about two city blocks, flanked by scattered houses on all four sides. The road here was patchy, badly in need of repair, but the homes were all vintage Victorian, small, simple, but well-built frame houses with peak roofs much like the Victorians Reuben had always loved in countless other old California towns. That several here and there were brightly painted with fresh pastel colors and white trim struck him as good for the town of Nideck. There were multicolored Christmas lights twinkling in windows here and there. And the cemetery itself, bound by an iron picket fence with more than one open gate, was rather a picturesque spot with well-kept grass and a great sprinkling of old monuments.

The rain had let up, and they didn't need the umbrellas they'd brought with them, though Reuben wound his scarf around his neck against the eternal chill. The sky was dark and featureless, and a white mist enveloped the top of the forest.

Small rounded tombstones made up most of the graves. Many had rich scrollwork and deep lettering, and here and there Reuben glimpsed a poetic epitaph. There was one small mausoleum, a house of stone blocks with a flat roof and an iron door, and this bore the name NIDECK in ornate letters, while several other Nideck tombstones were scattered to its left and right.

Felix had a key for the iron door.

It made Reuben very uneasy to hear the key grind in the old lock, but they were soon standing in a very dusty little passage illuminated by a single leaded-glass window in the back of the little building, with evidence of what must have been coffin-length crypts on either side.

Marchent had been laid to rest to the right, and a rectangular stone had been fitted in place near the head or the foot of the coffin, Reuben could not guess which. It gave her name, Marchent Sophia Nideck, the dates of her life, and a line of poetry, which surprised Reuben. It read: WE MUST LOVE ONE ANOTHER OR DIE. The poet was W. H. Auden, and his name was inscribed in small letters beneath the quote.

Reuben felt light-headed. He felt trapped and sick, and almost on the edge of collapsing in this little space.

Quickly, he hurried outside, back into the damp air, and left Felix alone inside the little building. He was trembling, and he stood still, fighting the nausea.

It seemed more than ever ghastly to him, perfectly ghastly, that Marchent was dead. He saw Celeste's face, he saw some sweetly illuminated image of the child he was now dreaming of, he saw all the faces of those he loved, including Laura, beautiful Laura, and he felt the grief for Marchent like a sickness that would turn him inside out.

So this is one of the big secrets of life, is it?—you cope with loss sooner or later, and then one loss after another most likely, and it probably never gets any easier than this, and each time you're looking at what is going to happen to you, only this won't happen to me. It won't. And I can't quite make that real.

He stared dully ahead of him and was only vaguely aware that a man was coming across the graveyard from a truck parked on the road, and that he was carrying a large bouquet of white roses, arranged in green ferns, that was fitted into what appeared to be a stone vase.

He thought of the roses he'd sent to Celeste. He felt like crying. He saw Marchent's tormented face again right near him, so near. He felt he was going to go crazy here.

He moved away as the man approached the little mausoleum but he could still hear Felix thanking the man and telling him that the flowers should be placed outside. He heard the rasp of the key in the lock. Then the man was gone, and Reuben was staring at a long row of yew trees, grown far too tall to be picturesque anymore, that divided the graveyard from the quaint and pretty houses across the way. Such pretty bay windows, outlined with red and green lights. Such pretty gingerbread trim. A mass of dark pines rose behind the houses. Indeed the dark woods encroached on all sides, and the houses in all directions looked small and bold against the giant fir trees. The trees were so horribly out of scale with the little streetscape and the community of small graves that slumbered here amid the velvet green grass.

He wanted to turn back, find Felix, say something comforting, but he was so deeply immersed now in the vision of last night, in seeing Marchent's face, feeling her cold hand on his hand, that he couldn't move or speak.

When Felix came up beside him, Felix said, "She's not here, is she? You don't sense any presence of her here."

"No," said Reuben. She is not here. Her suffering face is imprinted on my soul forever. But she is not in this place, and cannot be comforted here.

But where is she? Where is she herself now?

They headed for home, trolling the main street of Nideck, where the official town Christmas trimmings were going up with amazing speed. What a transformation, to see the three-story Nideck Inn already decked with tiny red lights to the rooftop, and to see the green wreaths on the shop doors, and the green garland wound around the quaint old lampposts. There were workmen busy on more than one site. They wore yellow rain slickers and boots. People stopped and waved. Galton and his wife, Bess, were just going into the Inn, probably for lunch, and they both stopped and waved.

All this cheered Felix, obviously. "Reuben," he said, "I think this little Winterfest is truly going to work!"

Only after they hit the narrow country road again did Felix say in a low, very gentle voice, his most protective voice,

"Reuben, do you want to tell me where you went last night?"

Reuben swallowed. He wanted to answer, but he couldn't think what to say.

"Look, I understand," said Felix. "You saw Marchent again. This was profoundly unsettling, of course. And you went out after that, but I so wish you had not."

Silence. Reuben felt like a bad schoolboy, but he didn't know the reason himself why he'd gone. Yes, he'd seen Marchent, and obviously it did have to do with that. But why had this triggered the need to hunt? All he could think of was the bloody triumph of the kill and that plunge through the forest afterwards, after he'd left little Susie Blakely and it seemed he'd been flying like Goodman Brown through the world's darkest wilderness. He knew he was blushing now, blushing with shame.

The car was following the narrow Nideck Road uphill through phalanxes of towering trees.

"Reuben, you know perfectly well what we're trying to do," Felix said, his patience as reliable as ever. "We're trying to take you and

Stuart to places where you can hunt unknown and unnoticed. But if you go out on your own, if you venture into the surrounding towns, the press will be on top of us all again. Reporters will be swarming all over the house, asking for some statement from you on the Man Wolf. You're the go-to guy when it comes to the Man Wolf, the one who's been bitten by the Man Wolf, the one who's seen the Man Wolf, not once but twice, the reporter who writes about the Man Wolf. Look, dear boy, it's a matter of surviving at Nideck Point, for all of us."

"I know, Felix, I'm sorry. I'm so sorry. I haven't even checked the news."

"Well, I haven't either, but the fact is you left your torn and bloody clothes, and a bloodstained blanket, of all things, in the furnace room, Reuben, and any Morphenkind can smell human blood. You've had a meal of somebody for certain, and this won't go unnoticed."

Reuben felt his face grow hot. Too many images of the hunt were crowding in on him. He thought of little Susie's tiny candle-flame face against his chest. He was disoriented, as if this normal body of his now was some sort of illusion. He longed for the other body, the other muscles, the other eyes.

"What stops us, Felix, from living in the forest always, encased in fur, living like the beasts that we are?"

"You know what stops us," said Felix. "We're human beings, Reuben. Human beings. And you will soon have a son."

"I felt like I had to go," Reuben said under his breath. "I just did. I don't know. I had to push back and I know it was foolish. And I wanted to go, that's the God's truth. I wanted to go alone." He blurted out in fits and starts the little story of the child in the trailer. He told how he'd buried the remains of the corpse. "Felix, I'm caught between two worlds, and I had to blunder into that other world, I had to."

Felix was quiet for a while, and then ventured, "I know it's all very seductive, Reuben, these people treating us like God's anointed."

"Felix, how many people are out there, suffering like that? That little girl wasn't fifty miles from here. They're all around us, aren't they?"

"This is part of the burden, Reuben. It's part of the Chrism. We cannot save all of them. And any attempt to do so will end in failure and in our own ruin. We can't make our territory into our kingdom. The time is long past for that. And I don't want to lose Nideck Point again so soon, dear boy. I don't want you to leave, or Laura, or any of us! Reuben, don't burn up your mortal life just yet, don't extinguish all ties with it. Look, this is all my fault and Margon's fault. We haven't let you boys hunt enough. We're not remembering what the early years were like. This will change, Reuben, I promise you."

"I'm sorry, Felix. But you know, those first days, those first heady days, when I didn't know what I was, or what would happen next—or whether I was the only man beast in the whole world—there was such a hedonistic freedom there. And I have to get over that, that I can't slip out at will and become the Man Wolf. I'm working on it, Felix."

"I know you are," said Felix with a sad little laugh. "Of course you are. Reuben, Nideck Point is worth the sacrifice. Whatever we become, wherever we go, we need a haven, a refuge, a sanctuary. I need this. We all need this."

"I know," said Reuben.

"I wonder if you do," said Felix. "How does a man who does not age, who does not grow old—how does such a man keep a family manse, a piece of land that is his? You cannot imagine what it means to leave all you hold sacred because you have to. You have to hide that you don't change, you have to annihilate the person you are to all those you love. You have to abandon your home and your family and return decades later in some alien guise to strangers, pretending to be the long-lost uncle, the bastard son. . . ."

Reuben nodded.

He had never heard Felix's voice so full of pain before, not even when he spoke of Marchent.

"I was born in the most beautiful land imaginable," said Felix, "near the River Rhine above a heavenly Alpine valley. I told you this before, didn't I? I lost it a long time ago. I lost it forever. The fact is I do own the property again now—that very land, those ancient buildings. I bought it all back—lock, stock, and barrel. But it's not my home, or my sanctuary. That can't be reclaimed ever. It's a new place for me now, with all the promise of a new home perhaps in a new time, and that's the best that it can be. But my true home? That's gone beyond reprieve."

"I understand," said Reuben. "I really do. I understand as far as I can understand. I don't know how but I do."

"But time hasn't swallowed Nideck Point for me," said Felix with that same low emotional heat. "No. Not yet. We still have time with Nideck Point before we have to slip away. And you have time, lots of time, with Nideck Point. You and Laura, and now your son, too, can grow up at Nideck Point. We have time to live a rich chapter here."

Felix broke off as though deliberately reining himself in.

Reuben waited, desperate for a way to express what he felt. "I will behave, Felix," he said. "I swear it. I won't ruin it."

"You don't want to ruin it for yourself, Reuben," Felix said. "Forget about me. Forget Margon or Frank or Sergei. Forget Thibault. You don't want to ruin it for yourself and for Laura. Reuben, you will lose everything here soon enough; don't throw away what you have now."

"I don't want to ruin it for you either," said Reuben. "I know what it means to you, Nideck Point."

Felix didn't answer.

A strange thought occurred to Reuben.

It took form as they drove up the sloping road from the gates to the terrace.

"What if she needs Nideck Point?" he asked in a soft voice. "What if it's Marchent's sanctuary? What if she's looked beyond, Felix, and she doesn't want to go beyond? What if she wants to remain here too?"

"Then she wouldn't be suffering, would she, when she comes to you?" Felix responded.

Reuben sighed. "Yes. Why would she be suffering?"

"The world might be full of ghosts for all we know. They might have found their sanctuaries all around us. But they don't show us their pain, do they? They don't haunt as she's haunting you."

Reuben shook his head. "She's here, and she can't break through. She's wandering, alone, desperate for me to see her and hear her." He thought about his dream again, the dream in which he'd seen Marchent in rooms filled with people who took no notice of her, the dream in which he'd seen her running through the darkness alone. He thought of those curious shadowy figures he'd seen vaguely in the dim forest of the dream. Had they been reaching out to her?

In a low voice, he described the dream to Felix. "But there was more to it," he confessed, "and now I've forgotten."

"That's always the way with dreams," Felix said.

They sat parked before the house. The end of the terrace along the cliff was scarcely visible in the mist. Yet they could hear the sounds of hammers and saws from the workmen down the hill at the guesthouse. Rain or shine, the men worked on the guesthouse.

Felix shivered. He drew in his breath, and then after a long pause, he placed his hand on Reuben's shoulder. As always it had a calming effect on Reuben.

"You're a brave boy," he said.

"You think so?"

"Oh yes, very," said Felix. "That's why she's come to you."

Reuben was bewildered, lost suddenly in too many shifting mind pictures and half-remembered sensations, unable to reason. Of all things, he heard that dreamy haunting song again that the ghost radio had played inside the ghost room, and that spellbinding beat paralyzed him.

"Felix, this house should be yours," he said. "We don't know what Marchent wants, why she haunts. But if I'm a brave boy, then I have to say it. This is your house, Felix. Not mine."

"No," Felix said. He smiled faintly, sadly.

"Felix, I know you own all the land around this property, all the land to the town and back and north and east. You should have the house back."

"No," said Felix gently but resolutely.

"If I deed it over to you, well, there's no way you can stop me from doing it—."

"No," Felix said.

"Why not?"

"Because if you did that," Felix said, his eyes glazing with tears, "it wouldn't be your home anymore. And then you and Laura might leave.

And you and Laura are the warmth shining in the heart of Nideck Point. And I can't bear the thought of your going away. I can't make Nideck Point my home again without you. Leave things as they are. My niece gave you this house to get rid of it, rid of her grief, and rid of her pain. Leave it as she willed it. And you brought me back to it. In a sense, you've given it to me already. Owning a great cluster of empty rooms might have meant little or nothing—without you."

Felix opened the door. "Now come," he said, "let's take a quick look at the progress on the guesthouse. We want it to be ready whenever your father comes to visit."

Yes, the guesthouse, and the promise of Phil coming to spend long leisurely visits with him. Phil had indeed promised. And Reuben wanted that so very much.

9

As it turned out, there was nothing on the news about the Man Wolf appearing again in Northern California. Reuben searched the web, and every local news source he knew. The papers, the television, all were silent on that score. But there was a big story, getting quite a bit of play in the *San Francisco Chronicle.*

Susie Blakely, an eight-year-old girl, missing since June from her home in Eureka, California, had at last been found—wandering near the town of Mountainville in northern Mendocino County. Authorities had confirmed that a carpenter, long suspected of the crime, had in fact abducted her, and kept her prisoner, often beating her and starving her until her escape from his trailer last night.

The carpenter was believed dead as the result of an animal attack, which the child, too traumatized by her ordeal, had witnessed but could not describe.

There was a picture of Susie, taken at the time she went missing. And there was that tiny radiant candle flame of a face.

Reuben Googled the old stories. Her parents, obviously, were extremely good people who had made numerous appeals to the media. As for the older lady, Pastor Corrie George, who had taken the child from Reuben, there was no mention of her on the news at all.

Had both the minister and the little girl agreed not to talk of the Man Wolf? Reuben was amazed. But he worried. How would the secret weigh upon both these innocent people? More than ever he was ashamed, yet had he not gone into the forest, would that precious little life have been snuffed out in that filthy trailer?

Over a late lunch, with only the housekeeper, Lisa, in attendance, Reuben assured the Distinguished Gentlemen that he would never again risk their security with this kind of careless behavior. Stuart made a few sulky remarks to the effect that Reuben should have taken him with him, but Margon cut him off with a quick and imperious gesture, and went on to toast Celeste's "marvelous news."

This didn't stop Sergei from lecturing Reuben at length on the risks of what he had done, and Thibault joined in as well. It was agreed that Saturday they would fly out for a couple of days, this time to the "jungles" of South America, and there hunt together before returning home. Stuart was ecstatic at the prospect. And Reuben felt a low arousal very much akin to sexual desire. He could already see and feel the jungles around him, a great swooshing fabric of moist greenery, fragrant, tropical, delicious, so very different from the bleak cold of Nideck Point, and the thought of prowling there in such a dense and lawless universe, in search of "the most dangerous game" caused him to fall quiet.

By suppertime, Reuben had conferred with Laura, who was genuinely overjoyed about the developments, and he and Lisa were removing all Laura's belongings to a new office on the east side of the house. This would suit Laura wonderfully, as the room was flooded with morning light, and a good deal warmer than anything on the ocean side of Nideck Point as well.

Reuben walked around the now-vacant bedroom for some half an hour, imagining the nursery, and then went to investigate all the necessary accoutrements online. Lisa chatted happily about the necessity of a good German nanny who would sleep in the room while the little boy was an infant, and all the marvelous Swiss shops from which the finest layette imaginable could be ordered, and the necessity of surrounding a sensitive little one with fine furnishings, soothing colors, the music of Mozart and Bach, and appealing paintings from the very start of his life.

"Now, you must leave the nanny to me," said Lisa forcefully as she straightened the white curtains in the new office. "And I will find the most marvelous of women to do this job for you. I have someone in mind. A beloved friend, yes, very beloved. You ask Master Felix. And you leave it to me."

Reuben was fine with it, yet something about her suddenly struck him as strange. There was a moment when Lisa turned and smiled at him that he had an uneasy feeling about her, that something was not quite right about her and what she was saying, but he shrugged it off.

He stood watching her as she dusted Laura's desk. Her mode of dress was prim, old-fashioned, even out-of-date. But she was spry in her movements and rather economical. It nudged at him, her whole demeanor, but he couldn't quite figure out why.

She was slender to the point of being wiry but unusually strong. He'd seen that when she forced the window which had been stuck fast with fresh paint. And there were other strange things about her.

Like now, when she seated herself before Laura's computer, turned it on, and quickly ascertained that it was in fact going "online" as it should.

Reuben Golding, you are a sexist, he said to himself silently. Why do you find it surprising that a forty-five-year-old woman from Switzerland would know all about checking that a computer was online? He'd seen Lisa often enough on the household computer in Marchent's old office. And she hadn't been merely pecking away.

She seemed to catch him studying her, and she gave him a surprisingly cold smile. Then giving his arm a squeeze as she passed, she moved out of the room.

For all her attractiveness, which he did like very much, there was something mannish about her, and as he heard her steps echoing down the hall they sounded like those of a man. More shameless sexism, he thought. She did have the prettiest gray eyes, and her skin had a powdery soft look to it, and what was he thinking?

He'd never paid much attention to Heddy or Jean Pierre, he realized. In fact, he was a little shy around them, not being used to "servants," as Felix so easily called them. But there was something a little strange about them too, about their whispering, their almost stealthy movements, and the way that they never looked him in the eye.

None of these people showed the slightest interest in anything ever said in their presence, and that was odd, when he thought about it, because the Distinguished Gentlemen talked so openly in front of them, at meals, about their various activities that you would have thought there would be a raised eyebrow, but there never was. Indeed no one ever dropped his voice when talking about anything just because the servants might hear.

Well, Felix and Margon knew them well, these servants, so who was he to be questioning them, and they couldn't have been more agreeable to everyone. So he ought to let it go. But the child was coming, and now that the child was coming, he was going to care about a lot of little things, perhaps, that he hadn't cared about in the past.

By evening, Celeste had changed the terms of her agreement slightly.

Mort, after some agonizing reflection, saw absolutely no reason why he should be the husband of record here, and neither did she. It was agreed that Reuben would drive down to San Francisco on Friday and marry Celeste in a simple legal ceremony at City Hall. No blood test or waiting period was required by California law, thank heaven, and a small "prenup" was being drafted by Simon Oliver that would guarantee a simple no-fault divorce settlement as soon as the child was born. Grace was taking care of the money involved.

Celeste and Mort had already moved into the guest bedroom at the Russian Hill house. They'd live with Grace and Phil until the baby came into the world and went to live with its father. But Mort didn't want to be around for the wedding.

Yes, Grace admitted, Celeste was angry, angry at the whole world. Prepare for some ranting. She was angry she was pregnant, and somehow Reuben had become an archvillain, but "We have to think of the baby." Reuben agreed.

A little dazed and angry himself, Reuben called Laura. She was fine with the marriage. Reuben's son would be his legal offspring. Why not?

"Would you consider going with me?" asked Reuben.

"Of course, I'll go with you," she said.

10

He was awakened in the middle of the night by the howling—the same lone Morphenkind voice he'd heard the night before.

It was about two a.m. He didn't know how long it had been going on, only that it had finally penetrated his thin chaotic dreams and nudged him towards consciousness. He sat up in the darkened bedroom and listened.

It went on for a long time, but gradually became fainter as if the Morphenkind was moving slowly and steadily away from Nideck Point. It had a tragic, plaintive quality as before. It was positively baleful. And then he couldn't hear it anymore.

An hour later when he couldn't get back to sleep, Reuben put on his robe and took a walk through the corridors of the second floor. He felt uneasy. He knew what he was doing. He was looking for Marchent. He found it an agony to wait for her to find him.

In fact, waiting for her was like waiting for the wolf transformation in those early days after he'd first changed, and it filled him with dread. But it soothed his nerves to make a circuit of the upstairs hallways. They were illuminated only by the occasional sconce, little better than night-lights, but he could see the beautiful polish on the boards.

The smell of floor wax was almost sweet.

He liked the spaciousness, the firm wood that barely creaked under his slippers, and the glimpse of the open rooms where he could just make out the pale squares of the undraped windows revealing the faint sheen of a wet gray nighttime sky.

He moved along the back hallway, and then turned into one of the smaller rooms, never occupied by anyone since he'd come, and tried to see out of the window into the forest behind the house.

He listened for that howling again, but he didn't hear it. He could make out a very dim light in the second floor of the service building to his left. He thought that was Heddy's room, but he wasn't sure.

But he could see precious little else of the dark forest itself.

A chill came over him, a pringling on the surface of his skin. He stiffened, keenly aware of the wolf hair bristling inside him, nudging him, but he didn't know why it had come.

Then very slowly, as he felt the prickling all over his face and scalp, he heard noises out there in the darkness, the dull crash of branches, and the sounds of grunts and snarls. He narrowed his eyes, feeling the wolf blood pulse in his arteries, feeling his fingers elongating, and he could just barely make out two figures beyond the end of the shed, in the clearing before the trees closed in, two wolfish figures who seemed to be pushing and shoving at each other, fending one another off, then gesticulating like human beings. Morphenkinder certainly, but which Morphenkinder?

Before this moment, he was certain he knew all the others by sight when they were in wolf coat. But now he was not certain at all who these two were. He was witnessing a violent quarrel, that much was clear. Suddenly the taller of the two threw the shorter Morphenkind against the doors of the shed. A dull reverberation went up from the wood as if it were the surface of a drum.

A high angry riff of syllables broke from the shorter figure, and then the taller figure, turning his back on the other, threw up his arms and let loose with a long, mournful, yet carefully modulated howl.

The shorter figure flew at the taller one; but the tall Morphenkind shoved him off and again appeared to lift his head as he howled.

The scene paralyzed Reuben. The transformation was coming over him fiercely now, and he fought desperately to stop it.

A sound interrupted him, the heavy tread of feet just behind him, and he started violently, turning to see the familiar figure of Sergei against the pale light of the hall.

"Leave them alone, little wolf," he said in his deep gravelly voice. "Let them fight it out."

Reuben shuddered all over. One violent chill after another passed through him as he fought the transformation and won. His skin felt naked and cold, and he was trembling.

Sergei had come up beside him and was looking down into the yard.

"They will fight it out and it will be over," he said. "And I know there is no way with those two but to leave them alone."

"It's Margon and Felix, isn't it?"

Sergei looked at Reuben with undisguised surprise.

"I can't tell," Reuben confessed.

"Yes, it's Margon and Felix," said Sergei. "And it doesn't matter. The Forest Gentry would eventually come whether Felix called them or not."

"The Forest Gentry?" asked Reuben. "But who are the Forest Gentry?"

"Never mind, little wolf," he said. "Come away and let them alone. The Forest Gentry always come at Midwinter. When we dance on Christmas Eve, the Forest Gentry will surround us. They will play their pipes and drums for us. They can do no harm."

"But I don't understand," said Reuben. He glanced back down at the clearing beyond the shed.

Felix stood alone now facing the forest, and raising his head he gave another of those plaintive howls.

Sergei was leaving. "But wait, please tell me," Reuben insisted. "Why are they fighting over this?"

"Is it so disturbing to you that they fight?" said Sergei. "Get accustomed to it, Reuben. They do it. They have always done it. It was Margon who brought the human family of Felix into our world. Nothing will ever divide Margon and Felix."

Sergei left him. He heard the door of his room close.

The sound of the howling came from far off.

Four a.m.

Reuben had fallen asleep in the library. He was sitting in Felix's leather wing chair by the fire, his feet on the fender. He'd done some computer work, trying to trace down the words "Forest Gentry," but could find nothing of any significance. And then he had sat by the fire, eyes closed, begging Marchent to come to him, begging her to tell him why she was suffering. Sleep had come but no Marchent.

Now he woke and at once sensed that some particular change in things around him had indeed awakened him.

The fire had burned low but was still bright in the shadows because a new log had been added to it; a big thick chunk of oak had been nestled in the embers of the fire he'd built two hours ago. Only shadows surrounded him in his chair before the brightness of the fire.

But someone was moving in the room.

Slowly he turned his head to the left, looking past the wing of the leather chair. He saw the slim figure of Lisa moving about. Deftly, she straightened the velvet draperies to the left side of the huge window. Bending easily, she stacked the books that lay on the floor there.

And in the window seat gazing at her with a look of fierce and tearful resentment sat Marchent.

Reuben couldn't move. He couldn't breathe. The scene struck perfect horror in him more surely than any other visitation—the spectacle of the living Lisa and the ghost in hideous proximity to each other. He opened his mouth but no sound came out.

Marchent's quivering eyes followed Lisa's smallest gestures. Agony. Now Lisa moved forward towards the ghostly figure, smoothing the velvet cushion of the window seat. As she drew nearer the seated figure, the two women looked at each other.

Reuben gasped; he felt he was smothering.

Marchent looked up furiously and bitterly at the figure who reached quite literally through her, and it seemed the obdurate Lisa stared right at Marchent.

Reuben cried out. "Don't disturb her!" he said before he could think or stop himself. "Don't torture her!" He was on his feet shaking violently.

Marchent's head turned as did Lisa's, and Marchent raised her arms, reaching towards him, and then vanished.

Reuben felt a pressure against him, he felt the pressure of hands on his upper arms, and then the soft tingling feeling of hair and lips touching him, and then it was gone, completely gone. The fire burst and crackled as if a wind had touched it. Papers on the desk rustled and then settled.

"Oh God," he said in a half sob. "You couldn't see her!" he stammered. "She was there, there on the window seat. Oh God!" He felt his eyes watering, and his breaths came uneasily.

Silence.

He looked up.

Lisa stood there behind the Chesterfield sofa with that same cold smile he'd seen on her narrow delicate features once before, looking both ancient and young somehow with her hair swept back so tight, and her black silk dress so prim to her ankles.

"Of course I saw her," she said.

The inevitable sweat broke out all over Reuben. He felt it crawling on his chest.

Her voice came again, unobtrusive and solicitous as she approached him.

"I have been seeing her since I came," she said. Her expression was faintly contemptuous, or at the very least patronizing.

"But you reached right through her as if she weren't there," Reuben said, the tears sliding down his face. "You shouldn't have treated her like that."

"And what was I to do?" said the woman, deliberately softening her manner. She sighed. "She doesn't know she's dead! I've told her, but she won't accept it! Should I treat her as if she is a living creature here? Will that help her!"

Reuben was stunned. "Stop it," he said. "Slow down. What do you mean she doesn't know she's dead?"

"She doesn't know," repeated the woman with a light shrug.

"That's . . . that's too awful," Reuben whispered. "I can't believe such a thing, that a person wouldn't know she was dead. I can't—."

She reached out and firmly urged him back towards the chair. "You sit down," she said. "And let me bring you some coffee now, as you're awake and it's useless for you to go back to bed."

"Please, leave me alone," said Reuben. He felt a massive headache coming on.

He looked into her eyes. There was something wrong with her, so wrong, but he couldn't figure what.

In what he'd seen of her deliberate movements, her strange demeanor had been as horrifying as the vision of Marchent crying there, Marchent angry, Marchent lost.

"How can she not know she's dead?" he demanded.

"I told you," said the woman in a low iron voice. "She will not accept it. It's common enough, I can tell you."

Reuben sank down into the chair. "Don't bring me anything. Let me alone now," he said.

"What you mean is you don't want anything from my hands," she said, "because you're angry with me."

A male voice spoke from behind Reuben. It was Margon.

It spoke sharply in German, and Lisa, bowing her head, immediately left the room.

Margon moved to the Chesterfield sofa opposite the fire and sat down. His long brown hair was loose down to his shoulders. He was dressed only in a denim shirt and jeans and slippers. His hair was tousled and his face had an immediate warm and empathetic expression.

"Pay no attention to Lisa," he said. "She is here to do her job, no more, no less."

"I don't like her," Reuben confessed. "I'm ashamed to say it, but it's true. However that's the smallest part of what concerns me right now."

"I know what concerns you," said Margon. "But Reuben, if ghosts are ignored, they often move on. It doesn't help them to look at them, acknowledge them, keep them lingering here. The natural thing is for them to move on."

"Then you know all about this?"

"I know you've seen Marchent," said Margon. "Felix told me. And Felix is suffering over this."

"I had to tell him, didn't I?"

"Of course you did. I'm not faulting you for telling him or any-one else. But please listen to me. The best response is to ignore her appearances."

"That seems so cold, so cruel," said Reuben. "If you could see her, if you could see her face."

"I did see her, just now," Margon said. "I hadn't seen her before, but I saw her in the window seat. I saw her rise and come towards you. But Reuben, don't you see, she can't really hear you or understand you and she can't speak to you. She's not a strong enough spirit, and please believe me, the very last thing you want is for her to become strong, because if she becomes strong she may stay forever."

Reuben gasped. He felt the maddest impulse to make the Sign of the Cross, but he didn't do it. His hands were shaking.

Lisa had returned with a tray, which she set down on the leather ottoman in front of Margon. The fragrance of coffee filled the room. There were two pots on the tray, two cups and saucers and the usual silver and old linen napkins.

Margon let loose a long stream of German words, obviously some sort of reproof, as he looked at Lisa. His words never became hurried or harsh, but there was a cold chastising tone to what he said nevertheless and the woman bowed her head again, as she had before, and nodded.

"I am so sorry, Reuben," said Lisa with soft sincerity. "Truly I am sorry. I am so rough, so perfunctory sometimes. My world is a world of efficiency. I am so sorry. You will, please, give me another chance, that you might think better of me."

"Oh, yes, of course," said Reuben. "I didn't know what I was say-ing." He felt immediately sorry for her.

"It was I who spoke badly," she said, her voice now an imploring whisper. "I will bring you something to eat. Your nerves are shattered and you must eat." She went out.

They sat there in silence, and then Margon said, "You'll get used to her and used to the others. There are one or two more coming. Believe me, they are expert at serving us or I wouldn't have them here."

"There's something unusual about her," Reuben confessed. "I can't put my finger on it. I don't know how to describe it. But really, she's been so helpful. I don't know what's the matter with me."

He took a folded Kleenex out of the pocket of his robe and wiped his eyes and nose.

"There are a lot of unusual things about all of them," said Margon, "but I've worked with them for years. They are very good with us."

Reuben nodded. "It's Marchent that worries me, you know that, because she's suffering. And Lisa said the most horrible thing! I mean—is it really possible that Marchent doesn't know she's dead? Is that conceivable, that the soul of a human being could be bound to this place, not knowing that it's dead, not knowing that we're alive and struggling to talk to us and not being able to do it? That's almost more than I can believe. I can't believe that life could be that cruel to us. I mean I know terrible things happen in this world, always, everywhere, but I thought that after death, after the cord had snapped, as they say, I thought there would be—."

"Answers?" offered Margon.

"Yes, answers, clarity, revelation," said Reuben. "Either that or, mercifully, nothing."

Margon nodded. "Well, maybe it's not so neat. We can't know, can we? We're bound to these powerful bodies of ours, aren't we? And we don't know what the dead know or don't know. But I can tell you this. They do eventually move on. They can. They have their choice, I'm convinced of it."

Margon's face showed only kindness.

When Reuben didn't answer or speak, he poured out a cup of fresh coffee for Reuben and, without asking, put two packets of artificial sweetener in it, which was what Reuben always took with his coffee, and after stirring the coffee, he offered it to Reuben.

There was the soft rustle of silk announcing Lisa, and the pungent smell of fresh-baked cookies. She held the steaming plate in her hand and then set it down on the tray.

"You eat now a little," she said. "Sugar wakes one in the early hours. It rouses the sleepy blood."

Reuben took a deep drink of the coffee. It did taste delicious. But the ugly and terrible thought struck him that Marchent could perhaps taste nothing. Perhaps she could smell nothing, savor nothing. Perhaps she could only see and hear, and this seemed penitential and awful.

When he looked up at Margon again, the compassion in Margon's face almost made Reuben cry. Margon and Felix had so much in common beyond the darker Asian skin, the dark eyes. They seemed so alike as to be from a common tribe but Reuben knew that wasn't possible, not if Margon was telling the truth with his ancient stories, and everything about Margon suggested that he always told the truth, even if others didn't like it or want to accept it. Right now, he looked like an earnest and a concerned friend, youngish, empathetic, genuine.

"Tell me something," said Reuben.

"If I can," said Margon with a little smile.

"Are all the elder Morphenkinder like you and Felix, and Sergei and the others? Are they all kind and gentle like you? Isn't there some scoundrel of a Morphenkind somewhere who's rude and hateful by nature?"

Margon laughed a low rueful laugh.

"You flatter us," he said. "I must confess there are some quite unpleasant Morphenkinder sharing this world with us. I wish I could say there were not."

"But who are they?"

"Ah, I knew you would immediately ask that. Will you accept that we're all better off if they leave us alone here, and keep to their own territory and their own ways? It's possible to go on for a very long time without coming in contact with them."

"Yes, I accept it. You're saying there's nothing to fear from them."

"Fear, no, there's nothing to fear. But I can tell you there are Morphenkinder in this world whom I personally despise. But you're not likely to encounter them, not as long as I'm here."

"Do they define evil in a different way that we define it?"

"Every single soul on earth defines evil in his or her own way," said Margon. "You know that. I don't have to tell you. But all Morphenkinder are offended by evil and seek to destroy it in humans."

"But what about in other Morphenkinder?"

"It's infinitely more complex, as you found out with poor Marrok. He wanted to kill you, felt he should, felt he'd no right to pass the Chrism to you, felt he had to annihilate his mistake, but you know how difficult it was for him, you and Laura being utterly innocent. And you, you had no difficulty in killing him simply because he was trying to kill you. Well, there you have the entire moral story of the human race and all the immortal races in a nutshell, don't you?"

"All the immortal races?"

"You and Stuart. If we answered every single question, we'd overwhelm you. Let it come gradually, please. And that way we can postpone the inevitable revelation that we don't know all the answers."

Reuben smiled. But he wasn't going to let this opportunity slip through his fingers, not feeling the pain he was feeling now.

"Is there a science of spirits?" asked Reuben. He felt the tears welling again. He picked up one of the cookies, which was still warm, and ate it easily in one mouthful. Delicious oatmeal cookie, his favorite kind, very thick and chewy. He drank the rest of the coffee, and Margon poured another cup.

"No, not really," said Margon. "Though people will tell you there is. I've told you what I know—that spirits can and do move on. Unless, of course, they don't want to move on. Unless, of course, they've made a career of remaining here."

"But what you mean is they disappear from your sight, don't you?" Reuben sighed. "I mean, what you're saying is they leave you, yes, but you can't know that they've gone on."

"There's evidence they go on. They change, they disappear. Some people can see them more clearly than others. You can see them. You get the power from your father's side of the family. You get it from the Celtic blood." It seemed he had more to say, and then he added, "Please listen to me. Don't seek to communicate with her. Let her go, for her sake."

Reuben couldn't answer.

Margon rose to go.

"Wait, Margon, please," Reuben said.

Margon stood there, eyes lowered, bracing himself for something unpleasant.

"Margon, who are the Forest Gentry?" Reuben asked. Margon's face changed. He was suddenly exasperated.

"You mean Felix hasn't told you?" he asked. "I should think he would have."

"No, he hasn't told me. I know you're fighting over them, Margon. I saw you. I heard you."

"Well, you let Felix explain to you who they are, and while he's at it, he might explain to you his entire philosophy of life, his insistence that all sentient beings can live in harmony."

"You don't believe they can?" Reuben asked. He was struggling to keep Margon there, keep Margon talking.

Margon sighed. "Well, let's put it this way. I'd rather live in harmony in this world without the Forest Gentry, without spirits in general. I'd rather people my world with those creatures who are flesh and blood, no matter how mutant, unpredictable, or misbegotten they may be. I have a deep abiding respect for matter." He repeated the word, "Matter!"

"Like Teilhard de Chardin," said Reuben. He thought of the little book he'd found before he'd met either Margon or Felix, the little book of Teilhard's theological reflections inscribed to Felix by Margon. Teilhard had said he was in love with matter.

"Well, yes," Margon said with faint smile. "Rather like Teilhard. But Teilhard was a priest, like your brother. Teilhard believed things I have never believed. I don't have an orthodoxy, remember."

"I think you do," said Reuben. "But it's your own godless orthodoxy."

"Oh, you're right, of course," said Margon. "And perhaps I'm wrong to argue for the superiority of it. Let's just say I believe in the superiority of the biological over the spiritual. I look for the spiritual in the biological and no place else."

And he left without another word.

Reuben sat back in the chair, gazing dully at the distant window. The panes were wet and clear and made up the many lead-framed squares of a perfect mirror.

After a long time and gazing at the distant reflection of the fire in a glass—a tiny blaze that seemed to float in nothingness—he whispered: "Are you here, Marchent?"

Slowly against the mirror, her shape took form, and as he stared fixedly at it, the shape was colored in, became solid, plastic and three-dimensional. She sat in the window seat again, but she did not look the same. She wore the brown dress she'd worn that day he'd met her. Her face was vividly moist and flushed as if with life, but sad, so sad. Her soft bobbed hair appeared combed. Her tears were glistening on her cheeks.

"Tell me what you want," he said, trying desperately to stifle his fear. He started to get up, to go to her.

But the image was already dissolving. There seemed a flurry of movement, the fleeting shape of her reaching out, but it thinned, vanished—as if made of pixels and color and light. She was gone. And he was standing there, shaken as badly as before, his heart in his throat, staring at his own reflection in the window.

II

REUBEN SLEPT TILL AFTERNOON, when a phone call from Grace awakened him. He had best come down now, she said, to sign the marriage documents and get the ceremony done tomorrow morning. He agreed with her.

He stopped on his way out only to look for Felix, but Felix was nowhere around, and Lisa thought he had perhaps gone down to Nideck to supervise plans for the Christmas festival.

"We are all so busy," said Lisa, her eyes glowing, but she insisted Reuben have some lunch. She and Heddy and Jean Pierre had the long dining room table covered in sterling-silver chafing dishes, bowls, and platters. Pantry doors stood open, and a stack of flatware chests stood on the floor by the table. "Now listen to me, you must eat," she said, quickly heading for the kitchen.

He told her no, he'd dine with his family in San Francisco. "But it's fun to see all these preparations."

And it was. He realized that the big party was only seven days away.

The oak forest outside was swarming with workmen, who were covering the thick gray branches of the oaks with tiny Christmas lights. And tents were already being erected on the terrace in front of the house. Galton and his carpenter cousins were coming and going. The magnificent marble statues for the crèche had been carted to the end of the terrace and stood in a wet confused grouping, waiting to be appropriately housed, and there was a flock of workmen building something, in spite of the light rain, that just might have been a Christmas stable.

He hated to leave but felt he had little choice in the matter. As for the journey ahead, well, he wouldn't be stopping for Laura, but she would meet the wedding party at City Hall tomorrow.

As it turned out, things went worse than he'd ever expected.

Caught in a downpour before he reached the Golden Gate Bridge, he took more than two hours to reach the Russian Hill house, and the storm showed no signs of letting up. It was the kind of rain that drenches one just running from the car to the front door, and he arrived disheveled and having to change immediately.

But that was the least of his problems.

The signing of the papers with Simon Oliver went smoothly, but Celeste was in a paroxysm of rage, which showed itself in unending resentful sarcastic comments as she signed over the baby to Reuben. Reuben inwardly gasped when he saw the amounts of money that were being transferred, but of course he said nothing.

He didn't know what it meant to carry a child and he never would, and he couldn't grasp what it meant to give one up. He was happy for Celeste that she'd walk away with enough cash to keep her secure for the rest of her life if she planned things right.

But after the lawyers had gone away, and the dinner had been endured in silence, then Celeste exploded in a tirade of rushing words, accusing Reuben of being one of the most worthless and uninteresting human beings ever born on the planet.

This wasn't easy at all for Grace or Phil to hear, but they remained at the table, Grace gesturing covertly to Reuben for patience. As for Jim, his expression was compassionate, but oddly fixed, as though this were a willful attitude rather than a reflective one. He was as always neatly dressed in his black clerical suit and shirtfront with his Roman collar, and every bit the movie star priest in Reuben's opinion, with his neat dark brown wavy hair and his extremely agreeable and engaging eyes. He was a handsome man, Jim, but nobody ever talked about it, not when they could talk about Reuben's looks instead.

Reuben said little or nothing for the first twenty minutes as Celeste castigated him as lazy, a pretty boy, a time waster, a ne'er-do-well, a glorified bum, the vapid airhead boy who dated the cheerleaders of the world, and an ambitionless brat to whom everything came so easy he had not the slightest moral fiber. Born beautiful and rich, he'd wasted his life.

After a while, Reuben looked away. Had her face not been red and knotted with anger and tears, he might have become angry himself. As it was he felt pity and a certain contempt for her.

He'd never been lazy in his life, and he knew this. And he'd never been the "vapid airhead boy who dated the cheerleaders of the world" but he had no intention of saying so. He began to feel a cool detachment, even a little sadness. Celeste had never known him at all, and maybe he'd never known her, and thank God this was a temporary marriage. What if they'd attempted to marry in earnest?

And each time she mentioned his "looks," he came to realize something ever more deeply. She despised him personally; she despised him physically. This woman with whom he'd been intimate countless times couldn't stand him physically. And this caused the tiny hairs to rise on his neck when he thought about it, and how ghastly a real marriage with Celeste might have been.

"And so the world just gives you a baby, the way the world's given you everything else," she said finally, apparently wrapping up, her fury spent, her lips quivering. "I'll hate you to my dying day," she added.

She was about to go on when he turned and looked at her. He no longer felt pity. He felt hurt and he eyed her without a word. She went silent looking into his eyes, and then for the first time, for the first time in months, she seemed slightly afraid. Indeed she looked afraid of him the way she had when he'd first experienced the influence of the Chrism, and when he'd begun to change in so many subtle ways before the wolf transformation. He hadn't understood then, and, of course, she'd never understood it. But she'd been afraid.

It seemed the others had sensed some deepening of the collective misery, and Grace started to speak, but Phil urged her to be quiet.

Suddenly, in a low tortured voice, Celeste said, "I've had to work all my life. I had to work hard when I was a kid. My father and mother left a small estate. I worked for everything." She sighed, obviously exhausted. "Maybe it's not your fault that you don't know what that means."

"That's right," said Reuben, the low sharp tone of his voice surprising him, but not stopping him. He was trembling but he struggled to hide it. "Maybe none of this is my fault. Maybe nothing in our relationship has ever been my fault except that I didn't acknowledge your blatant contempt for me sooner. But it takes courage to be unkind, doesn't it?"

The others were clearly stunned.

"Doesn't it?" he repeated. His pulse throbbed in his temple.

Celeste looked down for a moment and then up at him again. She seemed very small and vulnerable in her chair, face white and drawn, her pretty hair mussed. Her eyes softened. "Well, you do have a voice, after all," she said bitterly. "If you'd found it a little sooner, maybe none of this would have happened."

"Oh, lies and rubbish!" Reuben said. His face was hot. "Self-serving rubbish. If there's nothing further you want to say, I have things to do."

"Aren't you even going to say you're sorry?" she asked with exaggerated sincerity. She was on the edge of tears again. She was whitening before his eyes and shaking.

"Sorry for what? That you forgot to take a pill? Or that the pills didn't work? Sorry that a new life is coming into this world, and that I want that life and you don't? What is there to be sorry for?"

Jim gestured for him to slow down.

He looked steadily at Jim for a moment and then at Celeste. "I'm grateful to you that you're willing to have this baby," he said. "I'm grateful to you that you're willing to give it to me. Very grateful. But I'm sorry for absolutely nothing."

Nobody spoke, including Celeste.

"As for all the lies and foolishness you've spewed for the last hour, I've endured it as I've always endured your unkindness and your nastiness—to keep the peace. And if you don't mind, I'd like a little of that peace right now. I'm finished here."

"Reuben," said Phil softly. "Take it easy, son. She's just a kid the same as you are."

"Thanks, but I don't need your pity!" Celeste said to Phil, eyes flaming as she glared at him. "And I'm most certainly not a 'kid.'"

There was a collective gasp at the vehemence of it.

"If you'd ever taught your son one practical thing in this world about being an adult," Celeste went on, "things might be different now. People can't afford your tiresome poetry."

Reuben was furious. He didn't trust himself to speak further. But Phil didn't even flinch.

Grace rose abruptly and awkwardly from the table, and came around to Celeste and helped her out of the chair, though this was hardly physically necessary. "You're tired, really tired," Grace said in a soft solicitous voice. "In a way the exhaustion is one of the worst things."

It quietly amazed him, the way Celeste accepted this kindness without a word of gratitude, as if it were her just due.

Grace led her out of the room and up the stairs. Reuben wanted desperately to speak to his father, but Phil was now looking away, his face abstracted and thoughtful. He appeared to have removed himself completely from this time and place. How many times had Reuben seen that same expression on Phil's face?

The group sat in silence until Grace reappeared. She looked at Reuben for a long moment and then she said, "I didn't know you could get that angry. Wow. That was scary."

She laughed uneasily and Phil responded with a little half laugh and even Jim forced a smile. Grace placed her hand on Phil's and they exchanged a silent intimate glance.

"Was it scary?" asked Reuben. He was still quaking with anger. His soul was shaken. "Look, I'm no hotshot doctor like you, Mother, and I'm no hotshot lawyer like her. And I'm not a hotshot missionary priest in the slums like you, Jim. But I'm nothing like the man she's described here. And not a single one of you uttered a word in my defense. Not a single one of you. Well, I have my dreams and my aspirations and my goals, and they might not be yours but they are mine. And I've worked at them all my life as well. And I'm not the person she made me out to be. And you might have defended Dad here against her, even if you had no stomach to defend me. He didn't deserve her poison either."

"No, of course not," said Jim quickly. "Of course not. But Reuben, she can still abort this child—if she changes her mind. Don't you understand that?" He lowered his voice. "That's the only reason we sat here listening as we did. Nobody wants to risk her wrath against this baby."

"Oh, the hell with her," Reuben said dropping his voice against his anger. "She won't abort it, not with the money that's changed hands here. She's not insane. She's just mean-spirited and cowardly like all bullies. But she's not insane. And I won't put up with her abuse anymore." He rose to his feet. "Dad, I'm sorry about what she said to you. It was ugly and dishonest like everything that came out of her mouth."

"Put it out of your mind, Reuben," said Phil in a steady voice. "I've always felt very sorry for her."

This clearly surprised Jim and Grace as well, though Grace was obviously wrestling with a multitude of emotions. She was still holding tight to Phil's hand.

No one spoke, and then Phil went on. "I grew up the way she did, son, working for everything I got," he said. "It will be a long time before she can figure out what she really wants in this world. For the child, Reuben, for the child, be patient with her. Remember this child is liberating you from Celeste, and Celeste from you. That's not a bad thing at all, is it?"

"I'm sorry, Dad, you're right," said Reuben. And he was ashamed; he was completely ashamed.

Reuben left the gathering.

Jim came after him, following him silently up the stairs, and went right past Reuben into Reuben's bedroom.

The little gas fire was burning under the mantel and Jim took his old favorite upholstered wing chair beside the hearth.

Reuben stood at the door for a moment, and then he sighed, shut the door behind him, and went to his old leather chair opposite Jim's.

"Let me say something first," Reuben started. "I know what I've done to you. I know the burden I've put on you, telling you ghastly things, unspeakable things, in Confession and binding you to secrecy. Jim, if I had it to do over again, I wouldn't do it. But when I came to you, I needed you."

"And now you don't," said Jim dully, his lips quivering. "Because you have all your many werewolf friends at Nideck Point, correct?

And Margon, the distinguished priest of the godless, right? And you're going to bring up your son in that house with them. How are you going to do that?"

"Let's worry about that when the child is born," said Reuben. He thought for a moment. "You don't despise Margon and the others. I know you don't. You can't. I think you've tried and it hasn't worked."

"No, I don't despise them," Jim conceded. "Not at all. That's the mystery of it. I don't despise them. I don't much see how anyone could, not based on what I know of them, and based on how well they treat you."

"I'm relieved to hear that," Reuben said. "More relieved than I can say. And I know what I've done to you with these secrets. Believe me, I know."

"You care about what I think?" Jim asked. But it wasn't sarcastic or bitter. He looked at Reuben as if he earnestly wanted to know.

"Always," said Reuben. "You know I do. Jim, you were my first hero. You'll always be my hero."

"I'm no hero," said Jim. "I'm a priest. And I'm your brother. You trusted me. You trust me now. I'm desperately trying to figure out what I can do to help you! And let me tell you right now, I am not now or ever was the saint you think I am. I'm not the nice person that you are, Reuben. And maybe we should set the record straight on that now. That might be a good thing for both of us. I've done terrible things in my life, things you know nothing about."

"I find that very hard to believe," said Reuben.

But Jim's voice was raw and there was a look in his eyes Reuben had never seen before.

"Well, you need to believe it," Jim said, "and you need to simmer down with regard to Celeste. That's my first lesson here, my first concern. And I want you to listen. She could still abort this baby at any time. Oh, I know, you don't think she will and so forth and so on, but Reuben, just toe the line, will you, till this child is born." Jim broke off, as if he didn't know quite what he would say next. When Reuben tried to speak, Jim started up again.

"I want to tell you some things about me, some things that might help you understand about all this. I'm asking you to listen to me now. I need to tell you. Okay?"

This was so unexpected, Reuben didn't know quite what to say. When had Jim ever needed him? "Of course, Jim," he answered. "Tell me anything. How could I turn you down on such a thing?"

"Okay, then listen," said Jim. "I fathered a child once and I killed it. I did that with another man's wife. I did that with a beautiful young woman who trusted me. And I'll have that blood on my hands all my life. No, don't say anything but just listen. Maybe you will come to confide in me again and trust me, if you know just what kind of person I am and that you've always been a good deal better than me."

"I'm listening, but that just isn't—."

"You were about eleven when I quit med school," said Jim, "but you never really knew what went down. I hated it, studying to be a doctor, positively hated it. But that's another whole story, how I let myself be drawn into something just because of Mom and Uncle Tim, because of some idea we were a family of doctors, because of Grandfather Spangler and how he doted on them and on me."

"I figured you didn't want to do it. How else—?"

"That's not the important part," said Jim. "I was drinking myself to death at Berkeley. I was really pushing it. And I was having an affair with the wife of one of my professors, a beautiful Englishwoman. Oh, the husband didn't give a damn. Quite the contrary; he set it up. I realized that right off. He was twenty years older than her and wheelchair-bound since a motorcycle accident in England two years after they married. No kids, just him in his wheelchair, giving brilliant lectures at Berkeley, and Lorraine like some kind of angel caring for him as if he was her father. And he invites me to come study with him, at his house in south Berkeley, one of those beautiful old Berkeley homes with the dark paneling and the hardwood floors and the big old stone fireplaces, and the trees outside every window, and Professor Maitland turning in at eight o'clock and telling me to use the library as late as I wanted, spend the night in the guest room, you know, and 'Here's your own key.'"

Reuben nodded. "Cushy situation."

"Oh, yes, and Lorraine, so sweet, you have no idea. Sweet, that's the word I always come back to when I talk about Lorraine. So sweet. Gentle, thoughtful, with that silvery British accent, and the refrigerator filled with beer, an unending supply of beer, and the single malt Scotch on the sideboard, and in the guest bedroom, and I took advantage of the whole thing. I practically moved in. And about six months after this all started, I actually fell in love with her, if a twenty-four/seven drunk is capable of falling in love. I finally admitted how much I loved her. I was drinking myself into a stupor every night in that house, and pretty soon she was taking as much care of me as she did of the professor. She started handling all the messy stuff in my life."

Reuben nodded. This was all so new to him, so unimagined.

"She was exceptional, she really was," said Jim. "And I never knew if she fully understood the way Professor Maitland had set it all up. I knew, but she didn't know. At the same time, she was resolved we'd never hurt him if we kept this strictly secret, and never showed a particle of special affection for one another when he was around. But she tried to help me. She wasn't just sitting around filling my glass. She kept telling me, 'Jamie, your problem is booze. You've got to stop.' She actually dragged me to two AA meetings before I threw a tantrum. Time and again, she finished up my papers for me, worked out my little projects for me, got the books I needed from the University library, that kind of thing. But she kept saying, 'You've got to get help.' I was failing my classes and she knew it. Sometimes I played along, made a couple of promises, made love to her and then got drunk. Finally she gave up. She just accepted me the way I was, just like she accepted the professor."

"Were Mom and Dad suspicious about the drinking?"

"Oh, highly. I was ducking them. Lorraine helped me to duck them. Lorraine made excuses for me when they came over the bridge to see me and I was dead drunk in the guest room at her place. But I'll get to Mom and Dad in a minute. Lorraine got pregnant. It wasn't supposed to happen but it did. And that's when the crisis happened.

I just about went nuts. I told her she had to get an abortion and I left her house in a rage."

"I see," Reuben said.

"No, you don't. She came over to my apartment. She told me she'd never get an abortion, that she wanted this baby more than anything in the world. And that she'd leave Professor Maitland in a minute if I said the word. When Professor Maitland heard about the baby, he'd understand. He'd give her a divorce, no problem. She had a small income. She was ready to pack her bags and come to me. I was horrified, I mean in a state of shock."

"But you loved her."

"Yes, Reuben, I loved her, but I didn't want the responsibility of anybody or anything. That's why the affair with her had been so attractive. She was married! When she tried to lay anything on me, I could up and go back to my place and not answer the phone!"

"I understand."

"And here, it had turned into a nightmare. She was begging me to marry her, become a husband, a father. This was the very last thing I wanted. Look, I was so into booze at that point all I could really think about was laying in a stash of beer and whiskey, locking the door, and chilling out. I tried to explain all this to her, that I was damaged, bad for her, that she couldn't want me, that she had to get rid of the baby and now. But she wasn't buying it. And the more she talked the drunker I got. At one point she tried to take the glass out of my hand. That tipped me right over. We got into a fight, I mean a veritable brawl. It started with me throwing things, slamming doors, breaking things. I was falling down drunk, saying the meanest things to her but she wouldn't accept it. She kept telling me, 'That's the booze talking, Jamie. You don't mean these things.' I hit her, Reuben. I started slapping her, then beating her. I remember her face was covered in blood. I hit her over and over again, until she was down on the floor and I was kicking her, telling her she'd never understood me, she was a selfish bitch, a selfish slut. I said things to her that nobody should say to another human being. She curled up in a ball, trying to protect herself—."

"And that *was* the booze, Jim," said Reuben in a soft voice. "You would never have done it if it hadn't been for the booze."

"I don't know about that, Reuben," he said. "I was a pretty selfish guy. I am still basically a selfish guy. I thought the world revolved around me in those days. You were just eleven or twelve then. You had no idea what I was really like."

"She lost the child?"

Jim nodded. He swallowed. He was staring into the gas fire beneath the mantel. "I passed out at some point. Blacked out. And when I woke up, she was gone. There was blood all over, blood on the carpet, blood on the floor boards, blood on the furniture, the walls. It was horrible. You cannot imagine how much blood there was. I went and followed a trail of blood right down the steps, and through the garden and to the street. Her car was gone."

Jim stopped. He closed his eyes. There was the soft beat of rain on the panes. Otherwise the room was silent. The house was silent. Then he started talking again.

"I went on the longest worst bender I'd ever been on. I just shut the door and drank. I knew I'd killed that baby, but I was terrified that I might have killed her too. Any minute, I thought the police are going to be here. Any minute Professor Maitland is going to call. Any minute . . . I could easily have killed her beating her like that. The way I kicked her? It's a wonder I didn't. And for days I just lay in that apartment and drank. I'd always stockpiled enough booze to do this, and I don't know how long it was before the booze started running out. I wasn't eating. I wasn't bathing, nothing. Just drinking, drinking and crawling around that place on my hands and knees at times, looking for bottles to see if there was anything left in them. Well, you can figure what happened."

"Mom and Dad."

"Right. There came a banging on the door and it was Mom and Dad. It had been ten days, it turned out, ten days, and it was my landlord who'd called them. I was overdue with the rent. And he was worried. He was a nice guy. Well, the bastard probably saved my life."

"Thank God for that," said Reuben. He tried to picture all this, but he couldn't. All he saw was his brother, looking collected and strong in his Roman collar and clerics, sitting in the chair opposite, pouring out a story he could scarcely believe.

"I told them everything," Jim said. "I just broke down and told them the whole thing. I was drunk, you understand, so it was easy—to slobber, to cry, to confess all I'd done. Confessing things when you're blind drunk is a cinch. I felt so sorry for myself! I'd wrecked my life. I'd hurt Lorraine. I was flunking out of school. I told Mom and Dad all of it, I just let it loose. And when Mom heard how I'd beaten Lorraine, how I'd kicked her, kicked the life out of that child, well, you can imagine the look on her face. When she saw the bloodstains all over that carpet, on the floor, on the walls . . . And then Mom and Dad just put me in the shower, cleaned me up, and drove me straight south to the Betty Ford Center in Rancho Mirage, California, and I was there for ninety days."

"Jim, I'm so sorry."

"Reuben, I was lucky. Lorraine could have put me behind bars for what I did to her. As it turned out, she and Professor Maitland had gone back to England before Mom and Dad ever came knocking on my door. Mom found out all that. The professor's mother in Cheltenham had suffered a severe stroke. Lorraine had made all the arrangements with the university. So she was all right, it seemed. Mom was able to verify that. And the house in south Berkeley was up for sale. Whether Lorraine had checked into a hospital herself after I beat her, well, we never could find out."

"I hear you, Jim, I know what you're telling me. I understand."

"Reuben, I am nobody's hero, nobody's saint. If it wasn't for Mom and Dad, if they hadn't taken me to Betty Ford, if they hadn't stuck with me through that, I don't know where I'd be now. I don't know if I'd be alive. But look, listen to what I'm telling you. Play along with Celeste for the sake of the baby. That's lesson number one. Let her have that baby, Reuben, because you do not know how you might regret it to your dying day if she gets rid of it because of something that you say! Reuben, there are times when it is so painful for me to even see children, to see little kids with their parents, I . . . I tell you, I don't know if I could work in a regular Catholic parish, Reuben, with a school and kids. I just don't. There's a reason I'm deep in the Tenderloin. There's a reason my mission is working with addicts. There's a reason, all right."

"I understand. Look, I'm going to go talk to her now, apologize."

"Do it, please," said Jim. "And who knows, Reuben? Maybe somehow this child can keep you connected to us, to me, to Mom and Dad, to your flesh and blood family, to things that matter for all of us in life."

Reuben went at once to knock on Celeste's door. The house was quiet. But he could see the light was on in her room.

She was in her nightgown but immediately invited him in. She was frosty, but polite. He stood there and made his apologies to her as sincerely as he could.

"Oh, I understand," she said with a faint sneer. "Don't worry about it. This will all be over for us soon enough."

"I want you to be happy, Celeste," he said.

"I know that, Reuben, and I know you'll be a good father to this baby. Even if Grace and Phil weren't here to do the dirty work. I never had any real doubt about that. Sometimes the most childish and immature men make the best fathers."

"Thank you, Celeste," he said, forcing an icy smile. He kissed her on the cheek.

No need to repeat that parting shot to Jim when he went back to his room.

Jim was by the fire still and obviously deep in his thoughts. Reuben settled into his chair as before.

"Tell me," Reuben said, "is this the real reason that you became a priest?"

For a long moment Jim didn't respond. Then he looked up as if he were slightly dazed. In a low voice, he said, "I became a priest because I wanted to, Reuben."

"I know that, Jim, but did you feel you had to make amends for the rest of your life?"

"You don't understand," said Jim. He sounded weary, dispirited. "I took my time deciding what to do. I traveled. I spent months in a

Catholic mission in the Amazon. I spent a year studying philosophy in Rome."

"I remember that," Reuben said. "We'd get these great packages from Italy. And I couldn't figure out why you weren't coming home."

"I had a lot of choices, Reuben. Maybe for the first time in my life, I had real choices. And the archbishop asked me the very same question, actually, when I asked to enter the priesthood. We discussed the whole affair. I told him everything. We talked about atonement, and what it means to become a priest—to live as a priest year in and year out for the rest of one's life. He insisted on another year of sobriety in the world before he'd accept my application to the seminary. Usually he demanded five years of sober living, but admittedly, my period of drinking had been relatively short. And then there was Grandfather Spangler's donation and Mom's ongoing support. I worked every day at St. Francis at Gubbio as a volunteer during that year. By the time I entered the seminary, I'd been sober three years, and I was on strict probation. One drink and I would be out. I went through all that because I wanted to, Reuben. I became a priest because that's what I wanted to do with my life."

"What about faith?" Reuben asked. He was remembering what Margon had said, that Jim was a priest who didn't believe in God.

"Oh, it's about faith," said Jim. His voice was low now and more confidential. "Of course, it's about faith—faith that this is God's world and we're God's children. How could it not be about faith? I think if one truly loves God with all one's heart, then one *has* to love everybody else. It's not a choice. And you don't love them because it scores you points with God. You love them because you are trying to see them and embrace them as God sees and embraces them. You are loving them because they are alive."

Reuben was unable to speak. He just shook his head.

"Think about it," Jim said in a whisper. "Looking at each person and thinking, 'God made this being; God put a soul into this being!'" He sat back in the chair and sighed. "I try. I stumble. I get up. I try again."

"Amen," said Reuben in a reverent whisper.

"I wanted to work with addicts, with drunks, with people whose weaknesses I understood. Above all, I wanted to do something that mattered, and I was convinced that as a priest I could do that. I could make some difference in people's lives. Maybe I could even save a life now and then—save a life, imagine—to make some kind of amends for the life I'd destroyed. You could say that AA and the Twelve Steps saved me along with Mom and Dad. And yes, they led to my decision. But I had choices. And faith is part of it. I came out of the whole nightmare having faith. And a kind of crazy gratitude that I did not have to be a doctor! I can't tell you how much I really did not want to be a doctor! Medicine doesn't need any more coldhearted selfish bastards. Thank God, I got out of that."

"I can't quite understand it," said Reuben. "But I've never had much faith in God myself."

"I know," said Jim, looking into the little gas fire. "I knew that about you when you were a little kid. But I've always had faith in God. The creation speaks to me of God. I see God in the sky and in the falling leaves. That's always the way it was for me."

"I think I know what you mean," Reuben said in a low voice. He wanted Jim to go on.

"I see God in the little kindnesses people do for one another. I see God in the eyes of the worst down-and-out derelicts I deal with. . . ." Jim broke off suddenly, shaking his head. "Faith isn't a decision, is it? It's something you admit to having, or something you admit that you don't have."

"I think you're right about that."

"That's why I never preach to people about the supposed sin of not believing," said Jim. "You'll never hear me condemning a nonbeliever as a sinner. That makes no sense to me at all."

Reuben smiled. "And maybe that's why you sometimes give people the wrong impression. They think you don't believe when in fact you do."

"Yes, that does happen now and then," said Jim, with a soft smile. "But it doesn't matter. How people believe in God is a vast subject, isn't it?"

A silence fell between them. There was so much Reuben wanted to ask.

"Did you ever see or hear from Lorraine?" he asked.

"Yes," he said. "I wrote an amends letter about a year after I left Betty Ford. I wrote more than one. But they came back to me from the forwarding address she'd left in Berkeley. Then I got Simon Oliver to confirm that she was in fact in Cheltenham and at that address. I couldn't blame her for returning my letters. I wrote to her again, laying it all out in more candid terms. I told her how sorry I was, how in my eyes I was guilty of murder for what I'd done to the baby, how I feared I had irreparably hurt her so that she could never have a child. I got a brief but very compassionate note: she was all right; she was fine; not to worry. I had done her no lasting harm; I should go on with my life.

"Then before I went into the seminary, I wrote to her again, asking after her welfare and telling her of my decision to become a priest. I told her that time had only deepened my sense of the wrong that I'd done to her. I told her how the Twelve Steps and my faith had changed my life. I put too damned much of my own plans and dreams and ego in that letter. It was selfish of me really, now that I look back on it. But it was an amends letter, too, of course. And she wrote back an extraordinary letter. Just extraordinary."

"How so?"

"She told me, if you can believe it, that I had given her the only real happiness she'd known in recent years. She went on to say something about how miserable she'd been before I'd come into her life, how hopeless she had been until the day Professor Maitland brought me home. She said something about her life having been changed for the better completely by knowing me. And that she did not want me ever to worry that I had done her a particle of harm. She said she thought I would be a marvelous priest. Finding such a meaningful vocation in this world was indeed a 'wondrous' thing. I remember she used that word, 'wondrous.' She and the professor were doing 'splendidly,' she said. She wished me every blessing."

"That must have impressed the archbishop," said Reuben.

"Well, actually, it did."

Jim gave a short dismissive laugh. "That was Lorraine," he said. "Forever kind, forever considerate, forever generous. Lorraine was always so sweet." He closed his eyes for a moment and then went on. "About two years ago—I don't remember the date actually—I read a brief obit for the professor in the *New York Times*. I hope Lorraine has remarried. I pray that she has."

"Sounds like you did everything you could," said Reuben.

"I'm haunted by her and that child," Jim said. "When I think of all the things I might have done for that child. Whether I wanted it or not, think what I might have done for it. Sometimes I just can't be around children. I don't want to be any place where there are children. I thank God I'm at St. Francis in the Tenderloin and that I don't have to minister to families with children. It eats at me, what I could have provided for that child."

Reuben nodded. "But you're going to love this little nephew of yours who's coming down the pike."

"Oh, absolutely," Jim said, "with all my heart. Yes. I'm sorry. I didn't mean to say those things about children. It's just . . ."

"Believe me, I understand," said Reuben. "Maybe I shouldn't have put it that way."

Jim looked off into the fire again for a long moment, as if he hadn't heard.

"But all my life I'll be haunted by Lorraine and that child," he said. "And what might have been for that child. I don't expect to ever not be haunted. I deserve to be haunted."

Reuben didn't answer. He wasn't sure at all that Jim was right about all these many things. Jim's life seemed shaped by guilt, by remorse, by pain. There were so many questions he wanted to ask, but he couldn't figure how to ask them. He felt closer to Jim, immeasurably closer, and at a loss as to what to say. He was also very aware that he himself thrived in a realm in which he took human life without a particle of regret. He knew this. He saw all this. And it provoked no real crippling emotion.

"And several times in the last couple of years," Jim continued, "I've seen Lorraine. I think I have at any rate. I've seen Lorraine in church.

It's never more than a glimpse, and it's always during Mass when I cannot possibly leave the altar. I see her, way to the back, and then of course by the time I give the last blessing, she's gone."

"You don't think you're imagining it?"

"Well, I would except for her hats."

"The hats?"

"Lorraine loved hats. She loved vintage clothes and vintage hats. I don't know whether it's a British thing, or what, but Lorraine was always a very stylish person, and she positively loved hats. At any University function in the day, she'd have on some big brimmed hat, usually with flowers. And in the evening, she wore those black cocktail hats with veils, you know, that women used to wear years ago. Actually you probably don't know. She collected vintage clothes and vintage hats."

"And the woman you see at church is wearing a hat."

"Always and it's a real Lorraine Maitland hat. I mean, you know, a Bette Davis or Barbara Stanwyck hat. And then there's her hair, her long blond hair, straight hair, and her face, and the shape of her head and shoulders. You'd recognize me at a distance. I'd recognize you at a distance. And I'm sure it's Lorraine. Maybe she's living here now. Or maybe it's all something I'm imagining."

He paused, looking into the flames of the gas fire, and then he went on.

"I'm not in love with Lorraine now. I think I was once, booze or no booze. Yes, I was in love with her. But not now. And really I have no right to track her down if she is living here, no right to meddle in her life, to bring all those bad memories back to her. But selfishly, I'd love to know that she's happy, remarried, and maybe with children. If I could only know that for certain. She so wanted that baby! She wanted that baby more than she wanted me."

"I wish I knew what to say to you," Reuben said. "It breaks my heart to think of you going through this. And believe you me, I will go out to get Celeste pineapple at midnight if that is what it takes."

Jim laughed. "I think it's going to go well with her, if you just don't challenge her. Let her believe all the bad things she has to believe."

"I hear you."

"It's taking more courage for Celeste to give up this baby than she's admitting. So let her dump her anger on you."

"I'm with the program," said Reuben putting up his hands.

Jim was looking at the fire again, at the blue and orange flames licking the air.

"When was the last time you think you saw Lorraine?"

"Not that long ago," Jim said. "Maybe six months? And one of these days I'm going to catch up with her outside of church. And that will be when she decides it's time. And if she tells me that I hurt her so bad she couldn't have children anymore, well that will be exactly what I deserve to hear."

"Jim, if she'd been hurt that bad, she might volunteer it on her own. She could take you down even now for what happened, couldn't she?"

"Yes," said Jim. He nodded and looked at Reuben. "She certainly could. I was straight with my superiors about all of it, always, as I told you. But they were straight with me about it too. They knew that what I'd done had happened in a drunken brawl. I was a debilitated alcoholic. They didn't see it as premeditated murder. A man who murders cannot be a priest. But any scandal at any time could take me down. One letter to the archbishop, one threat of going public, that would do it. Lorraine could indeed take me down, and Jim's great personal mission in the slums of San Francisco would blink out like that."

"Well, she probably knows that," said Reuben. "Maybe she just wants to talk to you and she's building up the nerve."

Jim was pondering. "It's possible," he said.

"Or, you feel so guilty about it all that you think any pretty woman you see who's wearing a hat is Lorraine."

Jim smiled and nodded. "That could be true," he conceded. "If it is Lorraine, she'll probably try to protect me from the full truth about what I did to her. That was the tone of her letters. She is sweet, just so very sweet. She was the kindest person I ever met. I can only imagine what it was like for her when she left me that last day. How did she stand it? Going home sick, hemorrhaging, losing a baby and having to tell Maitland about that." He shook his head. "You don't know how protective she was with Maitland. No wonder he took her right out of there, and went back to England. Stroke. I don't believe his mother had a stroke. Boy, did I ever let him down. He brought me in to be a comfort to his wife, and I beat her within an inch of her life."

Reuben was at an utter loss.

"Well, listen, here's the second lesson," said Jim. "I'm no saint. I never was. I have a mean streak in me and always did, of which you know nothing. I work with addicts at my church because I am an addict. And I understand them and the things they've done. So stop thinking you have to protect me from the things that are happening to you now. You can come to me and tell me what's going on with you! And I can handle it, Reuben. I swear that to you."

Reuben felt he was gazing at Jim across a huge divide.

"But there isn't much you can do to help," said Reuben. "I'm not running away from what I am now."

"Have you thought about running away from it?" Jim asked.

"No. I don't want to," said Reuben.

"Have you thought about trying to reverse it?"

"No."

"You've never asked your august mentors whether or not it can be reversed?"

"No," Reuben admitted. "They would have told us, Stuart and me both, if it could be reversed."

"Would they?"

"Jim, it's . . . that's not possible. That's not discussable. You're not grasping the power of the Chrism. You've seen a Man Wolf with your own eyes, but you've never seen one of us experience the change. This isn't something that can be reversed in me. No."

Give up eternal life? Give up being immune to disease, to aging, to . . . ?

"But please," said Reuben. "Please know that I'm doing the best I can to use the Wolf Gift in the best way possible."

"The Wolf Gift," said Jim with a faint smile. "What a lovely little phrase that is." It was not sarcastic. He seemed to be dreaming for a moment, his eyes moving over the shadowy room, and fixing on the rainy windowpanes perhaps. Reuben could not quite tell.

"Remember, Jim," said Reuben. "Felix and Margon are doing all in their power to guide me and guide Stuart. This isn't a lawless realm, Jim. We're not without our own laws and rules, our own conscience! Remember, we can sense evil. We can smell it. We can pick up the scent of innocence and suffering. And if I'm ever to get to the bottom of what we are, what our powers are, what they mean, well, it will be through others like Margon and Felix. The world isn't going to help me with all this. It can't. You know it can't. You can't. It's impossible."

Jim appeared to consider this for a long moment and then he nodded. "I understand why you feel that way," he murmured. And then he seemed to slip off into his thoughts. "God knows, I haven't been a help so far."

"Now you know that's not true. But you know what my life is like at Nideck Point."

"Oh, yes, it's grand. It's marvelous. It's like nothing I ever imagined, that house, and those friends of yours. You've been embraced by some kind of monstrous aristocracy, haven't you? It's like a royal court, isn't it? You're all Princes of the Blood. And how can 'normal life' compete with that?"

"Jim, remember the movie *Tombstone*? Remember what Doc Holliday says to Wyatt Earp when Doc is dying. You and I saw that movie together, remember? Doc says to Wyatt: 'There's no such thing as normal life, Wyatt. There's just life.'"

Jim laughed softly under his breath. He closed his eyes for a brief moment and then again looked at the fire.

"Jim, whatever I am, I'm alive. Truly and completely alive. I'm part of life."

Jim gazed at him with another one of those faint winsome smiles of his.

Slowly, Reuben told him the story of what had happened with Susie Blakely. He didn't present it in a boasting or exuberant fashion. Leaving out all mention of Marchent's ghost, he explained that he'd gone out hunting, needing to hunt, breaking the rules set up by the Royal Felix and Margon, and how he'd rescued Susie and taken her to Pastor George's little church. Susie was now home with her parents.

"That's the kind of thing we do, Jim," he said. "That's who the Morphenkinder are. That's our life."

"I know," Jim responded. "I get it. I've always gotten it. I read about that little girl. You think I'm sorry you saved her life? Hell, you saved a busload of kidnapped kids. I know these things, Reuben. You forget where I work, where I live. I'm no suburban parish priest counseling married couples on common decency. I know what evil is. I know it when I see it. And in my own way I can smell it too. And I can smell innocence and helplessness, and desperate need. But I know the challenge of confronting evil without playing God!" He broke off, frowning slightly, pondering, and then he added, "I want to love like God, but I have no right to take life like God. That right belongs to Him alone."

"Look, I told you when I first came to Confession, you're free to call me about this anytime, you're free to bring up the subject. When you need to talk—."

"Do we have to make this about my needs? I'm thinking of you, I think of you slipping further and further from *ordinary* life. And now you want to take this child of yours up there to Nideck Point. Even the miracle of this child is not bringing you back to us, Reuben. Perhaps it can't."

"Jim, it's where I live. And this is the only human child I'll ever have."

Jim winced. "What do you mean?"

Reuben explained. Any children he fathered now would be with another Morphenkind and they too would be Morphenkinder, almost without exception.

"So Laura cannot conceive with you," Jim said.

"Well, she will be able to soon. She's becoming one of us. Look, Jim, I'm sorry. I'm sorry I brought all this to you, because there isn't anything you can do to help me, except keep my secrets, and keep on being my brother."

"Laura made this decision? On her own?"

"Of course she did. Jim, look at what the Chrism offers. We don't age. We're invulnerable to disease or degeneration. We can be killed, yes, but most injuries don't affect us at all. Barring accidents and mishaps, we can live forever. You can't guess the age of Margon, or Sergei, or any of the others. You know what I'm talking about. You know Felix. You've spent hours talking to these men. Did you think Laura would turn down everlasting life? Who has the strength to do that?"

Silence. The obvious question was, would Jim turn it down if it was offered to him, but Reuben was not going to go there.

His brother seemed dazed, crestfallen.

"Look, I want some time with my little boy," said Reuben. "A few years, anyway. And maybe after that he'll go to school in San Francisco and live with Mom and Dad, or maybe he'll go to some school in England or Switzerland. You and I never wanted that, but we could have had it. And my little boy can have it. I'll protect him from what I am. Parents always try to protect their kids from . . . something, from many things."

"I understand what you're saying," Jim murmured. "How could I not understand? I figure my son, he'd be what, twelve years old now, don't know . . ."

Jim looked tired, and old, but he didn't look defeated. His Roman collar and black clerics seemed a form of armor as they always had. Reuben tried to put himself in Jim's place. But it just didn't work. And the story about Lorraine and the baby only made him ache for Jim's well-being all the more.

How different this was from that night when in lupine form Reuben had entered the Confessional at St. Francis Church so desperately needing Jim in his pain and confusion. Now he only wanted to protect Jim from all this and he didn't know how to do it. He wanted to tell him about Marchent's ghost, but he couldn't do that. He couldn't add to the burden he'd already placed on Jim.

When Jim rose to leave, Reuben didn't stop him. He was startled when Jim came towards him and kissed him on the forehead. Jim murmured something softly, something about love, and then he left the room, closing the door behind him.

Reuben sat there quietly for a long time. He was fighting the need to cry. He wished he was at Nideck Point. And a crowd of worries descended on him: What if Celeste did abort the child? And how in the hell was Phil going to live under this roof with Celeste here, Celeste who couldn't conceal her perfect disdain for him? Hell, this was his father's house, wasn't it? Reuben had to support his father. He had to call, to visit, to spend time with Phil. If only the guesthouse at Nideck Point was finished! As soon as it was, he would call his father and urge him to come up for an indefinite stay. He had to find some way to show Phil how much he loved him and always had.

Finally he lay down and fell asleep, exhausted by the twists and turns of the races he was running in his mind, and only now did the submerged images of Nideck Point rise; only now did he hear Felix's reassuring voice, and reflect in that half world before sleep and dream that his time in this house was really over, and the future held bright and beautiful things. And maybe it would be that way for Celeste, too. Maybe she'd be happy.

The wedding was scheduled for eleven in the judge's chambers. Laura was waiting under the rotunda at City Hall when they came in. She at once kissed Celeste and told her that she looked good. Celeste warmed to her and told her she was glad to see her again, all this a bit breezy and predictable and ridiculous, Reuben thought.

They went immediately to the judge's chambers, and within five minutes it was finished. The whole affair was cheerless, and rather grim as far as Reuben was concerned, and Celeste ignored him as if he didn't exist even when she said, "I do." Jim stood in the corner of the room with his arms folded and his eyes down.

They were almost to the front doors of the building when Celeste announced that she had something to say, and asked that they all step to one side.

"I'm sorry for all I said yesterday," she said. Her voice was flat and unfeeling. "You were right. None of this is your fault, Reuben. It's my fault. And I'm sorry. And I'm sorry about what I said to Phil. I never should have gone off on Phil like that."

Reuben smiled and nodded gratefully, and once again, as he'd done last night, he kissed her on the cheek.

Laura was visibly confused and a little anxious, glancing from one of them to the other. But Grace and Phil were remarkably calm, as if they'd had some warning that this was coming.

"We all understand," said Grace. "You're carrying a child and your nerves are on edge. And everyone knows this. Reuben knows this."

"Anything I can do to make this easier, I'll do it," said Reuben. "You want me in the delivery room? I'll be there."

"Oh, don't be so damned obsequious," Celeste responded sharply. "I'm not capable of aborting a baby just because it's inconvenient. Nobody has to pay me to have a baby. If I could abort a baby, the baby would be gone by now."

Jim came forward at once and put his right arm around Celeste. He clasped Grace's hand with his left hand. "St. Augustine wrote something once, something I think about often," he said. "'God triumphs on the ruins of our plans.' And maybe that is what is happening here. We make blunders, we make mistakes, and somehow new doors open, new possibilities arise, opportunities of which we've never dreamed. Let's trust that that is what is happening here for each of us."

Celeste kissed Jim quickly, and then embraced him and laid her head against his chest.

"We're with you every step of the way, darling," Jim said. He stood there like an oak. "All of us."

It was a masterly performance, done with conviction, thought Reuben. It was plainly obvious to him that Jim loathed Celeste. But then again, maybe Jim was simply loving her, really loving her as he tried to love everybody. What do I know, Reuben thought.

Without another word, the little gathering broke up, Grace and Phil ushering Celeste away, Jim to go off back to St. Francis Church, and Reuben to take Laura to lunch.

When they sat down in the dim interior of the Italian restaurant, they finally spoke, and Reuben told Laura briefly and in a spiritless voice about what had happened last night and how he'd hurt Celeste. "I shouldn't have done it," he said, suddenly crestfallen. "But I just, I had to say something. I tell you I think being hated is painful, but being deeply disliked is even more painful, and that's what I feel coming from her. Intense dislike. And it's like a flame. And I've always felt it when I was with her, and it's made my soul wither. I know this now because I dislike her. And God help me, maybe I always did and I'm as guilty of dishonesty as she is."

What he wanted to talk about was Marchent. He needed to talk about Marchent. He wanted to be back in the world of Nideck Point, but he was caught here, out of his element, in his old world, and was eager to escape all of it.

"Reuben, Celeste never loved you," said Laura. "She went out with you for two reasons—your family and your money. She loved both and she couldn't admit it."

Reuben didn't answer. The truth was he couldn't believe Celeste capable of such a thing.

"I understood it as soon as I spent time with her," said Laura. "She was intimidated by you, by your education, your travel, your way with words, your polish. She wanted all those things for herself, and she was burning with guilt, burning. It came out in her sarcasm, her constant digs—the way she kept on even when you were no longer engaged, the way she just couldn't let it go. She never loved you. And now, don't you see, she's pregnant and she hates it but she's living in your parents' beautiful home, and she's taking money for the child, lots of money, I suspect, and she's ashamed and she can hardly stand it."

That *did* make sense. In fact, that quite suddenly made perfect sense, and it seemed a light had flared in his mind by which he could read his strange past with Celeste clearly for the first time.

"It's probably like a nightmare for her," said Laura. "Reuben, money confuses people. It does. That's a fact of life. It confuses people. Your family has plenty. They don't act like they do. Your mom works all the time, like a driven self-made woman, your father is an idealist and a poet who wears clothes he bought twenty years ago, and Jim comes off the same way, otherworldly, spiritual, driving himself to minister to others so that he's perpetually exhausted. Your dad's always strug-gling with his old work, or taking notes in a book as if he had to give a lecture in the morning. Your mother rarely gets a good night's sleep. And you come across a bit that way too, working night and day on your essays for Billie at the paper, pounding away on the computer till you practically fall asleep over it. But you do have money, and really no idea what it's like to be without it."

"You're right," he said.

"Look, she didn't plan it. She just didn't know what she was doing. But why did you ever listen to her, that's what I've always wondered?"

That rang a bell with him. Marchent had said something so very similar to him but now the words escaped him—something about the mystery being that he listened to those who criticized him and cut him down. And his family certainly did a lot of that and had done a lot of that before Celeste ever joined the chorus. Maybe they'd unwittingly invited Celeste to join the chorus. Maybe that had been her ticket in, though he and Celeste had never realized it. Once she'd taken up the relentless scrutiny of Sunshine Boy, Baby Boy, Little Boy—well, it was established that she spoke the common language. Maybe he'd felt comfortable with her for speaking that common language.

"In the beginning, I liked her a lot," he said in a small voice. "I had fun with her. I thought she was pretty. I liked that she was a smart. I like smart women. I liked being around her and then things started to go wrong. I should have spoken up. I should have told her how uncomfortable I was."

"And you would have in time," said Laura. "It would have ended in some completely natural and inevitable way, if you had never gone to Nideck Point. It *had* ended in a natural way. Except now there's the baby."

He didn't answer.

The restaurant was becoming crowded, but they sat in a little zone of privacy at their corner table, the lights dim, and the heavy draperies and framed pictures around them absorbing the noise.

"Is it so difficult for someone to love me?" he asked.

"You know it's not," she said smiling. "You're easy to love, so easy that just about everybody who meets you loves you. Felix adores you. Thibault loves you. They all love you. Even Stuart loves you! And Stuart's a kid who's supposed to be in love with himself at his age. You're a nice guy, Reuben. You're a nice and gentle guy. And I'll tell you something else. You have a kind of humility, Reuben. And some people just don't understand humility. You have a way of opening yourself to what interests you, opening yourself to other people, like Felix, for instance, in order to learn from them. You can sit at the table at Nideck Point and listen calmly to all the elders of the Morphenkinder tribe with amazing humility. Stuart can't do it. Stuart has to flex his muscles, challenge, tease, provoke. But you just keep on learning. Unfortunately some people think that's weakness."

"That's too generous an assessment, Laura," he said. He smiled. "But I like the way you see things."

Laura sighed. "Reuben, Celeste is not really part of you now. She can't be." Laura frowned, her mouth twisting a little as though she found this particularly painful to say, and then she went on in a low voice. "She'll live and die like other human beings. Her road will always be hard. She'll soon discover how little money will change it for her. You can afford to forgive her all this, can't you?"

He stared into Laura's soft blue eyes.

"Please?" she said. "She'll never know for one moment the kind of life that's opening now for both of us."

He knew what these words meant grammatically, intelligently, but he didn't know what they meant emotionally. But he did know what he had to do.

He picked up his phone, and he texted Celeste. He wrote in full and complete words, "I'm sorry. Truly I am. I want you to be happy. When this is all over, I want you to be happy."

What a cowardly thing to do, to tap it into his iPhone when he couldn't say it to her in person.

But in a moment, she'd answered. The words appeared: "You'll always be my Sunshine Boy."

He stared at the iPhone stonily and then he deleted the message.

They left San Francisco by three thirty, easily beating the evening traffic.

But it was slow go in the rain, and Reuben didn't reach Nideck point till after ten.

Once again, the cheerful Christmas lights of the house immediately comforted him. Every window on the three-story façade was now neatly etched with the lights, and the terrace was in good order. The tents were folded and to one side at the ocean end. And a large, well-built stable had taken shape around the Holy Family. The statues themselves had been hastily arranged under it, and though there was no hay or greenery yet, the beauty of the statues was impressive. They appeared stoical and gracious as they stood there under the shadowy wooden roof, faces glinting with the lights from the house, the cold darkness hovering around them. Reuben had some hint of how wonderful the Christmas party was going to be.

His biggest shock came, however, when he looked to the right of the house, as he faced it, and saw the myriad twinkling lights that had transformed the oak forest.

"Winterfest!" he whispered.

If it hadn't been so wet and cold, he would have gone walking there. He couldn't wait to do that, walk there. He wandered around the right side of the house, his feet crunching in the gravel of the drive, and saw that wood-chip mulch had been spread out thickly under the trees, and the festooned lights and the softly illuminated mulch paths went on seemingly forever.

Actually he had no idea how far the oak forest continued to the east. He and Laura had many times walked in it but never to the farthest eastern boundary. And the scope of this undertaking, this lighting of the forest in honor of the darkest days of the year, left him kind of breathless.

He felt a sharp pain when he thought of the gulf that now separated him from those he loved, but then he thought, They'll come to the Christmas gala, and they'll be here with us for the banquet and the singing. Even Jim will come. He promised. And Mort and Celeste would come, he'd make sure of it. So why feel this pain, why allow it? Why not think of what they would share while they could? He thought of the baby again, and he doubled back to the front and hurried along till he reached the stable. It was dark there and the marble Christ Child was barely visible. But he made out the plump cheeks and the smile on its face, and the tiny fingers of its extended hands.

The wind from the ocean chilled him. A thick mist suddenly stung him, rushing so fiercely against his eyes that they teared up. He thought of all the things he had to do for his son, all the things he'd have to assure, and one thing seemed absolutely certain, that he would never let the secret of the Chrism enter the life of his son, that he would shield his son from it even if it meant taking him away from Nideck Point when the time came. But the future was a little too vast and crowded for him to envision it suddenly.

He was cold and sleepy, and he didn't know whether Marchent was waiting for him.

Could Marchent feel cold? Was it conceivable that cold was all she felt, a bleak and terrible emotional cold that was far worse than the cold he was now feeling?

A fierce exhilaration came over him.

He went back to the Porsche, and took his Burberry out of the trunk. It was a fully lined Burberry and he'd never bothered to have it hemmed. He hated the cold and liked that it was long. He buttoned it up and down, pulled up the collar, and went walking.

He walked into the vast airy shadows of the oak woods gazing up at the miracle of the lights overhead and around him. On and on he walked, aware but unconcerned that the mist was thickening and that his face and hands were now damp. He shoved his hands into his pockets.

On and on the lighted boughs seemed to go, and everywhere the mulch was thick and safe for walking. When he glanced back the house was distant. The lighted windows were scarcely visible, an unshapen flickering beyond the trees.

He turned back and continued east. He had not come to the end of it, this exquisitely illuminated forest. But the thick mist was now shrouding the branches ahead of him and behind him.

Best to go back.

Very suddenly the lights went out.

He stood stock-still. He was in complete darkness. Of course he realized what had happened. The Christmas lights had been connected with all the outside lights of the property, the floods in front and at the back. And at eleven thirty the outside lights always went off, and so had the Christmas lights of this wonderland.

He turned abruptly and started back, immediately running smack into the trunk of a tree as his foot caught on a root. He could see nothing around him.

Far away the burnished light of the library and dining room windows did still reveal his destination, but this was faint, and at any moment someone might snap off those lights, never dreaming that he was out here.

He tried to pick up the pace, but he suddenly pitched forward and fell hard on the palms of his hands on the mulch.

This was a ridiculous predicament. Even with his improved sight he could see nothing.

He climbed to his feet and made his way carefully, feet inching along the ground. There was plenty of space for walking, he only had to keep to it. But once again he fell, and when he tried to get his bearings, he realized that he could no longer see any light in any direction.

What was he to do?

Of course he could bring on the change, he was certain of it, strip off these clothes and change, and then he'd see his way clearly to the house, of course he would. As a Morphenkind he'd have no problem even in this awful darkness.

But what if Lisa or Heddy were up? What if one of them were going around turning off the lights? Why, Jean Pierre would be in the kitchen as he always was.

It would be ridiculous for him to risk being seen, and the thought of enduring the change for reasons so mundane, and then quickly hiding again in his human skin and dressing hastily in the freezing cold outside the back door, seemed absurd.

No, he would walk carefully.

He started off again, his hands out before him, and immediately his toe caught again on a root and he went forward. But this time, something stopped him from falling. Something had touched him, touched his right arm and even caught hold of his right arm and he was able to steady himself and step over the roots and clear of them.

Had it been a bramble bush or some wild sapling sprung from the roots? He didn't know. He stood very still. Something was moving near him. Perhaps a deer had come into these woods, but he could catch no scent of a deer. And gradually he realized there was movement all around him. Without the slightest crackling sound of leaf or branch, there was movement virtually surrounding him.

Once again, he felt a touch on his arm, and then what felt like a hand, a firm hand, against his back. This thing, whatever it was, was urging him forward.

"Marchent!" he whispered. He stood still, refusing to move. "Marchent, is it you?" There came no answer from the stillness. The rural dark was so impenetrable that he couldn't see his own hands when he lifted them, but whatever this was, this thing, this person, whatever, it held fast to him and again urged him forward.

The change came over him with such swiftness he didn't have time to make a decision. He was bursting out of his clothes before he could even unbutton them or open them. He pushed off his raincoat and let it drop. He heard the leather of his shoes ripping and popping, and as he rose to his full Morphenkind height, he saw through the darkness, saw the distinct shapes of the trees, their clustered leaves, even the tiny glass lights threaded all through them.

The thing that had been holding him had backed away from him, but turning, he saw the figure now, the pale figure of a man, barely discernible in the moving mist, and as he slowly looked about he saw other figures. Men, women, even smaller figures that must have been children; but whatever they were, they were receding, moving without a sound, and finally he couldn't see them anymore.

He made for the house, easily sprinting through the trees, with the torn remnants of his clothes over his shoulder.

Beneath the dark and empty kitchen windows, he tried to will the change away, struggling violently with it, but it wasn't listening to him. He closed his eyes, willing himself with all his soul to change, but the wolf coat wouldn't leave him. He leaned back against the stones and he stared into the oak woods. He could see those figures again. Very slowly he made out the nearest figure, a man, it seemed, who was looking at him. The man was slender, with large eyes and very long dark hair, and a faint smile on his lips. His clothes looked simple, light, some sort of very old-fashioned shirt with balloon sleeves; but the figure was already paling.

"All right, you don't mean me any harm, do you?" he said.

A soft rustling sound came from the forest but not from the undergrowth or the overhead boughs. It was these creatures laughing. He caught the very pale outline of a profile, of long hair. And once again they were moving away from him.

He heaved a deep breath.

There was a loud snapping noise. Someone somewhere had struck a match. Pray it wasn't Lisa or the other servants!

Light leapt out from behind the north end of the house, and seemed to penetrate the mist as though it were made of tiny golden particles. And there they were again, the men, the women, and those small figures, and then they vanished altogether.

He struggled with the change, gritting his teeth. The light grew brighter and then flared to his left. It was Lisa. Dear God, no. She held the kerosene lantern high.

"Come inside, Master Reuben," she said, not in the least fazed that she was staring at him in his wolf shape, but merely reaching out for him. "Come!" she said.

He felt the most curious emotion as he looked at her. It was like shame, or the nearest thing to shame he'd ever known, that she was seeing him naked and monstrous and that she knew him by name, knew who he was, knew all about him and could see him this way, without his consent, without his desire for her to see him. He was painfully aware of his size, and the way his face must have appeared, covered in hair, his mouth a lipless snout.

"Go away, please," he said. "I'll come when I'm ready."

"Very well," she said. "But you needn't fear them. They are gone now anyway." She set the lantern on the ground, and left him. Infuriating.

It must have been some fifteen minutes before he made the change, cold and shivering as the thick wolf coat left him. Hastily, he put on his torn shirt and what was left of his pants. His shoes and raincoat were somewhere back in the forest.

He hurried inside, and was intent on running up the stairs to his room, when he saw Margon sitting in the dark kitchen, at the table, alone, with his head resting on his hands. His hair was tied back to the nape of his neck, and his shoulders were hunched.

Reuben stood there wanting to speak to Margon, desperate to speak to him, to tell him about what he'd seen in the oaks, but Margon quite deliberately turned away. It wasn't a hostile gesture, merely a subtle turning, his head bowed, as if he were saying, *Please do not see me, please do not talk to me now.*

Reuben sighed and shook his head.

Upstairs, he found the fire lighted in his room, and his bed turned down. His pajamas had been laid out for him. There was a small china pitcher of hot chocolate on the table with a china cup.

Lisa emerged from the bathroom with the air of one who was busy with a multitude of errands. She laid his white terrycloth robe out on the bed.

"Would you like for me to run you a bath, young master?"

"I take showers," Reuben said, "but thank you."

"Very well, master," she responded. "Would you care for some late supper?"

"No, ma'am," he replied. He was livid that she was there. Dressed in torn and filthy garments, he waited, biting his tongue.

She walked past him and around him and towards the door.

"Who were those creatures in the forest?" he asked. "Were they the Forest Gentry? Is that who they were?"

She stopped. She looked unusually elegant in her dress of black wool, her hands appearing very white against the cuffs of the black sleeves. She appeared to reflect for a moment and then,

"But surely you should put these questions, young sir, to the master, but not to the master tonight." She held up one emphatic finger like a nun. "The master is out of sorts tonight, and it is no time to ask him about the Forest Gentry."

"So that's who I saw," said Reuben. "And who the hell are they, exactly, this Forest Gentry?"

She looked down, visibly reflecting before she spoke, and then raised her eyebrows as she looked at him. "And who do you think they are, young master?" she asked.

"Not the forest spirits!" he said.

She gave a grave nod, and lowered her eyes again. She sighed. For the first time, he noticed the large cameo at her neck and that the ivory of the raised figures on the cameo matched her thin hands, which she clasped in front of her as though standing at attention. Something about her chilled his blood. It always had.

"That is a lovely way to describe them," she conceded, "as the spirits of the forest, for it's in the forest that they are most happy and always have been."

"And why is Margon so angry that they've come? What do they do that he's so angry?"

She sighed again and, dropping her voice to a whisper, she said, "He does not like them, that is why he is cross. But . . . they always come at Midwinter. I am not surprised they are here so early. They love the mists and the rain. They love the water. So they are here. They come at Midwinter when the Morphenkinder are here."

"You've been in this house before?" he asked her.

She waited before answering and then said with a faint icy smile, "A long time ago."

He swallowed. She was freezing his blood, all right. But he wasn't afraid of her, and he sensed she didn't mean for him to be afraid. But there was something proud and obdurate in her manner.

"Ah," he said. "I see."

"Do you?" she asked, but her voice and face were faintly sad. "I don't think that you do," she said. "Surely, young master, you do not think the Morphenkinder are the only Ageless Ones under heaven? Surely you know there are many other species of Ageless Ones bound to this earth who have a secret destiny."

A silence fell between them, but she didn't move to go. She looked at him as if from the depth of her own thoughts, patient, waiting.

"I don't know what you are," he said. He was struggling to sound confident and polite. "I really don't know what *they* are. But you needn't wait on me hand and foot. I don't require it, and I'm not used to it."

"But it is my purpose, master," she responded. "It has always been my place. My people care for your people and for other Ageless Ones like you. That is the way it has been for centuries. You are our protectors and we are your servants and that is how we make our way in this world and always have. But come, you are tired. Your clothes are in tatters."

She turned to the hot chocolate, and filled his cup from the pitcher. "You must drink this. You must come and be close to the fire."

He took the cup from her, and he did drink the thick chocolate in one gulp.

"That's good," he said. Strangely, he was less rattled now by her than he'd been in the past, and more curious. And he was infinitely relieved that she knew what he was and what they all were. The burden of keeping the secret from her and the others was gone, but he couldn't help but wonder why Margon hadn't relieved him of this burden before now.

"There's nothing for you to fear, master," she said. "Not from me and my kind ever, for we have always served you, and not from the Forest Gentry because they are harmless."

"The fairy people, that's what they are?" he said. "The elves of the woods?"

"Oh, that I would *not* call them," she said, her German accent sharpening slightly. "Those words, they do not like, I can tell you. And you will never see them appear in pointed caps and pointed shoes," she went on with a little laugh. "Nor are they diminutive beings with tiny beating wings. No, I would forget such words as 'the fairy people.' Here, please, let me help you take off these clothes."

"Well, I can understand that," said Reuben. "And actually it's a bit of a consolation. Would you mind telling me if there are dwarves and trolls out there?"

She didn't respond.

He was just miserable enough in his torn and wet shirt and pants

to let her assist, forgetting until it was too late that he had no underwear on, of course. But she had the terrycloth robe over his shoulders
instantly, quickly wrapping it around him as he slipped his arms into
it, and tying the sash for him as if he were a little boy.

She was almost as tall as he was. And her resolute gestures again
struck him as odd, no matter what she was.

"Now, when the master is not out of sorts, he will perhaps explain
everything to you," she said, her tone softening even further. She
dropped her voice, laughing under her breath. "If on Christmas Eve
they did not appear, he would be disappointed," she said. "It would be a
terrible thing in fact if they did not appear at that time. But he does not
like it at all that they are here now, and that they've been invited. When
they're invited, they become bold. And that irritates him considerably."

"Invited by Felix, you mean," Reuben asked. "That's what's been
going on. Felix howling—."

"Yes, invited by Master Felix, and it is his prerogative to tell you
why, not mine."

She gathered the soiled and torn clothes and made of them a little bundle, obviously for throwing away. "But until such time as the
august masters choose to explain about them to you and your young
companion, Stuart, let me assure you that the Forest Gentry cannot
possibly bring you the slightest harm. And you must not let them force
your . . . your blood to rise, as it were, as it seemed it did tonight."

"I understand," he said. "They caught me completely by surprise.
And I found them unnerving."

"Well, if you do want to unnerve them in return, which I do not
advise, by the way, under any circumstances, just refer to them as
the 'fairy people' or 'elves' or 'dwarves' or 'trolls' and that will do it.
Real harm they cannot do, but they can become quite an incredible
nuisance!"

With a loud sharp laugh, she turned to go, but then,

"Your raincoat," she said. "You left it in the forest. I'll see to it that
it is brushed and cleaned. Sleep now."

She went right out the door, shutting it behind her, leaving him
with all the questions on the tip of his tongue.

12

THE HOUSE WAS IN a pleasant uproar with people coming and going everywhere.

Thibault and Stuart were decorating the giant Christmas tree and commandeered Reuben to help them. Thibault wore a suit and tie as he almost always did, and with his wrinkled face and mossy eyebrows looked the schoolmaster next to Stuart, who, in cutoff jeans and a T-shirt, climbed the creaking ladder like a muscular young cherub to the top step to decorate the highest branches.

Thibault had put on a recording of old English Christmas carols sung by the choir of St. John's College at Cambridge, and the music was soothing and haunting.

The intricate lighting of every branch of the giant tree had already been done, and what was needed now was the hanging of countless gold and silver apples on the tree, little lightweight ornaments that sparkled beautifully amid the deep thick green pine needles. Here and there small edible cookie gingerbread men and gingerbread houses were to be added, and the gingerbread had a delicious aroma.

Stuart wanted to eat them, and so did Reuben, but Thibault forbade them sternly to even think of it. Lisa had decorated every single one herself, and there weren't enough as it was. The "boys" must "behave" themselves.

A tall elegant St. Nicholas with a gaunt but benevolent porcelain face and soft green velvet robes had been placed at the very top of the tree. And the branches from top to bottom had been dusted lightly with some sort of synthetic gold dust. The effect of it all was grand and impressive.

Stuart was his usual buoyant self, eternally smiling, freckles darkening when he laughed, explaining to Reuben that he'd been able to invite "everybody" to the Christmas gala, including the nuns from his high school, and all his friends, and the nurses he'd known in the hospital.

Thibault offered to help Reuben add any last-minute college or newspaper friends, but Reuben had taken care of all of this earlier when Felix had knocked on his door, offering to help him. Numerous phone calls had been made. Reuben's editor from the *San Francisco Observer* was coming with the entire staff of the paper. Three college friends were coming. His cousins from Hillsborough were also driving up; and Grace's brother, Uncle Tim from Rio de Janeiro, was flying in with his beautiful wife, Helen, as both wanted to see this fabulous house. Even Phil's older sister Josie, who lived in a nursing home in Pasadena, was making the trip. Reuben loved his aunt Josie. Jim was bringing a few people from St. Francis parish, and several of the volunteers who regularly helped with the soup kitchen there.

Meanwhile activity went on all around them. Lisa and the caterers had laid out hundreds of sterling knives and forks and spoons on the giant dining room table, and Galton and his men swarmed over the backyard area, clearing an old parking space behind the servants' quarters for the refrigerator trucks that would come the day of the banquet. A band of young teenagers, answering to Jean Pierre and Lisa— everyone was answerable to Lisa—were trimming every interior door and window frame with garland.

That might have looked absurd in a small house, so much greenery, but it was perfect here in these vast rooms, Reuben thought. Masses of thick red candles were being added to the mantelpieces, and Frank Vanderhoven brought in a cardboard box of old Victorian wooden toys to be placed under the tree when they were finished.

Reuben loved all this. It was not only distracting; it was restorative. He tried not to study Heddy and Jean Pierre as they passed, for clues of whatever nature they shared with the redoubtable Lisa.

And everywhere from outside came the noise of hammers and saws.

As for Felix, he left before noon to fly to Los Angeles to make "final arrangements" with the mummers and other costumed people who'd be working the Christmas fair in Nideck or the party up here after the

Christmas fair ended. He would stop in San Francisco before coming home to see to the adult choir and the orchestra he was assembling.

And Margon had gone to meet the arrival of the boys' choir from Austria, which would also be singing at the party. They'd been promised a week in America as part of their compensation. After he'd seen to all their arrangements at the hotels on the coast, he was headed on to make some other necessary purchases of additional oil heaters for the outdoors—or so Reuben and Stuart were being told.

Frank and Sergei, both very big men, came and went continuously with boxes of china and more silver flatware and other decorations from the lower storerooms. Frank was snappily dressed as always, in a polo shirt and clean, pressed jeans, and there was as ever that Hollywood sheen to him even as he toted and reached and lifted. Sergei, the giant of the household, his blond hair an unruly mop, sweated in his rumpled denim shirt and looked faintly bored but eternally agreeable.

A team of professional maids was inspecting all the extra bathrooms on the second floor, those on the inside of the corridors, to make sure each and every one was properly stocked for the banquet guests. The maids would stand outside these bathrooms to direct guests on Sunday.

Deliverymen rang the bell about every twenty minutes; and some reporters were outside braving the light rain to photograph the crèche statues and the ceaseless activity.

It was rather dazzling and comforting, actually—especially since neither Felix nor Margon could be reached with any questions about anything.

"You can expect the entire week to be this way," said Thibault casually as he handed the ornaments out of the box to Reuben. "It's been this way since yesterday."

At last they broke for a late lunch in the conservatory, the only place where decorating was not going on, its tropical blooms seeming woefully incongruous with the Christmas spirit.

Lisa brought plates for them piled high with freshly carved prime rib and huge potatoes already dressed with butter and sour cream, and bowls of steaming carrots and zucchini. The bread had been freshly baked. She opened Stuart's napkin for him and put it in his lap, and would have done the same for Reuben if she'd had the chance. She poured Reuben's coffee, put in the two sweeteners for him, and poured Thibault's wine and Sergei's beer.

Reuben sensed a gentleness in her he hadn't seen before but her gestures and movement were still odd, and a little while ago he'd seen her mount a five-step ladder before the front windows without holding on to anything, to wipe some blemishes from the glass.

Now she banked the little fire in the white Franklin stove, and stood about topping up drinks without a word as Sergei fell on his food like a dog, only using his knife now and then, shoving rolls of beef into his mouth with his fingers, and even breaking up the potato the same way. Thibault ate like a headmaster setting an example for schoolchildren.

"And that's how they ate in the day and age when you were born, right?" said Stuart to Sergei. He loved to tease Sergei at any opportunity. Only next to the giant Sergei did the muscular and tall Stuart look small, and Stuart more than seldom let his big blue eyes move slowly over Sergei's body as though he enjoyed the sight of it.

"Oh, you are dying to know precisely when I came into this world, aren't you, little puppy wolf?" said Sergei. His voice was deep and at times like this his Russian or Slavic accent thickened. He poked Stuart in the chest, and Stuart held firm deliberately, his eyes narrow and full of gleeful mock condescension.

"I bet it was on a farm in Appalachia in 1952," said Stuart. "You tended the pigs till you ran away and joined the army."

Sergei gave a deep sarcastic laugh. "Oh, you are such a clever little beast. What if I told you I was the great St. Boniface himself who brought the first Christmas tree to the pagans of Germany?"

"Like hell," said Stuart. "That's a ridiculous story and you know it. Next you'll tell me you're George Washington and you actually chopped down the cherry tree."

Sergei laughed again. "And what if I'm St. Patrick himself," asked Sergei, "who drove the snakes out of Ireland?"

"If you lived in those times at all, you were a thick-skulled oarsman in a longboat," said Stuart, "and you spent your time raiding coastal villages."

"Not far off the mark," said Sergei, still laughing. "Quite seriously, I was the first Romanov to rule Russia." He rolled his *r*s theatrically. "That's when I learned to read and write, and cultivated my taste for high literature. I'd been around for centuries before that. I was also Peter the Great, too, which was terrific fun, especially the building of St. Petersburg. And before that I was St. George who slew the dragon."

Stuart was tantalized by Sergei's mocking tone.

"No, I'm still betting on West Virginia," said Stuart, "at least for one incarnation, and before that you were shipped over here as a bond servant. What about you, Thibault, where do you think Sergei was born?"

Thibault shook his head, and blotted his mouth with his napkin. With his deeply creased face and gray hair, he looked decades older than Sergei but this meant nothing.

"That was long before my time, young man," Thibault said in his easy baritone. "I'm the neophyte of the pack, if I must confess it. Even Frank's seen worlds of which I know nothing. But it's useless asking these gentlemen for the truth. Only Margon talks of origins, and everyone ridicules him when he does it, including me, I must confess."

"I didn't ridicule him," said Reuben. "I hung on every word he said. I wish every one of you would bless us one day with your stories."

"Bless us!" said Stuart with a groan. "That might be the death of innocence for both you and me. And it might be our literal death from boredom. Add to that I sometimes break out in a fatal allergic rash when people start telling one lie after another."

"Let me make a guess with you, Thibault," ventured Reuben. "Is that fair?"

"Of course, by all means," Thibault answered.

"Nineteenth century, that was your time, and the place of the birth was England."

"Off by only a little," said Thibault with a knowing smile. "But I wasn't born a Morphenkind in England. I was traveling in the Alps at the time." He broke off as if this had sparked some deep and not-too-pleasant thought in him. He sat very still, then seemed to wake from it, and he picked up his coffee and drank it.

Sergei rattled off a long quote, sounding suspiciously like poetry, but it was Latin. And Thibault smiled and nodded.

"Here he goes again, the scholar who eats with his hands," said Stuart. "I can tell you right now, I won't be happy unless I grow to be as tall as you, Sergei."

"You will," said Sergei. "You're a Wonder Pup, as Frank always says. Be patient."

"But why can't you speak of where and when you were born in a casual way," said Stuart, "the way anyone would do it?"

"Because it isn't spoken of!" said Sergei sharply. "And when it is spoken of in a casual way, it sounds ridiculous!"

"Well, Margon of course had the decency to answer our questions immediately."

"Margon told you an old myth," said Thibault, "which he claims is true, because you needed a myth, you needed to know where we come from."

"What, you're saying it was all a lie?" asked Stuart.

"Indeed not," said Thibault. "How would I know if it was? But the teacher loves to tell stories. And the stories change from time to time. We aren't gifted with perfect memory. Stories have a life of their own, especially Margon's life stories."

"Oh, no, please, don't tell me this," said Stuart. He seemed genuinely upset by the idea, his blue eyes flashing almost angrily. "Margon's the only stabilizing influence in my new existence."

"And we do need stabilizing influences," said Reuben under his breath. "Especially stabilizing influences that tell us things."

"You're both in excellent hands," said Thibault quietly. "And I'm teasing you about your mentor."

"What he told us about the Morphenkinder," said Stuart. "That was all true, wasn't it?"

"How many times have you asked us that?" asked Sergei. His voice was a richer baritone than Thibault's voice and a little rougher. "What he told you was true to what he knows. What more do you want? Do I come from the tribe he described? I don't know whether I do or not. How can I? There are Morphenkinder all over the world.

But I will say this. I've never found one that didn't revere Margon the Godless."

That mollified Stuart.

"Margon's a legend among immortals," Sergei went on. "There are immortals everywhere who would like nothing better than to sit at Margon's feet for half a day. You'll find out. You'll see soon enough. Don't take Margon for granted."

"This is no time for all this," said Thibault with a little sarcasm. "We have too many things to do, practical things, small things, the things of life that actually matter."

"Like folding thousands of napkins," said Stuart. "And polishing demitasse spoons, and hanging ornaments and calling my mother."

Thibault laughed under his breath. "What would the world be without napkins? What would Western civilization be without napkins? Can the West function without napkins? And what would you be, Stuart, without your mother?"

Sergei gave a great loud laugh.

"Well, I know I can exist without napkins," he said, and he licked his fingers. "And the evolution of the napkin leads from linen to paper, and I know the West cannot exist without paper. That is a sheer impossibility. And you, Stuart, are far too young to try existing without your mother. I like your mother."

Sergei pushed back his chair, drank his beer down in one long pull, and headed out to find Frank and "get those tables out under the oak trees."

Thibault said it was time to return to work, and rose to lead the way. But neither Reuben nor Stuart moved. Stuart winked at Reuben. And Reuben glanced meaningfully in the direction of Lisa, who stood over his shoulder.

Thibault hesitated, and then shrugged and went on without them.

"Lisa, better give us a minute now," said Reuben, glancing up at her.

With a faint reproving smile, she left, closing the conservatory doors behind her.

Immediately Stuart let fly. "What the hell is going on! Why's Margon in a rage? He and Felix aren't even speaking. And what's with this Lisa, what's happening around here?"

"I don't know where to begin," said Reuben. "If I don't get to talk to Felix before tonight, I'm going to go crazy. But what do you mean about Lisa, what have you noticed about her?"

"Are you kidding? That's not a woman, that's a man," Stuart said. "Look at the way 'she' walks and moves."

"Oh, so that's it," said Reuben. "Of course."

"That's fine with me, of course," said Stuart. "Who am I to criticize her, if she wants to wear a ball gown around here. I'm gay; I'm a defender of human rights. If she wants to be Albert Nobbs, why not? But there are other weird things about her too and Heddy and Jean Pierre. They're not . . ." He stopped.

"Say it!"

"They don't use pot holders to touch hot things," said Stuart whispering now though it wasn't necessary. "They scald themselves when they're making coffee and tea, you know, let the boiling water splash or run over their fingers, and they don't get burned. And nobody bothers to be discreet when they're around about anything. Margon says we'll understand all this in time. How much time? And something else is going on in this house. I don't know how to describe it. But there're noises, like people are in the house who aren't visible. Don't think I'm insane."

"Why would I think that?" asked Reuben.

Stuart gave a droll laugh. "Yeah, right!" He said. His freckles darkened again as his face reddened a little, and he shook his head.

"What else are you sensing?" Reuben prodded him.

"I don't mean the spirit of Marchent," said Stuart. "God help me, I haven't see that. I know you have, but I haven't. But I tell you, there's something else in this house at night. Things moving, stirring, and Margon knows it and he's furious about it. He said it was all Felix's fault, that Felix was superstitious and crazy, and that it had to do with Marchent, and Felix was making a dreadful mistake."

Stuart sat back as if that was about all he had to report. He looked so innocent to Reuben suddenly, the way he had when Reuben had first seen him on that awful night when the thugs had killed Stuart's partner and lover, and Reuben in the melee had accidentally bitten Stuart and passed the Chrism.

"Well, I can tell you what I know about it," said Reuben. He'd made up his mind.

He wasn't going to treat Stuart the way they were treating him. He wasn't going to hold things back and play games, and make vague statements about waiting for the boss to speak. He told Stuart everything.

In detail, he described Marchent's visitations, and how Lisa could see Marchent. Stuart's eyes became huge as Reuben recounted this.

Then Reuben related what had happened to him the night before. He described the Forest Gentry, how they'd been gentle, and trying to help him in the dark, and how he'd freaked and changed. He described Margon sitting dejectedly in the kitchen and Lisa's strange words about the forest people. He recounted what Sergei had said. And then he confided the entire revelation from Lisa.

"My God, I knew it," said Stuart. "They know all about us. That's why nobody ever goes all 'discreet' when they're serving in the dining room! And you mean they're some kind of tribe of immortals themselves that exist to serve other immortals?"

"Ageless Ones, that's what she said," said Reuben. "I heard it with capital letters. But I don't care about her and them, whatever they are. What I care about is this Forest Gentry."

"It has to do with Marchent's ghost," said Stuart. "I know it does."

"Well, I figured that much, but what exactly? That's the question. How are they related to Marchent?" He thought of his dream of Marchent again, of Marchent running through the dark, and those shapes around her in the dark reaching out for her. He couldn't put it all together.

Stuart looked really shaken. He looked as if he was about to cry, about to turn into a little kid right before Reuben's eyes the way he'd done in the past, his face crumpling. But their little tête-à-tête was suddenly over.

Thibault had returned. "Gentlemen, I need you both," he said. He had a list of errands to be run for each of them individually. And Stuart's mother was calling again about her clothes for the party.

"Damn," Stuart said. "I've told her fifty times. Wear what she likes! Nobody cares. This isn't a Hollywood luncheon."

"No, that is not the approach with women, young man," said Thibault gently. "Get on the phone, listen to everything she says, dote upon one color or article of clothing she's described, tell her that really strikes a chord, and elaborate on that as best you can, and she will be marvelously satisfied."

"Genius," said Stuart. "Would you care to talk to her?"

"If you wish, I certainly will," said Thibault patiently. "She's a little girl, you know."

"Tell me!" said Stuart with a groan. "Buffy Longstreet!" He scoffed at his mother's stage name. "Who in the world goes through life with the name of Buffy?"

Frank was at the door.

"Come on, Wonder Pups," he said. "There's work to be done. If you're finished buzzing around the Christmas tree like a couple of little woodland spirits, you can come help with these boxes."

It was late afternoon before Reuben caught Thibault alone. Thibault had put on his black raincoat and was heading to his car. The whole property still swarmed with workmen.

"And Laura?" Reuben asked. "I was with her yesterday but she wouldn't tell me anything."

"There's nothing much to tell," said Thibault. "Calm yourself. I'm on my way there now. The Chrism's taking its time with Laura. This sometimes happens with women. There's no science to the Chrism, Reuben."

"So I'm told," said Reuben, but he was immediately sorry. "No science to us; no science to ghosts; and probably no science to spirits of the forest."

"Well, there's a lot of pseudoscience, Reuben. Wouldn't want to become involved in all that, would you? Laura's doing well. We are doing well. The Christmas gala will be splendid, and our Midwinter Yule will be more festive and joyful than usual—because we have you and Stuart and we will have Laura. But I have to get on the road. I'm late getting away as it is."

13

Wednesday morning, the small hours.

The house slept.

Reuben slept. Naked under the thick down comforter and quilts, he slept, his face against the cool pillow. Go away, house. Go away, fear. Go away, world.

He dreamed.

It was Muir Woods, and he and Laura walked alone in his dream amid the giant redwoods. The sun came down in soft dusty shafts to the dark forest floor. They were locked so close together they were as one, his right arm around her, her left arm around him, and the perfume of her hair was gently intoxicating him.

Far off in the trees, they saw a clearing where the sunlight broke violently and warmly on the earth, and they went to it and lay with their arms around each other. In the dream it didn't matter whether anyone came, whether anyone saw. Muir Woods was theirs, their forest. They took off their clothes; their clothes vanished. How marvelously free Reuben felt, as if he were in wolf coat, that free, that wondrously naked. Here was Laura beneath him, her opalescent blue eyes looking up into his eyes, her hair fanned out against the dark earth, such beautiful yellow hair, white hair, and he bent down to kiss her. *Laura.* Hers was a way of kissing like no other, hungry yet patient, yielding yet expectant. He felt the heat of her breasts against his naked chest, the moisture of her pubic hair against his leg. He rose high enough to guide his organ into her. Ecstasy, this little sanctum. The air was golden with the sun, dazzling on the leafy bracken that surrounded them in this temple of the high redwoods. Her hips rose just a little and then his weight brought her down firmly against the sweet, fragrant earth, and he fell into a great delicious rhythm riding her, loving her, kissing her soft delicious mouth as he took her, as he gave himself to her, *Love you, my divine Laura*. He came, his eyes shut, the wave of pleasure rising and rising until he could barely stand it, and he opened his eyes:

Marchent.

She lay under him in the bed, her tormented eyes pleading with him, her mouth quivering, her face streaked with tears.

He roared.

He shot up from the bed and slammed against the far wall. He was roaring, roaring in horror.

She sat up on the bed, grasping the sheet to her naked breasts—his sheets, her breasts—staring at him in panic. Her mouth opened but the words wouldn't come. Her arm reached out. Her hair was tangled and wet.

He was choking, sobbing.

Someone beat on his door, and then the door was flung open.

He sat crying against the wall. The bed was empty. Stuart was standing there.

"Jeez, man, what is it?"

Up the stairs came pounding steps. Jean Pierre stood behind Stuart.

"Oh, Mother of God!" Reuben sobbed. He couldn't stop the cries coming out of him. "Holy God." He struggled to stand up, then fell back on the floor, banging his head hard against the wall.

"Stop it, Reuben," cried Stuart. "Stop it! We're here with you now, it's okay."

"Master, here," said Jean Pierre, bringing his robe to him and covering his shoulders with it.

Lisa appeared in the door in a long plain white nightgown.

"I'm going to lose my mind," Reuben stammered, the words catching, his throat constricted. "I'm going to lose my mind." He shouted at the top of his voice, "Marchent!"

He put his face in his hands. "What do you want, what can I do, what do you want! I'm sorry, I'm sorry, I'm sorry, Marchent. Marchent, forgive me!"

He turned and clawed at the wall as if he could pass into it. He banged his head against it again.

Firm hands had ahold of him.

"Quiet, master, quiet," said Lisa. "Jean Pierre, change those sheets! Here, Stuart, you help me."

But Reuben lay crouched beside the wall, inconsolable. His body was clenched like a fist. His eyes were closed.

Moments passed.

Finally, he opened his eyes, and he let them help him to his feet. He hugged the robe to him as if he were freezing. Flashes of the dream returned: sun, smell of earth perfume of Laura; Marchent's face, tears, her lips, her lips, her lips, it had always been her lips, not Laura's. That had been Marchent's unique kiss.

He was sitting at the table. How did he get here?

"Where is Felix?" he asked. He looked up at Lisa. "When will Felix be home? I have to reach him."

"In a matter of hours, master," said Lisa comforting him. "He will be here. I will call him. I will make sure of it."

"I'm sorry," Reuben whispered. He sat back dazed, watching Jean Pierre remake the bed. "I'm so sorry."

"Incubus!" whispered Lisa.

"Don't say that word!" Reuben said. "Don't say that evil word. She doesn't know what she's doing! She doesn't know, I tell you! She's not a demon. She's a ghost. She's lost and she's struggling and I can't save her. Don't you call her an incubus. Don't use that demon language."

"It's okay, man," said Stuart. "We're all here now. You can't see her anymore, can you?"

"She is not here now," said Lisa shortly.

"She's here," said Reuben softly. "She's always here. I know she's here. I felt her last night. I knew she was here. She didn't have the strength to come through. She wanted to. She's here now and she's crying."

"Well, you must go back to bed and sleep."

"I don't want to," Reuben said.

"Look, man, I'll stay in here," said Stuart. "I need a pillow and a blanket. I'll be right back. I'll lie right here by the fireplace."

"Yeah, stay here, will you, Stuart?" said Reuben.

"Get the pillow and the blanket for him, Jean Pierre," said Lisa. She stood behind Reuben holding his shoulders, massaging his shoulders, her fingers like iron. But it felt good to him.

Don't let me go, he thought. Don't let me go. He reached up and took her hand, her firm cold hand.

"Will you stay with me?"

"Of course, I will," she said. "Now, you, Stuart, you lie down there by the fire, and you sleep there. And I will sit here in this chair and keep watch so that he can sleep."

He lay down on his back in the freshly made bed. He was afraid that if he tried to sleep, he'd turn and see her lying right beside him.

But he was too tired, so tired.

Gradually he drifted off.

He could hear Stuart softly snoring.

And when he looked at Lisa, she sat composed and still, staring at the distant window. Her hair was loose and down over her shoulders. He had never seen it that way before. Her white nightgown was starched and pressed, with faded flowers embroidered at the neck. He could see clearly that she was a man, a thin, delicate-boned man with impeccable skin and sharp distant gray eyes. And she stared at the window without moving, still as a statue.

14

THEY WERE GATHERED at the dining room table, the place of meeting, the place for history, the place for decisions.

The fire in the grate and the pure-wax candles were the only illumination, with one candelabrum on the table and one each on the dark oak hunter's boards.

Frank had gone off to be "with a friend" and wouldn't be back until time for the Christmas gala on Sunday. Thibault had left early to be with Laura.

So it was Stuart, white-faced, and plainly fearfully fascinated by the whole proceeding; and Sergei, the giant looking surprisingly interested; Felix, sad and anxious, eager for the meeting to take place; Margon, obviously short-tempered and displeased; and Reuben, still frayed from this morning's visitation. All were in casual clothes, sweaters, jeans of one sort or another.

They had had their supper, and the servants had "cleared away," and now only Lisa in her usual black silk, with the cameo at her throat, stood with arms folded by the fireplace. The coffee had been served, the pots set about, and the gingerbread and cream passed, along with the fresh apples and plums, and the soft creamy French cheese.

Faint scent of the wax, like incense, and of course the fire, always the comforting oak fire, and the lingering fragrance of wine now mingled with coffee.

Felix sat with his back to the fire; Reuben sat opposite. Stuart sat beside Felix. And Margon was as always to Reuben's left at the head of the table. Sergei was to the right of Reuben. It was the customary arrangement.

A bit of a gale beat on the windows. And the prediction was that it would get worse before morning. However, better weather was expected for Sunday's party.

The wind was screaming in the chimneys, and the rain on the glass sounded like hail.

The lights in the oaks had been shut off. But all the other outside lights were on. The workmen were gone from the property; and for the moment at least everything was "done" for the Christmas gala. Masses of holly and mistletoe as well as pine garland were wound around the mantelpiece and the sides of the fireplace, and about the windows and the doors, and the sweet scent sometimes filled the air and sometimes died away altogether, as though the greenery were now and then holding its breath.

Margon cleared his throat. "I want to speak first," he said. "I want to tell what I know about this audacious plan and why I'm against it. I want to be heard on this issue." His long hair was down around his face, and a little more brushed and combed than usual, perhaps because Stuart had been insisting he comb it, and he looked something like a dark-skinned Renaissance prince. Even his burgundy-colored velour sweater added to the effect, and the jeweled rings on his slender dark fingers.

"No, please, I beg you. Be quiet," said Felix with a small imploring gesture. His golden skin usually didn't show much color, but Reuben could see the flush in his cheeks now, and his brown eyes were sharpened with what was obviously anger. He seemed a much younger man now than the polished gentleman Reuben knew him to be.

Without waiting for Margon to speak, Felix looked at Reuben and said, "I've invited the Forest Gentry for a reason." He glanced at Stuart and back at Reuben. "They've always been our friends. And I've called them here because they can approach Marchent's spirit and invite her into their company, and comfort Marchent's spirit, and bring her round to realizing what's happened to her."

Margon rolled his eyes and sat back, folding his arms, rage exuding from every pore. "Our friends!" He spat the words contemptuously.

Felix went on. "They can do this," said Felix, "and they will if I ask them to do it. They will take her into their company, and if they will permit, she can elect to join them."

"Good God!" said Margon. "Such a fate. And this you do to your own blood kin."

"Don't speak to me of blood kin!" Felix flashed. "What do you remember of blood kin!"

"Guys, please, don't fight again!" said Stuart. Stuart was plainly shocked. He too had combed his thick curly hair for the meeting, even cut some of it maybe, which only made him look more like a giant freckled six-year-old.

"Since time immemorial they've lived in the forests," said Felix, glancing again at Reuben. "They were in the forests of the New World before *Homo sapiens* ever arrived here."

"No, they were not," said Margon disgustedly. "They've come here for the same reasons we came."

"They have always been in the forests," said Felix. He kept his eyes fixed on Reuben. "The forests of Asia and Africa, the forests of Europe, the forests of the New World. They have their stories of origin and their beliefs as to whence they came."

"Emphasis on the word 'stories,'" said Margon. "Better put it they have their preposterous fables and nonsensical superstitions like all the rest of us. All the Ageless Ones have their stories. Even the Ageless cannot live without stories, no more than humankind can live without them, because all the Ageless of this world come from humankind."

"We don't know that," said Felix patiently. "We know we were once human. That's all we know. And finally it doesn't matter, especially not with the Forest Gentry, because we know what they can do. What they can do is what matters."

"Does it matter if the Forest Gentry tell lies?" demanded Margon.

Felix was becoming more and more agitated.

"They are here and they are real and they will be able to see Marchent in this house, hear her, speak to her, and invite her to go with them."

"Go with them where!" said Margon. "To remain earthbound forever?"

"Please!" said Reuben. "Margon, let Felix talk. Let him explain the Forest Gentry. Please! I can't help Marchent's spirit. I don't know how." He had begun to tremble, but he wouldn't give up on this point. "This afternoon I walked all through this house. I walked the property in the rain. I talked to Marchent. I talked, and I talked and I talked. And I know she can't hear me. And every time I see her she's more miserable than the last!"

"Look, man, this is really true," Stuart said. "Margon, you know I worship the ground you walk on, man. I don't want to make you mad. I can't stand it when you're mad at me. You know that." His voice was getting husky and almost broken. "But please. You gotta understand what Reuben's going through. You weren't here last night."

Margon started to interrupt, but Stuart waved him aside. "And you guys have to start trusting us!" said Stuart. "We trust you but you don't trust us. You don't tell us what's going on around us." He glanced over his shoulder at Lisa. Lisa regarded him indifferently.

Margon threw up his hands, and then folded his arms again, looking off at the fire. His eyes flashed angrily at Stuart and then at Felix. "All right," he whispered. He gestured to Felix to speak. "Explain. Go on."

"The Forest Gentry are ancient," said Felix, now attempting to pick up his customary reasonable demeanor. "You've both heard tell of them. You heard of them in the fairy tales you learned as little ones, but the fairy tales have domesticated them, rendered them quaint. Forget the fairy tales, visions of elves."

"Yeah, like it's more like Tolkien."

"This is not Tolkien!" Margon seethed. "This is reality. Don't mention Tolkien again to me, Stuart. Don't mention any of your noble and revered fantasy writers! No Tolkien, no George R. R. Martin, no C. S. Lewis, do you hear me. They are marvelously inventive and ingenious, and even godly in the way they rule their imaginative worlds, but this is reality!"

Felix put up his hands for silence.

"Look, I saw them," said Reuben gently. "They appeared to be men, women, children."

"And so they are," said Felix. "They have what we call subtle bodies. They can move through any barrier, through any wall, and over any distance instantly. And they can take visible form, a form as solid as our form, and when they are in the solid form they eat, drink, and make love as we do."

"No, they don't," said Margon crossly. "They pretend to do these things!"

"The fact is, they believe they can do them," said Felix. "And they can be entirely visible to anyone!" He stopped, and took a drink of his coffee, and wiped his lips with his napkin. Then he resumed, his voice rolling easily and calmly once more. "They are distinct personalities, they have lineages and histories. But most important of all, they have the capacity to love." He emphasized the last word. "To love. And they are loving." Tears were rising in his eyes as he looked at Reuben. "And that is why I invited them."

"They are coming anyway, are they not?" said Sergei in a loud voice, gesturing impatiently with both his hands. He looked pointedly at Margon. "Won't they be here on Midwinter night? They are always here. If we build the fire, if our musicians play, if they play the drums and the flutes and we dance, they come! They play for us and they dance with us."

"Yes, they come and they may go as swiftly as they come," said Felix. "But I've begged them to come soon and remain so that I can implore them to help us."

"Very well," said Sergei, "so what is the harm? You think the workmen know they are here? They don't. Nobody knows except us, and we know only when they want us to know."

"Precisely, when they want us to know," said Margon. "They've been in and out of this house for days. They're likely in this room now." He was becoming more and more heated. "They're listening to what we're saying. You think when you snap your fingers they'll go? Well, they won't. They'll go when they have a mind to go. And if they have a mind to play pranks, they'll drive us crazy. Reuben, you think a restless spirit is a cross to bear? Wait till they start their tricks."

"I think they are here," said Stuart softly. "Really, Felix, I think they are. They can move things when they're invisible, can't they? I mean light things like curtains. And they blow out candles, or make the fire in the grate flare up."

"Yes, they can do all that," said Felix caustically, "but usually only when they're offended, or insulted, or overlooked, or denied. I don't mean to give them any offense. I mean to welcome them now, welcome them this very night into this house. Their capacity for mischief is a small price to pay if they can gather to themselves the suffering spirit of my niece." Now he was weeping and he didn't bother to conceal it.

This was bringing tears to Reuben's eyes too. He took out his handkerchief, and set it on the table. He gestured to Felix with it, but Felix shook his head, and took out his own.

Felix wiped at his nose and went on.

"I want to invite them in formally. You know what that means to them. They want food set out—the proper offerings."

"These are prepared," said Lisa softly from the fireplace. "I've put out their cream for them in the kitchen, and their butter cakes, the things they love. It's all set out there."

"They're a bunch of lying ghosts," said Margon under his breath. He took in Stuart and Felix with his eyes. "That's all they are and all they've ever been. They're spirits of the dead and they don't know it. They've built a mythology for themselves since olden times, lie upon lie, as they've grown stronger. They're nothing but lying ghosts, strong ghosts who've been evolving in power since the dawn of intellect and recorded memory."

"I don't get it," said Stuart.

"Stuart, everything is evolving on this planet," said Margon. "And ghosts are no exception. True, human beings die every minute and their souls ascend, or stumble into the earthbound sphere and roam in a self-made wilderness for years of earth time. But collectively, the inhabits of the earthbound sphere have been evolving. The earthbound have their Ageless Ones; the earthbound have their aristocracy; they have their myths now and their 'beliefs' and their superstitions. And above all, they have their powerful and brilliant personalities who have grown ever stronger over the centuries at holding their ethereal bodies together, and concentrating their focus so as to manipulate matter in ways that early ghosts on the planet never even dreamed of."

"You mean they've learned how to be ghosts?" asked Reuben.

"They've learned how to stop being mere ghosts and develop into sophisticated discarnate personalities," said Margon. "And finally, and this is most important, they have learned how to become visible."

"But how do they do it?" asked Stuart.

"Force of mind, energy," said Margon. "Concentration, focus. They draw to their subtle bodies, these ethereal bodies they possess, material particles. And the very strongest of these ghosts, the great nobility, if you will, can render themselves so visible and solid that no human looking at them, touching them, making love to them, could possibly know they were spirits."

"Good God, they could be walking around amongst us," said Stuart.

"They *are* walking around with us," said Margon. "I see them all the time. But what I'm trying to tell you is that these Forest Gentry are merely one tribe of these old and evolving ghosts, and of course they are among the most cunning, the most practiced and the most formidable."

"So why do they bother with fables about themselves?" asked Stuart.

Felix interjected. "They don't consider their origin stories mere fables," he said. "Not by any means, and it is offensive to suggest to them that their beliefs are mere fables."

Margon gave a faint sneer. His face was too agreeable for it to be a mean sneer and it vanished immediately.

"There is nothing under the sun," said Margon, "nor under the moon, no entity of intellect, that does not have to believe something about itself, something about its purpose, the reason for its suffering, its destiny."

"So what you're saying," said Reuben, "is that Marchent is a new ghost, a baby ghost, a ghost who doesn't know how to appear or disappear—."

"Exactly," said Margon. "She is confused, struggling, and what she's managed to achieve has depended on the intensity of her feelings— her desperate desire to communicate with you, Reuben. And to some extent her success so far has depended on your sensitivity to seeing her ethereal presence."

"The Celtic blood?" asked Reuben.

"Yes, but there are many sensitive seers of spirits in this world. Celtic blood is but one facilitating ingredient. I see spirits. I did not in the beginning of my life, but at some point I began to see them. And now I can see them sometimes before they're focused and intent on communicating."

"Let's cut to the chase," said Felix gently. "We don't know what really happens when a person dies. We know some souls or spirits detach from the body, or are released by the body and they move on and are never heard from again. We know some become ghosts. We know they appear confused and often unable to see us or see one another. But the Forest Gentry can see all ghosts, all souls, all spirits, and the Forest Gentry can communicate with them."

"They have to come, then," said Reuben. "They have to help her."

"Really?" asked Margon. "And what if there is some Maker of the Universe out there who has designed life and death? What if He doesn't want these earthbound entities lingering here, gaining power, lying to themselves, privileging their personal survival over the grand scheme of things?"

"Well, now, you just described us, didn't you?" said Felix. His voice was still strained, but he was calm. "You just described us personally. And who is to say that in the scheme of things ordained by the Maker of All Things, these earthbound spirits aren't fulfilling a divine destiny?"

"Ah, yes, all right, very well," said Margon wearily.

"But who do the Forest Gentry think they are?" asked Stuart.

"I haven't asked them of late," said Margon.

"In some parts of the world," said Felix, "they claim to have descended from fallen angels. In other places, they are the spawn of Adam before he coupled with Eve. What is curious is that humankind has countless such stories about them the world over; but one thread runs through it all. They are not descended from humans. They are another species of being."

"Paracelsus wrote of this," said Reuben.

"Right, he did," said Felix. He gave Reuben a sad smile. "Right you are on that," he said.

"But whatever the truth of the matter is, they can embrace Marchent."

"Yes," said Margon. "They do it all the time—invite the newly dead to join their ranks, when they find them strong and distinctive and interesting."

"Normally it takes centuries for them to notice a persistent earthbound soul," said Felix. "But they've come because I've asked them to come and I will invite them to welcome Marchent."

"I think I've seen them in a dream," said Reuben. "I had a dream. I saw Marchent and she was running through a dark wood and there were these spirits in the dream and they were trying to reach out for her, to comfort her. I think that's what was happening."

"Well, because I cannot prevent this from happening," said Margon wearily, "I give my consent to it."

Felix rose to his feet.

"But where are you going?" asked Margon. "They're here now. Ask them to show themselves."

"Well, isn't it fitting that I stand when I welcome the Forest Gentry into Reuben's house?"

He brought his hands together reverently as if in prayer.

"Elthram, welcome to Reuben's house," he said in a soft voice. "Elthram, welcome to the house of the new master of this forest."

15

THERE WAS A CHANGE in the atmosphere, a faint draft that made the candle flames shudder. Lisa straightened against the paneled wall and looked sharply towards the far end of the table. Sergei sat back heavily in his chair, sighing, with a smile on his lips as though he were enjoying this.

Reuben followed the direction of Lisa's gaze and then so did Stuart.

Out of the shadows there, something indistinct took shape. It was as if the darkness itself thickened. The candle flames settled on their wicks. And a figure gradually appeared—resembling first a faint projection of an image and then brightening, and becoming finally three-dimensional and vivid.

It was the figure of a large man, a man slightly taller than Reuben, rawboned, with a massive head of black shining hair. The frame of the man was enormous, and the bones of his face were prominent and beautifully symmetrical. His skin was dark, dark as caramel, but he had large almond-shaped light eyes, green eyes. These eyes shining out of the dark face gave him a slightly manic look, heightened by his thick straight eyebrows, and the faint smile on his large sensuous mouth. He had a high smooth forehead from which his unruly hair erupted in dark glossy waves.

His hair was so full that some of it was pulled back from his face, the great mass of it falling down on all sides to his shoulders. He appeared to be wearing a light beige-colored chamois shirt and pants. The belt he wore was very wide and dark and had a large bronze buckle in the shape of a face.

He had very big hands.

There was no classifying him as to race in Reuben's mind. He might have come from India. It was impossible to tell.

He looked at Reuben thoughtfully and made a little bow. Then he looked at each of the others in the same way, his face dramatically brightening when his eyes settled on Felix.

He came around the table behind Stuart to greet Felix.

"Felix, my old friend," he said in clear unaccented English. "How glad I am to see you, and how glad I am that you're returned to the Nideck woods." His voice was even, youthful.

They embraced.

His body seemed as real and as solid as Felix's body, and Reuben marveled that there was nothing even faintly frightening or horrible about this figure. In fact his fantastic materializing seemed like some natural revelation—that is, the uncovering of someone solid who had already been there, obedient to gravity, and breathing just like any one of them.

The man's eyes fixed on Reuben. Quickly Reuben rose and extended his hand.

"Welcome, young master of these woods," said Elthram. "You love the forest as we love the forest." He sounded contemporary, relaxed.

"I do love it," said Reuben. He was trembling and trying to conceal it. The hand that clasped his was warm and firm. "Forgive me," he stammered. "This is powerful, all this." The scent rising from the figure was the scent of the outdoors, of leaves, living things, but also of dust, very strongly of dust. But dust gives off a clean scent, doesn't it, Reuben thought.

"Indeed, and it's thrilling for me as well, to be invited into your house," said Elthram, smiling. "Many's the time our people have seen you and your lady walking in the woods here, and no human in these parts loves the woods any more than your beloved lady."

"She'll be so pleased to hear that," said Reuben. "I wish she were here now to meet you."

"But she has met me," said Elthram. "Though she hasn't known it. She's known me all her life, and I've known her—knew her when she was a child making her way through Muir Woods with her father. The

Forest Gentry know those who belong to the forest. They never forget those who are kind to the forest."

"I'll share all of this with her," said Reuben. "As soon as I'm able."

Some small derisive sound came from Margon.

The man's eyes fixed on Margon. To say the appearance of animation drained out of the man would be an understatement. He was immediately bruised and silenced. And it did seem that the entire figure grew paler for an instant, less reflective, the smooth shining skin fading to a matte surface, but this was at once corrected, though the man's eyes were narrow and quivering slightly as if fending off invisible blows.

Margon stood up and walked out of the dining room.

This was a terrible moment for Stuart, plainly, and he looked miserably after Margon and started to rise. But Felix reached down and put his right hand on Stuart's shoulder, saying "Stay with us" in a small but authoritative voice. He turned back to the man.

"Sit down, please, Elthram," said Felix and gestured to Margon's chair. It was the logical chair, of course, but the gesture seemed a little abrasive, to say the least.

"Now, Stuart, this is our good friend Elthram of the Forest Gentry, and I know you join me in welcoming him to the house."

"Absolutely!" Stuart responded. His face was flushed.

Elthram seated himself and immediately greeted Sergei, whom he also addressed as "old friend."

Sergei gave a low rolling laugh and a nod. "You look splendid, dear friend," said Sergei. "Simply splendid. You always take me back in mind to the most blissful—and the most tempestuous—times!"

Elthram acknowledged this with those intense eyes firing beautifully. Then he looked intently at Reuben.

"Let me assure you, Reuben," he said, "we did not mean to startle you in the forest. We meant to help you. You were confused in the darkness. And we did not know how quickly you would sense our presence. And so our attempts went wrong." His voice had a medium pitch, about like Reuben's or Stuart's voice.

"Oh, not at all," said Reuben. "I knew you were trying to help. I understood that. I just didn't know what you were."

"Yes," he said. "Often when we assist someone who is lost, that one is not so quick to realize that it is we who are doing it, you understand. We pride ourselves on subtlety. But you're gifted, Reuben, and we didn't realize how gifted, and so misunderstanding was the result."

Surely the green eyes in the dark face were the most startling trait of this man, and even if they'd been small they would have been startling. As it was, they were very large with large pupils and it seemed impossible they were mere illusion, but then again this wasn't mere illusion, was it?

And all this is particles, Reuben thought, drawn to an ethereal body? And all this can be dispersed? Now that seemed impossible. No revelation of a presence could compare in shock with the notion that something as solid and vital as this man could simply disappear.

Felix had seated himself again, and Lisa had set a large mug before Elthram, and was filling it from a cold silver pitcher with what appeared to be milk.

Elthram gave Lisa what was surely a bit of a mischievous smile and thanked her. Gratefully, in fact, with remarkably obvious pleasure, he looked at the milk. He lifted the mug to his lips but he did not actually drink the milk.

"Now Elthram," said Felix, "you know why I've asked you to come—."

"Yes, I do," said Elthram running over Felix's words. "And she is here, yes, most definitely here and lingering here and not wanting to go anywhere else. But she can't see us yet or hear us, but she will."

"Why is she haunting?" asked Reuben.

"She's grieved, and confused," said Elthram. The largeness of his face was slightly disorienting for Reuben, possibly because they sat so close to each other and the man was slightly taller even than Sergei, who was the tallest of the Distinguished Gentlemen. "She does know that she has passed, yes, she knows this. But she's still uncertain as to what caused her death. She knows her brothers are dead. But she doesn't grasp that they in fact took her life. And she searches for answers, and she fears the portal to the heavens when she sees it."

"But why, why fear the portal to the heavens?" asked Reuben.

"Because she is not a believer in life after death," explained Elthram. "She is not a believer in invisible things."

His speech was easily more contemporary sounding than the speech of the Distinguished Gentlemen, and his kind and inviting manner was extremely attractive.

"Reuben, when the newly dead see the portal to the heavens, they see a white light. Sometimes in that white light they see ancestors, or parents who have gone on. Sometimes they see only light. We often see what we think they see but we can't be sure. This light is no longer opening for her, or inviting her to move on. But it's clear that she doesn't know why she is still existing as herself, as Marchent, when she believed so firmly that death would be the end of what she was."

"What is she trying to tell me?" asked Reuben. "What does she want from me?"

"She's clinging to you because she can see you," said Elthram, "so in the main she wants you to know that she's here. She wants to ask you what happened to her and why it happened and what happened to you. She knows you're no longer a human being, Reuben. She can see this, sense it, probably she's witnessed you change into the beast state. I'm almost certain she's witnessed it. This frightens her, terrifies her. She is a ghost filled with terror and grief."

"This has to stop," said Reuben. He was trembling again, and he hated it when he started trembling. "She can't be allowed to suffer. She did nothing to deserve it."

"You're right, absolutely," said Elthram. "But do understand that in this world—in your world, and in our world, the world we share—suffering often has little to do with whether one deserves it."

"But you will help her," said Reuben.

"We will. We surround her now; we surround her when she is dreaming and unfocused and unaware. We attempt to rouse her spirit, to provoke it to focus so that she pulls her spirit body together and becomes a learner again."

"What do you mean, 'a learner'?" asked Reuben.

"Spirits learn when they are focused. Focus involves the concentration of the spirit body, concentration of the mind. When the newly dead first cross over, their biggest temptation in the earthbound state is to diffuse, to spread out, to become loose and like air, and to dream. A spirit can float in such a state forever, and the mind does not think in such a state so much as it dreams, if there is any narrative in that mind at all."

"Ah, that's exactly what I thought," said Stuart suddenly, but then he sank back and gestured in apology.

"You have studied this," said Elthram in a very genial manner to Stuart. "You and Reuben both have studied it on your computers, on the Internet, you've read all you can find about ghosts and spirits."

"A lot of jumbled theories," said Stuart. "Yes."

"I haven't studied it enough," said Reuben. "I've been too focused on myself, on my own suffering. I should have studied."

"But there's truth in much of those jumbled theories," Elthram continued.

"So when a dreaming spirit draws itself together," said Stuart, "when it focuses, then it starts to really think."

"Yes," said Elthram. "It thinks, it remembers, and memory is everything for the education and the moral fiber of a spirit. And as it grows stronger, so its senses become stronger; it can see the physical world in the old way again, though not perfectly. And it can hear physical sounds in the old way again, and even smell, and touch."

"And as it grows stronger, then it can appear," Reuben volunteered.

"Yes. It can appear to someone who is gifted more readily than to others, but yes, as it condenses its energy, as it envisions its own energy in the form of its old physical body, it can both accidentally and purposefully appear to anyone."

"I see. I'm getting it," said Stuart.

"Now do keep in mind that the spirit of Marchent doesn't know these things—she is responding when she sees or senses Reuben's presence. And she responds when Reuben responds to her. And the act of concentrating, of focusing, of pulling together, this happens without her fully grasping that that is what she's doing. This is how ghosts learn."

"And left to her own devices," asked Felix, "she will continue to learn?"

"Not necessarily," said Elthram. "She may remain as she is for years."

"That's too horrible," said Reuben.

"It is horrible," said Felix.

"Trust in us, old friend," said Elthram. "We will not abandon her. She's your blood kin, and you were master of these great woods for many a decade. Once she recognizes us, once she ceases to veer away from us and back into the buffer of her dreams, once she allows herself to focus on us, we can teach her more than I can now explain to you in words."

"But she could ignore you for years, too, couldn't she?" asked Felix.

Elthram smiled. It was the most compassionate smile. He extended his left hand and then, turning, placed both his hands over Felix's right hand. "She will not," he said. "I won't let her ignore me. You know how persistent I can be."

"So you're saying," asked Reuben, "that she turned away from the white light, the portal, as you call it, because she didn't believe in life after death?"

"There can be many tangled reasons why spirits don't acknowledge the portal," said Elthram. "I sense this was the reason in her case. And it was mingled with the fact that she feared notions of the hereafter for other reasons, that she would encounter there spirits she didn't want to encounter, the spirits of her parents, for instance, whom she hated by the end of their lives."

"Why did she hate them?" asked Reuben.

"Because she knew they'd been treacherous to Felix," said Elthram. "She knew."

"And all this you can extract simply by being here where her spirit is?" asked Stuart.

"We've been here for a very long time. We were here when she was growing up, of course. We were around her during many moments in her life. You might say we've always known her, because we have known Felix and known Felix's house and Felix's family, and we know much of what happened with her."

This was saddening Felix, almost crushing him. He put his face in his hands.

"Don't fear," said Elthram. "We are here now to do what you've asked us to do."

"What about the spirits of her brothers?" asked Reuben. "The men who stabbed her to death?"

"Gone from the earth," said Elthram.

"They saw the portal and went up?"

"I don't know," said Elthram.

"What about Marrok's spirit?" asked Reuben.

Elthram was quiet for a moment. "Not here. But Morphenkinder spirits almost never linger."

"Why not?"

Elthram smiled as if the question was surprising and even naïve. "They know too much about life and death," he offered. "It's those who don't know much about life and death that linger, those who aren't prepared for the transition."

"You help other spirits, lingering spirits?" asked Stuart.

"We do. We have. Our society is like many an earthly society. We meet, we come to know, we invite, we learn from. And so it goes."

"And your company, the Forest Gentry, you take in wandering spirits."

"We have. We do." Elthram seemed to be pondering for a moment. "Not everyone wants to join with us," said Elthram. "We are after all the Forest Gentry. But we are only one group of spirits in this world. There are others. And many a spirit needs no company and evolves from virtue to virtue on his own."

"This portal to the heavens," asked Reuben, "does it ever open for you?"

"I am not a ghost," said Elthram. "I have always been what I am. I chose this physical body; I constructed it for myself, and perfected it, and now and then alter it and refine it. Because I have never had an ethereal human body, but only an ethereal spirit body. I have always been spirit. And no, there is no portal to the heavens that opens for such as me."

There came the soft sound of someone walking into the room

again, and out of the gloom, Margon appeared and took the chair at the far end of the table.

Elthram's face was stricken. His eyes quivered again as though someone were hurting him. But he looked steadily at Margon in spite of this.

"If I offend you, I'm sorry," he said to Margon.

"You don't offend me," said Margon. "But you were flesh and blood once, Elthram. All of you Forest Gentry were once flesh and blood. You've left your bones in the earth like all living things."

These words were lacerating Elthram and he was flinching. His whole frame stiffened as if to hunker under an assault.

"And so you'll teach your clever skills to Marchent, will you?" demanded Margon. "You'll teach her to rule in the astral sphere as you rule. You'll use her intellect and memory to help her become a nonpareil of a ghost!"

Stuart looked as if he was going to cry.

"Please don't say any more," said Felix softly.

Margon kept his eyes on Elthram, who had drawn himself up, his open hands hovering in front of his face.

"Well, when you speak to Marchent," said Margon, "for the love of truth, remind her of the portal. Don't urge her to remain with you."

"And what if there is nothing beyond the portal?" asked Stuart. "What if it's a portal to annihilation? What if existence continues only for the earthbound?"

"If that's so, then that's the way it's probably meant to be," said Margon.

"How do you know what is meant to be?" asked Elthram. He was taking pains to be courteous. "We are the Forest People," he said gently. "We were here before you ever came into existence, Margon. And we do not know what is meant to be. So how can you know? Oh, the tyranny of those who believe in nothing."

"There are those who come from beyond the portal, Elthram," said Margon.

Elthram appeared shocked.

"You know there are those who come from beyond the portal," said Margon.

"You believe this and yet you say that we did not come from beyond the portal?" asked Elthram. "Your spirit was born of matter, Margon, and thrives in matter now. Our spirits were never rooted to the physical. And yes, we may have come here from beyond the portal, but we only know of our existence here."

"You become more clever all the time, don't you? And you grow ever more powerful."

"And why shouldn't we?" asked Elthram.

"No matter how clever you become, you'll never be able to actually drink that milk. You can't eat the food offerings you so relish. You know you can't."

"You think you know what we are, but—."

"I know what you are *not*," said Margon. "Lies have consequences."

Silence with the two staring at each other.

"Someday, perhaps," said Elthram in a low voice, "we will be able to eat and drink, too."

Margon shook his head.

"People of old knew ghosts or gods—as they called them—savored the fragrance of burnt offerings," said Margon. "People of old knew ghosts or gods—as they called them—thrived on moisture, thrived on the falling rain, and loved the brooks of the woodland or the fields, or liquids turning into steam. That feeds your electrical energy, doesn't it? The rain, the waters of a creek or a waterfall. You can dip to lap the moisture of a libation poured on a grave."

"I am not a ghost," whispered Elthram.

"But no spirit or ghost or god," Margon insisted, "can really eat or drink."

Elthram's eyes blazed with a painful anger. He didn't answer.

"Beings like this one, Stuart," said Margon as he glanced at Stuart, "have fooled humans since before recorded time—pretending to an omniscience they do not possess, a divinity they know nothing about."

"Please, Margon, I beg you," said Felix gently. "Don't go on."

Margon made an airy gesture of acceptance, but he shook his head. He looked off at the fire.

Reuben found himself glancing up at Lisa, who stood very still by the fireplace, staring at Elthram. She had no real expression except that of vigilance. Her mind might have been wandering for all he knew.

"Margon," said Elthram. "I will tell Marchent what I know."

"You'll teach her to invoke the memory of her physical self," said Margon. "That is, to move backwards—to strengthen her ethereal body to resemble her lost physical body, to seek for a material existence."

"It's not material!" said Elthram, raising his voice only slightly. "We are not material. We've taken bodies to resemble you because we see you and know you and would come into your world, the world you've made of the material, but we are not material. We are the invisible people and we can come and go."

"Yes, you are material, it's simply another kind of material," said Margon. "That's all it is!" He was becoming heated. "And you're burning to be visible in our world; you want it more than anything else."

"No, that is not true," said Elthram. "How little you know of our true existence."

"And look how your face reddens," said Margon. "Oh, you get better at this all the time."

"We must all get better at what we do," said Elthram with an air of resignation, his eyes appealing to Margon. "Why should we be different in that respect from you?"

Felix looked down, neither resigned nor accepting, but only unhappy.

"So, what, it's better to let Marchent suffer in confusion?" asked Reuben, "and hope that she slips permanently into dreams?" He couldn't keep silent any longer. "What does it matter what it's called or what science knows about it? Her intellect survives, doesn't it? She's Marchent and she's here and she's in pain."

Felix nodded to this.

"In dreams perhaps she can see the portal to the heavens," said Margon. "Once she becomes focused on the physical, perhaps she will never again see it."

"What if it's the portal to nonexistence?" asked Reuben.

"That's what it sounds like to me," said Stuart. "The white light, it flashes when the energy of the spirit disintegrates. That's what I think of this portal to heaven. That's all I think it might be."

Reuben shuddered.

Margon gazed across the long table at Elthram, Elthram's large eyes narrowed as if trying to fathom something about Margon that he could no longer describe in words.

Sergei, who'd sat there quiet all the while, gave a long eloquent breath.

"You want to know what I think?" said Sergei. "I think we leave here tonight, Margon, and me and these boy wolves and we go hunting. And we leave Felix here to keep preparing for the Christmas festival. And we leave Elthram and the Forest Gentry to their task."

"That sounds like an excellent idea," said Felix. "You and Thibault take the boys away from here. Satisfy their need to hunt. And Elthram, if there is anything I can do to cooperate with you, I will do it, you know that."

"You know the things I love," said Elthram, smiling. "Let us sup with you, Felix. Bring us to your table. Welcome us into your house."

"'Sup,'" scoffed Margon.

Felix nodded. "The doors are open, my friend."

"And I think this taking the boys away is an excellent idea," said Elthram. "Take Reuben away from here. And that will give me my best chance with Marchent."

He rose slowly, pushing back the chair and standing without using his arms or hands. Reuben noted this, and again noted his tremendous height. Six foot six, he calculated roughly, given that he himself was six foot three, and Stuart was taller than him, and Sergei was very slightly taller than that.

"I thank you for inviting us," said Elthram. "You can't know how we treasure your welcome, your hospitality, your invitation to come in."

"And how many more of you Forest Gentry are in this room right now?" asked Margon. "How many more of you are wandering this house?" It was meant to be accusatory, provocative. "Can you see better when you've assembled this physical body for yourself, when you've charged its particles with your subtle electricity, when you narrow your vision to look through those ravishing green eyes?"

Elthram looked stunned. He stood back away from the chair, blinking at Margon as if Margon were a bright light, Elthram's hands apparently clasped behind his back.

He appeared to say something under his breath, but it wasn't audible.

There came a soft series of sounds again, the woof of the air threatening the candles, and the fire, and then a great darkening of the gloom all around them, as a great mass of figures gradually came into view. Reuben blinked, trying to clear his vision, trying to make them more visible, but they were of their own becoming visible, as so many very long-haired women and children and men, all clothed in the same soft leather garments as Elthram, and quite literally of all sizes, and filling the entire room around them now, all along behind them and in front of them around the table and out to the corners.

Reuben was dazed, aware of shifting movements, gestures, and seeming whispers teeming almost like the drone of insects in midsummer around flowers, trying to fasten on this detail or that—long red hair, fair hair, gray hair, eyes flitting over him, dancing over the table, the wildly flickering candles, and even hands touching him, touching his shoulders, brushing his cheek, stroking his head. He felt he was going to slip out of consciousness. Everything he saw looked material, vital, yet it seemed moment by moment to be pulsing ever more rapidly, as if building to a pinnacle of some sort, while across from him Stuart looked frantically from right to left, his eyebrows knotted, his mouth open in what sounded like a moan.

Margon jumped to his feet and glared at them as if he were the least prepared for their number. Reuben couldn't see Lisa as too many crowded in front of her, and Felix merely looked up at them, appeared to be smiling at many of them, and nodding in agreement, and the crowd grew even more dense as if others were pressing the front lines slowly forward so that faces were now in the full glare of the candles, faces of all human shapes and sizes, Nordic, Asian, African, Mediterranean—Reuben didn't have the labels for them, only the associations—all rustic in dress and manner, yet all benign. Not a single face was disagreeable, or even curious, or in any way intrusive so much as passive and vaguely content-seeming at most. There came faint ripples of laughter like something drawn with a fine pen stroke, and again a sense of those around him soundlessly jostling, and he saw across from him two figures bending to kiss Stuart on either cheek.

Suddenly, with a gust of wind that shook the very rafters, the entire company vanished.

The walls creaked. The fire roared in the chimney, and the windows rattled as if about to break. A deep menacing rumble moved through the structure around them; plates and glasses on the hunter's boards tinkled and clattered, and a zinging sound came from the sparkling crystal on the table.

All of them gone, dematerialized. And like that.

The candles went out.

Lisa was plastered to the wall as if she were on a rolling ship, her eyes half closed. Stuart had gone stark white. Reuben resisted the urge to make the Sign of the Cross.

"Very impressive," said Margon sarcastically under his breath.

Suddenly sheets of rain were flung against the windows with such force that the glass groaned and strained in its framing. The whole house was creaking, writhing, and the high-pitched whistle of wind in the chimneys came from all sides. The rain pummeled the roofs and the walls. The windows rattled and boomed as if they'd explode.

And then the world, the soft familiar world around them, went quiet.

Stuart let out a long low gasp. His hands went up to his face, blue eyes peering through his fingers at Reuben. He was obviously delighted.

Reuben could scarcely repress a smile.

Margon, who was standing with his arms folded, had an oddly satisfied look on his face, as though he'd proven his point. But what that point was precisely Reuben couldn't figure.

"Never forget what you're dealing with here," Margon said to Stuart and Reuben. "It's so easy to tempt them to a display of power. I always marvel at it. And never forget that there may be multitudes around you at any moment, myriad homeless, restless, wandering ghosts."

Felix sat calm and collected, merely looking at the polished wood in front of him, where Reuben could see the reflected glare of the fire.

"Listen to them, my darling Marchent," Felix said with feeling. "Listen to them and let them dry your tears."

16

WHERE WERE THEY? Did it matter? Reuben and Stuart were so hungry they didn't care. They were exhausted too. The crumbling old villa was on the mountainside, and the writhing equatorial jungle was reclaiming it, the arched windows without glass, the Grecian columns peeling, the floors caked with decaying leaves and filth. A hoard of hungry creatures scurried through the fetid debris and the broken withered undergrowth that choked the passageways and stairs.

Their host, Hugo, was the only other Morphenkind they'd ever seen, except for the Distinguished Gentlemen, a great hulking giant of a man, with long snarled and matted brown hair, and maniacal black eyes, dressed in rags that might have once been a shirt and khaki shorts. Barefoot, covered in dirt.

And after he'd directed them to the filthy rooms in which they might sleep on soiled and rotting mattresses, Sergei said under his breath, "This is what happens when a Morphenkind lives as a beast all the time."

The villa had the smell of an urban zoo in the middle of summer. And indeed the heat was simmering and soothing after the relentless cold of Northern California. Yet it was like a toxin, wearying and weakening Reuben with every step.

In a small voice, Stuart asked, "Must we stay here? Like what about an American motel? A little B&B? Or a nice lodging with some old native in a hut somewhere?"

"We haven't come for the amenities of the house," said Margon. "Now listen to me, both of you. We don't spend all our lupine hours hunting humankind and there's never been a law that says we have to. We've come here to prowl the ancient ruins in these jungles—temples, tombs, the ruins of a city—the way men and women can't possibly do it—as Morphenkind—and we'll feed off the jungle rodents as we do it. We'll see things that no eye has seen in centuries."

"This is a dream," said Reuben. "Why didn't I think of such things?" A thousand possibilities were opening before him.

"Fill your bellies first," said Margon. "Nothing can hurt you here— not the beasts, not the serpents, not the insects, and not the natives if any dare to approach. Drop your clothes where you stand. Breathe and live as Morphenkinder."

At once, they obeyed him, stripping away shirts and trousers that were already soaked with sweat.

The wolf coat rose all over Reuben's body, sealing out the heat as it always did the cold. The enervating weakness in his limbs evaporated in a surge of power. At once the zinging, sighing, rippling voices of the jungle assailed him. Over the hills and valleys around them, the jungle seethed like one great undulating fungoid being.

They dropped down effortlessly from the cliff and into the rattling web of sharp-edged leaf and prickling vine, the night sky pink and luminescent above them, allowing themselves to slide fearlessly down the mountainside.

The noxious squirming brown-coated rodents slithered away from them everywhere. The hunting was easy, the prey large and pungent, gasping impotently with razor teeth, as the Morphenkinder ripped through fur and sinew to spouting blood.

They feasted together, thrashing and rolling noisily in the under- growth, the jungle around them erupting with the alarms of the living things who feared them, large and small. The night monkeys screamed in the treetops. Rotted crumbling branches and old tree trunks shat- tered beneath them, the tough fibrous vines whipped and torn by their simplest movements, snakes thrashing wildly through the foliage as the insects swarmed, seeking to blind them or stop them to no avail.

Again and again, Reuben brought down the fat succulent rats, big as raccoons, ripping back the twitching silky coat to bite into the meat. Always the meat. The same salty blood-soaked meat. The world devours the world to make the world.

At last all were satisfied and lay about in a bower of broken palm leaves and clawing branches, lazy and half dozing. How embracing was the hot motionless air, the deep rumble of malignant life all around them.

"Come," said Margon. He was the smallest of the Man Wolf pack, moving with a feline grace and swiftness that often dazzled Reuben.

They followed him on and on as he broke a tunnel through the dense growth, moving on all fours, springing upwards from time to time to chart a swift passage through the jungle high above the earth.

They came to a deep valley, slumbering beneath its writhing blanket of green.

Far off they could smell the sea, and for a moment Reuben thought he heard it, the rise and fall of the waves, equatorial waves, windless, and lapping again and again on an imagined beach.

There was no scent of humans here any more than there had been around the villa. The deceptive yet soothing quiet of the natural world reigned, with the simmering boiling sound of death, death in the treetops, death on the jungle floor—unbroken by a human voice.

It chilled Reuben suddenly to think of how long the world in its entirety had been like this place, devoid of human eyes or human ears or human language. Was Margon thinking of these same things? Margon, who'd been born in a time when the world had had no savage pedigree of biological evolution.

A terrible loneliness and sense of fatality came over Reuben. And yet this was a priceless perception, a priceless moment. And he felt wondrously alert, marveling at the universe of varying shapes and movements that he could pick from the airy darkness. He knew he was man and Morphenkind in one. Sergei rose on hind legs and threw his head back, his mouth gaping, fangs gleaming as if he were swallowing the breeze. Even the big shadowy brown wolf figure of Stuart, almost as big as Sergei, seemed content for the moment, crouched but not to spring, merely looking out with gleaming blue eyes at the valley beneath them and the distant slopes beyond.

Was Margon dreaming? He swayed slightly from one foot to the other, great hairy arms slack at his sides, as if the breeze were washing him clean.

"This way," Margon signaled finally. And they plunged with him now into what for human beings would have been an impassable tangle of knotted vines and sharp, prickling, and menacing leaves. Breaking loudly through pocket after pocket of fetid and wet underwood, they moved on, inexorably, birds screeching heavenward, lizards wriggling out of their path.

Ahead Reuben saw the great hulk of a pyramid. On all fours they traveled along its huge base, and then mounted its high steps, tearing loose like so much wrapping paper the living thatch that covered it.

How clear under the rosy sky were these curious twisted Mayan figures, so exquisitely carved, limbs seeming to writhe like the snakes and vines of the jungle around them, solemn faces in profile with half-closed eyes and noses like the beaks of great birds. Heads were wreathed in feathers. Bodies were embedded in mysterious configurations and patterns, as if imprisoned in the very fabric of the tropical world.

On and on they went, running their paws over these stone images as they yanked back the veil of foliage.

How private, how intimate, these moments seemed. Far back in the workaday world such relics were enshrined in museums, untouchable, and out of context, unconnected to such a night as this.

Yet here, against this monument, Reuben pressed the pads of his paws, and his forehead, relishing the rough surface and even the deep smell of the breathing, disintegrating stone.

He broke away from the others and bounded up the slope of the pyramid, clawed feet gaining easy traction as he moved—until he was under the infinitely faint and twinkling stars.

The blowing mist, filled with the light of the moon, was seeking to swallow the lamps of the heavens. Or so a poet might imagine, when in fact the whole odoriferous and quivering world around him, of earth and flora and helpless fauna, of gaseous cloud and humid air—all this sighed and sang at a million cross-purposes, and ultimately with no avowed purpose—an accidental chaos blindly serving up the unaccountable beauty he now saw.

What are we that this is beautiful to us? What are we that we are now powerful as lions and fear nothing, yet see this with the eyes and hearts of thinking beings—makers of music, makers of history, makers of art? Makers of the serpentine carvings that cover this old and blood-drenched structure? *What are we that we feel such things as I am feeling now?*

He saw the others running, stopping, and moving on. He went down again to join them.

For hours they prowled, over broken walls, low flattop buildings, and the pyramids themselves, searching out again and again the faces, forms, geometrical designs, until finally Reuben grew weary and wanted only to sit again under the sky, drinking in with all his senses the unmistakable ambience of this secret and neglected place.

But the little pack kept moving, towards the scent of the sea. He too wanted to see the shoreline. He dreamed suddenly of running on endless deserted sand.

Margon was in the lead with Sergei moving fast behind him. Reuben caught up with Stuart and on they traveled at the easy pace until Margon stopped suddenly. He rose to full height.

Reuben knew why. He too had caught it.

Voices in the night where there should have been none.

Up a small bluff they climbed.

The great warm ocean stretched beyond, sparkling wondrously under the bright incandescent clouds. So different from the cold northern Pacific, this inviting tropical sea.

Far below they saw a winding road leading on with a broken jagged beach beyond it. The sand appeared white, and the waves black with white foam as they crashed on the rocks.

The voices came from the south. Margon moved south. Why? What did he hear?

Then they all heard it as they followed him. Reuben saw the change in Stuart as he himself felt the delicious hardening of his body, the seeming expansion of his chest.

Voices crying in the night, the voices of children.

Margon began to run and they all tried frantically to keep up with him.

Further south they moved and further up onto a belt of cliffs where the vegetation died away, leaving only a rocky promontory.

The warm wind came strong and fresh, flooding over them as they found themselves standing there together.

Far below to their left, tucked into the mountainside, they saw the clear outline of an electrically lighted house and near it sprawling and manicured gardens, lighted swimming pools, and paved lots. The house was a conglomeration of tile roofs and broad terraces. Reuben could hear the low strum and rumble of machines. Cars crowded the lots like exotic beetles.

The voices rose, in a soft chorus of cries and desperate muted words. Children in this house. Boys, and girls, frightened, agitated, and without hope. And over the dismal choir of misery came the deeper voices of men, English-speaking men, mingling with one another in easy camaraderie. And the low drumbeat of women's voices in another language, speaking of discipline and pain.

"The best here, the very best," came a deep masculine voice. "You will find nothing like this anywhere in the world, not even in Asia."

A girl child wept without words. An angry, bruising woman's voice in a foreign tongue commanded obedience, so transparent the cajoling and bullying woven together.

Scent of innocence and suffering, scents of evil, and other scents, strangely ambiguous and unclassifiable, odious and ugly, rose all around them.

Margon dropped off the edge of the cliff, arms raised, falling down and down till he landed heavily on the tile roof. They all followed, landing silently on their padded feet. How could they not follow? A low rumble came from Stuart's chest that was not a roar, not a growl. Sergei answered.

Once more they dropped down, this time to a wide and spacious terrace. Ah, such a heavenly place, with soft, fluttering flowerbeds aglow in the gentle electric light, and the swimming pools shimmering and twinkling like rare jewels. The palm trees rattling in the caressing wind.

The walls of a villa rose before them, with glass windows and subtle soothing lights, sheer curtains billowing out into the night and twisting in the breeze.

Whisper of a child praying.

With a roar, Margon passed into the room as shrieks and screams rose all around him.

The children scrambled off the high-backed bed and ran for the corners as the woman and the half naked man fled for their lives.

"Chupacabra!" roared the woman. Smell of malice, old habitual malice. She hurled a lamp at the approaching Morphenkinder. A string of curses poured out of her like noxious fluid.

Margon caught the woman by the hair, and Stuart caught the man with her, the sniveling, sobbing man. Instantly, they were dead, remains dragged through the room and flung out over the terrace wall.

Naked, a boy and girl cowered, faces and limbs dark and twisted with terror, black hair shining. Move on.

But something was confusing to Reuben, something deviling him as they ran through the wide corridors, into room after room. There were men fleeing who gave no evil scent, only the rank smell of fear flying off them, and the reek of bowels cut loose, and urine gushing. And something else that might have been shame.

Against a wall two men stood, white men, men of ordinary build and ordinary clothes, stark terrified, faces wet and blanched, mouths loose and watering. How many times had Reuben seen that very attitude before, that helplessness, that blank stare of a broken human being on the verge of madness? But something was missing here, something was confusing, something was not right.

Where was the clear imperative? Where was the decisive scent? Where was the undeniable evidence of evil that had always goaded him to kill instantly in the past?

Margon stood beside him.

"I can't do it," Reuben whispered. "They're cowards," he whispered. "But I can't——."

"Yes, the ignorant and thoughtless clientele of these slave traders," said Margon under his breath, "the very tide of appetite that supports this foul business. They're everywhere in this house."

"But what do we do?" asked Reuben.

Stuart stood helplessly there, waiting for the command.

Below people were running and screaming. Ah, now there was the scent, there was the old stench that galvanized Reuben and sent him flying down the staircase. Evil, hate you, kill you, full-blown evil, reeking like a carnivorous plant. How easy it was to take them down, the hard-bitten, the scum, one after another. Were these the old habitual predators, or their servants? He didn't know. He didn't care.

Gunshots rang out in the plaster rooms. *"Chupacabra, chupacabra."* Wild volleys of Spanish burst forth like the crack of artillery.

There was a car starting out there in the night, and the roar of an accelerating engine.

Through the broad open doors of a terrace, Reuben saw the giant figure of Sergei bounding after the car and easily overtaking it, springing first on the roof, and then dropping down in front of the windshield as the vehicle swerved, screeched into a circle, and came to a halt, glass exploding.

Another one of those craven men knelt right in front of Reuben with his arms up, his bald head bowed, wire glasses glinting, prayers issuing from his lips, Catholic prayers, words tumbling out of him meaninglessly and like the mumblings of a maniac.

"Holy Mary Mother of God, Jesus, Joseph, and all the saints, dear God, please, Mother of God, God, please, I swear, no, please, please, no . . ."

And again, no clear and unequivocal stench of evil, no scent that commanded it, made it clear, made it possible.

People were dying above.

Those men were dying above, those men that Reuben had left alive. Over the staircase railing fell one of those bodies, landing on its face, or what was left of its face, blood streaming from it.

"Do it!" whispered Margon.

Reuben felt he couldn't. Guilty, yes, guilty, soaked in shame, yes, and fear, unspeakable fear. But wholly evil, no, by no means. That was the horror. This was something else, something more rank and hideous and defeating in its own way than purposeful evil, the purposeful break from all things human, this was something boiling with helpless hunger and agonizing denial.

"I can't."

Margon killed the man. He killed others.

Sergei appeared. Blood and blood and blood.

Others ran through the gardens. Others were rushing out the doors. Sergei went after them and so did Margon.

Reuben heard Stuart's tortured voice, "What can we do with these children?"

Sobbing, sobbing everywhere around them.

And the clusters of women, accomplices, yes, terrified, damaged, defeated, down on their knees too. *"Chupacabra!"* He heard it woven into their prayerful pleading cries, *"Ten piedad de nosotros."*

Margon and Sergei returned, the blood clinging to their fur in gouts.

Sergei paced before the terrified group on its knees, murmuring in Spanish words that Reuben could not catch.

Women nodded their heads; the children prayed. Somewhere a telephone rang.

"Come, let's leave here. We've done what we can," said Margon.

"But the children!" said Stuart.

"People will come," said Margon. "They will come for the children. And the word will spread. And fear will do its work. Now we are going."

Back in the ruined villa of the Morphenkind Hugo, they lay on the mattresses, sweating, bone weary, and tormented.

Reuben stared at the blotched and broken plaster ceiling. Oh, he had known this moment was coming. He had known it had all been too simple before, the Brotherhood of the Scent, the brotherhood that acted like the right hand of God, incapable of error.

Margon sat cross-legged against the wall, his dark hair loose over his naked shoulders, his eyes closed, lost in his meditations or his prayers.

Stuart climbed up off the mattress, and paced back and forth, back and forth, unable to stop.

"There will be such times," Margon said finally. "You will encounter them, yes, and situations even more baffling and defeating. All over the world, day after day and night after night, victims tumble down into the abyss with the guilty, and the weak and the corrupt who don't deserve death pay with their lives one way or another for what they do and what they don't do."

"And we leave," Stuart cried. "We just leave the children?"

"It's finished," said Margon. "You take the lessons with you."

"Something was accomplished," Sergei said, "make no mistake of it. The place is shattered. They'll all clear out; the children will have some chance for escape. The children will remember. They will remember that someone slew the men who had come to use them. They will remember that."

"Or they'll be shipped to another brothel," said Stuart dismally. "Christ! Can we make a war on them, a consistent war?"

Sergei laughed under his breath. "We're hunters, little wolf, and they are the prey. This is not a war."

Reuben said nothing. But he had seen something he would not forget, and he marveled that it hadn't surprised him. He had seen Margon and Sergei slay at will those who didn't give off the fatal scent, those ugly, compromised souls driven by unholy appetites and inveterate weakness.

If we can do that, he thought, then we can fight amongst each other. The scent of evil does not make us what we are, and once we are beasts we can kill like beasts, and we have only the human part of us, the fallible human part, to guide us.

But these ideas were abstract and remote. Only the recollections were immediate—boys and girls racing in terror, and the women, the women screaming for mercy.

Somewhere off in this filthy villa, Margon was talking to the mysterious Hugo.

Had a plan been made to destroy the seaside brothel?

No doubt it was deserted by now. Who in his right mind would have remained?

He fell asleep, hating the dirt and grit of this mattress, waiting for the car that would come before daylight to take them to the luxury hotel where they would bathe and dine before the flight home.

17

IT WAS SATURDAY EVENING about 9:00 p.m. when they returned, and never had the property looked more warm, more welcoming, more beautiful. Through the rainy mist as they came up the road, they could make out the lighted gables along the front and the neat squares and rectangles of three stories of windows.

Felix came out of the front door to greet them all in the driveway with a warm embrace and to show them the preparations for tomorrow's banquet. His exuberance was positively contagious.

The entire terrace was now one great lighted and decorated pavilion, with the giant tented rooms flowing into one another on either side of a great covered corridor that led to the immense Christmas stable.

It stood with its back to the sea surrounded by a forest of dense and beautiful Douglas fir trees, all splendidly lighted like everything else. The white-marble figures of the crèche were artfully illuminated and perfectly arranged amid a bed of green pine branches, and a more splendid Christmas grouping Reuben had never seen. Even Stuart got wistful and almost sad looking at it. It excited Reuben terribly that all his family would see this. And he could have stood alone by the crèche for a long time, just looking at the white-marble faces of Mary and Joseph and the beaming Christ Child. On the pediment of the stable a great white-marble angel had been fixed with brackets and bolts, who, bathed in golden light, looked down on the Holy Family.

The forest of tall potted Douglas firs extended to the right and the left of the stable, against a newly constructed wooden wall, and this functioned as an excellent windbreak. Nobody after dark could have seen the ocean anyway.

To the left of the stable in the vast tented space was a massive grouping of little gold-painted music chairs, ready and waiting, with black-wire music stands, for the orchestra, while on the far right side were the chairs for the adult choir and for the boys' choir, which would alternate and at times sing together.

There were other choirs, too, Felix quickly added, and they'd be singing in the house and in the oaks. He'd conferred with everyone today, and seen to everything.

The rest of the pavilion was beautifully furnished with hundreds of small white draped tables and white dressed chairs, all trimmed in gold ribbon. Each table had its trio of candles in a glass shade, surrounded with holly.

Every few yards it seemed there were station tables or bars already stocked with silver coffee urns, china, and cases of glassware as well as cases of soft drinks and tubs for the ice that would be delivered tomorrow. Mountains of linen napkins lay in waiting, along with piles of sterling spoons and dessert forks.

The metal framing beneath the high white roofs of the tents was all concealed in fresh pine garland, bound here and there with red velvet ribbon; a lot of holly had been worked into this as well. And the flagstones of the entire terrace had been cleaned and polished to a high luster.

Tall treelike oil heaters were in place all over, and some were already lighted to keep the air not only warm but dry. Tiny multicolored lights were strung everywhere. But soft white floodlights provided the real illumination.

The pavilion opened in two places along the east side to accommodate incoming guests from the driveway and those wandering out into the oak forest, and the door of the house itself opened into the pavilion.

In sum, it had become a huge sprawling extension of the house, and Reuben confessed he'd never seen anything on this scale before, not even at the largest weddings.

The rain was falling only lightly now and Felix had high hopes that it would die off for a little while tomorrow. "But still, it will be entirely possible to walk in the forest," he said, "as the branches are so thick. Well, let's hope, and if not, well, it's splendid to look at."

Yes, indeed it was.

"You should see the town," Felix said. "Everything's ready for the fair. The Inn's full, and people have been renting out spare bedrooms in their homes to the merchants. We have a marvelous range of crafts. Just wait. And think what we can do for next year when we really have time to do things properly."

He brought the company into the main room, and stood with arms folded as they acknowledged the perfection of everything.

It had all been "done," or so they had thought when they left, but it seemed a multitude of refinements had been added. "Those are pure bayberry candles on all the mantels," Felix said, "and the holly. Do note the holly." It was everywhere, with sharp dark glistening leaves and bright red berries, nestled into the garland around the fireplaces, the doorways, and the windows.

To the giant tree, already a masterpiece before they left, countless little gold ornaments had been added, most representing nuts or dates, and also a whole sprinkling of gold angels.

And to the right of the front door stood a giant dark heavily carved German grandfather clock, "to chime on New Year's Eve," said Felix.

In the dining room, the great table was covered in Battenberg lace, and laid out, like the hunter's boards, with sterling chafing dishes and heavy serving pieces. In the corner a long bar was set up with a dazzling array of name-brand liquors and wines, and there were round tables here and there with potbellied silver coffee urns and piles of sparkling china cups and saucers.

China plates in ten or more patterns at least were piled at the ends of the long table along with stacks of heavy sterling dinner forks. Chefs would carve the turkey and the ham for a "fork meal," said Felix, as some people would have to balance a plate on their knees, and he wanted them to be entirely comfortable.

Reuben was completely in the spirit. Only the absence of Laura hurt him, and also the worry about Marchent. But judging from Felix's excitement, perhaps there was no cause now to worry about Marchent.

Nevertheless the thought of Marchent here or Marchent gone struck equal terror in Reuben's heart. But he didn't want to say so.

They had their supper in the kitchen, crowding around the rectangular table by the window, Lisa ladling up a pungent beef stew into their bowls, while the men served themselves their drinks, and Jean Pierre served a crisp green salad. Stuart devoured half a loaf of French bread before even touching the stew.

"Don't worry about this kitchen," Felix said. "It will be turned out like everything else. And don't be shocked at all the garland upstairs. We can take it all down off the doors after the party."

"I'm kind of loving it," Stuart said. And he did appear dazed as he looked around at the trimmings on the kitchen window which hadn't been there before, and the masses of candles on the sideboard. "It's a shame it can't be Christmas all year."

"Oh, but the spring will bring its festivals," said Felix. "Now we must get our rest. We have to be down in the village by ten a.m. tomorrow for the fair. Of course we can take breaks. We don't have to be there all day; well, I have to be there all day, and, Reuben, it would be good if you were with me."

Reuben agreed immediately. He was smiling at the sheer scope of all this, and wondered who would be first in his family to ask how much it had cost and who was paying for it. Maybe Celeste would ask that question, but then maybe again she wouldn't dare.

It was Stuart now who asked this very question.

Felix clearly didn't want to answer, and Sergei said, "A banquet like this is a gift to everyone who comes, you wait and see; it's that way. You can't measure it in dollars and cents. It's an experience. And people will be talking about it for years. You give them something priceless with all this."

"Yes, but they give us something priceless too," said Felix, "in that they come, they are part of it, and what would it be without every one of them?"

"True," said Sergei, and then looking at Stuart he said gravely in his crackling baritone, "In my time, of course, we ate the captives of other tribes at Midwinter, but before cooking them, we put them to death painlessly."

Felix laughed out loud before he could stop himself.

And Stuart shot back, "Oh, yeah, right!—You're a farm boy from West Virginia and you know it. Probably worked in a coal mine for a little while. Hey, I'm not knocking it. Just sayin'."

Sergei laughed and shook his head.

Margon and Felix exchanged a secretive look, but said nothing.

After supper, Reuben and Felix headed up the steps together. "You must tell me if you see her," said Felix. "But I don't think you will. I think Elthram and his people have been successful."

"Did Elthram tell you this?"

"More or less," he said. "I hope you sleep well tonight, and I so appreciate you're coming with me to the village tomorrow—because you are the lord of the manor, you know, and they all so want to see you. It's going to be a long day and evening, but it's only once a year, and they'll all love it."

"I'm going to love it too," said Reuben. "And what about Laura?"

"Well, she'll be with us tomorrow in the village for a little while . . . and then later on Christmas Eve, of course. That's all I know. Reuben, we must let her do things her own way. That's what Thibault is doing—letting her decide things."

"Yes, sir," said Reuben with a smile. He kissed Felix quickly, in the European style on both cheeks, and then went off to bed.

He was asleep the moment he hit the pillow.

18

THE DAY DAWNED GRAY but rainless. The air was moist, as if at any moment the featureless sky would dissolve into rain, but by ten a.m., it hadn't happened.

Reuben had awakened marvelously refreshed with no dreams or hints of Marchent's presence. And he was downstairs at nine for a quick breakfast.

Big refrigerator trucks were already arriving, and caterers swarmed the kitchen and the backyard, unloading portable ovens, ice makers, and other equipment, while the teenagers who would function as guides all over the house and the woods were there for "orientation" with Lisa.

All the Distinguished Gentlemen were present and smartly dressed in dark suits, and at nine thirty, Felix, Reuben, Stuart, and Margon headed to "the village" while Thibault, Sergei, and Frank stayed behind to get ready for the banquet.

The town was reborn. Either that, or Reuben had simply never seen it before. Now with every façade etched in decorative lights, for the first time he appreciated the Old West storefronts with their overhanging roofs that sheltered the sidewalks, and how gloriously the three-story Inn dominated the main street, sitting right in the middle of the three-block stretch as it faced the old theater.

The old theater, though in the midst of restoration, had been opened for just one of the many crafts markets, and the booths were already doing business to a lively early bird crowd of families with children.

Cars were bumper to bumper for the three-block stretch that was the downtown and being directed to the side streets to parking lots blocks away.

Every shop was occupied and bustling, and a group of musicians in Renaissance garb was already playing beside the Inn doors while another group a block and a half away was singing Christmas carols near the town's only gas station. Several people were selling lightweight see-through umbrellas, and vendors were selling gingerbread cookies and small mince pies from smoking hot tables or trays they carried through the crowd.

People swamped Felix as soon as he stepped out of the car. Reuben was being greeted too on all sides. Margon took off to see how things were going at the Inn. And Reuben, Stuart, and Felix made their slow and deliberate progress down one side of the street with the aim of doubling back up the other.

"Ah, the Forest Gentry are going to love all this," said Felix.

"Are they here now?" asked Stuart.

"I don't see them yet, but they'll come. They absolutely love this sort of thing, people descending on the forest and its neglected little towns, gentle people, people who love the cold crisp pine-scented air. You'll see. They'll be here."

More than one huge empty shop had been turned into a veritable arcade of booths. Reuben glimpsed quilts for sale, along with hand-made cloth puppets, rag dolls, baby clothes, and a whole variety of linens and laces. But it was impossible to focus on any one particular booth because so many people wanted simply to shake his hand and thank him for the festival. Again and again, he explained that Felix had been the genius behind it. But it was soon clear that people saw him as the young lord of the castle, and even said so in exactly those terms.

By eleven a.m. cars were directed off the street, and it became a pedestrian mall. "Should have done that immediately," said Felix. "And we'll be certain to do that next year."

The crowds increased steadily while the rain came and went. The cold wasn't stopping anybody. Kids wore caps and mittens; and there were caps and mittens aplenty for sale. The hot-chocolate vendors were doing great business, and whenever the rain cleared, the crowd flowed out into the middle of the street.

It was more than two hours before they'd made their circuit of downtown—what with stopping for a puppet show and several choruses of "Deck the Halls"—and there was nothing to do but begin it all again as new people were arriving all the time.

Only a few people asked Reuben about the famous Man Wolf attack at the big house, and if he'd seen or heard any more of the Man Wolf. Reuben had the distinct feeling many more wanted to ask but didn't think it in keeping with the festivities. He was quick to answer that no one in Northern California, to the best of his knowledge, had ever seen the Man Wolf again after that "horrible night," and as for what happened, well, he could scarcely remember it. The old cliché "It all happened so fast" was coming in handy.

When Laura arrived, she fell into Reuben's arms. Her cheeks were beautifully rosy and she wore a pink cashmere scarf with her long finely cut navy blue coat. She was thrilled by the festival and embraced Felix warmly. She wanted to see the rag-doll dealers, and of course the quilt dealers, and she'd heard there was someone selling French and German antique dolls too. "And how did you achieve this in only a few weeks?" she asked Felix.

"Well, no entry fee, no license requirements, no rules, no restrictions, and some cash incentives," said Felix exuberantly. "And a lot of repeated personal invitations by phone and e-mail, and networks of phone helpers, and voilà, they have come. But think about next year, darling, what we can do."

They broke for a quick lunch at the Inn, where a table was ready for them. Margon was in fast conversation with a table of real estate agents and potential investors, and eagerly stood to greet Felix and introduce people all around. Stuart, with two of his old high school buddies, was holding forth from another table.

A state senator had been looking for Reuben, and two state representatives, and several people wanted to know what Felix thought about widening and improving the road to the coast, or whether it was true he was going to build a planned community back of the cemetery, and could he talk a little about the architectural theme he had in mind?

Reporters came and went. They did ask right off about the Man

Wolf attack at the house, with the same old questions and Reuben gave them the same old answers. There were a few local news cameras from the surrounding towns passing through. But the Christmas festival was the real news, and the banquet later at "the castle." Would this be a yearly tradition? Yes, indeed.

"And to think," Laura said to Margon, "he made this happen, he brought together all this life where essentially there was no life. . . ."

Margon nodded, drinking his hot chocolate slowly. "This is what he loves to do. This is his home. He was like this years ago. It was his town, and now he's back and free once again to be mentor and the creative angel for another couple of decades and then—." He broke off. "Then," he repeated looking around, "what will we do?"

After lunch, Laura and Reuben hit the antique-doll table and two of the quilt tables, and Reuben carried all the goods for Laura to her Jeep. She'd parked on the very edge of the cemetery, and to Reuben's amazement he found the cemetery crowded with people who were photographing the mausoleum and the old tombs.

The place appeared picturesque enough, as always, yet he couldn't prevent a frisson from paralyzing him at he looked at the graves. A huge arrangement of fresh flowers stood before the iron gates of the Nideck mausoleum. He closed his eyes for a moment and whispered a silent prayer of sorts for Marchent, an acknowledgment of what? That she could not be here, could not see or taste or feel, or be part of this vibrant and shifting world?

He and Laura stole a few quiet moments in the Jeep before she took off. This was Reuben's first chance to tell her about the Forest Gentry, to tell her the strange and moving things that Elthram had said about her, and having known her when she walked the forest with her father. She was speechless. Then after a long pause she confessed that she'd always felt the presence of the spirits of the wood.

"But then everyone does, I think, everyone who spends any time alone in the forest. And we tell ourselves it's our imagination, just as we do when we feel the presence of ghosts. I wonder if we offend them, the spirits, the dead, when we don't believe in them."

"I don't know, but you will believe this spirit," he said. "He appeared as real as you do to me now or I to you. He was solid. The floor creaked when he walked. The chair creaked when he sat down. And there was a scent coming from him; it was, I don't know, like honeysuckle and green things, and dust, but you know dust can be a clean smell, like in the first rain, when the dust rises."

"I know," she said. "Reuben, why are these things making you sad?"

"But they're not," he protested.

"Yes, they are. They're making you sad. Your voice changed just now when you talked about these things."

"Oh, I don't know, if I am sad it's a sweet sadness," he said. "It's just that my world's changing, and I'm caught betwixt and between, or I'm part of both, and yet the real world, the world of my parents, of my old friends, it can't know this new world, and so it can't know that part of me which is so changed."

"But I know it," she said. She kissed him.

He knew if he took her in his arms, he couldn't stand it, stand not having her, stand being here with her in the Jeep, with people passing as they made their way to their cars. This was so painful.

"You and I, we make a new covenant, don't we?" he asked. "I mean we make a new covenant in this new world."

"Yes," she said. "And when I see you on Christmas Eve, I want you to know that I'm yours, I'm your bride in this world, if you'll have me."

"Have you? I can't exist without you." He meant it. No matter what fear he felt of her transforming into the she-wolf, he meant it. He would get past that fear. Love for her would carry him past it, and there was no doubt that he loved her. With every passing day of being without her, he knew that he loved her.

"I will be your spouse on Christmas Eve," he said. "And you will be my bride, and yes, this will be the sealing of our covenant."

This was the hardest parting from her yet. But finally, kissing her quickly on both cheeks, he slipped out of the Jeep and stood by the side of the road to watch her go.

It was two o'clock as she headed for the highway.

Reuben headed back to the Inn.

He ducked back into the private bedroom set aside for him and his party long enough to use the bathroom and then he completed a quick little story on the festival for the *Observer* and e-mailed it to his editor, Billie Kale, with the note that he'd have more to add if she wanted it later on.

Billie had already left for the banquet, but he knew she'd hired a chauffeured car for herself and the staff so she could pass judgment on the story from the road.

Indeed the answer came back, "Yes, and yes," as he was leaving the Inn again with Felix and the others under the first sunshine that had broken through all afternoon. She texted that his Christmas-traditions essay was now the most e-mailed story on the paper's website. But she'd like to add a short paragraph to today's story, about the Man Wolf being nowhere in sight during the village fair. "Yes," Reuben said, and tapped out the paragraph just as she'd requested.

After greeting a group of television reporters, Reuben and Felix broke off from Stuart and Margon to inspect all of the booths in earnest, as Felix wanted to hear from the craftsmen and merchants as to how sales were for them and what he could do to make the fair better in coming years.

Reuben grew almost groggy as he moved from table to table, inspecting the highly glazed pottery, the unique bowls and mugs and plates, and then the dried-apple dolls, and the quilts again, always the quilts. There were leather craftsmen selling belts and purses, dealers in brass and pewter belt buckles, fine gold and silver jewelry, and the inevitable flea-market professionals marketing obvious machine-made goods, and even one merchant selling what might have been stolen hardcover best sellers at half price.

Felix took time with everybody, nodding again and again to this or that compliment or complaint. He had pockets filled with business cards. He accepted cups of mead and ale from the vendors but seldom drank more than a sip.

And through all of this Felix appeared deliriously happy, even a little manic, needing from time to time to escape to a back room or a restroom or a back alley, where he and Reuben found themselves in the company of the guilty outcast smokers who puffed on their verboten cigarettes furtively and with apologies before going back to join the "saved."

There were times when Reuben felt dizzy, but it was a beautiful kind of dizzy, what with the Christmas carols rising and falling in the general hubbub of voices, and the giant Christmas wreaths on door frames all around him, and the smell of pine needles, and the fresh, moist breeze.

Finally he lost Felix. He lost everybody.

But that was fine. He stopped now and then to jot notes for the next article, thumbs hammering on his iPhone, but mostly he drifted, soothed and fascinated by the movement and color, the squeals and laughter of the children, the slow hesitating yet incessant movement of shoppers that seemed at moments rather like dance.

Arcades and artisans were running together in his mind. He saw table after table of little fairy and elf Christmas ornaments and angels, and displays of fascinating handmade wooden toys. There were dealers in perfumed soaps and bath oils everywhere he looked, booths of buttons, dyed yarns, ribbons, and lace trim, and booths of fantasy hats. Or were those vintage hats? Somebody had recently been talking about hats, hats like those with big brims and flowers. He couldn't quite remember. Hand-dipped Christmas candles were for sale every few feet it seemed, and so was incense, and handmade notepaper.

But here and there was the rare exceptional artisan presenting a display of unique wood-carved animals and figurines that didn't resemble the more commercial big-eyed woodland critters at the next table, or the jewelry maker whose gold and silver brooches were truly spectacular creations, or the man who painted his silk and velvet scarves with entirely eccentric and original figures.

And then there was the painter who put out nothing but his original and fascinating canvases, with no apology or explanation whatsoever, or the woman who assembled huge baroque decoupage ornaments out of bits of lace and gold braid and brightly colored figures clipped from old Victorian prints. There were wooden flutes for sale, Tibetan brass bells and singing bowls, zithers and drums. There was one dealer who sold old sheet music, and another with a table of tattered and broken vintage children's books. And a woman who'd made beautiful napkin rings and bracelets from old sterling spoons.

The sky was white overhead, and the wind had died down.

People were buying, said the merchants. Some of the food vendors had sold out. One potter confessed she wished she brought all of her new mugs and bowls, as she was now left with almost nothing to sell.

There was at least one dealer doing a great business in handmade leather shoes.

Finally Reuben rested against a storefront, and through a break in the crowd tried to gain perspective on the mood of the festival. Were people really enjoying themselves as much as they seemed? Yes, undoubtedly. Balloon artists were doing a brisk business with the little kids. Cotton candy was being sold, and even saltwater taffy. And there were face paint artists for the children too.

To his right sat a tarot card reader at her velvet-draped card table, and a few feet beyond a palm reader who had a client opposite in a folding chair.

One whole shop across from him was selling Renaissance costumes, and people were laughing with delight at the lace-trimmed shirts that were selling for "great prices." And beside the shop was a used-book vendor presiding over tables of books about California and its history and the history of the redwoods and the geology of the coast.

Reuben felt drowsy and comfortable, unnoticed for the moment, and almost ready to close his eyes. Then he made out two familiar figures in the shadowy open door of the Renaissance shop. One figure was most definitely the tall raw-boned Elthram in his familiar beige chamois shirt and pants, his black hair long and bushy and even tangled with bits of dried leaf; and the other figure, the slender and graceful woman who stood right beside him, groomed and seemingly poised, was Marchent.

For a moment he could not believe it, but then he knew that this was exactly true. Nothing distinguished them from those around them except what would have distinguished them had they been alive.

Elthram towered over Marchent, his large eyes glittering as he smiled, whispering to her, it seemed, whispering with moist smiling lips, with his right arm tightly around her, and she, turned just slightly towards Elthram, her hair neatly combed, was looking straight at Reuben as she nodded her head.

The world went silent. It seemed to empty except for the two of them, Elthram now casting a slow glance at Reuben, and Marchent's eyes holding him steady as she continued to listen, to nod.

The crowd shifted, moved, closed the gap through which Reuben had seen them. The noise around him was deafening suddenly. Reuben hurried out into the middle of the street. There they were, the two of them, solid and vivid down to the tiniest details, but they turned their backs now, and they appeared to be walking into the enveloping darkness of the shop.

The sights and sounds of the fair went dim again. Someone bumped into Reuben, and he yielded without thinking or responding, barely conscious of a hand on his arm. There was a stab in his intestines, and a heat rising in him threatening to be pain.

Someone else had come up close beside him. But he only stared off into the inevitable gloom of the shop, searching for them, waiting for them, his heart pounding as it always did when he saw Marchent, and he tried to reconstruct the details of what he'd seen. There had been no clear indication that Marchent had really seen him; perhaps she'd only been looking forward. Her face had been calm, thoughtful, passive. He couldn't know.

Suddenly he did feel a hand on his arm and he heard a very familiar voice say, "Well, that's one very interesting-looking man."

He woke as if from a dream.

It was his dad standing beside him. It was Phil, and Phil was staring into the shop.

"There are a lot of really interesting people here," said Phil in the same half murmur. Reuben stood dazed as out of the shadows the two figures emerged once more, Elthram still smiling, his arm fastened as tightly as before to Marchent, and Marchent looking so delicate in her brown wool dress and brown boots, such a thin frail figure, in the very long soft dress she'd worn the day she died. This time her pale eyes fastened on Reuben and she offered the faintest acknowledging smile. Such a winsome distant smile.

And then they were gone.

Simply gone. Subtracted from the shifting world around them, subtracted as though they'd never been there at all.

Phil sighed.

Reuben turned to Phil, glaring at him, unable to say what he wanted to say. Phil was still looking at the door of the shop. Phil had to have seen them disappear.

But Phil said nothing to Reuben. Phil just stood there in his heavy gray tweed jacket, gray scarf around his neck, his hair blowing slightly in the breeze—looking at the open shop as before.

The pain in Reuben's guts was sharpened, and his heart ached. If only he could tell his father everything, absolutely everything, if only he could bring his father into the world in which he, Reuben, was struggling, if only he could access the wisdom that had always been there for him, and which he'd wasted too often in his life.

But how could he even begin? And half measures were as intolerable as this silence.

A dream flared in his heart. Phil would eventually move to the guesthouse at Nideck Point. They'd certainly talked of his visiting often enough.

And after Phil moved to the guesthouse, and surely Phil would, they would sit together and Reuben would, with the blessing of the Distinguished Gentlemen, pour out the whole tale. They'd sit in candlelight with the sea banging on the cliffs below, and talk and talk and talk.

But as the dream flared, an awesome and horrifying vista opened for him on the coming years. The divide could only become greater and greater between him and his father. His loneliness felt like a shell in which he was suffocating. A great sadness filled him. He felt a lump in his throat.

He looked away, more into his thoughts than at anything particular, and as his eyes moved over the street, he now saw them everywhere, the shaggy-haired, leather-clad figures of the Forest Gentry, some in dark green, others in varying shades of brown, some even in bright colors, but all distinct in that soft chamois cloth, with their abundant hair, their windblown tangled hair. Their skin was radiant and their eyes sparkled. They exuded happiness and excitement. It was so easy to see them as they passed, as they walked among the human beings, so easy to know who they were. He recognized here and there women and children he had glimpsed in that eerie moment in the dining room when they had all crowded in on the table before vanishing into the night.

And they were observing him, too, weren't they? They were nodding to him. One woman with long red hair made him a little curtsey quickly before disappearing behind a crowd of others. And they were looking at Phil.

Phil stood as passive and silent as before, his hands in his coat pockets just watching the great parade go by. "Look at that woman," he said airily, "in that beautiful old hat. Such a beautiful old hat."

Reuben glanced in that direction and caught a glimpse of her, a fellow human being, not one of the Forest Gentry, a slender figure with her arms out, guiding a whole troop of youngsters through the crowd. And it was a gorgeous hat, made of green felt with crushed silk flowers. Something about hats. Why, of course. How could he have forgotten? Lorraine, and Jim's dreadful story of pain and suffering with Lorraine. Lorraine had loved vintage hats. The woman was gone now with her flock of children. Could that have been Lorraine? Probably not.

The rain began to spatter down.

At first people ignored it, but then they began to home to the covered porches and the little arcades. The sky darkened, and more lights flashed on in the shops and windows, and the streetlamps, the quaint old black-iron streetlamps, went on.

Within moments a new air of festivity had swept through the fair, and it seemed the noise of the crowd was louder than ever. The strings of colored lights above the street shone with a new brightness.

Stuart and Margon appeared suddenly, and said it was almost four o'clock, that they ought to head back to the house to change.

"It's black tie tonight for us all, as we're hosting," said Margon.

"Black tie?" Reuben all but stammered.

"Oh, not to worry. Lisa's laid out everything for us. But we should go home now to be ready when the first people start leaving the fair."

Felix waved at Reuben from down the street, but then was blocked inevitably by more greetings and more thanks, though he kept moving.

Finally, they were all together. Phil headed off to get his car, as he'd driven up alone ahead of the rest of the family.

Reuben took one last look at the fair before he turned to go. The carolers were singing clearly and beautifully in front of the Inn as if the darkness had excited them and urged them to come together again, and this time there was a fiddler there with them, and a young boy playing a wooden flute. He stared at the distant figure of that boy, long-haired, clad all in brown chamois leather, playing that wooden flute. And far to the right in the shadows, he saw Elthram with Marchent, her head almost touching Elthram's shoulder, their eyes fixed on the same young musician.

19

THE TERRACE PAVILION WAS ABLAZE with light and sound and streaming with people when they got out of the car. The orchestra was rehearsing with the boys' choir in a positively magical blend of glorious sound. Phil was already there, standing with his arms folded, listening to the music in obvious awe, while reporters and photographers from the local papers took pictures, and groups of mummers in medieval costume—teenagers mostly—came up to greet them until Felix introduced himself and told them how pleased he was, and instructed them to take up a position in the nearby oaks.

Reuben hurried upstairs to change. He took the fastest shower in human history, and Lisa helped him dress, handling the studs on his boiled shirt for him, and tying his black silk tie. The jacket had been "perfectly measured" for him, she was right about that. And he was pleased that she'd arranged a black vest for him and not a cummerbund, which he hated. The shining patent-leather shoes were also a good fit.

He had to laugh when he saw Stuart, because Stuart looked so uncomfortable in his black-tie finery, but he looked pretty terrific at the same time, freckles and curly hair and all.

"You're growing right before my eyes," said Reuben. "You must be as tall as Sergei now."

"Rampant cell division," muttered Stuart. "There's nothing quite like it." He was anxious, uneasy. "I gotta find my friends, and the nuns from school, and the nurses. And my old girlfriend who threatened to kill herself when I came out of the closet."

"You know what? This place is done up so beautifully and this is all going to be so much fun, you don't have to do any heavy lifting. And your old girlfriend, she's okay now, right?"

"Oh yes," said Stuart. "She's getting married in June. We're e-mail buddies. I'm helping her to pick out her wedding dress. Maybe you're right. This is going to be fun, isn't it?"

"Well, let's make it fun," Reuben said.

The main floor was filled with people.

Caterers were rushing back and forth from dining room to kitchen. The table was laden from end to end with what appeared to be the first course—hot hors d'oeuvres of countless kinds, hot chafing dishes of meatballs in sauce, fondue, plates of crudités, nuts, wheels of French cheese, sugared dates, and a huge china tureen of pumpkin soup to be ladled into mugs for the asking by a stiff young attendant who waited with hands clasped behind his back.

The raw and beautiful sound of a string quartet suddenly broke through the murmuring of the crowd all around him, and Reuben caught the soft heartbreaking strains of the "Greensleeves" carol. The music drew him as much as the food—he drank down a mug of the thick soup immediately—but he wanted to see that orchestra outside. It had been too long since he'd seen a live orchestra of that size and he headed through the press in the front room to the door.

To Reuben's surprise, Thibault appeared and explained that he was taking Reuben out to stand with Felix at the large east entrance of the pavilion.

"You will help him greet the guests, won't you?" Thibault looked entirely comfortable in his formal clothes.

"But what about Laura?" Reuben whispered as they pushed through the crowd. "Why aren't you with Laura?"

"Laura wants to be on her own tonight," said Thibault. "And she will be all right, I assure you. I wouldn't have left her if that were not the case."

"But Thibault, you mean then the change has happened."

Thibault nodded.

Reuben had come to a halt. Maybe he'd had some vain childish hope all along that Laura would never change, that the Chrism would somehow not work, that Laura would always be Laura! But it had happened. At last, it had happened! He was suddenly powerfully excited. He wanted to be with Laura.

Thibault embraced him just as a father might embrace him, and said, "She is doing exactly what she wants. And we must let her do things in her own way. Now come, Felix is hoping you'll join him."

They moved out into the crowded pavilion. Dozens of people were already milling, and the caterers were serving both coffee and drinks to those already seated at the tables.

Margon, his long brown hair tied back to the nape of his neck with a thin leather thong, was escorting Stuart's petite mother, Buffy Longstreet, up to see the crèche. Buffy, in spike heels and a short white sleeveless silk turtleneck dress and diamonds, looked every bit the starlet, and not old enough to be the mother of Stuart, who was welcoming her with open arms. Frank Vanderhoven was making her a stately bow, and turning on that Hollywood charm for her, and she was seemingly ecstatic.

Quite suddenly the voices of the boys' choir broke forth with the spirited lyrics of "The Holly and the Ivy," drowning out the murmur everywhere of conversation. Reuben stopped just to savor the sound of it, vaguely conscious that others too were turning their heads to listen. The voices of the adult choir soon joined in, and the entire glorious wave of sound proceeded without the need of the waiting orchestra. At the far end very near the choir, Reuben could see Phil alone at a table clearly rapt as he'd been when Reuben first arrived.

But there was no time to go to Phil now.

Felix stood at the large eastern entrance of the pavilion greeting each and every person coming in, and Reuben quickly took his place beside him.

Felix was beaming, his eager dark eyes fixing every single face. "How do you do, Mrs. Malone, and welcome to the house. I'm so glad you could join us. This is Reuben Golding, our host, whom I'm sure you've already met. Do come in. The girls will show you to the coatroom."

Reuben was soon clasping hands, repeating more or less the same welcome, and finding himself meaning it.

Out of the corner of his eye, he could see Sergei and Thibault stationed at the steps to the door of the house, also clasping hands, answering questions perhaps, welcoming. There was a remarkably tall and handsome woman right beside Sergei, a dark-haired woman in a striking red velvet gown, who gave Reuben a soft affectionate smile.

All the locals were streaming in, Johnny Cronin, the mayor, the three-person town council, and most of the merchants who'd been down in the village, all plainly curious and eager for the experience of the banquet. Soon there was a crush outside the entrance, and Thibault arrived along with Stuart at his side, to help speed things along.

People were enthusiastically announcing themselves and where they'd come from and thanking Reuben or Felix for the invitation. A whole group of the clergy came in, all in black clerics and Roman collars, having been invited from the Archdiocese of San Francisco, and dozens of people who had come from Mendocino on the coast, and other towns in the wine country.

The nurses from Stuart's hospital arrived, and powerfully excited, Stuart embraced each and every one of them. Then came pretty Dr. Cutler, who'd treated him for his injuries, overjoyed to see him in such wonderful shape, and asking when Grace would arrive. There were five or six doctors with her, and other people from Santa Rosa. In came Catholic priests from Humboldt County, thanking Felix for including them, and there were ministers arriving too from churches up and down the coast, expressing the same ardent thanks.

Uniformed maids and teenage volunteers took heavy coats and wraps, and brought people to the waiting tables or invited them to go into the house, as the pavilion was filling rapidly. Other boys and girls were passing trays of hors d'oeuvres. Frank appeared and reappeared to escort guests to various destinations.

The pure and soaring voices of the choir were singing "Coventry Carol," and there were moments when Reuben gave in to a sudden lock on the music, shamefully tuning out the introductions that he could hardly hear, but warmly shaking hands and urging the guests to be welcome.

Again and again, Felix drew his attention to this or that guest,

"Judge Fleming, let me present Reuben Golding, our host," and Reuben would gladly respond. The state senator he'd met in the village soon arrived, and other people from Sacramento. More clergymen arrived, and two rabbis, both with black beards and black yarmulkes. Frank obviously knew the rabbis, greeting them both by name, and he eagerly led them into the thick of the party.

The excitement was infectious, Reuben had to admit, and now when the orchestra began to play with the choir, he felt that this was perhaps one of more exhilarating experiences he'd ever had.

People were in all manner of dress, from cocktail attire and black tie to business suits and even jeans and down jackets, kids in Sunday best, little girls in long dresses. Phil didn't look at all out of place in his tweed jacket and open shirt collar. And there were plenty of women in hats, fantasy hats and vintage hats, and those little cocktail hats with veils that Jim had described.

The sheriff came along in a blue suit with his fashionably dressed wife and his good-looking college-age sons, and there were other deputies from his office, some in uniform and some in civilian dress with wives and children.

Suddenly the word came that dinner was being served in the dining room, and there was a shift in the crowd, as many sought to go into the house, while a long line came streaming out with plates laden with food to find tables.

At last Grace came, with Celeste and Mort, their faces radiant and curious and warm as though the party had already affected them as they'd waited to enter. Grace, in one of her typically handsome white cashmere sweater dresses, wore her red hair loose and down to her shoulders in a delightfully girlish manner.

"Good Lord," she said. "This is just fabulous." She was waving at a couple of doctors she knew, and rattling off their names. "And the archbishop is here, how incredible!"

Celeste looked breathtakingly pretty in black sequined silk. She seemed actually happy as she and Mort made their way into the crowd.

Indeed the splendor of the pavilion swept people right through the entrance and into the swim of things.

Immediately, Rosie, the family housekeeper arrived, looking very pretty and girlish in a bright red dress with her full dark hair combed free. Husband Isaac and their four girls were with her. Reuben hugged Rosie. There were few people in the world he loved as much as Rosie. He was dying to show her the entire house, but watched her disappear into the party with Grace and Celeste.

Reuben's Hillsborough cousins flooded in suddenly with squeals and hugs and breathless questions about the house. "Did you really see this Man Wolf thing!" Cousin Shelby whispered into Reuben's ear, but when he stiffened she immediately apologized. "Just had to ask!" she confessed.

Reuben said he didn't mind. And he didn't. He'd always loved Shelby. She was his uncle Tim's oldest daughter, and a redhead like Tim and Grace, and used to babysit Reuben when he was a kid. Reuben loved Shelby's eleven-year-old son, redheaded Clifford, born out of wedlock when Shelby was still in high school. Clifford, a handsome and solemn little boy, was beaming now at Reuben, clearly impressed with the scope of the party. Reuben had always admired Shelby for bringing up Clifford, though she'd never identified the boy's father to anyone. Grandfather Spangler had been furious about it at the time, and Grace's brother, Tim, a recent widower, had been brokenhearted. Shelby had become a model mother to Clifford. And of course they'd all come to adore him, especially Grandfather Spangler. Grace doubled back at once to take Shelby and Clifford and the other cousins in hand. And then when Phil's gray-haired sister, Josie, arrived, in her wheelchair with a very sweet elderly nurse to take care of her, Phil came to collect her and bring her up to where she might better hear the choir.

Finally Felix said they had been greeting people for an hour and a half now, and they could break to have supper themselves.

People were now moving back and forth through the entrance freely. And some people, especially those who had worked at the daylong fair, were even headed home.

Reuben wanted more than anything in the world to wander off in the oaks and see what that was like for the guests, but he was also starving.

Thibault and Frank took over at the door.

Several exceptionally beautiful women were coming in, clearly friends of Frank's. Hmmm. Friends of Thibault's as well. Dressed in impressive and revealing gowns and full-length evening coats, they had the sheen of film actresses, or models, but Reuben had no real idea who they were. Maybe one of these beauties was Frank's wife.

All over the library, the main room, and the conservatory people were eating, many with the aid of little folding tray tables covered with white Battenberg place mats, and the young catering staff refilled wine, and cleared away old glasses and coffee cups. The fires were blazing in every fireplace.

Of course there were furtive whispers of "the Man Wolf," and "the window" as here and there people pointed to the library window through which the notorious Man Wolf had jumped the night he'd appeared at this house and slaughtered two mysterious and unsavory Russian doctors. But few were asking about the Man Wolf out loud, and Reuben was grateful for that.

Reuben could hear the thunder of feet on the old oak staircase, and the low rumble of those walking overhead.

He grabbed a plate full of turkey, ham, and roast goose, raisin dressing, and mashed potatoes, and moved to the dining room windows to look out on the wonderland forest.

It was just as he had imagined it would be, with families following the pathways, and a band of musicians playing just below him on the gravel drive.

The medieval mummers were making a snaking dance through the crowd. How remarkable they were, their green costumes covered in ivy and leaves; one wore a horse's head, another a skull mask, and yet another the mask of a demon. One man wore an actual wolf skin cloak, with the wolf's head on top of his head. Another wore the skin and head of a bear. Two played fiddles and one was piping on a flute, and the "demon" was playing a concertina. The others played tambourines and little drums attached to their waists. The last in line was giving out what appeared to be large gold coins—perhaps some sort of party favor.

Other costumed men and women were passing out cups of mulled wine; and a tall white-haired St. Nicholas figure, or a Father Christmas, in streaming green velvet robes, moved about, handing out little wooden toys to the children. These appeared to be little wooden boats and horses and locomotives, small enough to go in a parent's pocket. But from his big green velvet sack, he also took tiny little books, and little porcelain dolls with flopping arms and legs. The children were charmed and delighted as they crowded around him, and the adults were clearly pleased as well. There was that blond woman he'd glimpsed in the village, with all her crowd of youngsters, but she no longer wore her pretty green flowered hat. Could that be Jim's Lorraine? Reuben was not about to ask. He'd never find Jim in time to ask anyway. There must have been a thousand people milling around the house and the woods.

Reuben didn't have long to gobble his food, which was what he was doing. Several old friends from Berkeley had found him and were full of questions about this house and what in the world had happened to him. They talked around the Man Wolf as best they could without ever directly mentioning him. Reuben was vague, reassuring but not very forthcoming.

He led the gang back to the table, this time for more roast goose, roast partridge, and big sweet yams, and kept eating no matter who said what. Actually he was glad to see his friends, and to see them having such a great time, and it wasn't hard at all to deflect their questions by asking questions of his own.

At one point, he heard Frank at his side, and Frank whispered, "Don't forget to look around, Wonder Pup. Don't forget to enjoy it." He himself seemed marvelously alive, as though he'd been born for events such as this. Surely he was the twentieth-century Morphenkind; but then Thibault had described himself as the neophyte, hadn't he? Ah, it was impossible to figure them all out. And he had plenty of time to do it, that was the strange thing. He had not yet begun to think of time as something that would extend beyond a normal life span.

But speaking of time, was he taking the time to enjoy what was happening all around him?

He had been looking down the long length of the massive table dazzled by the array of sauced vegetables, and the big boar's head in the center. Again and again the caterers refilled dishes of cream peas, Brussels sprouts, sweet potatoes, mounded rice and bread-crumb dressings, and platters of freshly carved turkey, beef, pork. There were steaming bowls of red and golden fruit sauce, and even fresh orange slices sparkling on lettuce, and an egregious whipped-cream ambrosia filled with all manner of chopped fruit. Every kind of rice dish imaginable was offered, and heaps of raw carrots, broccoli, and tomatoes, which the health conscious were eagerly piling on their plates.

The masked mummers were now in the house, winding through the dining room, in fact, and Reuben put out his hand for one of the golden coins they were distributing. He could see now that the wolf skin and bear skin were clever fakes, and that the demon was the German Christmas devil, Krampurs, with his wild goat's horns. They weren't singing now, merely playing their little drums and tambourines, and taking special delight in amusing the children. There were so many children.

The gold coin was of course not gold at all, but a large imitation of a coin, light, and inscribed in old-fashioned scrollwork with the words YULETIDE AT NIDECK POINT on one side, and an impressive image of the house on the other with the date beneath it. Where had Reuben seen trinkets like this before? He couldn't think, but it was a marvelous souvenir. Surely Felix had thought of everything.

Off to one side stood Jean Pierre, of all people, explaining to a small group that in Old Europe people has often "donned the skins of wild beasts" at Yuletide.

To the left, Reuben's mother and Dr. Cutler were talking tête-à-tête, and just beyond them he could see Celeste, her condition beautifully disguised in her flowing black dress, in fast conversation with one of the Sacramento politicians. Quite suddenly, Grace's brother, Tim, appeared with his new Brazilian wife, Helen.

Grace burst into tears. Reuben went at once to greet his uncle. It was always a bit unnerving to see Tim because Tim seemed the twin of his mother, with the very same red hair and the same rather fierce blue eyes. It was like seeing his mother in a man's body, and he didn't entirely like it but he could never look away from it, either, and Tim was also a doctor and a surgeon and he had that same hard and direct stare that Grace had, and this fascinated and repelled Reuben at the same time. Tim had a way of demanding, "What are you doing with your life?" But this time he did not. All he talked about was the house. "And I have heard all those crazy stories," he confided. "But this is no time for that. Look at this place." His Brazilian wife, Helen, was petite and sparkling with generous enthusiasm. Reuben had never seen her before. Yes, he'd seen Shelby and Clifford, said Tim, and yes, they were staying in Hillsborough with the family there through Christmas.

Mort commandeered Reuben to tell him in anxious whispers how happy he was for him with the baby coming, but his face said he was anxious, and Reuben told him that everybody would do everything possible between heaven and earth to make Celeste comfortable.

"Well, she says she can't wait to hand over that baby to Grace, but I just don't know if she's being realistic," Mort said, "but I can tell you, this is a great place for that little boy to grow up, just a great place."

Again, those exceptional women caught Reuben's eye. A pair of them—ravishing in their exquisitely draped dresses—were embracing Margon, who had a rather cold cynical smile on his face, and another, olive-skinned woman with jet-black hair and enormous breasts was still with Thibault, who had greeted her when she arrived.

The woman's eyes were large and black and almost tender. She smiled generously at Reuben, and when Thibault turned to glance at Reuben, he blushed and moved away.

Well, of course the Distinguished Gentlemen had women friends, did they not? But were they Morphenkinder? The very idea gave him chills. He didn't want to stare, but then everyone was more or less looking them over. They were robust, extremely well shaped, and were elaborately dressed and decked with jewels precisely to draw admiration. So why not?

Margon beckoned to Reuben and quickly presented him to his mysterious companions—Catrin and Fiona.

Up close, they were perfumed and provocative—no scent but the usual human scent smothered in artificial sweetness. Reuben tried not to stare at their half-naked breasts but it was difficult. Their skimpy dresses were glorified nightgowns.

"A pleasure to meet you at last," said Fiona, a striking and obviously natural blond with long wavy hair to her shoulders and pale almost-white eyebrows. She looked Nordic, like Sergei, with large bones and exquisitely angular shoulders and hips but her voice was simple and contemporary. She wore the largest diamonds Reuben had ever seen on a woman, in a choker around her neck, and on her wrists and two of her fingers.

Reuben knew if he looked closely enough into her shapeless low-cut bodice he would see her nipples. So he tried to focus on the diamonds. Her skin was so fair he could see the blue veins beneath it, but it was fresh and healthy, and her mouth was large and extremely pretty.

"We have heard so very much about you," said the other, Catrin, who seemed a little less bold than Fiona, and did not extend her hand as Fiona did. Catrin's long hair was brown, perfectly straight, strikingly simple. Like Fiona she was practically naked, with the tiniest straps holding up the dark beaded sack of a dress in which she appeared squeezable and devourable. She glanced at Fiona as she spoke, as if to watch her every reaction, but her brown eyes were warm and her smile almost girlish. She had a dimpled chin.

"Such an unusual and impressive house," said Catrin, "and such a remote and beautiful spot. You must love it."

"I do, I very much do," said Reuben.

"And you're as handsome as everyone said you were," said Fiona in her more forthright manner. "I had thought surely they were exaggerating." She spoke it like a criticism.

And what do I say now, Reuben thought, as always. One doesn't return a compliment with a compliment, no, but what's the proper response? He didn't know any more now than he ever did.

"And we've met your father," said Catrin suddenly, "and he is the most charming man. And what a name, Philip Emanuel Golding."

"He told you his entire name?" asked Reuben. "I'm surprised. He doesn't usually do that with people."

"Well, I pressed him on it," said Fiona. "He's not like a lot of the people here. He has a remote and lonely look in his eye and he talks to himself and doesn't care if people see it."

Reuben laughed out loud. "Maybe he's just singing along with the music."

"Is it true he's likely to remain living with you here?" Fiona asked. "Under this roof? That is your plan and his plan?"

This plainly startled Margon, who glanced at her sharply, but she merely kept her eyes on Reuben, who honestly didn't know what to say and didn't see why, really, he should say anything.

"I heard this man was coming here to live," said Fiona again. "Is this true?"

"I like him," said Catrin, stepping closer to Reuben. "I like you, too. You look like him, you know, but with the darker coloring. You must be very fond of him."

"Thank you," Reuben stammered. "I'm flattered—I mean, I'm pleased." He felt awkward and stupid and just a little offended. What did these women know about Phil's plans? Why should they care about this?

There was something positively dark in Margon's expression, something distrustful, uneasy, unreadable to Reuben. Fiona's eyes moved over Margon coldly, a bit dismissively, and then back to Reuben.

Suddenly Margon was spiriting the ladies away. He took Fiona's arm almost roughly. Fiona flashed him a contemptuous look, but she followed him, or allowed him to pull her along.

Reuben tried not to stare at Fiona as she moved off, but he didn't want to miss it entirely either, the way her hips and flanks moved in that skimpy dress. She put him off and yet she fascinated him.

There was Frank by the far window with another one of the striking women. Was that his wife? And was she too a Morphenkind? She looked remarkably like Frank with the same very glossy black hair and flawless skin. She wore a conservative velvet jacket and long skirt, with a lot of ruffled white lace, but she had the same presence as the others, and Frank was clearly talking intimately with her. Was Frank angry as he spoke to her, and was she begging him to be patient about something with little hand gestures and imploring eyes? Reuben was probably imagining it.

Suddenly Frank glanced at him, and before Reuben could turn away, Frank approached and presented Reuben to his companion. "My beloved Berenice," he called her. They were so strikingly similar in appearance—same clear skin, and playful dark eyes, even something of the same gestures, though she was of course delicate and shapely, whereas Frank had the squared-off jaw and hairline of a film star. Off they went, as Berenice, with a soft almost affectionate backward glance, moved on to see more of the house, with Frank obviously eager to show it to her.

A wave of musicians and choristers came in for their dinner break, the boys looking proverbially angelic in their choir robes, and the musicians hastening to tell Reuben how much they were loving all this, and they'd be willing to come up from San Francisco anytime for events here.

Suddenly Grace accosted him and told him she'd had to take a plate out there to Phil, who wouldn't move away from his privileged spot right by the choir for anything. "I think you know what's happening, Baby Boy," she said. "I think he's brought his suitcases and won't be driving back tonight."

Reuben didn't know what to say, but Grace was not unhappy. "I don't want him to be a burden to you, that's all, I really don't think that's fair to you and your friends here."

"Mom, he's no burden," said Reuben, "but are *you* ready for him to come live here?"

"Oh, he won't stay forever, Reuben. Though I have to warn you, he thinks he is. He'll spend a few weeks, maybe worst case a few months, and then he'll be back. He can't live away from San Francisco. What would he do without his walks in North Beach? I just don't want him to be a burden. I tried to talk with him about this but it's useless. And having Celeste in the house doesn't make it any easier. She tries to be nice to him but she can't stand him."

"I know," said Reuben crossly. "Look, I'm glad he's come to stay, as long as you're okay with it."

A small string orchestra had just come into the dining room, now that the crowds around the table had eased, and they began to play, along with a lovely female soprano who was singing a decidedly Eliz-abethan carol he'd never heard before, her voice purposely sad and plaintive.

He marveled as he listened to her. All his life he'd loved live music, and heard so little of it, existing as most of his friends did in a luxuri-ous world of recordings of every type of music imaginable. This was heaven to him, hearing the soprano, and indeed just watching her, watching the expression on her face as she sang, and watching the graceful attitudes of the violinists as they played.

Wandering off half reluctantly, he ran into his editor Billie Kale and the gang from the *Observer*. Billie apologized for their photogra-pher snapping pictures everywhere. Reuben was fine with it. Felix was fine with it. There were fellow journalists from the *Chronicle* here too, and several television people who'd been down in the village earlier.

"Look, we need a picture of that library window," said Billie. "I mean we have to say something about the Man Wolf having been here!"

"Yes, go right ahead," said Reuben. "It's the big east window. Take all the pictures you want."

His mind was on other things.

What was it with those exceptional women? He saw another one, a dark-skinned beauty with a mass of raven hair and bare shoulders in fast conversation with Stuart. How intense she seemed, and how fascinated was Stuart, who took her off with him apparently to see the conservatory, disappearing in the crowd. Maybe Reuben was imagin-ing things. There were a lot of beautiful women here, he reminded himself. What made those particular ladies shine out?

More people were taking their leave, what with the long day in the village and the long drive home. But it seemed others were just coming in. Reuben accepted thanks to the right and to the left for the party. He'd stopped long ago mumbling that Felix was responsible for it. And he realized that he didn't have to make himself smile and shake hands. It was coming naturally to him, the happiness around him contagious.

There was that woman again, the one who'd worn the lovely hat in the village. She was seated on the couch beside a young girl who was crying. The girl looked about eleven or twelve. The woman was patting the little girl and whispering to her. A young boy sat on her other side, with his arms folded, rolling his eyes and staring at the ceiling with an air of mortification. Good heavens, what could be wrong with the little girl? Reuben started to make his way towards her but a couple of people interrupted with questions and thanks. Someone was telling him a long story about an old house remembered from childhood. He'd been turned around. Where was the woman with the little girl? She was gone.

Several old high school friends approached him, including an old girlfriend, Charlotte, who had been his first love. She already had two children. He found himself studying the fat-cheeked baby in her arms, a writhing mass of lively pink flesh that kept pushing and stretching and kicking to escape his mother's patient arms as she took it in stride, her older girl, now three years old, clinging to her dress and staring up at Reuben in glum wonder.

And my son is coming, Reuben thought, and he'll be like this, made of pink bubble gum with eyes like big opals. And he will grow up in this house, under this roof, wandering through this world and inevitably taking it for granted, and that will be a wonderful thing.

He couldn't find his old high school love at all in Charlotte. But a song was nudging at him, what was it? Yes, that strange unearthly song "Take Me As I Am," by the October Project. Mingled suddenly with memories of Charlotte were memories of that song seeping out of Marchent's room from a spectral radio.

Again, he made his way to the eastern window, this time in the library, and though the window seat was occupied from end to end, he managed to look out again on the sparkling forest. Surely people were watching him, wondering about the Man Wolf, wanting to ask questions. He heard a faint whisper of those words behind him, and "right through that window."

The music had become noise, as the sounds from the dining room met with the great swell from the pavilion, and he felt that old familiar drowsiness come over him that so often did when he was at busy and crowded events.

But the forest did look fantastical.

The crowds were thicker than ever, even though a light rain was falling. And gradually Reuben realized there were people high in the trees everywhere. There were shaggy-haired men and women and pale lean little children in the trees, many of them smiling down on the people below and some of them talking to the people below, and these mysterious beings all, of course, wore the familiar soft chamois leather. And the guests, the innocent guests, thought them to be part of the tableau. For as far as he could see, the Forest Gentry were there, dusty, bedraggled with leaves, and even here and there clothed in ivy, sitting or standing on the heavy gray branches. The more he looked, the more detailed and bizarre and vivid they became. The myriad lights twinkled in the falling rain and he could almost hear the mingled laughter and voices as he looked out on them.

He shook himself all over and stared again. Why was he dizzy? Why was there a roaring in his ears? Nothing had changed in the scene. He did not see Elthram. He did not see Marchent. But he could see a constant shifting and reshuffling amongst the Forest Gentry because innumerable members of the tribe were disappearing and others appearing right before his dazzled eyes. He became fascinated with it, trying to catch this or that lean and feline figure as it vanished or burst into visible color, but he was making himself even more dizzy. He had to break the spell. This had to stop.

He turned and began to drift through the party as he'd drifted through the village fair. The music surged. Real voices played on his ears. Laughter, smiles. The sense of the bizarre, the horror of the bizarre, left him. Everywhere, he saw people in animated conversation, infused with the excitement of the party, and unusual meetings of locals with friends he knew. More than once he studied Celeste from afar and noted how much fun she was having, how often she laughed.

And again and again he marveled at the Distinguished Gentlemen and how they helped the party along. Sergei was introducing people to one another, and directing the orchestra musicians to the dining table, and answering questions and even accompanying people to the stairs.

Thibault and Frank were always in conversation and motion, with or without their women companions, and even Lisa, who was busy with the management of the feast on every level, took time to talk to the boy choristers and point out things to them about the house.

A young man approached her, whispering in her ear, to which she answered, "I do not know. No one told me where the woman died!" and she turned her back to the man.

How many were asking that very question, Reuben thought. Surely they were wondering. Where had Marchent fallen when she'd been stabbed? Where had Reuben been discovered after the attack?

A constant parade moved up the oak stairs to the upper floors. Standing at the foot Reuben could hear the young docents describing the William Morris wallpaper and the nineteenth-century Grand Rapids furnishings, and even such things as the kind of oak used in the floorboards and how it had been dried before construction, things Reuben knew nothing about himself. He caught a female voice saying, "Marchent Nideck, yes. This room."

People smiled at Reuben as they made their way up.

"Yes, please, do go up," he said earnestly.

And behind it all was the mastermind, the ever-charming Felix, who moved so rapidly that he seemed to be in two places at one time. Ever smiling, ever responding, he was on fire with goodwill.

At some point, Reuben realized, slowly realized, that the Forest Gentry were in the house as well. It was the children he noticed first of all, pale, thin little creatures in the same dusty leaf-strewn rustic dress as their elders, darting through the crowds this way and that as if they were playing some kind of personal game. Such hungry faces, dirt-streaked faces, urchin faces! It sent a stab into his heart. And then he saw the occasional man and woman, eyes aflame yet secretive, drifting about as he had been drifting about, studying the human guests as if they were the curious ones, indifferent to those who eyed them.

It unnerved him that these small emaciated children might be the earthbound dead. It positively made his heart quiver. It made him faintly sick. He couldn't stand the thought of it suddenly that these towheaded boys laughing and smiling and dodging amongst the guests here and there were ghosts. Ghosts. He could not imagine what it signified, being this size and this shape forever. He couldn't grasp how this could be desirable or inevitable. And all that he didn't know about the new world around him frightened him. But it also tantalized him. He caught a glimpse of one of those unusual women, those strangely alluring women, bejeweled and sequined and passing through the crowd slowly with long lingering glances to her right and left. She seemed a goddess in some brutal yet indefinable way.

His anxieties suddenly collected around him, crowding him, dimming the radiance of the party, and making him aware of how sharp and unusual the emotions and experiences of his new life actually were. What had he ever known of worry before? What had the Sunshine Boy ever known of dread?

But all he had to do, he thought, was not look at the Forest Gentry. Not look at that strange woman. Not speculate. Look instead at the very real and substantial people of this world who were everywhere having such a remarkably good time. He was desperate suddenly to do that, to not see the unearthly guests.

But he was doing something else. He was searching. He was searching now from left to right and straight ahead for the one figure he most dreaded in all the world, the figure of Marchent.

Did someone behind him just say, "Yes, in the kitchen, that's where they found her"?

He moved past the giant Christmas tree towards the open doors of the conservatory, which was as crowded as every other room. Under countless Christmas bulbs and golden floods the huge masses of tropical foliage here looked almost grotesque; guests were everywhere among the trellises and pots, but where was she?

There was a slender woman near the round marble-top table before the fountain where Reuben and Laura had so often taken their meals. His skin was pringling and singing as he moved towards this slim blond-haired figure, this delicate figure, but quite suddenly as he stood beneath the arching branches of the orchid trees, the woman turned and smiled at him, flesh and blood like countless others, another nameless happy guest.

"Such a beautiful house," she said. "You'd never think anything terrible happened here."

"Yes, you're right," he said.

So many words seemed on the tip of her tongue, but she said only it was a great joy to be here, and she moved on.

Lifting his eyes, he looked up into the purple blossoms of the trees. The noise pressed in around him, but he felt remote and alone. He was hearing Marchent's voice when they'd talked of orchid trees, beautiful orchid trees, and it was Marchent who'd ordered these trees for this house and for him. These trees had been brought over hundreds and hundreds of miles on account of the living Marchent, and they were alive now and bent low with shivering blossoms and Marchent was dead.

Someone had approached, and he ought to turn around, he knew it, and acknowledge the greeting or the good-bye. A couple was here, with plates and glasses in hand, obviously hoping to commandeer the table, of course, and why not?

And just as he did turn, he saw far across the giant room the person for whom he'd been searching, the unmistakable Marchent, almost invisible in the shadows against the dark and shining glass panes of the wall.

Her face was marvelously realized, however, and her pale eyes were fastened on him just as they'd been in the village when she'd stood there in semi-profile listening to the smiling Elthram who'd stood at her side. An unnatural light seemed to pick her out of the artificial twilight, subtle but sourceless, and in that light he saw the sheen of her smooth forehead, the gleam of her eyes, the luster of the pearls around her neck.

He opened his mouth to call her name and no sound came out. As his heart shook, the figure appeared to grow brighter, to shimmer, and then to fade completely away. A volley of raindrops hit the glass roof overhead. Silver rain slid down the many panes all around him, and the very walls shimmered everywhere that he looked. *Marchent.* The grief and the longing felt like a pain through his temples.

His heart stopped.

There had been no misery, no tears, no desperate reaching in her face. But what had the expression in those serious eyes, those thoughtful eyes, actually meant? *What do the dead know? What do the dead feel?*

He put his hands up to his head. He shivered. His skin was hot under his clothes, terribly hot, and his heart would not stop skipping. Someone asked him if he was okay.

Oh, yes, thank you, he answered and he turned and left the room.

The air in the main room was cooler, and sweet with the scent of pine needles. Soft swelling music came from the orchestra beyond the open windows. His pulse was returning to normal. His skin was cooling. A glistening gaggle of teenage girls passed him, giggling and laughing and then rushing into the dining room, obviously on a mission to explore.

Frank appeared, the ever-genial Frank with his high Cary Grant polish, and without a word put a glass of white wine in Reuben's hand. "Want something stronger?" Frank asked, eyebrows raised. Reuben shook his head. Gratefully Reuben drank the wine, good Riesling, cold, delicious, and found himself alone by the fire.

Why had he gone to look for her? Why had he done that? Why had he sought her out in the very midst of all this gaiety? Why? Did he want for her to be here? And if he retreated now to some sealed-off room, presuming he could find one, would she come at his bidding? Would they sit together and talk?

At some point, he saw his father through the crowd. It was Phil, all right, that old gentleman in the tweed jacket and gray pants. How much older than Grace he looked. He was not heavy, no, and he wasn't frail. But his face, never surgically tightened, was soft, natural, and heavily lined like that of Thibault, and his thick thatch of hair, once strawberry blond, was now almost white.

Phil was standing in the library, quite alone among the people drifting in and out, and he was looking fixedly at the big picture of the Distinguished Gentlemen over the mantelpiece.

Reuben could almost see the wheels turning in Phil's mind as he studied the picture, and the sudden awful thought came to him: He will figure it out.

After all, wasn't it obvious that the Felix of today was the spitting image, as everyone said, of the man in the photograph, and that the men around him, the men who should now be some twenty years or more older than they'd been when the picture was taken, were exactly the same now as they'd been then? Felix had come back as his own illegitimate son. But how to explain Sergei or Frank or Margon not having aged in the slightest during the last two decades? And what about Thibault? One might grant men in their prime another twenty years of remarkable vigor, and the young ones did appear to be men in their prime. But Thibault had looked like a man of sixty-five or perhaps seventy in the photograph and he looked exactly like that now. How was such a thing possible, that someone so advanced in years when the photo was taken should have the very same appearance now?

But maybe Phil wasn't noticing all these things. Maybe Phil didn't even know the date of the picture. Why would he? They'd never discussed it before, had they? Maybe Phil was studying the foliage in the photograph and thinking of mundane things, like where it might have been taken, or observing details about the men's clothing and guns.

People interrupted Reuben—wanting to say thanks, of course, before they left.

When he finally reached the library, Phil was nowhere in sight. And who should be sitting in the window seat, on the red velvet cushion looking out over the forest, but the inimitable Elthram, his dark caramel skin and savage green eyes veritably glowing in the firelight, as if he were a demon fueled by fires no one in this room could possibly see. He didn't even look up as Reuben drew close to him. Then finally he did turn and give Reuben a radiant confidential smile before vanishing as he had in the village, without a thought for those who might have been watching, as if such things didn't really matter. And as Reuben glanced around at the people talking and laughing and nibbling from their plates he realized that nobody had noticed, nobody at all.

Suddenly and without a sound Elthram appeared beside him. He turned and looked into Elthram's green eyes, as he felt the pressure of the man's arm around his shoulder.

"There's someone here who must speak to you," Elthram said.

"Gladly, only tell me who," said Reuben.

"Look there," he said, gesturing towards the great front room. "By the fire. The little girl with the woman beside her."

Reuben turned, fully expecting to see the woman and the young girl who'd been crying. But these were different people, indeed.

At once Reuben realized he was looking at little Susie Blakely, at her grave little face with her eyes fixed on him. And the woman beside her was Pastor Corrie George, with whom Reuben had left her at the church. Susie wore a lovely old-fashioned smock dress with short puffed sleeves and her hair was beautifully combed. There was a gold chain around her neck with a cross on it. Pastor George wore a black pantsuit with a lot of pretty white lace at the neck, and she too was staring fixedly at Reuben.

"You must be wise," Elthram whispered. "But she needs to talk to you."

Reuben's face was burning. There was a throbbing in his palms. But he went directly towards them.

He bent down as he smoothed the top of Susie's blond head.

"You're Susie Blakely," he said. "I've seen your picture in the paper. I'm Reuben Golding, I'm a reporter. You're much much prettier than your picture, Susie." It was true. She looked fresh, radiant, undamaged. "And your pink dress is beautiful. You look like a little girl in a storybook."

She smiled.

His heart was racing, and he marveled at the calm sound of his voice.

"Are you having a good time?" He smiled at Pastor George. "What about you? Can I get anything for you?"

"Can I talk to you, Mr. Golding?" asked Susie. Same clear crisp little voice. "Just for a minute, if I could. It's really really important."

"Of course you can," said Reuben.

"She does need to talk to you, Mr. Golding," said Pastor George. "You must forgive us for asking you like this, but we've come a long way tonight, just to see you, and I promise this won't take but a few minutes."

Where could he visit with them in quiet? The party was as crowded as ever.

Quickly, he drew them out of the great room and down the hallway and up the oak stairs.

His room was open to all the guests, but fortunately only a couple were having some eggnog at the round table and they quickly yielded when he brought the little girl and the woman in with him.

He shut the door and locked it, and made sure the bathroom was empty.

"Sit down, please," he said. "What can I do for you?" He gestured for them to sit at the round table.

Susie's scalp looked as pink as her dress, and she blushed suddenly as she sat down on the straight-backed chair. Pastor George took her right hand and held it in both of hers as she sat near the child.

"Mr. Golding, I have to tell you a secret," said Susie. "A secret I can't tell anybody else."

"You can tell me," said Reuben, nodding. "I promise you, I can keep a secret. Some reporters can't but I can."

"I know you saw the Man Wolf," said Susie. "You saw him in this house. And the time before that, he bit you. I heard all about it." Her face puckered as if she was about to cry.

"Yes, Susie," said Reuben. "I did see him. All that was true." He wondered if he was blushing as she was blushing. His face was hot. He was hot all over. His heart went out to her. He would have done anything at this moment to make her comfortable, to help her, protect her.

"I saw the Man Wolf, too," said Susie. "I really did. My mom and dad don't believe me." There was a flash of anger in her small face, and she glanced uneasily at Pastor George who nodded to her.

"Ah, that's how you were rescued," said Reuben. "That's how you got away from the man."

"Yes, that's what happened, Mr. Golding," said Pastor George. She dropped her voice, glancing anxiously at the door. "It was the Man Wolf who rescued her. I saw him too. I spoke to him. Both of us did."

"I see," said Reuben. "But there wasn't anything about it in the papers. I didn't see anything on television."

"That's because we didn't want anybody to know," said Susie. "We didn't want anybody to capture him and put him in a cage and hurt him."

"Yes, right, I see. I understand," said Reuben.

"We wanted to give him time to get away," said Pastor George. "To clear out of this part of California. We wanted to figure some way not to ever tell anybody. But Susie needs to tell people, Mr. Golding. She needs to talk about what happened to her. And when we tried to tell her parents, well, they didn't believe us! Either of us!"

"Of course she needs to talk about it," said Reuben. "You both do. I understand. If anyone should understand, I should."

"He's real, isn't he, Mr. Golding?" asked Susie. She swallowed and the tears came up in her eyes, and suddenly there was a listlessness in her face as if she'd lost the thread.

Reuben took her by her shoulders. "Yes, he's real, darling," he said. "I saw him and so did a lot of other people, downstairs in the big room. Many people have seen the Man Wolf. He's real all right. You don't ever have to doubt your senses."

"They don't believe anything I say," she said in a small voice.

"They believe about the bad man who took you, don't they?" he asked.

"Yes, they do," said Pastor George. "His DNA was all over the trailer. They've connected him to other disappearances, too. The Man Wolf saved Susie's life, that's perfectly obvious. That man killed two other little girls." She stopped suddenly and glanced at Susie with concern. "But you see, when her parents didn't believe her about the Man Wolf, and others didn't—. Well, she doesn't want to talk anymore about any of it, not any of it at all."

"He did save me, Mr. Golding," said Susie.

"I know that he did," said Reuben. "I mean I believe every single word you're saying. Let me tell you something, Susie. Lots of people don't believe in the Man Wolf. They don't believe me. They don't believe the people who were with me here, the other people who saw him. We have to live with that, that they don't believe us. But we have to tell what we saw. We can't let the secrets fester inside us. Do you know what that means?"

"Yes, I know what it means," said Pastor George. "But you see, we don't want to trumpet it to the media either. We don't want people hunting him down, killing him."

"No," said Susie. "And they will. They'll get him and kill him."

"Well, listen, honey," Reuben said. "I know you're telling the truth, both of you. And don't you ever forget that I saw him too. Look, Susie, I wish you were old enough for e-mail. I wish—."

"I am old enough," said Susie. "I can use my mom's computer. I can write down my e-mail address for you right now."

Pastor George took a pen out of her pocket. There was a writing pad already on the table.

Quickly Susie began to carve out the letters of her e-mail, her teeth biting into her lower lip as she wrote. Reuben watched, quickly entering the e-mail into his iPhone.

"I'm e-mailing you now, Susie," he said, his thumbs working. "I won't say anything that anybody else would understand."

"It's okay. My mom doesn't know my e-mail address," said Susie. "Only you do and Pastor George."

Pastor George wrote out her e-mail and gave it to Reuben. At once he recorded it and fired an e-mail off to her address.

"Okay. We're gonna e-mail, you and me. And any time you have to talk about what you saw, you e-mail me—and look." He took the pen. "This is my phone number, the number of this phone here. I'll e-mail this to you too. You call me. You understand? And you, too, Pastor George." He tore off the sheet of paper and gave it to the woman. "Those of us who've seen these things have to stick together."

"Thank you so much," Susie said. "I told the priest in Confession and he didn't believe me either. He said maybe I imagined it."

Pastor George shook her head. "She just doesn't want to talk anymore about any of it now, you see, and that's no good. That's just no good."

"Really. Well, I know a priest who'll believe you," said Reuben. He was still holding his iPhone in his left hand. Quickly, he texted Jim. "My bedroom upstairs now, Confession." But what if Jim couldn't hear his phone over the music downstairs? What if his phone was shut off? He was four hours away from his parish. He might have shut it off.

"She needs to be believed," said Pastor George. "I can live with people's skepticism. The last thing I want is the press on my doorstep anyway. But she does need to talk about all of what happened to her, and a lot—and that's going to be true for a long time."

"You're right," he said. "And when you're Catholic, you want to talk to your priest about the things that matter most to you. Well, some of us do."

Pastor George gave a little shrug and an offhand gesture of acceptance.

There was a knock at the door. It couldn't be Jim, he thought, not this quickly.

But when he opened the door, Jim was there all right, and behind him Elthram stood leaning against the wall of the corridor.

"They said you wanted to see me," said Jim.

Reuben gave a grateful nod to Elthram and let Jim into the room.

"This little girl needs to talk to you. Can this woman stay with her while she goes to Confession?"

"If this little girl wants the woman to stay, certainly," said Jim. He focused intently on the little girl, and then nodded to the woman with a soft formal smile. He seemed so gentle, so capable, so effortlessly reassuring.

Susie stood up out of respect for Jim. "Thank you, Father," she said.

"Susie, you can tell Father Jim Golding anything," said Reuben. "And I promise you, he will believe you. And he'll keep your secrets too, and you can talk to him anytime you want, just as you can talk to me."

Jim took the chair opposite her, gesturing for Susie to sit down.

"I'm going to leave you now," said Reuben. "And Susie, you e-mail me any time you want, honey, or you call me. If it goes to voice mail, I promise, I'll get back to you."

"I knew you'd believe me," said Susie. "I knew you would."

"And you can talk to Father Jim about all of it, Susie, whatever happened out there in the woods with that bad man. And anything about the Man Wolf. Honey, you can trust him. He's a priest and he's a good priest. I know because he's my big brother."

She beamed at Reuben. What a beautiful and radiant creature she was. And when he thought of her crying in that trailer that night, when he thought of her small dirt-streaked face as she'd cried and begged him not to leave her, he was silently overcome.

She turned and looked eagerly and innocently at Jim.

And Reuben said, without thinking,

"I love you, darling dear."

Susie's head turned as if jerked by a chain. Pastor George turned too. They were both staring at him.

And it came back to him, that moment in the forest outside the church, when he'd left Susie with Pastor George and he had said in that very same tone of voice, "I love you, darling dear."

His face reddened. He stood there silently looking at Susie. Her face seemed ageless suddenly, like the face of a spirit, stamped with something profound and at the same time simple. She was gazing at him, without shock or confusion or recognition.

"Good-bye, honey," he said and he went out closing the door behind him.

At the foot of the stairs, Reuben's editor, Billie, accosted him. Wasn't that Susie Blakely? Had he gotten an exclusive with Susie Blakely? Did Reuben realize what that meant? No reporter had been able to talk to that little girl since she'd been returned to her parents. This was huge.

"No, Billie, and no, and no," Reuben said lowering his voice to soften his outrage. "She's a guest in this house, and I do not have any right or any intention of interviewing that child. Now, listen, I want to get back to the pavilion and hear some of the music before the party's over. Come with me, come on."

They plunged into the thick of the crowd in the dining room and mercifully he could no longer hear Billie or anyone else. Billie drifted away. He shook hands here, nodded to thanks there, but steadily moved towards the music coming through the front door. Only now did he think about Jim hating so much to be around children, hating to see them, but surely he'd had to call Jim for Susie. Jim would understand. Jim was a priest first and foremost, no matter what personal pain he might feel.

The pavilion was no less crowded. But it was easier to make his way through the tables, exchanging greetings, acknowledging thanks, merely nodding at those he didn't know, and who didn't know him, until he came near to the solemn artfully lighted crèche.

The chain of medieval mummers was passing through, handing out their golden commemorative coins. Waitresses and waiters everywhere were replenishing plates or collecting them, offering fresh glasses of wine, or cups of coffee. But all of this faded as he moved into the soft dreamy light of the manger. This had been his destination all along. He smelled the wax of candles; the voices of the choir were blended and heartbreaking yet faintly shrill.

He lost track of time as he stood there, the music close and beautiful and engulfing. The boys' choir began a mournful hymn now to the accompaniment of the whole orchestra:

> *In the bleak mid-winter*
> *Frosty wind made moan,*
> *Earth stood hard as iron,*
> *Water like a stone.*

Reuben closed his eyes for a long moment, and when he opened them he looked down on the smiling face of the Christ Child, and he prayed. "Please show me how to be good," he whispered. "Please, no matter what I am, show me how to be good."

A sadness overwhelmed him, a terrible discouragement—a fear of all the challenges that lay ahead. He loved Susie Blakely. He loved her. And he wanted only all that was good for her forever and always. He wanted good for every single person he'd ever known. And he could not think now of the cruelty he'd visited on those whom he'd judged as evil, those whom he'd taken out of this world with a beast's thoughtless cruelty. Silently with his eyes closed he repeated the prayer in a profound and wordless way.

The inner silence, the engulfing song, seemed to go on forever, and gradually he felt a quiet peace.

All around him people seemed rapt in the music. Nearby to his left, Shelby stood with her son, Clifford, and her father. They were singing, as they gazed at the choir. And others crowded in whom he didn't know.

The choir went on with the soft, beautiful hymn.

> *Enough for Him, whom cherubim*
> *Worship night and day,*
> *A breastful of milk*
> *And a mangerful of hay;*
> *Enough for Him, whom angels*
> *Fall down before,*
> *The ox and ass and camel*
> *Which adore.*

At some point he heard a tenor voice, a familiar voice, singing beside him, and when he opened his eyes, he saw it was Jim. Jim was with Susie, standing in front of him, Jim's hands on her shoulders and beside Jim was Pastor Corrie George. It seemed an age had passed since he left them. Now they were all singing the hymn together, and Reuben sang along with them, too.

> *What can I give Him,*
> *Poor as I am?*
> *If I were a shepherd*
> *I would bring a lamb,*
> *If I were a wise man*
> *I would do my part,*
> *Yet what I can I give Him,*
> *Give my heart.*

Gathered all round them were the volunteers from Jim's parish soup kitchen whom Reuben knew from past meals there when he'd worked with them as he had last Christmas and the Christmas before. Jim stood still merely looking down at the white-marble Christ Child in the manger of real hay with a curious wondering expression on his face, one eyebrow raised, and an overall sadness pervading him—so like what Reuben felt.

Reuben didn't talk. He caught a glass of sparkling water from a passing tray and sipped it quietly, and the choir started up again. *"What child is this who laid to rest in Mary's arms is sleeping . . ."*

One of the volunteer women was crying softly, and two others were singing along with the choir. Susie sang clearly and loudly, and so did Pastor George. People came and went around them, as if paying visits to the altar. Jim remained, and Susie and Pastor George remained, and then slowly Jim's eyes moved up over the serene face of the angel on the pediment of the stable and over the trees massed behind it.

He turned and saw Reuben as if shaken out of a dream. He smiled and put his arm around Reuben and kissed Reuben's forehead.

The tears sprang to Reuben's eyes.

"I'm happy for you," said Jim in an intimate voice under the sound of the choir. "I'm happy your son is coming. I'm happy you're with your remarkable friends here. Maybe your new friends know things I don't know. Maybe they know more things than I ever dreamed it was possible to know."

"Jim, whatever happens," said Reuben in a low confidential voice, "these are our years, our years to be brothers." His voice broke and he couldn't continue. He didn't know what more to say anyway. "And about the little girl, I mean I know what you said about it being painful, painful to be around children, but I had to—."

"Nonsense, not another word," said Jim with a smile. "Understood."

They both turned, allowing others to step between them and the crèche. Pastor George led Susie to a vacant pair of chairs at one of the tables, and Susie waved at Jim and at Reuben and, of course, they both smiled.

They stood together facing the huge pavilion. To their right the orchestra played the old "Greensleeves" melody beautifully and the voice of the choir was one voice. *The King of Kings salvation brings; Let loving hearts enthrone Him."*

"They're all so happy," said Jim as he looked at the crowded little tables, at the waiters and waitresses weaving in and out with their trays of drinks. "All so happy."

"Are you happy, Jim?" Reuben asked.

Jim suddenly broke into a smile. "When have I ever been happy, Reuben?" He laughed, and this was maybe the first time he'd laughed this way, in his old way, with Reuben since Reuben's life had changed forever. "Look, there's Dad. I think that man talking to him has him trapped. Time for a rescue."

Did the man have Phil trapped? Reuben hadn't seen this man before. He was tall with long full white hair down to his shoulders, much like Margon's hair, something of a lion's mane, and he was dressed in a worn belted suede jacket with dark leather patches on the elbows. He was nodding as Phil talked, and his dark eyes were coolly regarding Reuben. Beside him sat a lovely but rather muscular blond woman with slightly upturned eyes and severe cheekbones. Her straw-colored hair was free like that of the man, a small torrent, falling to her shoulders. She too was looking at Reuben. Her eyes appeared colorless.

"This is a world traveler, this man," said Phil, after presenting his two sons. "He's been regaling me with stories of Midwinter customs the world over—of ancient times and human sacrifice!" Reuben heard the man say his name, Hockan Crost, in a mellow deep voice, an arresting voice, but he heard the word *Morphenkind.*

"Helena," said the woman extending her hand. "Such a lovely party." Obvious Slavic accent, and the smile very sweet, but there was something faintly grotesque about her, about her strong proportions, and the very large bones of her beautifully painted face, and her long throat and firm shoulders. Her sleeveless dress was crusted with sequins and beads. It looked heavy, like a carapace.

Morphenkinder, both of them.

Maybe there was a scent to his own kind, male and female, that his body recognized even when his mind didn't acknowledge it. The man regarded Jim and Reuben almost coldly from beneath heavy black eyebrows. He had a hard-cut face but it wasn't ugly. He looked weathered, with colorless lips and massive shoulders.

He and the lady rose, bowed, slipped away.

"Some fascinating people here tonight," said Phil. "And why they keep introducing themselves to me I have no idea. I sat here to listen to the music. But this is a lot of fun, Reuben. I have to hand it to your friends, and the food is spectacular. That Crost is a remarkable man. Not many people claim to sympathetically understand Midwinter human sacrifice." Phil laughed. "He's quite a philosopher."

Dessert service began, and people were heading for the big dining room once more, the air filled with aroma of coffee and the freshly baked mince and pumpkin pies. The waiters brought trays of plum pudding, "humble pie," and mince pies in the shape of the Christmas crib to those who remained in the pavilion. Phil loved the pecan pie with the real whipping cream. Reuben had never had "humble pie" and he loved it.

At the next table little Susie was eating ice cream and Pastor George gave Reuben a secretive reassuring nod and smile.

More and more people were slipping away. Felix came through the tables urging everyone please to wait for the closing music. Some clearly could not. There was talk of the long drive to here and to there, and how it had been worth it. People flashed the commemorative gold coins with thanks, saying they'd be saving them. People so loved "this house."

The caterers were now giving out small white candles, each cradled in a little paper holder, and directing everyone to the pavilion for the "closing music."

What was happening? The "closing music"? Reuben had no idea.

The pavilion was suddenly packed. People in the main room of the house were crowded against the open windows looking into the pavilion, and the double doors to the conservatory were wide open with many crowded there as well.

The overhead floods were being turned off, reducing the light throughout to a beautiful gloom. Candles were being lighted every-where, with people offering their candles to one another. Soon Reu-ben's small candle was lighted and he was shielding it with his hand.

He rose and pressed towards the orchestra again, and finally found a comfortable place opposite against the stone wall of the house itself just below the far-right front-room window. Susie and Pastor George moved closer to the crèche and orchestra, too.

Felix was at a microphone to one side of the crèche, and in a soft rolling genial voice he said that the orchestra and the adult choir and the boys' choir would now be singing "the most loved Christmas carols in our tradition" and everybody was most welcome to join in.

Reuben understood. There had been many lovely old hymns and songs heard up until now, and some grand church music, but not the great lusty heavy hitters. And when the orchestra and the choirs burst forth with "Joy to the World" in high vigor, he was thrilled.

Everywhere around him, people were singing, even the most unlikely people, like Celeste, and even his dad. In fact, he could hardly believe that Phil was standing there with a small lighted candle singing in a loud clear voice, and so was Grace. His mother was actually sing-ing. Even his uncle Tim was singing, along with his wife Helen, and Shelby and Clifford. And Aunt Josie in her wheelchair was singing. Of course Susie was singing, and so was Pastor George. And so were Thibault and all the Distinguished Gentlemen whom he could see. Even Stuart was singing, along with his friends.

Something communal was happening that he could never have anticipated, never thought possible, not here in this place or this time. He'd thought the emotional temperature of his world far too cool for such a thing.

The orchestra and choirs went right into "Hark! The Herald Angels Sing" with the same vigor and after that "God Rest Ye, Merry Gentle-men." A whole string of English carols followed, each one more exu-berant than the other. There was a jubilant authority to the music, and a spirit that seemed to engulf all present.

When a single soprano led the magnificent "O Holy Night," people actually began to cry. So powerful was her voice, and so lustrous and beautiful the song itself, that the tears came to Reuben's eyes. Susie leaned against Pastor George, who held her close and tight. Jim was beside Pastor George.

Stuart had come up to stand beside Reuben, and he too was singing as the orchestra moved into a solemn and urgent "O Come, All Ye Faithful" with the choir soaring over the rapturous strings and the deep throbbing French horns.

A silence fell with the rustling of the little paper candleholders and a few coughs and sneezes as one might hear in a packed church.

A thickly accented German voice spoke through the microphone. "And now I give the baton to our host, Felix Nideck, with pleasure."

Felix took the baton and held it high.

Then the orchestra struck up the first famous notes of Handel's "Hallelujah Chorus," and people seated throughout the giant pavilion rose to their feet. Even those slightly confused by this were rising on account of the others. Aunt Josie struggled to rise with the help of her nurse.

When the chorus broke forth with the first "Hallelujah" it was like the blast of a trumpet, and on and on the voices went rising, falling, and rising again, declaring with the orchestra surging beneath them the gorgeous anthems of the chorus.

All around Reuben people were singing, falling in and out of riffs of lyrics that they knew and humming with those they didn't know. On the voices roared: *"And he shall reign forever and ever!"*

Reuben pushed forward. He moved closer and closer towards the overwhelming sounds, until he stood close to Felix between the orchestra and the chorus, vigorously conducting with his right hand, the baton in his left.

"King of kings. Forever and ever!"

On and on in frenzy the music coursed towards its inevitable climax until there came the last great: "Ha Le Lu Jah!"

Felix's arms dropped to his sides, and he bowed his head.

The pavilion roared with applause. Voices broke out everywhere in a delirium of convivial thanks and praise.

Felix straightened and turned, his face positively glowing as he smiled. At once he broke and rushed to embrace the conductor, the choirmasters, and the concertmaster and then all the players and singers. On and on came the applause as they took their bows.

Reuben pushed his way towards him. When their eyes met, Felix held him closely. "Dear boy, for you, this Christmas, your first at Nideck Point," Felix whispered in his ear.

Others were reaching for Felix, calling his name.

Thibault took Reuben by the arm. "Easiest thing now is to stand by the door, or they'll all be stumbling around trying to find you to say good-bye."

And he was right.

They all took up their positions by the main entrance, including Felix. The medieval mummers and the tall gaunt St. Nicholas were also there, reaching into green sacks for coins and toys to give everyone.

For the next forty-five minutes people filed out, voicing their exuberant thanks. Some of the kids wanted to kiss St. Nicholas and feel his natural white mustache and beard, and he gladly obliged, offering his toys to the adults when there were no more children.

All the musicians and singers were soon gone, some declaring this the best Christmas festival they'd ever played for or attended. The night was filled with the rattle and throb of diesel buses pulling away.

Stuart's mother, Buffy Longstreet, was crying. She wanted Stuart to come with her back down to Los Angeles. Stuart was comforting her and explaining gently that he just couldn't do this as he walked her out to her car.

The exceptional women came to say their farewells together, and with the singular man, Hockan Crost, and that cinched it. Morphenkinder, had to be. Another, a dark-haired woman whom Reuben hadn't met before, confided her name to be Clarice as she took Reuben's hand, and told him how much she'd enjoyed the entire festival. She was his height in flat evening slippers, and wore a decidedly politically incorrect white fox-fur coat.

"You thrive in the public eye, don't you?" she said, her speech so very heavily accented that he found himself leaning forward, the better to hear her. "I am Russian," she explained, sensing the difficulty. "I am always learning English but never mastering it. This is all so innocent, so normal!" She made a soft scoffing sound. "Who would ever dream this was Yule?" The others were waiting a bit impatiently to say their good-byes, it seemed, and sensing it, she gave a petulant shrug and embraced Felix tightly, confiding something to him under her breath that made him smile a little tightly as he released her.

The other ladies embraced him in turn. Berenice, the pretty brunette who so closely resembled Frank, gave him long lingering kisses, and seemed suddenly sad, the tears plainly rising in her eyes. The woman he'd seen with Thibault introduced herself as Dorchella, and offered her thanks warmly as she left. The tall pale Fiona of the diamonds appeared to be rushing the others. She kissed Reuben brusquely on the cheek. "You bring a strange new life to this great house," she whispered. "You and all your family. Aren't you afraid?"

"Afraid of what?" he asked.

"Don't you know?" she asked. "Ah, youth and its eternal optimism."

"I'm not following," said Reuben. "What is there to be afraid of?"

"The attention, of course," said she quickly. "What else?"

But before he could respond, she'd turned to Felix.

"I marvel that you think you can get away with all this," she said. "You don't learn, do you, from experience?"

"Always learning, Fiona," said Felix. "We are born into this world to learn, to love, and to serve."

"That's the dreariest thing I've ever heard," said Fiona.

He flashed a brilliant and perfect smile on her. "How very good of you to come, young Fiona," he said with seeming sincerity. "Delighted to have you as a guest under this roof anytime. Don't you agree with me, Reuben?"

"Yes, absolutely," said Reuben. "Thank you so much for coming."

A deep anger darkened Fiona's face, her eyes moving quickly over both of them. Does anger have a scent, and what would her scent be if she weren't a Morphenkind? Behind her, the woman named Helena pressed in, and put a hand on Fiona's shoulder.

"You think you can get away with anything, Felix," said Fiona, voice uglier than before, a flush beating in her cheeks. "I think you like heartbreak."

"Good-bye, my dear," said Felix with the same even courtesy. "Safe journey." The two women withdrew without another word. Catrin went with them, flashing a smile at both Felix and Reuben.

Yes, Morphenkinder, because some scent of malice would have arisen from all that, but there had been nothing.

Hockan Crost's eyes lingered on Reuben for a long moment, but Felix at once spoke up in his usual convivial manner, "Always good to see you, Hockan, you know that."

"Oh, indeed, old friend," said Hockan in his deep melodious voice. There was something wistful in his expression. "We need to meet, we need to talk," he said emphasizing the word *need* both times.

"I'm more than willing," said Felix earnestly. "When have I ever closed my doors to you? And during Midwinter? Never. I hope we see you soon again."

"Yes, you will," said the man. He looked troubled, and there was something immediately appealing about him, in the way he let his feelings come to the fore, in the imploring way in which he spoke. "There are things I have to say, beloved Felix." He was pleading with dignity. "I want you to hear me out."

"Indeed, and we will have the chance to talk together, won't we?" said Felix. To Reuben he said, "This is my old and dear friend, Reuben. Hockan Crost. He should always be welcome day or night here."

Reuben nodded and murmured his approval.

Then the man, glancing at the guests crowding towards the exit, and sensing that this was not the time and the place for any more talk, moved on.

And they were gone, the mysterious ones, all this confusing and unsettling talk having taken no more than two or three minutes. Felix gave Reuben a pointed and meaningful glance, and then sighed audibly with eloquent relief.

"You recognized your kindred, didn't you?" he asked.

"Yes," said Reuben. "Most definitely yes."

"And for now, forget about them," said Felix, and he went back to the farewells with renewed spirit.

Susie Blakely gave Reuben a hug as she came to say good-bye. Pastor George whispered, "You can't imagine the change in her! I can't tell you. She actually had fun!"

"I saw it. I'm so happy for her. And please, stay in touch with me."

Off they went.

Of course the family and closest friends remained for a while longer, together with Galton, Mayor Cronin, and Dr. Cutler, and some of Stuart's old gay boyfriends. But then even Celeste and Mort said they were tired and had to be going, and Grace, after hugging each of the Distinguished Gentlemen in turn, kissed Reuben good-bye, leaving with Aunt Josie, Cousin Shelby and Clifford, and Uncle Tim and his wife, Helen.

Finally Stuart's friends wandered out into the night also, one of them singing the "Hallelujah Chorus" at the top of his lungs, the mayor and Galton left arguing with each other over something to do with the village festival, and the giant plastic flaps of the tent doors came down on the damp and gusty darkness. The windows to the main room were being shut up and locked.

Then it was to the kitchen, where Felix wanted to personally thank the maids and the entire catering team. Would Reuben please join him? And he would show Reuben just how he liked to do these things.

Reuben was eager to learn. Tipping people had always made him very nervous.

Lisa appeared right beside them with a large leather purse from which Felix took one white envelope after another to present to each individual cook, server, waiter or waitress, and maid as he gave thanks. Soon he deferred to Reuben and handed the envelopes to him to give to the workers, and Reuben did his level best to assume the same gracious manner, discovering how easily the awkward matter of tipping could be handled if he just looked people right in the eye.

Last, they handed out envelopes to the surprised teenage volunteers who had been the upstairs docents and guides and who had not expected any such special consideration. They were delighted.

The other Distinguished Gentlemen had wandered off. Soon only Lisa and Jean Pierre and Heddy were left putting this or that little thing in order, and Felix had flopped down in the wing chair by the library fire, kicking off his patent-leather dress shoes.

Reuben stood there drinking a cup of hot chocolate and looking down into the flames. He wanted so to tell Felix about having seen Marchent, but he couldn't bring himself to confide this just yet. It would alter Felix's mood too dramatically, and perhaps it would alter his own mood as well.

"This is where I secretly and quietly relive every minute of the evening," said Felix happily, "and ask myself what I might have done better and what I might do next year."

"You know these people mostly had never seen anything like this," said Reuben. "I don't think my parents in all their lives ever contemplated giving a large party let alone something even remotely like this." He sat down in the club chair and confessed how he himself had only been to the symphony maybe four times in his entire life, and had only heard Handel's *Messiah* once, during which he had fallen asleep. The fact was, parties had always been a bore to him, and mostly involved tiny hors d'oeuvres on plastic plates, white wine in plastic glasses that wouldn't stain anybody's carpet or linen, and people who couldn't wait to leave. The last time he'd had this much fun was at a "bring your own bottle" party in Berkeley where the only food had been pizza and there hadn't been much of that.

Then, quite suddenly with a violent start, he remembered Phil. Was Phil still here? "Good God, where is my dad?"

"Taken care of, dear boy," said Felix. "He's in the best room in the middle of the east side. Lisa took him up, saw to it that he had everything he needed. I think he's here to stay, but he doesn't want to presume."

Reuben sat back. "But Felix, what does that mean about our own Yuletide?" he asked. Never mind the sadness he felt that his parents were in fact drifting apart, far apart. That was nothing new, after all.

"Well, Reuben, we will ask for his indulgence on that night when we go out into the forest. We'll call it a European thing, you know.

Something like that. I'll speak with him about it. I'm sure he will gladly allow us our private Old World customs. He knows so much history, your father. He knows so much about the old pagan ways in Europe. He's a reader of wide scholarship. And he has that Celtic gift."

Reuben felt uneasy.

"Is it a powerful gift?" he asked.

"Well, I think it is," said Felix, "but don't you know?"

"We've never talked about it, me and Phil," he said. "I do recall his saying his grandmother saw ghosts and that he'd seen them, but that was all there was to it. In our house, people weren't very receptive to that kind of talk."

"Well, there's a great deal more, I'm sure. But the main thing is you needn't be the least concerned. I'll explain that on Christmas Eve we have our private customs."

"Yeah, sure," said Reuben. Lisa was filling his cup with hot chocolate again. "That's how we'll handle it, of course.

"Listen, there's something I have to confess," said Reuben. He waited until Lisa had left the library. "There was a little girl here tonight—."

"I know, dear boy. I saw her. I recognized her from the papers. I greeted her and her friend when they came in. They didn't expect to be admitted so easily. They asked to speak to you. I told them everyone was welcome. I insisted they join the party. I told them they'd find you in the main room. And I saw you later with them by the crèche. You had quite a good effect on the little girl's spirits."

"You know, I didn't reveal anything to her, not deliberately in any event. I was just trying to assure her that yes, the Man Wolf was real, and what she'd seen was real—."

"Don't worry. I knew that's what you would do. I trusted that you would handle it beautifully, and I saw that you did."

"Felix, I think maybe she suspected . . . because I might have said something, just something offhand that made her recognize me, I mean, for a minute anyway. I'm not sure."

"Don't worry, Reuben. Do you realize how few people tonight even mentioned the Man Wolf, or asked about the scene here? Oh, there was a lot of whispering, but it was the party that mattered tonight.

Let's enjoy our pleasant memories of the party. And if the little girl is troubled, well, we'll deal with that when the time comes."

There was a moment of silence and then Felix said, "I know you were quite mystified with Hockan Crost and a number of the others tonight," he said. "Stuart's no doubt puzzled by them as well."

Reuben's heart skipped a beat. "Morphenkinder, obviously."

Felix sighed. "Oh, if you knew how little I care for their company."

"I think I understand. They made me curious, that's all. I guess it's only natural."

"They've never approved very much of me and my ways," said Felix. "This house, my old family. And the village, they've never understood my love of the village. They don't understand the things I do. And they blame me for some of my own misfortune."

"So I gathered," said Reuben.

"But at Midwinter Morphenkinder never turn away their own kind. And it's never been my policy to turn away others at any time, really. There are ways to live this life, and my way has always been one of inclusion—of our own kind, of all humankind, of all spirits, of all things under the sun. It's not a virtue with me. I don't know any other way to move through the world."

"But you didn't actually invite them."

"I did not invite them, no, but then all the world was invited. And they knew that. And I'm not surprised that they came, and it's understood that they may join us for the Yule celebration. And if they come, we will of course include them. But frankly, I don't think they will. They have their own ways of celebrating Yule."

"That man, Hockan Crost, you seemed to like him," Reuben ventured.

"Did you?"

"He's very impressive," said Reuben. "His voice is positively beautiful."

"He's always been something of a poet and an orator," said Felix, "and he is magnetic, and I daresay immensely attractive. Those black eyebrows of his, those black eyes, and the white mane of hair; he's quite unforgettable."

"And is he old and experienced?" asked Reuben.

"Yes," said Felix. "Oh, nothing as old as Margon. There is no one as old as Margon, and no one as widely respected as Margon. And Hockan is kin to us, I mean quite literally kin to us. We have our differences but I can't dislike him. There are times when I've deeply appreciated Hockan. It's Helena one has to be wary of, and Fiona."

"I caught that, but why? What is it that so offends them?"

"Anything and everything I do," he said. "They have a way of interfering in the business of others, but only when it suits them." He seemed annoyed. "Helena's hearty, proud of her age, of her experience. But the truth is she's very young in our world, and so is Fiona—and certainly in our company."

Reuben remembered Fiona's unusually intrusive question as to whether Phil was coming to live at Nideck Point. He repeated the exchange to Felix. "I couldn't imagine why this concerned her."

"She's concerned because he's not one of us," said Felix. "And she can damn well keep out of it. I have always lived among human beings, always. My descendants lived here for generations. And this is my home and this is your home. She can keep her bloody notions to herself." He sighed.

Reuben's head was swimming.

"I'm sorry," said Felix. "I didn't mean to become so very unpleasant. Fiona has a way of provoking me." He extended his hand suddenly. "Reuben, don't let me alarm you with all this. They're not a particularly frightening bunch of kindred. They're a little bit more, well, brutal than we are. It's just that right now they share the Americas with us, so to speak. It could be worse. The Americas are enormous, aren't they?" He laughed under his breath. "There could be a lot more of us."

"Are they a pack, then, a pack with a leader in Hockan?"

"Not exactly," he said. "If there is a pack there, it's the women under Helena, and excluding Berenice. Berenice used to spend a lot of time with us, though not lately. But Hockan's been with them off and on for a very long time now. Hockan has suffered his own losses, his own tragedies. I think Hockan's under the spell of Helena. They used to confine themselves to the European continent, this bunch, but it's sim-

ply too hard now for Morphenkinder in Europe, especially Morphenkinder who believe in human sacrifice at Midwinter." He gave a scornful
laugh. "And the Morphenkinder of Asia are more jealous of territory
than we tend to be. So they're here, in the Americas, now, been here for
decades actually, searching perhaps for some special locale. I don't
know. I don't invite their confidences. And frankly, I wish Berenice
would leave them, and come live with us, if Frank could bear it."

"Human sacrifice!" Reuben winced.

"Oh, it's not all that horrifying, really. They select an evildoer, some
utterly reprehensible and unredeemable scoundrel, some murderer, and
they drug the poor bastard till he's in a perfect stupor, and then they
feast on him at midnight on Christmas Eve. Sounds worse than it
really is, considering what we're all capable of. I don't like it. I won't
make the killing of evildoers ceremonial. I refuse to incorporate it into
ritual. I refuse."

"I hear you."

"Put it out of your mind. They talk big but lack a certain collective
or personal resolve."

"I think I see what's happened," said Reuben. "You were gone from
here for twenty years. And now you're back—all of you—and they've
come to look the place over again."

"That's it, exactly," said Felix with a bitter smile. "And where were
they when we were captive and struggling to survive?" His voice grew
heated. "Didn't see hide nor hair of them. Of course they didn't know
where we were, or so they've said. And said. And said. And yes, we're
back in North America, and they are, shall we say, curious? They make
me think of moths collecting around a bright light."

"Are there others, others besides these, who might show up at the
Yule?"

"Not likely."

"But what about Hugo, that strange Morphenkind we met in the
jungles?"

"Oh, Hugo never leaves that ghastly place. I don't think Hugo has
found his way out of the jungles now for five hundred years. Hugo
moves from one jungle outpost to another. When his present shelter

ultimately collapses, he'll seek another. You can forget about Hugo. But as to whether others might come, well, I honestly don't know. There's no universal census of Morphenkinder. And I'll tell you something else if you promise to put it out of your mind immediately."

"I'll try."

"We aren't all the same species either."

"Good God!"

"Why did I know you'd turn the color of ashes when I told you that? Look. Truly, it doesn't matter. Now, don't get agitated. This is why I so hate to inundate you with information. Leave the others to me for the time being. Leave the world to me, and all its myriad predatory immortals."

" 'All its myriad predatory immortals'?"

Felix laughed. "I'm playing with you."

"I wonder if you are."

"No, truly. You're easy to tease, Reuben. You always respond."

"But Felix, are there universally accepted rules about all this?—I mean do all Morphenkinder agree on this or that law, or—?"

"Hardly!" he said with thinly concealed disgust. "But there are customs among our kind. That's what I was referring to earlier, the Yuletide customs. We receive each other at Yuletide with courtesy, and woe to one who breaks those customs." He paused for a moment. "Not all Morphenkinder have a place to celebrate the Yule as we do. And so if others join us on Modranicht, well, we welcome them."

"Modranicht," said Reuben with a smile. "I've never heard that name for the Yule spoken aloud."

"But you know the word, don't you?"

"Night of the Mother," said Reuben. "From the Venerable Bede, in describing the Anglo-Saxons."

Felix laughed softly. "You never let me down, my beloved scholar."

"Night of the Mother Earth," said Reuben, relishing the words, the thought, and Felix's pleasure.

Felix went silent for a moment, and then went on:

"In the old days—the old days for Margon, that is—Yuletide was the time to come together, to pledge fidelity, to pledge to live in peace, to reaffirm the resolves to love, to learn, and to serve. That's what the teacher taught me a very long time ago. That's what he taught Frank, and Sergei, and Thibault as well. And that's what Yule still means to us, to *us,*" he emphasized, "a time of renewal and rebirth, no matter what the hell it means to Helena and the others."

Reuben repeated it: "To love, to learn, and to serve."

"Well, it's not as dreadful as I've made it sound," said Felix. "We don't make speeches, we don't offer prayers. Not really."

"It doesn't sound dreadful at all. It sounds like one of those concise formulas I've been searching for all my life. And I saw it tonight, I saw it in the party, I saw it infecting the guests like some kind of wonderful intoxicant. I saw so many people behaving and responding in the most unusual way. I don't think my family has ever much held with ceremonies, holidays, any celebration of renewal. It's as if the world's gone past all that."

"Ah, but the world never does go past all that," said Felix. "And for those of us who cannot age, we must find a way to mark the passage of the years, to celebrate our own determination to renew our spirits and our ideals. We're fastened to time, but time doesn't affect us. And if we don't watch it, if we live as if there were no time, well, time can kill us. Hell, Yuletide is when we resolve to try to do better than we have in the past, that's all."

"New Year's resolutions of the soul," said Reuben.

"Amen. Come, let's forget about the others and go walk in the oaks. The rain has stopped. I never had a chance to walk in the oaks while the party was in full swing."

"Me either, and I so want to do that," said Reuben.

Quickly getting their coats, they went out together into the marvel of the lighted forest.

How still and quiet it was in the soft lovely illumination, rather like the enchanted place it had been when he'd first wandered out here alone.

Reuben looked around in the shadowy tangles of gray limbs, wondering if the Forest Gentry surrounded them, if they were up high in the branches above them.

On and on they walked, past the scattered party tables, and deeper and deeper into the fairy-tale gloaming.

Felix was quiet, deep in his own thoughts. Reuben so hated to disturb him, to ruin his contentment and his obvious happiness.

But he felt he had to do this. He had no choice. He had put it off long enough. It ought to be happy news, he thought, so why was he hesitating? Why was he torn?

"I saw Marchent today," he confessed. "I saw her more than once, and it was markedly different."

"Did you?" Felix was obviously startled. "Where? Tell me. Tell me everything." There came that immediate distress that was completely unnatural to Felix. Even with all the talk of the other Morphenkinder, he hadn't been this suddenly anguished.

Reuben explained that long glimpse in the village when he'd seen her in company with Elthram, moving about with him as if she were fully material, and then the moment in the dark corner of the conservatory as if she'd answered his summons. "I'm sorry I didn't immediately tell you. I can't explain exactly. It was so intense."

"Oh, I understand," said Felix. "That doesn't matter. You saw her. That's what matters. I couldn't have seen her, whether you told me about it or not."

Felix sighed.

He held the backs of his arms with his hands, that gesture Reuben had seen in him when they had first spoken of Marchent's spirit.

"They have broken through," he said sadly. "Just as I hoped they would. And they can take her away now when she's willing to go. They can provide their way, their answers."

"But where do they go, Felix? Where were they when you called to them?"

"I don't know," he answered. "Some of them are always here. Some of them are always wandering. They are wherever the woods are thickest and darkest and most quiet and undisturbed. I called them together. I called to Elthram, that's what I did. Whether they ever really go far away, I can't say. But it's not their way to gather in one place, or to repeatedly show themselves."

"And she will become one of them?"

"You saw what you saw," he said. "I would say it's already happened."

"Will there be no moment in which I can actually talk to her?" asked Reuben. He had lowered his voice to a whisper—not because he feared the Forest Gentry would hear, but because he was opening his soul to Felix. "I had thought, perhaps, there would be some moment. And yet when I saw her in the conservatory, I didn't ask for this. I felt a kind of paralysis, an absence of any rational thought. I didn't let her know how badly I wanted to talk to her."

"It was she who came to you, remember," said Felix. "It was she who tried to speak, she who had the questions. And maybe now they've been answered."

"I pray that's true," said Reuben. "She looked content. She looked whole."

Felix stood silent for a moment, merely reflecting, his eyes moving gently over Reuben's face. He gave a faint smile.

"Come, I'm getting colder and colder," he said. "Let's go back. She has time in which to speak to you. Plenty of time. Keep in mind the Forest Gentry won't leave before Christmas Day and probably not before New Year's. It's too important to them to be here when we make our circle. The Forest Gently will sing with us and play their fiddles and their flutes and their drums."

Reuben tried to envision it. "That's going to be indescribable."

"It varies from time to time, what they bring to the ceremony. But they're always gentle, always good, always filled with the true meaning of renewal. They're the essence of the love for this earth and for its cycles, its processes, its ever renewing itself. They have no taste for human sacrifice at Midwinter, I can tell you. Nothing would drive them away sooner than that. And of course they like you, Reuben, very much."

"So Elthram said," said Reuben. "But I suspect it was Laura walking in the woods who stole their hearts."

"Ah, yes, well, they call you the Keeper of the Woods," said Felix. "And they call her the Lady of the Woods. And Elthram knows what you've suffered with Marchent. I don't think he means to abandon you without some resolution with Marchent. Even if the spirit of Marchent moves on, Elthram will have something to say to you before New Year's, I'm certain of it."

"And what do you hope for, Felix, with regard to Marchent?"

"That she'll soon be at peace," he said. "The same thing you hope for, and that she's forgiven me for all the things I did that were wrong, and unwise, and foolish. But do keep in the mind that the Forest Gentry are distractible."

"How do you mean?"

"All spirits, ghosts, the bodiless—they're distractible," said Felix. "They're not rooted in the physical and so they're not fastened to time. They lose track of the things that cause such pain in us. This is not infidelity on their part. It's the ethereal nature of spirits. It's only in the physical that they are focused."

"I remember Elthram using that word."

"Yes, well, it's an important word. It's Margon's theory that they cannot truly grow in moral stature, these spirits, unless they're in the physical. But we're too deep in this woods to be uttering Margon's name." He laughed. "Don't want to anger anyone unnecessarily."

The rain was starting again. Reuben could see it swirling in the lights as if the drops were too light to fall to the ground.

Felix stopped. Reuben stood beside him waiting.

Slowly, he saw the Forest Gentry materializing. They were in the branches again as they'd been earlier. He saw their faces coming clear, saw their dark shapeless clothes, knees crooked, soft booted feet on the branches, saw the impassive eyes regarding them, saw those tiny child faces like flower petals.

In the ancient tongue, Felix said something to them, what sounded like a soft rush of greeting. But he kept walking. Reuben kept walking.

There was a lot of snapping and rustling in the trees, and a shower of tiny green leaves appeared suddenly, leaves that swirled like the rain, only gradually falling to the earth. The Forest Gentry were vanishing.

They continued on in silence.

"They're still around us, aren't they?" Reuben asked.

Felix only smiled.

Alone in his room, in his pajamas and robe, Reuben tried to write about the entire day.

He didn't want to lose the vivid mind pictures crowding his brain, or the questions, or the sharp remembrances of special moments.

But he found himself merely listing all the many things that had happened, in loose order, and listing the people he'd seen and met.

On and on went his list.

He was simply too stimulated and dazed to really absorb why it had all been so much fun, and so unlike anything he'd ever done or known. But again and again, he recorded details, the simplest to the most complex. He wrote in a kind of code about the Forest Gentry, "Our woodland neighbors" and their "wan" children, and just when he thought he could remember nothing else he began describing the carols played and sung, and the various dishes that had covered the table, and the descriptions of those memorable beauties who'd walked like goddesses through the rooms.

He took some time describing the Morphenkinder women— Fiona, Catrin, Berenice, Dorchella, Helena, Clarice. And as he tried to remember each one as to hair coloring, facial features, and lavish dress it struck him that they had not all been conventionally beautiful, not by any means. But what had marked them all was luxuriant hair and what people call demeanor. They had possessed what someone might call a regal demeanor.

They had dressed themselves and carried themselves with exceptional confidence. A fearlessness surrounded them. But there was something else, too. A kind of low seductive heat came off these women, at least as Reuben saw it. It was impossible to revisit any one in his imagination without feeling that heat. Even the very sweet Berenice, Frank's wife, had exuded this kind of inviting sexuality.

Was it a mystery of beast and human intermingled in the Morphenkind where hormones and pheromones of a new and mysterious potency were working on the species subliminally? Probably. How could it not be?

He described Hockan Crost—the man's deep-set black eyes, and his large hands and the way the man had looked him over so obviously before acknowledging him. He noted how different the man had seemed when saying his farewells to Felix, how warm, how almost needful. And then there was that low, running voice of his, the exquisite way he pronounced his words, so persuasive.

There had to be some way male Morphenkinder knew one another too, he figured, whether or not the erotic signals were forthcoming. Hadn't he felt some very similar set of tiny alarm bells the first time he'd met Felix? He wasn't sure. And then what about the first few moments of the disastrous encounter with the doomed Marrok? It was as if the world was reduced to pen and ink when a Morphenkind was on the scene and the Morphenkind was done in rich oil paint.

He didn't write the word "Morphenkind." He would never write it down, not in his most secret computer diary. He wrote, "The usual questions abound." And then he asked: "Is it possible for us to despise one another?"

He wrote about Marchent. He described the apparitions in detail, searching his memory for the smallest things that he might remember. But the apparitions were like dreams. Too many key details had faded. Again, he was so careful with his words. What he'd written might have been a poem of remembrance. But he was comforted that Marchent's entire aspect had changed, that he'd seen nothing of misery or pain at all in her. But he had seen something else, and he didn't know what that was. And it had not been entirely consoling. But was it conceivable that he and this ghost could actually speak to one another? He wanted that with his whole soul, and yet he feared it.

He was half asleep on the pillow when he woke thinking of Laura, Laura on her own in the forest to the south, Laura having changed unimaginably into a full and mysterious Morphenkind, Laura, his precious Laura, and he found himself uttering a prayer for her and wondering if there was a God who listened to the prayers of Morphenkinder. Well, if there was a God, perhaps he listened to everyone, and if he didn't, well, what hope was there at all? Keep her safe, he prayed, keep her safe from man and beast, and keep her safe from other Morphenkinder. He could not think of her and think of that strange overbearing Fiona. No. She was his Laura, and they would travel this bizarre road into revelation and experience together.

20

It was one of the fastest weeks of Reuben's life. Having his dad in residence was infinitely more fun than he'd ever imagined, especially since the entire household welcomed Phil, and everyone assumed that Phil had come to stay. It took Reuben's mind off absolutely everything else.

Meanwhile, the house recovered from the banquet and moved towards Christmas Eve.

The pavilion had been completely cleared by evening on Tuesday, the wooden wind barrier, the tents, and the rented furniture all hauled away. The great marble crèche and stable, with all its lighting and fir trees, had been immediately moved down to the village of Nideck, where it had been set up for the public in the old theater across from the Inn.

The beautiful lighting of the house—of all its windows and gables—and the lighting of the oak forest remained as before. Felix said the lights would remain until Twelfth Night—January 6, or the Feast of the Epiphany—as was the tradition, and there would be people coming up now and then to wander through the woods.

"But not on Christmas Eve," said Felix. "That night the property is dark for us and our Yule."

Phil's books arrived on Wednesday, and so did a venerable old trunk that Phil's grandfather Edward O'Connell had brought from Ireland. At once Phil started telling Reuben all about the old man, and their times together when Phil was a boy. By the time he was twelve, Phil had lost his grandparents, but he remembered them vividly. Reuben had never in all his life heard Phil talk about this. He wanted to ask all about the grandparents. He wanted to ask about the gift of seeing ghosts, but he didn't dare to broach the subject. Not now, not so soon, not so close to Christmas Eve, when a veil had to come down between him and his father.

All this took Reuben's mind off the faintly disturbing memory of the Morphenkinder at the party, and his driving anticipation for the Yuletide reunion with Laura.

At breakfast on Thursday, Margon had told them all offhandedly to pay little mind to the "strange uninvited guests" who'd come to the banquet. To Stuart's immediate barrage of questions, he replied, "Our species is ancient. You know that. You know there are Morphenkinder throughout the world. Why wouldn't there be? And you can see well enough how we come together in packs as wolves do, and packs have their territory, do they not? But we are not wolves, and we do not fight those who come now and then into our territory. We bear with them until they move on. That has always been our way."

"But I can see damn well that you don't like those others," said Stuart. "And that Helena, she was frightening. Is she lovers with that man, Hockan? And when you talk about our inherent sense of good and evil, well, I can't connect it to that dislike. What happens when you hate a perfectly innocent and upright fellow Morphenkind?"

"That's just it, we don't hate!" said Sergei. "We are resolved never to hate, and never to quarrel. And yes, from time to time, there is trouble. Yes, I admit, there is trouble. But it's over quickly, as it is with wolves, and then we go, finding our own peaceful parts of the world, laying claim to them."

"That might be what's bothering them the most," said Thibault softly. He glanced at Margon, and when Margon didn't interrupt, he continued. "We have laid claim once more to this part of the world, and we have an enduring strength which others find—well, enviable."

"Doesn't matter," said Margon, raising his voice. "This is Yule and we receive all others as we've always done—even Helena and Fiona."

It was Felix who brought the discussion to a decisive close, announcing that the guesthouse was now completely ready for Phil, and he wanted to take father and son down now to see it. He confessed that he was mildly annoyed the workers hadn't had it ready before the ban-quiet, but then he'd pulled them off the guesthouse to work on the party and, well, it just didn't get done. "It's ready now for your father," he said to Reuben, "and I can't wait to show him the place."

At once they went up to collect Phil, who'd just finished his own breakfast, and the three proceeded down the cliff in the light rain.

The workmen were gone, all the plastic draping and debris had been taken away, and Felix's "little masterpiece," as he called it, was ready for inspection.

It was a spacious gray-shingled cottage with a high-peaked roof and stone chimney. Trellises on the front flanked its double doors where vines would be replanted in spring, said Felix, and the garden beds would be full of flowers. "I'm told that's how it used to be," said Felix, "one of the most charming spots on the whole property." There was quite a little patio now restored in front of the cottage, of old flags uncovered and patched, where Phil could sit out in the spring and summer, and that too would be wreathed in spring flowers. This was the place for geraniums, said Felix. Geraniums love the ocean air. And he promised that it would be spectacular. Giant old rhododendrons grew beyond the trellises in both directions, and when they came into bloom, said Felix, they would be a vision of purple blossoms. In the old days, he'd been told that the house was always covered in honeysuckle, and bougainvillea and ivy, and it would be once again.

A giant sprawling scrub oak stood just below the house on the edge of the patio and there was an old iron bench circling its immense gray trunk.

Reuben had seen little really of the building when first he ventured here with Marchent, to a half-burnt ruin surrounded by Monterey pines and hidden by weeds and bracken.

The little guesthouse hung right on the cliff over the ocean, its large small-paned windows having an unobstructed view of the slate-colored sea. Thick scatter rugs covered the highly polished wide-plank floors, and the bathroom had been upgraded to a marble shower and tub fit for royalty, or so Phil claimed.

There was plenty of room in the parlor bedroom for an oak rocking chair by the large Craftsman-style fireplace opposite a leather recliner, and a rectangular oak table under the window. The bed was on the far north wall opposite the fireplace with a curved lamp at the head for reading. And a good-sized oak desk facing the room fitted comfortably in the far right corner.

A wooden corkscrew stair to the left of the front door went up to a huge finished attic. The window from there had the best view of the sea and the surrounding cliffs as Reuben saw it, and Phil might eventually work up there, yes, he said, but for now the coziness of the house proper was perfect for him.

Felix had picked these furnishings, but assured Phil that he must make the place his own and replace or remove anything that wasn't to his liking.

Phil was grateful for all of it. And Phil was comfortably ensconced by nightfall.

On the desk he set up his computer and favorite old brass desk lamp, and tolerated the newly installed telephone though he said he would never answer it.

Built-in bookshelves flanking the large fieldstone fireplace were soon filled from the cardboard boxes arriving from San Francisco, plenty of wood was stacked nearby, and the little kitchen was fitted out with Phil's special espresso machine, and a microwave, which was all he needed, he claimed, to live the hermit life of his dreams. There was a small table beneath the window just big enough for two people.

Lisa stocked the refrigerator for him with yogurt, fresh fruit, avocados, tomatoes, and all the raw stuff he ate all day. But she had no intention, she declared more than once, of leaving him to his own devices here.

A faded patchwork quilt appeared on the daybed, which Phil explained had been made by his grandmother Alice O'Connell. Reuben had never seen this before, and was vaguely fascinated that such family relics even existed. Phil said it was the wedding-ring pattern, and his grandmother had made it before she was married. A couple more things came out of the trunk, including a little white cream pitcher that had belonged to Grandma Alice, and several old silver-plate spoons with the initials O'C on the handles.

And he takes out these old treasures, Reuben thought, that he's had all these years, and puts the quilt on his bed here because he feels that he can do that now.

Though Phil claimed he didn't need the huge flat-screen TV over the fireplace, he soon had it turned on with the sound down constantly, as he played one DVD after another from a library of his treasured "great films."

The rocky paths from the guesthouse to the terrace or to the road were no problem at all for Phil, who had dug out yet another family heirloom from his trunk, an old shillelagh that had belonged to Edward O'Connell. It was a thick and beautifully polished stick with a weighted knob at the end for popping people over the head, presumably, and made the perfect staff for long walks, during which Phil wore a soft gray-wool flat cap that had once belonged to old Edward O'Connell, as well.

With that cap and staff, Phil disappeared for hours on end, rain or shine, into the broad Nideck forests, often not appearing till well after supper when Lisa would force him to sit down at the kitchen table and take a meal of beef stew and French bread. Lisa went down every morning, too, with his breakfast, though often he was gone before she got there, and she left the meal for him on the counter in his little kitchen while she cleaned the guesthouse and made his bed.

A number of times Reuben had roamed down to talk to him, but finding him typing away furiously on the computer, he'd stood outside for a while and then wandered back up the slope. Towards the end of the week, Sergei or Felix might be found visiting with Phil, in fast conversation about some matter of history or the history of poetry or drama. Felix borrowed Phil's two-volume *Mediaeval Stage* by E. K. Chambers and sat for hours in the library poring over it, marveling at Phil's carefully written notes.

It was all going to work out, that was the point, and Felix cautioned Reuben not to worry about it for a single moment more.

The fact was, the Distinguished Gentlemen all loved Phil and were obviously glad of the one night he did come to the big table for the evening meal.

Lisa had all but dragged Phil to it, and the conversation had been great, having to do with the peculiarities of Shakespeare that people mistakenly took as representative of the way people had written in Shakespeare's time, but were not at all typical, and rather a bit mysterious—as Phil so loved to explore. Margon knew vast blocks of Shakespeare by heart and they had fun going back and forth with chapter and verse of *Othello*. But it was *King Lear* that fascinated Phil above all.

"I should be mad and raving on the heath," said Phil. "By all rights, that's exactly where I should be, but I'm not. I'm here, and I'm happier than I've been in years."

Of course Stuart threw out the schoolboy questions about the play. Wasn't the king crazy? And if he was, how could it be a tragedy? And why had he been such a fool as to give all his property to his kids?

Phil laughed and laughed, and never really gave a direct answer, saying finally, "Well, maybe the genius of the play, son, is that all that's true, but we don't care."

Each and every one of the Distinguished Gentlemen, and even Stuart, told Reuben individually how much they liked Phil and how much they wished he'd come to dinner every night, Stuart summing it up with "You know, Reuben, you are so lucky, I mean even your dad is completely exceptionally cool."

What a far cry from the house on Russian Hill where no one paid the slightest attention to Phil, and Celeste had so often secretly remarked that he was almost unendurable. *I feel so sorry for your mother.*

There was evidence that certain other mysterious people also loved Phil. On Friday evening, Phil had wandered into the cottage, badly stung by bees on his face and on his hand. Reuben had immediately been alarmed and called Lisa in the main house for Benadryl. But Phil waved it all away. Could have been so much worse than it was.

"They were in a hollowed-out oak," he said, "and I tripped and fell against it. They were swarming, but fortunately for me, your friends came along, those forest people, you know the ones who were at the fair and the party."

"Right. Which people exactly?" asked Felix.

"Oh, you know, the green-eyed man with the dark skin, that amazing man—Elthram. That's his name, Elthram. I tell you the fellow is strong. He carried me away from those bees, just picked me up and carried me. This could have been a lot worse. They got me three times here, and he laid his hands on it, and I'm telling you he has some gift. It was really swelling. Not hurting now at all."

"Better take the Benadryl anyway," said Reuben.

"Well, you know, those are nice people, those people. Where do they live, exactly?"

"All through the forest, sort of," said Reuben.

"No, but I mean where do they live?" asked Phil. "Where's their home? They were the nicest. I'd like to invite them in for coffee. I'd love to have them as company."

Lisa came rushing in.

Reuben already had a glass of water ready.

"You need to stay out of that area," she said. "Those were African killer bees, and they're very aggressive."

Phil laughed. "Well, how on earth do you know where I was roaming, Lisa?"

"Because Elthram told me," she said. "Good thing he was looking out for you."

"I was just saying to Reuben that they are the nicest people, that family. He and that beautiful redheaded Mara."

"I don't think I've ever met Mara," said Reuben, struggling to say this in a normal believable voice.

"Well, she was at the fair in the town," said Phil. "Don't know that she came to the party. Beautiful red hair, and clear skin, like your mother."

"Well, stay out of that part of the woods, Philip," said Lisa sharply. "And take these pills now before you get a fever."

On Saturday Reuben went into San Francisco to pick up his gifts for family and for friends. Everything had been purchased by phone or online through a rare-book dealer, and Reuben inspected each selection personally before having each wrapped with the appropriate card. For Grace, he'd found a nineteenth-century memoir by an obscure doctor who described a long and heroic life in medicine on the frontier. For Laura, the *Duino Elegies and the Sonnets to Orpheus* of Rilke in a first edition. For Margon he had an early special edition of T. E. Lawrence's autobiography, and for Felix, Thibault, and Stuart fine and early hardcovers of several English ghost-story writers—Amelia Edwards, Sheridan Le Fanu, and Algernon Blackwood—whom Reuben especially treasured. He had vintage travelers' memoirs for Sergei and for Frank, and Lisa; and books of English and French poetry for Heddy and Jean Pierre. For Celeste, he had a special leather-bound copy of the autobiography of Clarence Darrow; and for Mort a vintage edition of Hawthorne's *The House of the Seven Gables,* which he knew Mort loved.

For Jim, he had books on filmmakers Robert Bresson and Luis Buñuel and a first edition of Lord Acton's essays. For Stuart, a couple of great books on J. R. R. Tolkien, C. S. Lewis, and the Inklings, as well as a new verse translation of *Sir Gawain and the Green Knight.*

Lastly for Phil, he had managed at last to score all the small individual hardcover volumes of Shakespeare's plays edited by George Lyman Kittredge—the little Ginn and Company books which Phil had so loved in his student days. This was a crate of books, all clean of markings and in excellent condition, on good paper and with good print.

After that, he rounded up some newer books to be added to the mix—books by Teilhard de Chardin, Sam Keen, Brian Greene, and others—and then he shopped for some personal gifts for his beloved housekeeper Rosie—perfume, a purse, some pretty things. For Lisa he had found a particularly fine cameo in a San Francisco shop, and for Jean Pierre and Heddy cashmere scarves. And finally he called it quits.

The Russian Hill house was empty when he got there. After putting all the family gifts quietly under the tree, he headed for home.

Sunday, he spent the entire morning writing a long piece for Billie on the evolving concept of Christmas and New Year's in America, since the ban on all Christmas celebrations in the early colonies to the condemnations today of the commercial nature of the feast. He realized how happy he was writing this kind of informal essay, and how much he preferred this to any kind of reporting. He had it in his mind to do a history of Christmas customs. He kept thinking of those medieval mummers whom Felix had hired for the party and wondering how many people knew that such performers were once an integral part of Christmas.

Billie wasn't asking him to take any assignments. (She said she understand about Susie Blakely too many times. These were nudges, reminders, which he came to ignore.) She was pleased with his essays and told him so at every opportunity. The essays gave the *Observer* heft, she said. And when he found old Victorian pen-and-ink sketches to go with his work, that also pleased her. But she wondered how he might feel about covering the arts in Northern California, maybe reviewing some little-theater productions in various towns, or musical events in the wine country. That sounded very good to Reuben. What about the Shakespeare Festival in Ashland, Oregon? Yes, Reuben would love to cover that, he said. Immediately he thought of Phil. Would Phil like to go up there with him?

Two more "employees" had arrived from Europe on Friday, a young woman and a young man, both of whom were designated as secretaries and assistants for Felix—Henrietta and Peter—but by the next day, it was clear that both worked under Lisa at just about any task that was required. They were fair-haired, possibly a brother and sister, Swiss by birth, or so they said, and they said very little of anything, moving about the house without a sound, attending to the wants of everyone under the roof. Henrietta did spend hours in Marchent's old kitchen office, working on household receipts. Stuart and Reuben exchanged secretive glances as they studied the movements of the pair and the way they seemed to be communicating with each other without speaking out loud.

Reuben received one brief e-mail written by Susie Blakely saying "I loved the party and will remember it all my life." He imagined it had been a chore for her to write that much and spell it correctly. He wrote her back to say that he hoped she had the very best Christmas ever and he was here for her anytime that she wanted to write or call. Pastor George sent him a longer e-mail, explaining that Susie was now doing much better, and was willing to confide in her parents again though they still did not believe Susie had been rescued by the famous Man Wolf. Pastor George was driving to San Francisco to have lunch with Father Jim and see his church in the Tenderloin.

Night after night, Reuben woke in the small hours. Night after night, he took a long slow walk around the upstairs hallways and the lower floor, quietly opening himself to a visit from Marchent. But never was there the slightest inkling of her presence.

Sunday afternoon, when the rain let up, Phil and Reuben took a long walk in the forest together. Reuben confessed he'd never covered the entire property. Felix had explained at lunch that he was having the entirety of it fenced, including the Drexel and Hamilton acreages. This was an immense undertaking, but Felix felt in this day and age it was something he wanted to do and of course Reuben was in agreement.

Felix promised that after Christmas, he would take Reuben and Phil to see the old Drexel and Hamilton houses, both big old Victorian country homes that could be remodeled and updated without losing their charm.

The fencing was chain link, and six feet in height. But there would be numerous gates; and Felix would make certain that ivy and other attractive vines covered every ugly inch of it. Of course people could still hike the woods, yes, definitely. But they would enter by the front gate, and Reuben and Felix would have some idea of who was out there. And, well, there would be times when he opened all the gates and people could roam freely. It was wrong to "own" this woods, but he wanted to preserve it and he wanted to get to know it again.

"Well, that won't keep Elthram and his family out of the woods, will it?" Phil asked.

Felix was startled but quickly recovered. "Oh, no, they're always welcome in the woods whenever and wherever. I would never dream of trying to keep them out of the woods. These woods are their woods."

"That's good to know," said Phil.

That night, Reuben came upstairs to find a long dark green velvet robe on his bed, and a pair of heavy green velvet slippers. The robe had a hood and was full length.

Margon explained that this was for Christmas Eve, for him to wear into the forest. The robe was very similar to a monk's habit, long, loose fitting, with large sleeves, except that it was padded and lined in silk, and had no waist or belt, and closed down the front with loops and gold buttons. There was tiny fine gold embroidery along the hem and the edges of the sleeves in what seemed a curious pattern. It might have been writing, like the mysterious writing that the Distinguished Gentlemen shared, the writing that looked Eastern in origin. It conveyed an air of mystery and even sanctity.

The usefulness of this garment was obvious. The group would become wolves in the woods, and they would drop these robes easily at their feet and it would be a simple manner to put on these robes afterwards. Reuben was so eager for Christmas Eve that he could scarcely contain it. Stuart was already being a little cynical. Just what sort of "ceremony" were they going to have, he wanted to know. But Reuben knew this was going to be marvelous. Frankly he didn't care what they did. He wasn't worried about Hockan Crost or the mysterious women. Felix and Margon appeared completely calm and quietly eager for the all-important night.

And Reuben would see Laura. At last, Reuben would be with Laura. Christmas Eve had taken on the character and solemnity of their wedding night for him.

Felix had already explained to Phil about their celebrating some Old World customs in the forest, and asked for Phil's indulgence. Phil had been more than fine with it. He'd spend Christmas Eve as he always did, listening to music, and reading, and probably be asleep well before eleven o'clock. The last thing Phil wanted was to be a nuisance. Phil was sleeping wonderfully out here with the windows open to the ocean air. He'd been falling asleep as early as 9:00 p.m.

At last it was Christmas Eve morning, a cold crisp day with a bright white sky that just might show some sunshine before twilight. The foaming sea was dark blue for the first time in days. And Reuben walked down the windy slope to the guesthouse with his box of gifts for his father.

At home in San Francisco, they'd always exchanged gifts before going to Midnight Mass, so Christmas Eve was the big day in Reuben's mind. Christmas Day had always been informal and a time for leisure, with Phil going off to watch films of Dickens's *Christmas Carol* in his room, and Grace having an informal buffet for her hospital friends, especially the personnel who were far from home and family.

Phil was up and writing, and immediately poured a mug of Italian roast coffee for Reuben. The little guesthouse was the epitome of the word "cozy." Sheer white ruffled curtains had been put over the windows, a remarkably feminine touch, Reuben thought, but they were pretty, and they softened the stark vision of the endless sea, which was something unsettling to Reuben.

They sat by the fire together, Phil presenting Reuben with one small book wrapped in foil, which Reuben opened first. Phil had made it himself, illustrating it with his own freehand drawings, "in the style of William Blake," he said with a self-mocking laugh. And Reuben saw that it was a collection of the poems Phil had written over the years expressly for his sons, some of which had been published before, and most of which had never been read by anybody.

For My Sons was the simple title.

Reuben was deeply touched. Phil's spidery drawings surrounded each page, weaving images together rather like the illuminations in medieval manuscripts, and often amounted to frames of foliage with simple domestic objects embedded in them. Here and there in the dense, squiggly drawings was a coffee mug or a bicycle, or a little typewriter or a basketball. Sometimes there were impish faces, crude but kindly caricatures of Jim and Reuben and Grace and Phil himself. There was one primitive whole-page drawing of the Russian Hill house and all its many crowded little rooms filled with cherished furniture and objects.

Never had Phil put together anything like this before. Reuben loved it.

"Now your brother has his own copy coming to him by FedEx today. And I sent your mother one too," said Phil. "You mustn't read a word of it now. You take that up to the castle, and you read it when you want to read it. Poetry should be taken in small doses. Nobody needs poetry. Nobody needs to make himself read it."

There were two other gifts, and Phil assured Reuben that Jim was receiving identical ones. The first was a book Phil had written called simply *Our Ancestors in San Francisco—Dedicated to My Sons*. Reuben couldn't have been happier. For the first time in his life, he really wanted to know all about Phil's family. He'd grown up under the gargantuan shadow of his Spangler grandfather, the real estate entrepreneur who had founded the Spangler fortune, but had heard little or nothing of the Goldings, and this was not typed, this book, it was written in Phil's old-fashioned and beautifully readable cursive. There were old photographs reproduced here that Reuben had never seen before.

"You take your time with that, too," said Phil. "You take the rest of your life, if you like, to read it. And you pass it on to your boy, of course, though I intend to tell that child some of the stories I never told you and your brother."

The last gift was a soft tweed flat cap, or ivy cap, which had belonged to Grandfather O'Connell—just like the cap Phil had been wearing on his walks. "Your brother got the very same thing," said Phil. "My grandfather never went out without one of these caps. And I have another couple in my trunk for that boy who's coming."

"Well, Dad, these are the best presents anyone's ever given me," said Reuben. "This is an extraordinary Christmas. It just keeps getting better and better." He concealed the low burning pain he felt—that he'd had to lose his life to really understand the value of it, that he'd had to leave the realm of human family to want to know and embrace his antecedents.

Phil looked at him gravely. "You know, Reuben," he said. "Your brother Jim is lost. He'd buried himself alive in the Catholic priesthood for all the wrong reasons. The world in which he struggles is shrunken and dark. There's no magic in it, no wonder, no mysticism. But you have the universe waiting for you."

If only I could tell you the smallest part of it, if only I could confide and seek your guidance. If only . . .

"Here, Dad, my presents," Reuben said. And he brought in the big box of carefully wrapped little volumes and set it before Phil.

Phil was in tears when he opened the first one, seeing the little Ginn and Company hardcover of *Hamlet,* the very textbook version he'd cherished as an undergraduate. And as he came to see that the complete plays were here, every single one of them, he was overwhelmed. This was something he hadn't even dreamed of—the entire collection. These books had been out of print even when he first came upon them in secondhand shops in his student days.

He choked back the tears, talking softly of his time at Berkeley as the richest period of his life, when he was reading Shakespeare, acting Shakespeare, living Shakespeare every day, spending hours under the trees of the beautiful old campus, wandering the Telegraph Avenue bookstores for scholarly works on the Bard, thrilled every time some piercing critic gave him a new insight, or brought the plays to life for him in some new way. He'd thought then he would love the academic world always. He wanted nothing more than to stay in the atmosphere of books and poetry forever.

Then had come teaching, and repeating the same words year after year, and the endless committee meetings, and tiresome faculty parties, and the relentless pressure to publish critical theories or ideas that he didn't even have in him. Then had come weariness of it all, and hatred even, and his conviction of his own utter insignificance and mediocrity. But these little volumes took him back to the sweetest part of it—when it had been new, and filled with hope, before it had become a racket for him.

About that time, Lisa appeared with a full breakfast for both of them—scrambled eggs, sausage and bacon, pancakes, syrup, butter, toast, and jam. She had it set up quickly at the little dining table, and put on fresh coffee. Jean Pierre appeared with the carafe of orange juice, and a plate of the gingerbread cookies which Phil couldn't resist.

After they'd demolished the meal, Phil stood for a long time at the large rectangular window looking out at the sea, at the dark blue horizon lying beneath the brighter cobalt of the clear sky. Then he said how he had never dreamed he could be this happy, never dreamed he had this much life left in him.

"Why don't people do what they really want to do, Reuben?" he asked. "Why do we so often settle for what makes us devoutly unhappy!

Why do we accept that happiness just isn't possible? Look what's happened. I'm ten years younger now than I was a week ago, and your mother? Your mother's perfectly fine with it. Perfectly fine. I was always too old for your mother, Reuben. Too old in here, in my heart, and just plain too old in every other way. When I get the slightest doubt about her being happier, I call and I talk to her and I listen to the timbre of her voice, you know, the cadence of her speech. She's so relieved to be on her own."

"I hear you, Dad," Reuben said. "I feel a little the same way when I think of my years with Celeste. I don't know why I woke up every morning with the idea that I had to adjust, had to accept, had to go along with."

"That's it, isn't it?" Phil said, turning from the window. He shrugged and made a resigned gesture with his hands. "Thank you, Reuben, for letting me come here."

"Dad, I don't ever want you to leave," said Reuben.

The expression in Phil's eyes was the only response he needed. Phil went over to the box of Shakespeare books and took out the copy of *A Midsummer Night's Dream*. "You know, I can't wait to read parts of this to Elthram and Mara. Mara said she's never heard of *A Midsummer Night's Dream*. Elthram knew it. He can recite parts of it by heart. You know, Reuben? I'm going to give my old copy of the comedies to Elthram and Mara. It's here somewhere. Well, I have two. I'll give them the one without the notes, the clean one. I think that would be a good present for Elthram and Mara. And look what they gave to me." He turned and pointed to a small bouquet of brightly colored wildflowers on his desk, with streams of ivy trailing from it. "I didn't know there were that many wildflowers in the woods this time of year. They gave me that early this morning."

"It's beautiful, Dad," said Reuben.

That afternoon, they drove to the coast and to the town of Mendocino, to have a walk around while the weather held. And it was worth it. The little downtown of beach Victorian buildings was as cheerfully decorated as the village of Nideck, and bustled with last-minute Christmas shoppers. The sea was calm as well as beautifully blue, and the sky overhead, filled with scudding white clouds, was glorious.

But by four o'clock, as they drove home, the slate-colored sky was rolling over them, and the evening gloom was falling around them. Tiny raindrops struck the windshield. Reuben thought to himself how little it would matter when he was in full wolf coat whether a storm descended on Nideck Point, and he settled into his own quiet growing anticipation. Would they hunt tonight? They had to hunt. He was starving for the hunt and he knew that Stuart was starving for it too.

He stayed long enough in Phil's little house to call Grace and Jim and wish them both the happiest of Christmases. Jim would say Midnight Mass tonight at St. Francis at Gubbio Church as always, and Grace, Celeste, and Mort would be there. Tomorrow they'd all serve Christmas dinner at the St. Francis dining room for the homeless and the poor of the Tenderloin.

Finally, it was time to take leave of Phil. It was Christmas Eve at last. It was full dark, and the rain had become a fine mist outside the windows. The forest beckoned.

As he came up the slope, Reuben realized all the outside lights of Nideck Point had been turned off. The cheerful three-story house so well drawn on the night with bright Christmas lights had vanished, leaving in its place a great dark apparition of glinting windows with only the faintest light within, gables invisible in the shrouding mist.

Only a few candles lighted his way up the stairs. And in his room, he found the green velvet hooded robe laid out for him, with the slippers.

Another spectacular item had been added—a very large drinking horn trimmed in gold and beautifully carved with tiny gold-filled figures and symbols. There was a band of hammered and decorated gold beneath the lip, and a gold tip on the end, and a long thin leather shoulder strap for carrying it. It was a beautiful thing, too big for a buffalo or sheep horn, obviously.

A knock on his door interrupted him as he inspected it. He heard Felix's faintly muffled voice say: "It's time."

21

ONLY ONE CANDLE LIGHTED his way down the staircase, and he felt the emptiness and the vastness of the house.

From far off came the ominous beat of drums.

When he stepped out onto the back steps, he could barely see the five hooded figures in the heavy darkness. The distant drums sounded a bizarre and faintly menacing cadence. And just below the sound of the wind, he heard the faint melody of flutes. The rain was no more than a thick mist now that he could feel but not hear, though a wind gusted through the distant trees and he heard that awful moaning that can come with the wind.

An instinctive fear gripped him. Far off, he saw the lurid flickering of a fire. It was a huge fire, a fire so huge it struck a deep chord of alarm in him. But the rain-drenched forest was in no danger from the fire. He knew that.

Gradually he made out more clearly the outlines of those nearest him. There was the loud crack of a kitchen match and a little blaze flared revealing Margon with a long slender torch in his hand.

At once, the torch was ignited and the other figures emerged in the burgeoning light.

Reuben could smell the pitch or the tar of the torch, he didn't know for sure which it was.

They began to walk through the forest with Margon, torch in hand, leading the way. It seemed the distant drums knew they were coming. There came the deep insistent throbbing of big drums, and the relentless goading sound of other smaller drums, and then the horns soaring above them. Another instrumental voice joined in that might have been the Irish pipe, high, nasal, and almost baleful.

All around them the forest rustled, snapped, and moved in the shadows. As they struggled over rocks and fallen bracken moving steadily onwards, he heard hushed and secretive laughter. He could see the dim white faces of the Forest Gentry, mere flashes on either side of the irregular path they followed, and suddenly the faintest eeriest music rose to accompany them—in time with the greater sound summoning them from afar—the roughened mournful notes of wooden pipes, the tap and jingle of tambourines, a restless humming.

He felt the chills come up on the back of his arms and his neck, but they were pleasurable chills. His nakedness beneath the robe felt erotic.

On and on they walked. Reuben began to feel the deep pringling that meant the change. But Felix's hand gripped his wrist. "Wait," he said gently, falling into stride beside Reuben, steadying him when he stumbled or almost fell.

The drums in the distance grew louder. The deepest drums slowed to the ominous and terrifying sound of a knell, and the deep whine of the Irish pipes was hypnotic. Overhead the high remote branches of the redwoods groaned and creaked with the Forest Gentry. Sharp sounds came from the underbrush as of vines ripped in the blackness, and of branches beating the underbrush.

The fire was a great red glare in the mist ahead, flashing in a vast mesh of tangled vine and branches.

This way and that they turned as they walked. He had no idea now in which direction he was going except that they were drawing closer and closer, always, to that glare.

In front of him, the hooded figures looked anonymous in the distant light of the lone flickering torch, and it seemed suddenly only Felix was real to him, Felix who was beside him, and his heart went out to Stuart. Was Stuart afraid? Was he himself afraid?

No. Even as the drums grew louder, and as the spectral musicians around him answered and wove their low, harsh threads of melody around the drumbeat, he was not afraid. Again, the prickling began and he could feel the hairs of his scalp wanting to be released, feel the wolf hair in him raging against the skin of the man. Did the wolf in him respond to the drums? Did the drums hold a secret power over the beast of which he'd been unaware? Bravely yet deliciously he struggled against it, knowing it would burst forth soon enough.

The distant fire grew brighter, and seemed to swallow the feeble light of Margon's torch. There was something so horrific about the quivering, throbbing glare of the fire that he did feel again a deep and terrible alarm. But the fire was calling them, and he was eager for it, reaching out suddenly and taking firm hold of Felix's arm.

Suddenly the anticipation he felt was intoxicating and it seemed to him that he'd been moving through this dark forest forever, and it was the greatest of experiences, this, to be with the others, heading towards the distant blaze that flared and flickered so high above them as if from the throat of a volcano or some dark chimney invisible beneath its light.

Pungent scents caught his nostrils, the deep rich and living scent of the wild boar he'd hunted all too seldom, and the sweet and seductive fragrance of simmering wine. Cloves, cinnamon, nutmeg, the sweet smell of honey, all this he caught with the smell of smoke, the smell of pine, the smell of the wet mist. It was flooding his senses.

Out of the night, he thought he heard the deep-throated cry of the wild boar, a guttural scream, and again his skin was on fire. Hunger knotted his insides, hunger for living meat, yes.

A vast wordless song rose from the invisible beings all round them as ahead they drew up to a veritable wall of blackness above which the sparks flew heavenward from the raging fire they could no longer clearly see.

Suddenly the small torch in Margon's hand was moving upwards, and dimly Reuben saw the outlines of the gray boulders that he'd once glimpsed by daylight, and all at once he was climbing a steep and rocky incline and entering at Felix's bidding a narrow, jagged passage through which he could barely move. The drums beat loud against his ears, and the pipes soared again, throbbing, urging, calling to him to move quickly.

Ahead the world exploded with lurid dancing orange flames.

The last of the dark figures in front of him had stepped aside and into the clearing, and he stumbled down now and found his footing on the packed earth, the fire for a moment blinding him.

It was a vast space.

Some thirty yards away the great exploding bonfire raged and crackled, its dark heavy scaffolding of logs plainly visible within the furnace of its yellow and orange flames.

It appeared to define the very center of a vast arena. To the right and left of him he saw the boulders spreading out into the inevitable shadows, how far he couldn't guess.

Right by the mouth of the passage through which they'd just come stood the company of musicians—all recognizable in their green velvet hooded finery. It was Lisa pounding the kettledrums whose deep rolling booms shook Reuben's very bones, and around her were gathered Henrietta and Peter playing the wooden flutes, and Heddy with a long narrow drum, and Jean Pierre playing the huge Scottish bagpipes. From high above came the wordless singing of the Forest Gentry and the unmistakable sound of violins and metal flutes, and the twanging notes of dulcimers.

All contrived to make a song of expectation and reverence, of unquestioned solemnity.

Between the boulders and the fire ahead stood a giant golden cauldron over a low-simmering fire that glowed as if made up of coals, and Reuben realized that this cauldron defined the center of the circle which the Morphenkinder were now forming around it.

He stepped forward, taking his place, the fumes of the spiced mixture in the cauldron rising in his nostrils enticingly.

The music slowed now and softened all around him. The air seemed to hold its breath, with the drum rolling as softly as thunder.

There came the screams of the wild boar, the grunts, the deep guttural growls, but these animals were safely penned somewhere, he sensed this. He trusted in it.

Meanwhile, the Morphenkinder drew in as close to the heat of the cauldron as they could, the circle not small enough for them to touch one another, yet small enough for every face to be visible.

Then from the dancing shadows beyond the blaze to his right emerged a strange figure to join the circle, and as she lifted her green hood back from her face, Reuben saw it was Laura.

His breath went out of him. She stood opposite him, smiling at him through the faint steam rising from the huge cauldron. A chorus of cheers and murmured greetings rose from the others.

Margon raised his voice:

"Modranicht!" he roared. "The night of the Mother Earth, and our Yule!"

At once the others raised their arms and roared in response, Sergei giving a deep-throated howl. Reuben raised his arms, and ached to let loose the howl that was inside him.

Suddenly the kettledrums went into a deafening roll, shaking Reuben to the core, and the flutes rose in piercing melody.

"People of the Forest, join us!" declared Margon, his arms raised. From the boulders all around came a clamor of drums and flutes and fiddles and the shock of brass trumpets.

"Morphenkinder!" cried Margon. "You are welcome."

And out of the darkness came more hooded figures. Reuben saw plainly the face of Hockan, the face of Fiona, and the smaller feminine shapes that had to be Berenice, Catrin, Helena, Dorchella, and Clarice. The circle widened, admitting them one by one.

"Drink!" cried Margon.

And all converged on the cauldron, dipping their horns into the simmering brew, and then stepping back to swallow mouthful after mouthful. The temperature was perfect, to make a fire in the throat and in the heart—to ignite the circuits of the brain.

Again, they dipped their horns and again they drank.

Suddenly Reuben was rocking, falling, and Felix on his right had reached out to steady him. His head swam and a low boiling laughter came out of him. Laura's eyes blazed as she smiled at him. She lifted the gleaming horn to her lips. She saluted him. She said his name.

"This is no time for the words of humankind—for poetry or sermons," cried Margon. "This is no meeting for words at all. Because we all know the words. But how are we to mourn the loss of Marrok if we don't speak his name?"

"Marrok!" cried Felix. And stepping up to the cauldron, he dipped his horn and drank. "Marrok," said Sergei, "old friend, beloved friend." And one by one all were doing the same. Finally Reuben had to do it, had to lift the horn and call out of the name of the Morphenkind he'd killed. "Marrok, forgive me!" he cried out. And he heard Laura's voice echoing the same words: "Marrok, forgive me."

Sergei gave a roar again and this time Thibault and Frank roared with him and so did Margon. "Marrok, we dance for you tonight," cried Sergei. "You've gone into the darkness or the light, we know not which. We salute you."

"And now, with joy," cried Felix, "we salute the young amongst us: Stuart, Laura, Reuben. This is your night, my young friends, your first Modranicht amongst us!"

He was answered this time with terrific howls from the entire company.

The robes were being thrown aside. Felix had stripped, and throwing up his arms was becoming the Man Wolf. And opposite Reuben, Laura suddenly rose up naked and white, her breasts beautifully visible through the rising steam from the cauldron. Sergei and Thibault stood naked, the wolf hair rising on them as they flanked her.

Reuben let out a terrified gasp. Waves of desire rose in him with the waves of drunken giddiness.

His robes lay at his feet and the cold air stole over him, awakening him and emboldening him.

They were all changing. Howls rose from all now irresistibly. The music rose in a deafening clamor. The icy pringling covered Reuben's face and head first, then raced over his trunk and limbs, his muscles aching for one split second as they expanded into their glorious new strength and flexibility.

But it was Laura that he was seeing, as if there were no one else in the marvelous expanding universe but Laura, as if Laura's transformation was his transformation.

A dreadful horror gripped Reuben, a fear as terrible as the fear he'd known the very first time when, as a boy, he'd seen a photograph of the mature female sex organ, that wondrous and terrible secret mouth, so moist, so raw, so veiled in tangled hair—awful as the face of Medusa, magnetizing him and threatening to turn him to stone. But he couldn't look away from Laura.

He was seeing the dark gray hair spring out on the top of her head, as the hair sprang from his own, hair pouring down to her shoulders as the mane poured down to his. He saw the sleek shining fur sheathe her cheeks and her upper lip, her mouth becoming that black and silken band of flesh that was the same as his mouth, the gleaming white fangs descending, the thick bestial coat closing over her shoulders, swallowing her breasts and her nipples.

Petrified now, he saw Laura's eyes smoldering from the massive face of the beast, and saw her rise to greater height, her powerful wolf arms lifted, her claws reaching for the sky above them.

Fear and desire pumped through him, maddening him infinitely more than the scent of the boar, or the pounding music, or the deafening fiddles and pipes of the Forest Gentry.

But the group opposite was in movement. Laura was shifting places with Thibault, and then with Hockan and then with Sergei and then with another and another until she stood beside Reuben.

He reached out with his claws and caught the wolf mask of her face in his paws, staring right into her eyes, staring, determined to penetrate the full mystery of the monstrous face he saw before him, hideously beautiful to him with its gray hair and gleaming teeth.

Suddenly she closed her powerful arms around him, stunning him with her strength, and he returned the embrace, his mouth opening over her mouth, his tongue plunging between her teeth. They were sealed together, the two in the glorious concealment and nakedness of the wolf coat, and the others were all crying their names: "Laura, Reuben, Laura, Reuben."

The music was softening, boiling into an obvious dance, and in the dancing glare of the fire, Reuben saw the Forest Gentry closing in, Elthram and the others, with long garlands of ivy and flowering vine with which they decked Reuben and Laura, winding the ivy and vine around their shoulders. From out of the air it seemed flower petals were falling down on them. Petals of white and yellow and pink—rose petals, dogwood petals, the broken fragile petals of wildflowers. And all around, the Forest Gentry pushed in singing, and covering them with light, airy scentless kisses, kisses that had only the scent of the flowers.

"Laura," he whispered in her ear, "Laura, bone of my bone, flesh of my flesh!" He heard her deep bestial voice answering him, her words softened and sweet. "My beloved Reuben, wither thou goest, I will go, and where thou lodgest, I will lodge."

"And I with thee," he answered. And the words sprang out of his memory and to his tongue. "And thy people shall be my people."

Horns of wine were thrust at them, and they took the horns and drank, and exchanged horns and drank again, the wine flowing out of their mouths, down their heavy coats. How little did it matter. Someone had poured a horn of wine over Reuben's head and he now saw Laura anointed in the same manner.

He crushed his face against hers and felt the hot pressure of her breasts against his chest, the heat pounding through the fur.

"And the hairy ones shall dance!" cried Margon. "'Round the cauldron."

The drums took up the dancing beat, and the pipes fell into a dancing rhythm.

At once they were swaying, rocking, leaping, and rushing to the right, all of them, the circle picking up speed.

The drums described the rhythmic shape of a dance and they were indeed dancing, arms out, knees bent, figures springing up into the air, twisting, turning. Sergei caught Reuben and swung him around, and then moved on to Laura. Again and again, others came together then broke apart, the drive to the right around the cauldron continuing.

"'Round the fire!" roared the giant Sergei, whose rich bass voice in wolf form was unmistakable, and he leapt out of the circle and the others streamed after him, Reuben and Laura together pounding after them as fast as they could.

The great full circle of the enclosure was theirs as they raced full speed one behind the other.

The thumping speed of those passing Reuben prodded him on as much as the drums, Laura keeping pace right beside him, in his watchful eye, her flanks now and then crashing against his as they plunged forward together.

He knew the roars that cut the air, he knew the howls of Frank, Thibault, Margon, Felix, Sergei. He heard the strange high savage cries of the other female Morphenkinder. And then he heard Laura's voice, beside him, full throated, higher, sweeter than his, and exquisitely savage as she roared past him.

He tore after her, losing sight of her as others moved more swiftly than he could.

Never in all his life had he run this fast, had he leapt so far, had he felt himself positively taking flight as he sped along—not even on that long-ago night when he'd pounded over the miles to find Stuart. Too many obstacles had lain in his path; too much fear of injury had inhibited him. But this was ecstasy, as though he were smeared with the secret salve of the witches, and like Goodman Brown he was truly traveling the night air, released from the pull of the Mother Earth, yet buoyed by her winds, touching down not even long enough to feel the ground beneath him.

A new riff of guttural howls and raw cries rose against the insistent goading throb of the music.

"Modranicht!" came the cries, and "Yule!," the words perhaps unintelligible to human ears as they came from the deep throats of the Morphenkinder. Ahead of Reuben two racing figures collided with one another and began to roll on the earth, snarling, growling, playfully nipping at each other, and then one raced off leaving the other to chase after it.

A figure pounced full weight on top of Reuben and he rolled away from the fire towards the encircling stones, throwing off the other, and then lunging for its throat with a mock thrust as the figure struck out at him like a monstrous feline. He turned and ran on, not caring who this had been, not caring suddenly about anything, but stretching every sinew of his powerful frame, and springing as wildly from the pads of his hands and feet as he could, dashing over the slower figure ahead of him, rounding the great bonfire for perhaps the fifth or sixth time now, he didn't know, and greedy for the wind on his face as if he were devouring the wind, the menacing shadows thrown by the gargantuan blaze, and driven by the deep rolling drums and the wild grinding song of the pipes.

The thick musky scent of the wild boar came at him full force. He cried out. There was no human left in him. Suddenly ahead he saw the huge bulk of a monstrous male running as fast and furiously as he was running. Before he could mount it another Morphenkind had overtaken it and had sunk his teeth into the boar's huge neck and was riding it doggedly, legs flying over the boar's back.

Yet another boar and another Morphenkind ripped past him. After them at top speed he went, the hunger exploding in his belly.

And again, he saw the boar brought down.

Horrid squeals from the wounded and furious animals filled the night, and roars from the Morphenkinder.

He pounded on until he saw the figure ahead of him that he knew to be Laura. Quickly he overtook her and they fell into the same stride.

Suddenly he heard the hooves right by his ears, and he felt the sharp screaming pain of a tusk in his side. He pivoted, enraged, and opening his mouth wide in a delicious roar brought his teeth down on the side of the animal's neck. He felt the thick musky hide tear, the muscles shred, his claws rending the rough bristling coat, and the delicious taste of the meat overwhelmed him.

Laura on top of the beast ripped into its lower flank.

He turned over and over with the shrieking grunting beast suddenly as it struggled for its life, ripping one chunk of live meat from it after another. At last his face found its underbelly, his claws slicing it open for his hungry tongue. Laura sank her teeth into the feast right beside him.

He gorged himself on the hot bleeding meat, chomping into the flank, as the last life went out of the creature, its hoofed feet still twitching. Laura lapped at the blood, ripped at the strips of bloody muscle. He lay there watching her.

It seemed an eternity passed in which the squeals and grunts had died away, the pounding of the hooves had died away, and only the distinct sharp roars of the Morphenkinder pierced the night within the hushed cloud of the spellbinding music.

Reuben was drunk and satiated with the meat, almost unable to move. The hunt was finished.

A stillness had fallen over the immense clearing in which the monstrous fire burned and the music played on.

Then a cry went up: "Bones into the bone fire!"

A huge crashing sound erupted from the heart of the blaze, and then came another as if the fire were a spitting volcano.

Reuben rose and picking up the torn and bleeding carcass of the boar on which he'd feasted he hurled it into the fire. He could see others doing the same, and soon the stench of burning animal flesh rose all around him, sickening and yet somehow tantalizing. Laura tumbled against him, leaning heavily on him, her breaths coming in hoarse gasps. They were knowing the heat of the wolf coat, the thirst in the wolf coat.

The figure of Sergei appeared beside him, telling him to come back, to join the others by the cauldron. They found the others crowded about, drinking from their horns, and exchanging horns. Reuben made out the seven who were not of his pack, but he could not tell the identity of the female wolves. Hockan he knew. Hockan had a large heavy wolfen body like that of Frank or Stuart, and his fur was almost entirely white, streaked here and there with gray, powerfully setting off his black eyes. Other dark-eyed Morphenkinder had no such advantage.

Nothing clearly distinguished the females except their smaller size and their slightly feline movements. Their breasts and intimate organs were covered in long hair and fur, their height varying as did the height of the men, their limbs obviously powerful. Everywhere he looked, he saw hairy faces clotted with blood and bits and pieces of shivering boar flesh, torsos smeared with blood, chests heaving with deep breaths. Again and again, the horns were dipped into the seemingly inexhaustible cauldron. How natural it all seemed, how perfect, to slake his thirst like this, with draft after draft, and how divine the drunkenness he felt, the utter safety of the moment.

Sergei backed up near the gathered musicians, and then giving a horrific roar, he cried out: "Through the need fire!"

He took off with a fierce leap, touching down once before he bounded straight into the flames. Reuben was terrified for him, but at once, the others began running, circling and racing to the fire in the same manner, soaring up into the heights of the fire, their powerful cries of triumph rising as they cleared the inferno and landed on their feet.

Reuben heard Laura's voice calling to him, and in a flash he saw her break from the group, running towards the musicians, then turning and racing forward as Sergei had done, her body sailing upwards and into the hungry flames.

He couldn't stop himself from following. Terrified as he was of the flames, he felt invulnerable, he felt eager, he felt crazed with the new and seductive challenge.

He ran at top speed and then sprang upwards as he had seen the others do, the fire blinding him, the heat engulfing him, the smell of his own burning fur filling his nostrils until he broke free into the cold wind and came crashing down on the ground to begin the race once more around the circle.

Laura had waited for him. Laura was running beside him. He saw her paws flying out before her, like two front feet, saw her powerful shoulders churning under the dark gray wolf coat.

Round the cauldron they ran and then made the mad dash once more, springing high into the licking flames.

When next they approached the cauldron, the company was gathered together, on hind legs forming the circle again. At once, they fell in.

What was happening? Why had the music slowed, why had it fallen into an ominous syncopated rhythm?

The goading song of the flutes was slowed in time with it, every fourth beat stronger than the three before. And the others were rocking back and forth, back and forth, and Margon was singing something in that ancient tongue, to which Felix added his voice, and then came the thundering bass of Sergei. Thibault was humming; the unmistakable figure of Hockan Crost, the nearest thing to a white wolf in the group, was also humming as he was rocking—and a kind of moaning hum rose from the other females.

Suddenly Hockan rushed past Felix and Reuben, grabbing with both paws for Laura.

Before Reuben could come to her defense, Laura hurled Hockan backwards right into the cauldron which almost went over, the hot liquid splashing upwards like molten metal.

Fierce growls had broken out from the Sergei, Felix, and Margon, all of whom surrounded Hockan. Hockan threw up his paws, claws extended, snarling at them as he backed away. And said in his deep brutal wolf voice, "It's Modranicht." He let out a threatening growl.

Margon shook his head, and gave the lowest most menacing and guttural response Reuben had ever heard from a Morphenkind.

One of the females broke through the press and shoved Hockan playfully but powerfully with both paws, and as he lunged at her, she took off, racing around the fire with him close behind her.

The tension went out of the protective males.

Another female came pounding Frank with her paws, and Frank, accepting the challenge, went after her.

It was happening now all around them, Felix going after the third of the women, and Thibault after the fourth. Even Stuart was suddenly courted and seduced and had gone tearing away in hot pursuit of his female.

Laura moved to Reuben, her powerful breasts pumping against his chest, her teeth grazing his throat, her growls filling his ears. He tried to pick her up off the ground but she threw him over and they wrestled, rolling into the shadows against the boulders.

He was on fire for her, opening his mouth on her throat, and licking at her ears, at the silken fur of her face, at the soft black flesh of her mouth, his tongue sliding in over her tongue.

At once, he was inside her, pumping into a tight, wet sheath that was deeper and more muscular than her human sex had been, closing against him so hard that it almost, almost but not quite, hurt him. His brain was gone, gone down into the beast, into the loins of the beast, and this thing, this thing that so resembled him, this powerful and menacing thing that had been Laura was his as surely as he was hers. Her muscular body shook with spasms beneath him, her jaws opening, the hoarse roar issuing out of her as if she had no control of it. He let loose in a torrent of thrusts that blinded him.

Stillness. The thin silver rain came down without a sound. Not so much as a hiss from the great fire with its dark slowly collapsing logs, its high flaming towers of timber.

The music was low, furtive, patient, like the breath of a beast who was dozing, and dozing they were, Laura and Reuben. Wrapped in the shadows and against the rocks, they lay in one another's arms, heart pounding against heart. There was no nakedness in the wolf coat; only total freedom.

Reuben was groggy and drunken and half dreaming. Words floated to the surface of his mind—*love you, love you, love you, love the inexhaustible beast in you, in myself, in us, love you*—as he felt the weight of Laura against his chest, his claws dug deep into the tangled mane of her head, her breasts hot against him, hot as they'd been when she was a woman, hotter than the rest of her, and he felt the heat of her sex in that same old way against his leg. Her soft clean scent, which wasn't a scent at all, filled his nostrils and his brain. And this moment seemed more intoxicating than the dance, the hunt, the kill, the lovemaking, this strange suspension of all time and all worry, with the beast yielding so effortlessly to this fearless drowsiness, this half sleep of mingled sensation and perplexing contentment. Forever, like this, with the spitting and crackling of the giant Yule fire, with the sharp cold air so close, the soft wet rain little more than a mist, so close, yes, not really rain, and all things revealed, all things sealed between him and Laura.

And will she love me tomorrow?

His eyes opened.

The music had quickened; it was a dance again, and the tambourines were playing, and as he let his head roll to one side, he saw between him and the immense blaze the leaping, dancing figures of the Forest Gentry. Silhouetted against the flames, they danced arm in arm, and swinging in circles like old peasant people have always danced, their lithe and graceful bodies beautiful in silhouette against the fire as they ran on around it, then stopped to make their fancy circling steps again, laughing, whooping, calling to one another. Their song was rising, falling, in time with their steps, a blending of glorious soprano voices and deeper tenor and baritone. For one moment, it seemed they shimmered, became transparent as if they would dissolve, and then were solid once more, with the thud of their feet on the earth beneath them.

He was laughing with delight as he watched them, their hair flying, the women's skirts flying, the little children forming chains to circle the elders.

And here came the Morphenkinder with them.

There was Sergei marching, leaping, turning, with them, and here came the familiar figure of Thibault.

Slowly, he rose, rousing Laura with nuzzling and wet kisses.

They climbed to their feet and joined the others. How ancient and Celtic the music sounded now, joined again with violins and stringed instruments far deeper and darker than violins, and the clear metallic notes of the dulcimer.

He was drunk now. He was terribly drunk. Drunk from the mead, drunk from making love, drunk from gorging on the living flesh of boar—drunk on the night and on the sizzling, hissing flames against his eyelids. An icy wind gusted into the clearing, raking the fire into a new fury, and tantalizing him with the very light fistfuls of rain.

Hmmm. Scent on the wind, scent mingled with the rain. Scent of a human? Not possible. Worry not. This is Modranicht.

He kept dancing. Turning, twisting, moving along, and the music bubbled and boiled and pushed and hurried him along, the drums pounding faster and faster, one rolling riff crashing into another.

Someone cried out. It was a male voice, a voice full of rage. A loud strangled scream tore the night. Never had he heard a Morphenkind scream in that fashion.

The music had stopped. The singing of the Forest Gentry had stopped. The night was empty, then suddenly filled with the crackling and exploding of the fire.

He opened his eyes. They were all rushing round the fire now to the place of the musicians and the cauldron.

There was that scent, stronger now. A human scent, distinctly human like nothing in this clearing, like nothing that should have been in this clearing or in these woods tonight.

In the flickering half-light all the Morphenkinder were crowded into a circle, but the cauldron was not the center of this circle. That was way off to the side. There was something else in the center of this circle. The Forest Gentry hung back whispering and murmuring restlessly.

Hockan was roaring at Margon, and from the other male voices he knew came a rising chorus of fury.

"Dear God," said Laura. "It's your father."

22

REUBEN PUSHED HIS WAY through the Morphenkinder blocking him, with Laura right behind him.

There stood Phil facing the fire, his eyes wide with shock, his body swaying and stumbling as he sought to stand upright. He wore the old gray sweatpants and sweatshirt he always wore for sleep, and his feet were bare in the dirt. He seemed on the verge of passing out, and suddenly one of the female Morphenkinder grabbed him roughly by the shoulder, jerking him upright.

"He should die for this," she roared. "Coming unbidden to our revels. I tell you, he should die! Who dares to say otherwise?"

"Stop, Fiona," cried Felix. He rushed forward just as Reuben did, and gripped Fiona's arm, quickly overpowering her with his masculine advantage and forcing her back as she moaned in rage, struggling against him.

Reuben reached out and grabbed Phil under the arms to steady him, but what in God's name could he say to Phil? How could he make himself known to Phil without further shattering his sanity, and it was clear that Phil was losing all semblance of reasoning as he stared around him.

Suddenly as Reuben let him go, so as not to frighten him more, there came a gleam of recognition into Phil's pale eyes, and he cried out: "Elthram, Elthram, help me. I don't know where I am. I don't know what this is! What's happening to me?"

Out of the shadows Elthram came towards him saying loudly, "I'm here, my friend. And no harm, I swear it, will come to you!"

At once three of the female Morphenkinder began to roar, advancing on Phil and Felix and Reuben. "Back, out of here," screamed Fiona.

"The dead don't talk at our revels. The dead don't say who lives or dies amongst us!" The others were closing in as well, roaring at Elthram and menacing him with barks and growls.

"Get back!" Felix roared. Sergei, Thibault, and Frank moved in. The taller figure of Stuart charged up to Felix's shoulder.

Elthram did not move. There was a faint smile on his lips.

"This is a matter of flesh and blood!" cried Fiona, one paw raised. "Who didn't know the utter folly of these Morphenkinder to bring this human being right to their own hearth? Who did not see this coming?"

Margon took up a spot directly behind Fiona, unseen by her, but not unseen by those with her. Slowly, one female was moving away. Surely this was Berenice. She moved silently away from the females and towards Frank, taking up her stand behind him.

"No one is harming this man!" said Felix. "And no one will say one more word about death on this hallowed night and on this hallowed ground! You want a human sacrifice! That's what you want. And you won't have it here."

All of a chorus the women roared.

"Death has always been a part of Modranicht!" said one of the women, surely the Russian, but Reuben could not clearly picture her now or recall her name. "Sacrifice has always been a part of Modranicht." The other females gave their loud assent, stepping forward and then back and then dangerously forward again.

"Modranicht!" Phil whispered.

"Not in our time!" declared Sergei. "And not here on our land, and not this man who is blood kin to one of us. Not this man who *is an innocent man*!" Growls of assent came from the males.

It seemed every figure present was in some kind of motion, yet some dynamic tension held back the inevitable brawl.

"You came to our secret revels," Fiona cried out as she faced Phil, the stubbed fingers of her hairy hand visible as she spread them out, claws fully extended. "You dared come when you were told not to come. Why should you not be the sacrifice? Aren't you a gift from fortune, you blundering fool?"

"No!" Phil cried. "I didn't come! I don't know how I got here."

Right through the band of females came Lisa suddenly, throwing back her hood, the glare of the fire full on her face. Margon motioned for her to stay back and so did Sergei but she would not.

"Look at Philip," she shouted, her voice sharp but unequal to the others. "Look at his bare feet. He didn't come here of his own accord. Someone brought him here."

Fiona lunged at her, but Felix and Sergei caught Fiona and held her as Hockan drew close, threatening them. It was only with great effort that the two males could hold Fiona.

Lisa stood her ground, her face as cold and calm as it had ever been.

She went on, "These are lies. Philip didn't walk through the woods like this. How could he? I gave him the drink to make him sleep. I saw that he drank every drop. He was sleeping like the dead when I left him. This is treachery beneath the Morphenkinder. Where is your conscience? Where is your code?"

The females were outraged.

"And now we listen on Modranicht to the voices of servants?" cried Fiona. "What right have you to speak here? Maybe your usefulness is at an end." Two of the other females made snorting noises of contempt and outrage. The protective males moved in closer.

"Hockan, speak for us!" Fiona roared. The other took up the same cry. But the white wolf stood apart staring without a sound.

Reuben could smell the fear and the innocence of his father. But he could catch no scent of evil from these female Morphenkinder. It was maddening to him. If this was not evil, then what was evil? But all his senses told him this would end in a violent frenzy in which Phil could be instantly killed.

Lisa would not be moved.

Phil stumbled again as if his knees were giving out, and once more Reuben's arm encircled his back and steadied him. Phil was staring at Lisa and then he looked again to Elthram. "Lisa's telling the truth. I don't know how I got here. Elthram, is this a nightmare? Elthram, where is my son? My son will help me. This is his land. Where is my son?"

Elthram started to come towards Phil with his arms out, and at once the females menaced him as they'd menaced Lisa, with Fiona jerking herself free of Felix and dealing Felix one fine blow that sent him stumbling backwards. Thibault quickly came to his rescue. Margon rushed at Fiona but Fiona would not back off. Elthram pressed in as before.

Fiona made a great swiping gesture at Elthram, which appeared to go right through his solid body without so much as causing it to flicker. A gasp came from Phil as he saw this, and Lisa remained close.

"No harm will come to you, master," Lisa said to Phil. "We won't let this happen."

Other shadowy figures moved on either side of Elthram, unsubstantial but visible, and seeming to multiply before Reuben's very eyes.

"You brought him here, Fiona!" said Elthram. "How do you hope to deceive us? How do you hope to deceive anyone?"

"Silence, I warn you, unclean spirit!" she said in a low seething voice. "You go back to the woods until you're called. You have no voice here. As for the man, his fate is sealed. He's seen us here. His death is inevitable. You and your unclean brethren should leave here now."

"You brought him here," Elthram continued. "You planned this. You and your cohorts, Catrin and Helena, you went for him and brought him here to force this bloody travesty. The man will not die in our forest, I warn you."

"You warn me? You?" Fiona was howling. But for every advancing step taken by any of the females, the males countered while others moved this way and that behind them ready to spring.

There were outraged roars on all side. Only Hockan remained motionless on the periphery, not uttering a sound.

Stuart now stood directly behind Phil. Laura had taken up her place on the other side of him from Reuben. Indeed things were happening so fast, words were spoken so swiftly that Reuben could scarcely follow the thread.

"What are you now, Margon and Felix?" asked Fiona. "Sorcerers, that you call the spirits to defend your unholy actions? You think these insubstantial spirits have power over us! Hockan, speak for us!"

The white wolf did not respond.

"You, Felix, this is on your head, this death," cried the other female. "And it can't be extirpated, what you've done, you with your dreams and your schemes and your risks and your madness."

"Back off, Fiona," cried Frank. "Leave here now. Get out of here, all of you. Fiona, lead your pack out of here. You take on every single one of us if you persist with this." Berenice remained silent at his side.

There came snarls from the other females.

"And what?" Fiona spat back. "Stand idly by while you drag us into yet another chain of fiascoes? You with your glorious Nideck dominion—your festivals, your village of sheepish serfs, your splendid displays of hubris? Is no one's safety and secrecy sacred to you, you arrogant greedy Morphenkinder? Show your loyalty now to us by punishing this human! Stand with us and our customs or it will be war. Modranicht demands a sacrifice—a sacrifice from you, Felix!"

Margon stepped to the front. "The world's big enough for all of us," he said in a low commanding voice. "Leave now and there's no harm done—."

"No harm done?" came that Slavic accent from the female wolf beside Fiona. Surely it was Helena. "This man has seen us as we are. He's seen too much to live. No, you can be certain on one thing now; this man will not live!"

Reuben was in a rage. Weren't they all in a rage? What held them all back? It was driving Reuben mad. Beside him, Stuart uttered a long low menacing growl as he looked at the women. When the explosion finally happened, Reuben would throw himself over Phil to protect him. What else could he do?

Margon raised his arms for calm.

"Go!" declared Margon. His lupine voice rose with a power he never exerted in human form. "Stay and this is to the death," he said, the words rolling out slowly and forcefully. "And it won't be this innocent man's death unless you slay every single one of us."

Phil was staring wildly at Margon. Plainly he must have been recognizing the cadences of these many voices, Reuben thought, and

Reuben didn't dare to speak, dare to confide that he was the monster standing beside his father.

"We will not go!" said Helena, the sharp accent once more defining her. "You've done more to harm us in these times than any others the world over, what with your passion for human display and human kin. You tantalize the most dangerous enemies we've ever known, and you carry on, and on, and on as if this is nothing! Well, I say an end to it. Enough of you and your Nideck world. It's time that house was burnt to the ground."

"You can't do such a thing!" Laura screamed. A roar went up from the males. "You wouldn't dare to do such a thing!" There were low contemptuous protests from all sides. The tension was unbearable. But Felix called for silence.

"What harm have I done, and to whom and when?" demanded Felix. "You've never suffered on account of me, not a single one of you." It was his old reasonable approach, but what good was it going to do here? "It's you who bring the treachery here—seeking to divide us—and you know it. It's you who violate our code!"

As if on cue, the males sprang at the females.

Fiona and Helena ducked and rushed Phil, their powerful arms snatching him out of Reuben's grasp and away from Laura in a split second, their mouths closing on Phil's shoulder and chest as swiftly as any animal of the wild moves to slay. Reuben was thrown down forcefully, and Laura was fighting as if for her life.

At once, all the male Morphenkinder were on top of Fiona and Helena, dragging them backwards, as the other females—except for Berenice—assaulted the males. Reuben, freed from his attacker, managed to smash a fist into Fiona's bloody fangs. He felt hot breath on his face and the maddening stab of fangs into his throat. But Margon hurled his assailant away from the frenzy.

Phil had fallen to the ground, white faced and gasping, the blood streaming from his torn shoulder and side. Lisa had thrown herself on top of him.

From everywhere came the Forest Gentry surrounding Elthram and sliding between the male Morphenkinder and the two rebellious

females and surrounding the females with countless bodies and countless embraces, as the two prisoners fought in vain with furious protests.

"Modranicht!" chanted the Forest Gentry in a deafening chorus.
"Modranicht!" shouted Elthram.

Hockan was suddenly roaring in protest, Hockan who had been
silent all this while. "Stop them, Margon. Felix, stop them!"

Louder and louder came the chant. "Modranicht."

Margon appeared dazed and Felix too stood motionless.

The great compact and irresistible mass of the Forest Gentry
absorbed the futile blows of the frantic female Morphenkinder and
the desperate white wolf, Hockan, as they sped their helpless prisoners
towards the bonfire. Even Berenice, Frank's wife, ran at them, trying
to claw her way into them; but they absorbed her blows and remained
intact. The crush of Forest Gentry was suddenly beyond any count,
and the chant of "Modranicht" drowned out all other sounds.

And into the fire the Forest Gentry threw the two wailing, roaring
females, Fiona and Helena.

A great howl went up from Hockan.

The females roared.

The chanting stopped.

Reuben had never heard such anguish from beast or human as the
wails of Hockan and Berenice and the other females.

He stood stock-still watching all in horror. A low gasp broke from
Sergei. This had all happened in seconds.

Out of the inferno came horrific screams, but the Forest Gentry
held fast. The flames ate the figures of the Forest Gentry but could not
burn and could not devour them as the Forest Gentry shimmered and
shivered and resubstantiated themselves. The great dark timber scaffolding of the fire shifted and crackled, and the fire belched and leapt
against the sky.

The other females were down on their knees wailing. Hockan had
gone quiet. Frank and Sergei stood silent staring as did Margon. Felix
stood transfixed, his great hairy arms and paws crossed over the top of
his head.

A soft despairing sound came from Margon.

The ghastly cries from the bonfires ceased.

Reuben looked down at Phil. Phil lay on his back. Sergei and Thibault were beside him, licking at his wounds as fiercely as they could. Lisa knelt at a distance, her hands clasped in prayer in front of her face.

Elthram suddenly appeared on his knees beside Phil, between Sergei and Thibault. "Hands, hands," said Elthram, and other Forest Gentry crowded around Phil, all laying their hands on him. Elthram appeared to be pressing with great strength on the gushing wound in Phil's side and the deep vicious wound in Phil's shoulder.

Reuben struggled to get close to Phil, but Sergei said, "Be patient. Let them do their work."

Thibault and Margon crouched on the other side of Phil from his injuries; and carefully turning Phil's head, Margon lowered his fangs to bite gingerly into Phil's neck, then drew back, his long pink tongue lapping at the tiny wound he'd made.

Felix, on his knees, had Phil's right hand in his great hairy paws, and he sank his teeth gently into that hand. Phil convulsed as he felt the pain.

But Phil's eyes appeared blind. He was staring up into the night sky as though he were seeing something, something very particular, that no one else could see, and then softly he said, "Reuben? You're here, aren't you, son?"

"Yes, Dad, I'm here," said Reuben. He knelt behind Phil's head, the only place he could find room, and spoke softly in Phil's ear. "I'm with you here, Dad. They're giving you the Chrism to heal you. Each one is giving you the Chrism."

Elthram rose to his feet and the other Gentry backed away like melting shadows. "The bleeding is stopped," said Elthram.

Berenice and Frank now licked Phil's wounds, and Felix and Margon withdrew, as if this new infusion of the Chrism would have some added potency.

The remaining females of the other pack were sobbing in deep, hoarse wolfish sobs. Hockan stood staring into the fire which burned on and on, inevitably dissolving the remains of those it had devoured.

"Modranicht," said Phil softly, eyes still wide and seemingly blind, his eyebrows knit, his mouth quivering slightly. He looked so pale, so moist. It was almost as if he were gleaming.

"The spirit remains well rooted to the body," said Elthram to Reuben. "The Chrism will have its chance now."

Reuben saw Lisa come around and stand over his dad crying softly into her hands. Henrietta and Peter had brought two of the discarded velvet cloaks to cover Phil and bundle him warmly. Lisa was murmuring in an old-fashioned and mournful way, "Oh, Philip, my Philip."

Hockan's low measured voice suddenly rose above Lisa's crying.

"I call all to hear me," he said. "I won't be silent about what's happened here."

No one challenged him. The female wolves remained on their knees, weeping quietly.

"Beware what you've done here," Hockan said, pointing to Margon and to Felix. His rough wolfish voice had given way to a deep yet more human timbre. "Never in all my time have I seen such a thing as this. Spirits roused to shed the blood of the living? This is evil! This is undeniable evil." He turned to look at Reuben, and at Stuart. "Beware, young ones, your citadel is made of glass, your leaders are as blind as you are!"

"Go before you meet the same fate," said Elthram, his face and form brightening. How perfectly terrifying he looked, his green eyes large and menacing as he stared at Hockan. The fire glinted on his dark skin, his black hair. "You and your companions brought malice and foul dealings to the forest. Your companions have paid the price."

"Destroy me you very well might," said Hockan steadily. His voice was still the voice of the beast, but also very much the voice of the man, with its distinct melodic power. "But you cannot destroy the truth." He looked around, taking in each figure individually before he went on. "What I see here is evil, terrible evil."

"Enough," said Margon under his breath.

"Is it enough? It is not enough!" said Hockan. "Your ways, Felix, have always been evil. Your houses, your estates, your greedy attachment to your mortal blood kin, your preening before the eyes of the living. Your seduction of the living. It is evil."

"Stop," said Margon in the same low voice. "You brought the treachery here tonight, and you know this."

"Ah, but it was your sinfulness that provoked it," said Hockan calmly, and with obvious conviction. "Felix, you destroyed your mortal family with your filthy secrets. Your children turned against you and your Morphenkind brothers—selling you for profit—and you shed their blood to punish them. But who had roused the greed of the men of science who bought and paid for you and put you in cages? Who drew them to our secrets? Yet you shed the blood of stupid blundering mortals."

A deep angry sound of protest came from Sergei. He took a small step closer to Hockan. Margon gestured for patience. Hockan ignored them.

"Oh, what a withering shadow you threw over the life of your last descendants, Felix," he said, his voice fast attaining an eerie beauty. "And how they shriveled from the poison of your legacy. The ghost of your murdered niece walks this forest even now, in agony, paying for your sins! Yet you hold a revel in the very house where she was cut down by her own brothers!"

Margon sighed but said nothing. Felix was staring at Hockan, and it was impossible to read into his wolfen face or posture any response. It was the same with all of them. Only a voice or a gesture could reveal a response. And now only Hockan was speaking. Even the mourning females had gone silent. For Reuben to hear these harsh and frightening words spoken with such a beautiful voice was crushing.

"What arrogance, what pride," said Hockan, "what greed for undeserved admiration. And do you think you've seen the last of greedy doctors and government men who would put a price on our heads and hunt us for their laboratories like vermin?"

"Stop," said Margon. "You misjudge everything."

"Do I?" asked Hockan. "I misjudge nothing. You put us all at risk with your revels and your games. Fiona was right, you learned nothing from your own blunders."

"Oh, go away from here, you pompous fool," said Sergei.

Hockan turned and looked at Reuben and Stuart.

"Young ones, I caution you," he said. "Move away from the living; move away from those of flesh and blood who were your kin, for your sake, and for theirs. Mothers, brothers, sisters, friends, unborn child—forswear them. You have no right to them or their affections. The lie you live can only contaminate and destroy them. See what Felix's evil has done already to this one's father."

Margon made a low disgusted and derisive sound. Felix remained still and quiet.

"Oh, yes," said Hockan. His voice now had become tremulous. "Fiona and Helena were unwise, and meddlesome and reckless. I don't deny it. Young Morphenkinder, untried and unchastened and now gone forever. Forever, when they might have lived till the end of time. Into the need fire, the bone fire of Modranicht! What is it now, this fire? What have your Forest Gentry made of it? An unclean funeral pyre. But who provoked those two, our sisters? Who gave them scandal? Where did it all start, that is what you must ask yourselves."

No one answered him.

"It was Felix who drew this innocent man into his web," said Hockan. "Nideck Point is his snare. Nideck Point is his public shame. Nideck Point is his abomination." His voice rose. "And it was Felix who roused the spirits of the forest to an unholy and bloody violence never witnessed before! It is Felix who has strengthened them, emboldened them, enlisted them like dark angels in his unholy designs."

He was visibly trembling, but he drew himself up, and caught his breath and then went on in the same exquisitely modulated voice as before.

"And so now you have these murderous spirits on your side," he said. "Ah, such a wonder. Are you proud, Felix? Are you proud, Margon?"

From Elthram there came a low hiss, and suddenly the same rose from all the Forest Gentry everywhere in the clearing, a storm of hissing in derision.

Hockan stood still regarding them all.

"Young ones," he said. "Burn Nideck Point." He pointed to Reuben, then to Stuart. "Burn it to the very foundations!" His voice rose again until it was just below a roar. "Burn the village of Nideck. Erase it from the earth. That should be your penance at the very least for this, all of you! What right have you to human love, or human adulation! What right have you to darken innocent lives with your duplicity and evil power!"

"Enough from you!" cried Elthram. He was plainly in a rage. All around him, the Forest Gentry collected in vivid color in the glare of the fire.

"I have no stomach for war with you," said Hockan, "any of you. But you all know the truth. Of all the misbegotten immortals roaming this earth, we pride ourselves on rectitude and conscience!" He beat his chest silently with his paws. "We, the protectors of the innocent, are known for the singular gift of knowing good from evil. Well, you have made a mockery of this, all of you. You have made a mockery of *us*. And what are we now but another horror?"

He walked right up to Elthram and stood before him, peering into his eyes. It was a frightful image, Elthram surrounded by his kindred, glaring at the powerfully built white Man Wolf, and the Man Wolf poised as if to spring, but doing nothing.

Slowly, Hockan turned and drew closer to Reuben. His posture shifted from one of confrontation to weariness, his body shuddering.

"What will you say to the mournful and broken soul of Marchent Nideck who seeks your comfort, Reuben?" he asked. His words came on, smooth, seductive. "It's to you that she reveals her sorrow, not to Felix, her guardian and her kin who destroyed her. How will you explain to the murdered Marchent that you share her great-uncle's cursed and pestilential power, feasting now so happily and greedily in this beautiful realm which she gave to you?"

Reuben didn't answer. He couldn't answer. He wanted to protest, with all his soul he wanted to protest, but Hockan's words overwhelmed him. Hockan's passion and conviction had overwhelmed him. Hockan's voice had woven some crippling spell around him. Yet he knew, positively knew, that Hockan was wrong.

Helplessly, he looked down at Phil, who lay half conscious on the ground, his head turned to the side, his body tightly covered by the green velvet cloaks, yet plainly shuddering beneath them.

"Oh, yes, your father," said Hockan, his voice lower, words coming more slowly. "Your poor father. The man who gave you life. And he's ripped out of life now as you were ripped. Are you happy for him?"

No one stirred. No one spoke.

Hockan turned away, and with a series of small eloquent grunts and noises beckoned his remaining female cohorts to go with him, and off they ran except for one, vanishing into the darkness.

That one was Berenice. She remained kneeling close to Phil, and now Frank went to her, and helped her to her feet in the most tender and human manner.

Elthram backed away from the center, out of the direct glare of the bonfire. All around the great arena, against the pale boulders, stood the Forest Gentry watching, waiting.

"Come on, let's take him back home," said Sergei. "Let me carry him."

Gently he scooped up the body of Phil and laid Phil gently against his shoulder. Lisa secured the warm wrappings around Phil, walking beside Sergei as he moved towards the passage out of the clearing.

The other Morphenkinder were all in motion, moving ahead and behind, Laura moving right with them.

The Forest Gentry began to melt away as if they'd never been there. Elthram had vanished.

Reuben wanted to go along with the others, but something held him back. He watched them as they made their way into that narrow passage just beyond where the discarded drums and pipes lay in the dust. The gold-trimmed drinking horns lay about everywhere. And the cauldron still gave off steam on its bed of coals.

Reuben groaned. With his whole soul he groaned. He felt a pain in his belly. It grew bigger and bigger, constricting his heart, throbbing in his temples. The cold air lacerated him, bruised him, and he realized the wolf hair had fallen away from him, leaving him naked.

He saw his naked white fingers trembling before him and felt the wind tear at his eyes.

"No," he whispered. And he willed it to return. "You come back to me," he said in a half whisper. "I won't let you go. Be mine now." And at once the old tingling surged in his hands and in his face. The hair once more grew thick and smooth over him spreading with the inexorable force of water. His muscles sang with the old lupine strength and the warmth enclosed him.

But the tears had risen in his eyes. The bonfire hissed and spat and rustled in his ears.

From his right, Laura approached, this comely gray she-wolf whose face and form resembled his own, this savage pale-eyed monster who was so unutterably beautiful in his eyes. She had come back for him. He fell into her arms.

"You heard him, you heard all the terrible things that he said," Reuben whispered.

"Yes," she said. "I did. But you are bone of my bone, and flesh of my flesh. Come. We will make our truth together."

23

FOR DAYS, ELTHRAM SAT in the cottage by Phil's bed. Phil slept. A powerful drink was given to Phil over and over again to make him sleep, this drink concocted by Elthram and Lisa, and Phil dozed sometimes moaning or singing under his breath, his wounds visibly healing, his fever rising and ebbing and finally dying away.

Slowly, the subtle changes began to appear—the thickening of his white hair with its reddish blond streaks, the restlessness in his legs and arms as his muscles grew stronger. And his eyes, of course, his pale hazel eyes were now a deeper shade of green when from time to time he opened them.

All this time Reuben slept either on the floor near Phil's bed, or in a chair by the fire, or from time to time in the spacious attic above, on a simple mattress bed Lisa made up for him.

Laura brought down Reuben's laptop computer for him, and spent the nights on the attic mattress by his side or alone as he remained below, in the leather recliner by the fire, listening in a half sleep to the rhythm of Phil's breathing. But Laura was often gone. She could not yet control the transformation, and she and Thibault slipped off again and again together in the forest.

Felix and the others looked in on Phil often. A terrible gloom gripped Felix, but he showed no desire to talk with anyone about it. It was as if a dark and tortured soul had taken up residence in Felix's body, claiming Felix's face and voice for his own, though it could not be Felix.

Reuben went out to him and they stood in silence in the rain, merely embracing one another in shared and wordless grief for the terrible twists and turns of Modranicht. Then Felix wandered off alone, and Reuben returned to his vigil.

Margon whispered that they must all leave Felix alone, in the wake of Hockan's scathing excoriations. Sergei snorted with contempt. "Hockan, the judge," he said. "He is the high priest of words and words and words. His words couple with his words and breed more words. His words run rampant."

Stuart appeared from time to time, as tormented as the others. "And so there can be war amongst us," he said to Reuben in anxious whispers. "There can be terrible strife. I knew it." Stuart needed to talk to Reuben and Reuben knew this, but he couldn't leave Phil just now. He couldn't take his mind off Phil. He couldn't answer Stuart's many questions. Besides, who better to answer those questions than Margon, if only Margon would.

Lisa told Reuben that the first thing Felix had done on Wednesday morning was to commence plans for a sprinkler system to protect the house, hooked to the county water supply, but also to a huge reserve tank that would be installed in the parking area behind the servants' wing.

"Nobody will ever burn down Nideck Point," said Felix. "Not while I have breath in my body." Other than those few words, nothing more on the horrors of Modranicht came from Felix.

"He is in Marchent's old room," said Lisa. "He sleeps there on top of her bed. He won't disturb anything. This is not good, this must stop." She shook her head.

But what of Margon, Reuben asked Lisa in furtive whispers—Margon, who was so opposed to the Forest Gentry on general principles? Was he not alarmed that the Forest Gentry had marshaled such physical power on Modranicht? How many times had Reuben been told that the Forest Gentry never harmed anyone?

Lisa waved all this away with the soft answer, "Margon loves your father. He knows why they did what they did."

From time to time, Margon checked on Phil with the careful scrutiny and precision of a doctor, with Stuart always nearby. Margon was easy with Elthram there. They nodded to one another, as if nothing unusual had occurred in the history of the Forest Gentry, as if they had not massed together to kill two Morphenkinder before everyone's eyes.

Finally Phil was out of all danger.

Yet now and then Phil cried out in his sleep, and Lisa knelt beside him whispering. "In the beginning he was with the living and the dead," she told Reuben. "Now he is only with the living."

Elthram spoke to no one. If he could sleep in his material form, he gave no evidence of it. Each morning, people of the Gentry came to bring fresh flowers, which Elthram arranged in vases and glasses around on the windowsills and the tables.

Lisa was as easy with Elthram's presence as she'd ever been. And Sergei and Thibault spoke to him casually now and then when they came to visit the guesthouse, though Elthram only nodded, rarely taking his eyes off Phil.

But surely the massive show of physical power by the Forest Gentry had meant something to the others. It had to have shocked them all. This was much on Reuben's mind. The Forest Gentry could indeed do harm to others when they chose. Who could deny it now?

Yet he felt comfortable with Elthram, indeed, more comfortable perhaps than he'd ever been. Elthram's presence had a soothing affect on him. If Phil took a turn for the worse, Elthram would be the first to see it, and call attention to it. Of that Reuben was sure.

One early morning while Laura slept, Reuben wrote out all that he could remember of Hockan's condemnations. He did not attempt a reconstruction of the speech so much as an accurate record of it. And when he was finished, he lay restless in the warm dry quiet of the attic, the window a patch of white light, feeling a deep dull misery.

On the morning of the fourth day—December 28—Reuben went up while it was still dark to shower and shave, and get fresh clothing. He and Laura made love in their bedroom, and Reuben fell helplessly to sleep afterwards in Laura's arms. It wasn't good, however. It had not been enough. Reuben wanted her in the beast shape; he wanted both of them coupling in the forest, savage as they'd been by the Yule fire. But that would have to wait.

It was ten a.m. when he awakened, alone, filled with guilt and worry for Phil. How could he have left Phil like this? Hastily he pulled on his jeans and his polo shirt, and searched for his shoes and jacket.

It seemed to take him forever to reach the cottage. He came in to find Phil at his desk, writing in his diary. Lisa was assembling his breakfast in the kitchen. Setting down the tray and carafe of coffee, with cups and plates for father and son, she slipped out of the cottage. Elthram was gone.

On and on Phil wrote, and then finally, he shut the diary and rose to his feet. He wore a fresh black sweatshirt and black sweatpants. His dark green eyes regarded Reuben calmly, but abstractly, as though he were struggling to bring himself out of his deepest and most crucial thoughts.

"My boy," he said. He gestured to the breakfast on the table before the window.

"You know what's happened to you?" asked Reuben. He sat down at the table with the window to his left. The sea was a steel blue beneath a bright white sky, and the inevitable rain fell hard in silent sheets of sparkling silver.

Phil nodded.

"What do you remember, Dad?"

"Just about all of it," Phil said. "If I've forgotten anything, well, I don't know what that would be." Hungrily he sliced through the fried eggs, making a mixture of them with the bacon and grits. "Come on, aren't you hungry? A man your age is always hungry."

Reuben stared at the food. "Dad, what do you remember?"

"All of it, son, I told you," said Phil. "Except being carried through the woods, that I don't remember. It was the cold that brought me around, and it took a few minutes. That and the light of the fire. But I remember everything after that. I never lost consciousness. I thought I would. But I never went completely under."

"Dad, did you want us to do what we did?" asked Reuben. "I mean, what we did to save your life. You know now what's happened to you, don't you?"

Phil smiled. "There's always plenty of time to die, isn't there, Reuben?" he answered. "And plenty of opportunity. Yes, I know what you did, and I'm glad that you did it." He looked youthful, vigorous in spite of the familiar creases in his forehead and the slight jowls he'd had for years. His white hair was shot through with thick locks of reddish blond.

"Dad, have you no questions about what you saw?" asked Reuben. "Don't you want an explanation for what you saw? Or what you heard?"

Phil swallowed a couple more forkfuls of food, scooping up plenty of the thick grits with the eggs. Then he sat back and ate the last of the bacon with his fingers.

"Well, you know, son, it wasn't a shock, though to see it that way was a shock all right. But I can't say I was entirely surprised. I knew you'd gone out there to celebrate Modranicht with your friends, and I pretty much figured how that might go for you, the old Yuletide customs being what they are."

"But Dad, you mean you knew?" Reuben asked. "You knew all along what we were, all of us?"

"Let me tell you a story," said Phil. His voice was the same as ever, but his sharp green eyes kept startling Reuben. "Your mother doesn't drink much, you know that. I don't know that you've ever seen your mother drunk, have you?"

"One time, tipsy, maybe."

"Well, she stays off the sauce because she tends to go crazy on it, and always did, and then she blacks out and she can't remember what happened. It's bad for her, bad for her because she becomes emotional and carries on and cries and then she can't own what happened."

"I remember her saying all that."

"And of course, she's a surgeon, and when that phone rings she wants to be ready to go into the operating room."

"Yes, Dad. I know."

"Well, right after Thanksgiving, Reuben, I think it was the following Saturday night, your mother gets completely drunk all by herself and comes into my room crying. Of course she'd been telling the newspapers and the televisions twenty-four/seven that she'd seen the Man Wolf with her own eyes, seen him here at Nideck Point when he broke in the front door and killed those two Russian scientists. Yes, she'd been telling everybody who asked that it was no myth, the California Man Wolf, and that it was some kind of physical mutant, you know, an anomaly, a one-off as she kept saying—a biological reality for which we'd all soon have an explanation. Well, anyway, she comes into my room and she sits down on the side of my bed, just sobbing, and she tells me that she knows, just knows in her heart, that you and all your friends up here are the very same species—'They're all Man Wolves,' she sobs, 'and Reuben's one of them.' And on and on she goes explaining that she knows this to be true, just knows, and knows that your brother Jim knows, because Jim can't talk about it, which can mean only one thing—that Jim can't reveal what was told him in Confession. 'They're all in it together. Did you see that big picture of them all over the library fire? They're monsters, and our son is one of them.'

"Well, of course, I helped her back to bed, and I lay down with her until she stopped crying and went to sleep. And then in the morning, Reuben, she didn't remember a thing except that she'd gotten drunk and she'd cried over something. She was humiliated, terribly humiliated like she always is over any excess emotion, any loss of control, and she swallows half a bottle of aspirin, and goes to work like nothing happened. Well, what do you think I did?"

"You went to see Jim," said Reuben.

"That's exactly right," said Phil with a smile. "Jim was saying the six a.m. Mass as usual when I got there. There was, what, fifty people in the church? Probably half that many. And the street people were all lined up outside waiting to get in to go to sleep in the pews."

"Right," said Reuben.

"And I caught Jim right after Mass, right after he'd said farewell to the people at the front door, and he was heading back up the aisle towards the sacristy. And I told him what she'd said. 'Now you tell me,' I said to Jim, 'is this conceivable? That this Man Wolf creature is not some simple freak of nature, but that there's a tribe of them, and that

your brother is in fact part of that tribe? That this is some secret species that's always existed, and when Reuben was bitten up there in that
house in the dark, he became one of them?'"

Phil stopped and took a deep swallow of the hot coffee.

"And what did Jim say?" asked Reuben.

"That was just it, son. He didn't say anything. He just looked at me
for a long time, and the expression on his face, well, I don't have words
to describe it. And then he looked up at the high altar. And I saw he
was looking at the statue of St. Francis and the Wolf of Gubbio. And
then he said, in the most sad, discouraged voice, 'Dad, I don't have any
light to shed on this.'

"And I said, 'Okay, son, we'll let it go, and your mother can't
remember any of this anyway.' And I just went on out, but I knew. I
knew it was all true. I knew it was true, really, when your mother was
laying it out, I felt it was true, felt it, felt it in here. But I knew it
was true then when I watched Jim walking on back to the sacristy
behind the altar—because there were a million things he might have
said if it had been nonsense, and he didn't say any of them."

He wiped his mouth with his napkin, and refilled his mug with
coffee. "You do know that Lisa makes the best coffee in the world,
don't you?"

Reuben didn't answer. He was feeling so sorry for Jim, so sorry that
he'd ever burdened Jim, yet what would he do without Jim? Well, there
was time to deal with Jim, to made amends, to give thanks, to thank
him for taking over with Susie Blakely.

"But, Dad, if Mom knew," Reuben asked, "why ever did she let you
come up here to live with us?"

"Son, she blacked out that night, I told you. What she'd revealed
had come from someplace deep down inside that's closed off to her
when she isn't drinking. And the next day she didn't know. And she
doesn't know now."

"Ah, but she does," said Reuben. "She does. What the liquor did
was let her speak of it, confess it, face it. And she also knows she can't
do anything about it, that she can never mention it out loud to me, she

can never become an accessory to it. The only way she can live with it is to pretend she doesn't have an inkling."

"Maybe so," he said. "But to get back to your question, what did I think when I saw all of you out there in the forest on Christmas Eve? Well, I was shocked. I'll grant you that. It was as shocking a spectacle as anything I've ever seen in my life. But I wasn't surprised, and I knew what was happening. And I knew that wily Helena, I knew her by her Polish accent when she picked me up out of my bed with her great hairy arms, when she said, 'Are you willing to die for your son, to teach him and his friends a lesson?'"

"She said that to you?"

He nodded. "Oh yes. That was her scheme, apparently, and I knew the voice of Fiona, who was with her. Ah, such monsters! And right here in this room. 'Foolish man,' she said, that Fiona. 'That you ever came here. Most humans have better instincts.'"

He sipped the coffee, then put his elbows on the table and ran his hands back through his hair. He seemed a man some twenty years younger now, whatever the stamp of age on his face. His shoulders were remarkably straight and his chest was broader. And even his hands were larger and stronger than they had been.

"I blacked out after they appeared here," he said. "But when I came to in the forest, I understood their evil plan, those two, to use me as the living proof that Felix's way with Nideck Point, of living in the very midst of human beings, of carrying on as if he were a living man, a normal man, a generous man—that this was all, as Fiona called it, folly. I saw and heard all that when the spectacle unraveled."

"Then you know what happened to Fiona and Helena," said Reuben.

"Not at first I didn't," said Phil. "That is the one part that wasn't clear, that was puzzling me. But as I was lying there in that bed, I was having nightmares some of the time, nightmares that they'd burn down Nideck Point, and burn down the village."

"She spoke about those very things," said Reuben.

"Right, I'd heard that part," said Phil. "But what wasn't clear to me was that she and Helena were gone. I hadn't seen what happened to them. The nightmares were terrible. I grabbed hold of Lisa and tried to get her to understand that Nideck Point was in danger from those two. And that's when Lisa told me, told me how Elthram and the Gentry had driven them into the fire. She explained to me who the Gentry were, or at least she tried to. She said something about them being the 'woodland spirits' and not people like us." He laughed softly under his breath, shaking his head. "I should have known. Well, Lisa said no one had ever seen the Forest Gentry do such a thing. But the Forest Gentry would never have done it without 'grave cause.' And then Elthram was there, I mean by my bed, right beside Lisa. I saw him looking down at me. And he placed one of his warm hands on me. And Elthram said, 'You are all safe.'"

"That's what happened," said Reuben.

"And then I knew they weren't coming to harm anybody, and I better understood all the rest of what I'd heard—what I'd heard Hockan saying out there, with his voice like Giazotto's notorious Adagio in G Minor."

Reuben gave a little bitter laugh. "Yes, it's exactly like that, isn't it?"

"Oh, yes, that Hockan has quite a voice. But then they all do. Felix has a voice like a Mozart piano concerto, always full of light; and Sergei, well, Sergei sounds like Beethoven."

"Not Wagner?"

"No," said Phil, smiling. "I like Beethoven better. But about Hockan, I sensed a sadness in him at the banquet, a kind of deep broken melancholy, I guess I'd call it, and how he seemed to love that Helena even though she frightened him. I could see that. Her questions to me frightened him." He shook his head. "Yeah, Hockan, he's the violin in the Adagio in G Minor all right."

"And it is all right with you what's happened," asked Reuben. "That they used the Chrism to save your life, and that you're now one of us."

"Didn't I just say that it was?" asked Phil.

"Can I be blamed for asking a question like that twice?" asked Reuben.

"No, of course not," said Phil gently. He sat back and looked at Reuben with the saddest smile. "You are so young, and so naïve and so truly good of heart," he said.

"Am I? I always wanted you with us!" Reuben whispered.

"I knew what I was doing when I came here," said Phil.

"How could you have really known?"

"It wasn't the mystery that drew me," Phil explained. "It wasn't mad speculation as to whether these friends of yours really had the secret of living forever. Oh, I knew there was a possibility of that, yes. I'd been putting it together for some time, just as your mother had. It wasn't only the picture in the library, or the unusual personalities of the men who were living with you. It wasn't just their curious anachronistic speech, or the odd points of view they hold. Hell, you've always had a way of speaking that made us joke about your being a little change-ling." He shook his head. "So it wasn't all that surprising that you'd cultivate some group of otherworldly friends who sounded as strange as you sometimes sound. No, it's overwhelming and irresistible, surely, immortality. It is. But I don't know that I quite believed that part of it all. I don't know that I believe it now. It's easier to believe that a human being can turn into a beast than it is to believe he'll live forever."

"I understand that perfectly," said Reuben. "I feel exactly that way, myself."

"No, it was something more mundane than that yet infinitely more profound and meaningful that brought me here. I was coming to live with you in this anointed place, because I had to do it! I just had to. I had to seek this refuge against the world to which I'd given my long and dreary and inconsequential life."

"Dad—."

"No, son. Don't argue with me. I know who I am. And I knew I had to come. I had to be here. I had to spend my remaining days some-where that I truly *wanted* to be, doing the things that mattered to me, no matter how trivial. Walking the woods, reading my books, writing my poems, looking out at that ocean, that endless ocean. I had to. I couldn't keep moving towards the grave step by step—choked with regret, choked with bitterness and disappointment!" He sucked in his breath as though he were in pain. His eyes were fixed on the barely visible line of the horizon.

"I understand, Dad," said Reuben quietly. "In my own way, my young and naïve way, I felt the same thing the first day I came here. I can't say I was on a dreary path to the grave. I just knew I'd never lived, that I'd been avoiding living—like I'd learned early to decide against life rather than for it."

"Ah, that's beautiful," Phil said. His smile brightened again as he looked at Reuben.

"Dad, do you understand the things that Hockan said? Did you follow the thread?"

"Most of it," said Phil. "It was a bit like a dream. I was lying right on the earth and the earth was cold, but I was warm under those coverings. And I was listening to him. I knew he was aiming his powerful arrows at Felix and at you and Stuart. I heard him. I put it all together. And in the nights since I've been going over and over it, with Lisa's little whispers here and there, patching it together."

Reuben screwed up his courage, and then he asked, "Do you think there was truth in what Hockan said? Do you think he was right?"

"What do you think, Reuben?" asked Phil.

"I don't know," said Reuben, but the words were lame. "Each time I talk about it with myself, each time I see Felix or Margon or Sergei—I come to realize a little more that I have to make up my mind, my own mind, as to what I feel about the things Hockan said to us."

"I understand that. I respect that."

Reuben reached inside his jacket and withdrew a folded piece of paper, and then he handed that to Phil.

"That's everything he said to us, written down there," Reuben explained. "That's every word. Exactly as I recall it."

"My son, the honor student," said Phil. He unfolded the page, and read the words slowly, thoughtfully, and then closed up the page again.

He looked expectantly at Reuben.

"It's had a devastating effect on Felix," said Reuben. "He's deeply discouraged."

"That's understandable," said Phil. He had more to say, but Reuben continued.

"Margon does not seem moved, one way or the other," he said, "and Sergei and Stuart seem absolutely to have forgotten all of it, to have swept it aside like it never happened. They certainly aren't afraid of Elthram and the Forest Gentry. They seem as comfortable with them as they ever were."

"And Laura?"

"Laura has asked the obvious question: 'Who is Hockan? Is Hockan an oracle? Or is Hockan a fallible creature like the rest of us?'"

"So the ones who've been really hurt by this are you and Felix?"

"I don't know, Dad. I can't get his words out of my head! I've never been able to get the negative voices of my life out of my head. I've struggled all my life to find my own truth and I find myself smothered by other people's words. It's as though they're always shouting at me, bullying me, shaking their fists, and half the time I can't find what I think."

"Don't sell yourself short, son," said Phil. "I think you do know what you think."

"Dad, know this," said Reuben. "I love that house, this place, this part of the world's great forest. I want to bring my son here. I want to be here with you. I love them all, my new family. I love them more than I can say. Laura, Felix, Margon, Stuart, Thibault, Sergei, all of them. I love Lisa, whoever and whatever she is. I love the Forest Gentry."

"I hear you, son," said Phil, smiling. "I'm extremely fond of Lisa, too." He gave a short secretive laugh. "'Whoever and whatever' she might be."

"The thought of leaving Nideck Point behind, of breaking off all contact with my mom, of giving my son over to Mom to bring up, of never seeing Jim again—these are things I can hardly bear to think about. My heart's breaking."

Phil only nodded.

"I feel larger and stronger here than I've ever felt anywhere," said Reuben. "That day at the village fair and the banquet here, I sensed a creative energy all around me. I felt a creative spirit that was infectious. I don't know any other words to describe it. I felt it was good, all that Felix had done, all that Felix had brought into being. It was like magic, Dad. Over and over he made something out of nothing. A bleak winter, a dying town, a great empty house, a day that might have been like a thousand other days. He transformed all this. And it was good. I swear it was. Yet here comes Hockan's judgment, Hockan's dark reading of the script to make some other story out of it."

"Yes, Reuben, that's just what Hockan did," said Phil.

"Hockan calls this great house a snare, an abomination."

"Yes, son, I heard him."

"What is Felix's sin, Dad? That he wants to live in fellowship with all living creatures—with spirits, ghosts, Morphenkinder, with Ageless Ones like Lisa, with human beings? Is that really evil? Is that the Original Sin here that killed Marchent?"

"What do you think, Reuben? Is it?"

"Dad, I have no idea what immortality is. I've admitted that before. I just don't know. But I do know I'm struggling here for the finer feeling, for the finer understanding. Whatever I am, I have a soul. I've known that always. And I can't believe that Marchent's out there lost and suffering because of the dreadful secret of what we are, because of the sins of Felix in loving her and her parents and keeping our secrets from them. Felix would never have left Marchent if those evil men hadn't taken him prisoner."

"I know, son. I know the story. Hockan provided all the missing pieces of the puzzle to me as I was lying there in that clearing."

"And I can't lay the blame on Felix that the Forest Gentry astonished everyone. They did something that no one knew they could do. That's obvious. But was that Felix's doing because he called them and invited them here?"

"No. I don't think it was," said Phil. "The Forest Gentry have always had their own reservoir of power."

"If only I could talk to Marchent!" said Reuben. "If only I could hear her voice. I've seen her, seen her tears, seen her misery. Hell. I've even made love to her, Dad, held her in my arms. But no voice comes from her. No truth comes from her."

"And what could she tell you, Reuben?" Phil asked. "She's a ghost, not a deity or an angel. She's a lost soul. Beware of what she might say, just as you should beware of Hockan."

Reuben sighed. "I know that. I know that. I keep wanting to ask Elthram. Surely he knows why she haunts. He must know."

"Elthram knows what Elthram knows," said Phil. "Not what Marchent knows, if she knows anything."

They were quiet. Phil drank another mug of coffee. And outside the rain picked up, shimmering and singing on the windows. Such an intimate sound, the rain gusting on the panes. The colorless sky unaccountably brightened in spite of the rain, and far out to sea a ship moved on the distant horizon. It was barely visible in the gray dazzle of the sea.

"You won't tell me what to do, will you?" asked Reuben.

"You don't want me to tell you what to do," said Phil. "You need to discover that for yourself. But I will tell you this. You've taken my mind off my rapidly fading aches and pains; you've done me wonders. And whatever happens, whatever you decide, whatever Felix decides, nobody will separate you from me or me from you and Laura."

"That's true. That is absolutely true." He looked at his father. "You're happy, aren't you, Dad?"

"Yes," Phil answered.

24

IT WAS THEIR FIRST DINNER together since Modranicht. They sat around the dining room table, eagerly feasting on the baked fish, roast chicken, and sliced pork with platters of hot steaming buttered greens and carrots. Lisa had baked fresh bread, and apple pies for dessert. And the chilled Riesling was sparkling in the crystal decanters and glasses.

Reuben was in his usual place, to the right of Margon, and Laura sat beside Reuben. Then came Berenice and Frank, and Sergei, while opposite sat Felix as always with Thibault on his left and Stuart next with Phil beside him.

It was easy and quiet as if they'd dined this way a hundred times before, and when the conversation erupted, it was of ordinary things, like the little New Year's Eve party scheduled for the village Inn, or the unchanging weather.

Felix was silent. Utterly silent. And Reuben could hardly bear the expression on Felix's face—the shadow of dread in his eyes as they stared listlessly at nothing.

It seemed that Margon was being uncommonly gentle with Felix, and more than once tried to talk to him about unimportant or neutral matters, but when no answer came from Felix, Margon didn't press it, as if he knew this would defeat his kind purpose.

At one point, Berenice said in a casual polite way that the other female wolves had gone back to Europe, and that she might soon be joining them. This was obviously not news to Frank, but it was news to the other men, yet not a single one asked what Reuben wanted to ask: had Hockan not gone with them?

Reuben wasn't going to utter the name "Hockan" at this table.

Finally Margon said, "Well, Berenice, you are certainly welcome to remain here if you don't want to go. Surely you know that."

She only nodded. There was a look of deliberate resignation on her face. Frank was simply staring off as if this were of no concern to him.

"Look, Berenice," said Thibault. "I think you should stay with us. I think you should forget your old ties to those creatures. There's no reason why we can't attempt a pack of males and females again. And this time we ought to make it work. Indeed, my dear, we have Laura with us now."

Berenice was startled, but not offended. She only smiled. Laura was watching all this, with obvious concern.

In a soft voice, Laura said, "I would like it if you stayed, but of course this is your affair, not mine."

"We'll all like it if you stay," said Frank dismally. "Why do women so often form their own packs? Why can't we live in peace together?"

No one said a word.

Just before the end of the meal, when they'd had their fill of the apple pie and the espresso and Sergei had gulped down an enormous quantity of brandy, in came Elthram, dressed in his familiar beige chamois leather, and without a word, he seated himself in the armchair at the foot of the table.

Margon welcomed him with an agreeable nod. Elthram sat back, almost slouching in the armchair, and smiled at Margon as he made a little helpless shrugging gesture.

All this was so puzzling to Reuben. Why wasn't Margon furious that the Forest Gentry had done what they did? Why was he not claiming that he had foreseen such a grisly possibility? Or that he'd been right to warn against their involvement? But Margon had not been saying such things, and now he sat comfortably with Elthram at the foot of the table.

Stuart was drinking in every detail of Elthram with a kind of startled fascination. Elthram gave him a gentle smile, but the company continued in its miserable silence.

One after another was slipping away. Berenice and Frank headed off to drive down to the village for a nightcap at the Inn. Stuart went up to finish the novel he'd been reading. Suddenly Sergei was gone along with the brandy. And Thibault asked Laura if she might help him with his usual frustrating computer difficulties.

Phil rose to take his leave, pleading utter exhaustion, and refused all offers of assistance, saying he had not the slightest difficulty now in walking or seeing his way to the cottage in the darkness.

And it was the "cottage" now, wasn't it, not the "guesthouse."

Elthram sat there staring fixedly at Margon. Something silent seemed to pass between them. Margon rose, and giving a quick warm embrace to Felix, who did not acknowledge it at all, he went out towards the library.

Silence.

No sound came from anywhere, not the low fire in the grate or the kitchen. The rain had died away completely, and the lighted forest beyond the windows was a sweet yet sad spectacle.

Reuben looked up to see Elthram watching him.

Only Reuben and Felix and Elthram remained.

Then after a long period of quiet, Elthram said: "Go now, both of you. Go to the clearing, if you would see her."

Felix gave a violent start. He glared at Elthram. Reuben was stunned. "You mean it?" Reuben asked. "She'll be there?"

"She wants you to come," said Elthram. "Go now, while the rain is slacking. A fire burns there. I've seen to it. She wants to come through. It's in the clearing that she'll be strongest."

Before Reuben could say another word, Elthram was gone.

Quickly and quietly, Felix and Reuben went to the closet for their overcoats and scarves, and went out the back door. The forest sang of the rain but there was no rain now, just the high branches releasing their soft trickling downfall.

Felix walked ahead rapidly through the darkness.

Reuben struggled to keep up, realizing that once they were beyond the house lights and the lights of the oak forest, he'd be utterly lost without Felix.

It seemed an eternity that they struggled along one narrow uneven path after another. Reuben managed to put on his leather gloves without slowing his pace, and he wrapped his scarf high around his face against the wind.

The deep woods trembled and whispered with the collected rain, and the earth beneath their feet was often muddy and slippery.

Finally, Reuben saw a pale flickering gleam against the sky, and he made out in the light of that gleam the line of the approaching boulders.

Through the narrow pass, they slipped as before, and into the vast clearing. The strong smell of soot and ashes rose in Reuben's face. But the cold air seemed at once to dilute it and diffuse it.

All the debris of Modranicht was gone—the scattered instruments, the drinking horns, the coals, the cauldron. A great black circle was all that remained of the bonfire, and in the center of it stood another small blaze, made up of thick oak logs, flames leaping in the swirling mist.

To this blaze they went, walking through the charred and shiny bits and pieces of the old fire. Reuben was painfully aware that Fiona and Helena had died here. But there was no time for mourning the two who had attacked Phil.

They stood as close to the little fire as they could, and Reuben stripped off the gloves and buried them in his pockets. He and Felix stood side by side warming their hands. Felix shivered in the cold. Reuben's pulse was racing.

And what if she doesn't come, Reuben thought desperately but didn't dare to speak the words. And what if she does and what she says to us is terrible, more lacerating, more wounding, more damning than any words that came from Hockan?

He was shaking his head, biting into his lower lip, fighting the sheer misery of the anticipation, when he realized that another figure was standing directly opposite, on the other side of the fire, quite visible above the leaping flames, gazing at him.

"Felix," he said, and Felix looked up and saw the figure as well.

A low moan came from Felix's lips. "Marchent."

The figure grew suddenly brighter than it had been, and Reuben saw her fully realized face, fresh and supple as it had looked on the last day of her life. Her cheeks were rosy from the cold and her lips were faintly pink. Her gray eyes were sparkling in the firelight. She wore a simple gray garment with a hood, and beneath the hood, he saw her short blond hair framing her oval face.

She was not four feet away from them.

The only sharp sound came from the lively fire, and beyond a soft series of sighs came from the great forest.

Then came the sound of Marchent's voice for the first time since the night of her death.

"How can you think that I am unhappy that you are here together?" she asked. Ah, that voice, that voice which Reuben had never forgotten, so crisp, so distinct, so gentle. "Reuben, this house, this land, I wanted so for you to have it; and Felix, I wanted so for you to be conscious and alive and well, and beyond the reach of anyone who could ever harm you. And you two, whom I've loved with all my soul, you are now friends, you are now kindred, you are now together."

"My darling, my blessed darling," said Felix in the most broken and bruised voice. "I love you so much. I always did."

Reuben was shaking violently. The tears spilled down his face. Clumsily he wiped at them with his scarf, but truly he didn't care about them. He kept his eyes focused on her, as her voice came again with the same distinct and muted power.

"I know this, Felix," she said. She was smiling. "I always knew. Do you think that, living or dead, I've ever laid blame on you for anything? Your friend, Hockan, and he is your friend, enlists me in a cause for which I have no sympathy."

Her face was absolutely warm and expressive as she spoke, her voice as lyrical and natural as it had been that last day.

"Now, please, both of you listen to me. I don't know how much longer I have to say these things to you. When the invitation comes again, I must accept it. Your tears hold me here now, and I must set you free, that I too might be free."

She gestured naturally with her hands as she spoke, and it seemed she moved closer to the fire, impervious to its heat.

"Felix, it was not your secret power that darkened my life," she said tenderly. "It was the unspeakable treachery of my loveless parents. I died at the hands of those who were diseased and blind. You were the sunshine of my life in the garden you planted here for your descendants. And in my darkest hour, when all the vibrant world defied my reach, it was you, Felix, who sent the gentle spirits of the forest to bring me light and understanding."

Felix wept softly, soundlessly. He wanted to speak, Reuben could see that, but Marchent's eyes had shifted to Reuben.

"Reuben, your loving face has been my lamp," she said. It was the same manner she'd taken with him on the fatal day, naturally kind and almost tender. "Let me be your lamp now. I see your innocence abused again—not by your old family—but this time by one who speaks with bitterness and feigned authority. Look well at the dark intelligence he offers you. He would cut you off from those you love and those who love you in return—from the very school in which all souls imbibe the greatest wisdom." She lowered her voice, underscoring her outrage with understatement. "How dare a living soul consign you to the ranks of the damned, or devise for you a bleak and penitential path of fetters and circumscription? You are what you are, not what others would have you be. And who does not struggle with life and death? Who does not face the chaos of the living breathing world as you and Felix do? Reuben, resist the curse that claims the power of Scripture. Resist my words, Reuben, if they offend the deepest longings of your honest spirit."

She paused but only to include both of them now as she continued.

"Felix, you left this house and land to me. I gifted it in your memory to Reuben. And now I leave you both, bound by ties as strong as any under heaven. The lamps burn bright again at Nideck Point. Your future stretches to infinity. Remember me. And forgive me. Forgive me for what I didn't know, and didn't do, and failed to see. I will remember you wherever I go, as long as memory itself survives in me."

She smiled. There was the tiniest trace of apprehension, of fear in her face and her voice. "This is farewell, my darlings. I know that I go on, but I don't know to what, or where, or if I will ever see you again.

But I see you now, vital and precious, and filled with an undeniable power. And I love you. Pray for me."

She went still. She became the picture of herself, eyes looking forward, lips softly closed, her expression one of faint wonder.

Then her face began to waver, to fade. And soon all that was left of her was the outline of her figure drawn on the darkness. Finally that too vanished.

"Good-bye, my darling," whispered Felix. "Good-bye, my precious girl."

Reuben was crying uncontrollably.

The wind was soughing in the dark invisible trees that towered all around the clearing.

Felix wiped his tears with his scarf and then put his arms around Reuben, and steadied him.

"She's gone now, Reuben, gone home," said Felix. "Don't you see? She has set us free, just as she said she wanted to do." He was smiling through his own tears. "I know she'll find the light; her heart's too pure, her courage too strong, for anything else."

Reuben nodded, but all he could feel for the moment was grief, grief that she was gone, grief that he'd never hear her voice again, and only slowly did he come to realize that a great consolation was being given to him.

When he turned and looked again into Felix's eyes, he felt a deep calm, a trust that somehow the world was the good place he'd always believed it to be.

"Come," said Felix, hugging him close, and then letting him go, his eyes filled now with the old vigor and light. "They must all be waiting for us, and they must be so afraid. Let's go to them."

"It's all perfectly all right again," said Reuben.

"Yes, dear boy, it is," said Felix. "And we will disappoint her terribly if we don't realize it."

Slowly they turned and made their way back across the field of ash and cinders, to the narrow passage between the boulders, and began the long walk to the house in easy silence.

25

PASTOR GEORGE CAME IN the afternoon. She'd called Reuben the night before and asked to see him privately. And he could not refuse.

They met in the library. She was dressed prettily again, as she had been for the Christmas party, this time in a red pantsuit with a white silk scarf wound around her neck. Her short gray hair was nicely curled, and she wore a bit of powder and lipstick, as if this was an important visit for her.

Reuben invited her to take the wing chair by the fire. He sat on the Chesterfield sofa. The coffee and pound cake was already set out, and he poured for her.

She seemed quite calm and pleasant and as soon as he asked about Susie, she explained that Susie was doing remarkably well. Once Father Jim had believed Susie, then Susie had been willing to talk to him and her parents about "the other things" that had happened to her when she was abducted, and Susie was now a happy child.

"I cannot thank you enough for all you did," said Pastor George. "Her parents have taken her in to see Father Jim twice," she said. "They attended Midnight Mass at his church."

Reuben couldn't disguise his satisfaction and relief, but Pastor George only knew half of it. No, Jim couldn't and wouldn't ever break the seal of Reuben's Confession. But Jim had been able to believe Susie, to do good for Susie.

Pastor George went on a bit about how nice Father Jim was, and how he was the first Catholic priest she'd ever personally known. He'd agreed to come speak at her little church on the needs of the homeless, and she was profoundly grateful. "I didn't think a priest would come to a little nondenominational church like mine, but he's more than willing. And we're so glad."

"He's a good guy," Reuben said with a quick smile. "And he's my brother. I've always been able to rely on Jim."

Pastor George fell silent.

Now what, Reuben was thinking. How will she talk around it, speculate on the mystery of the Man Wolf, how will she lead up to it, and then back off from it? He braced himself, still not certain at all as to what he would do and say to distance himself from the mystery, to keep the conversation abstract and vague.

"You're the one who rescued Susie, aren't you?" asked Pastor George.

He was stunned.

She looked directly at him, calm as before. "That was you, wasn't it?" she asked. "You brought her to my door."

He knew he was blushing. And he could feel the tremors in his legs and in his hand. He said nothing.

"I know it was you," she said in a low confidential voice. "I knew when you said good-bye to her that way, upstairs here, when you said, 'I love you, darling dear.' I knew it from other things, from what people call demeanor—the way you moved, the way you walked, the sound of your voice. Oh, it wasn't the same, no, but there's a . . . a cadence to a person's voice, a personal cadence. It was you."

He didn't answer. He didn't know precisely what to do or what to say, only that he could not ever admit this to her. He could not be drawn into any sort of admission, now or ever; and yet he hated the idea of lying to her, hated it with his whole being.

"Susie knows, too," said Pastor George. "But she doesn't have to come here and ask you about it. She knows, and for her now, that's enough. You're her hero. You're her secret friend. She can tell your brother, Jim, that she knows because he's a priest and can never tell anyone what he's heard from her in Confession. And so she doesn't have to tell anyone else ever who you are. I don't either. Neither of us has to tell. But I had to come here. I had to say it. I don't know why I had to come here, why I had to ask you but I do. Maybe because I'm a pastor, a believer, somebody for whom the mysterious is just, well, very real." Her voice was even, almost emotionless.

He held her gaze without saying a word.

"The police have it all wrong, don't they?" she asked. "They've been searching up and down the coast for some Yeti or Sasquatch when in fact the Man Wolf changes into what he is, and changes back. The Man Wolf is a werewolf. I don't know how he does it. But they haven't a clue."

The blood was pounding in his cheeks. He looked down. He reached for his cup of coffee but his hand was shaking far too badly to manage it, and he laid his hand gently on the arm of the sofa. Slowly, he looked at her again.

"I just had to know if I was right," she said. "I had to know that it wasn't all vague suspicions on my part, that it was you. Believe me, I bear you no ill will. I can't judge something or someone like you. I know you saved Susie. She'd be dead by now if you hadn't saved her. And when Susie needed you, here at this house, you were here for her and you connected her with the man who could help her heal. I bear you no ill will."

Images more than thoughts were rushing through Reuben's mind, jumbled and jarring images of the Yule fire, of the Forest Gentry, of the horrific immolation of the two Morphenkinder, of that miserable man who'd kidnapped Susie, of his bloodied broken body as Reuben had held it in his paws. Then his mind went black. He'd looked off again and now he focused once more on Pastor George. His head was throbbing but he had to keep looking into her eyes.

She was simply looking at him, her face broad and placid and agreeable.

She picked up her cup of coffee and drank. "That's good coffee," she said under her breath. Then she set the cup down again, and looked into the fire.

"I want only the best things in this world for Susie," said Reuben, his voice quavering as he struggled to keep it under control.

"I know," she said. She nodded, eyes still on the flames. "I want the same. I want the best things in this world for everybody. I don't ever want to cause any being harm." The words seemed chosen carefully and they were spoken slowly. "I'll tell you. The most radical thing about a conversion to God is the determination to love, to really love in His name."

"I think you're right," said Reuben.

"Well, that's what your brother Jim says too."

When she looked at him again, she smiled. "I wish you every good thing in the world, Mr. Golding." She rose to her feet. "I want to thank you for letting me come here."

He rose with her and he walked with her slowly to the door.

"Please understand, I had to know," she said. "It was as if my sanity depended upon it."

"I do understand," he said.

He threw his arm around her as he walked her out onto the terrace. The wind was fierce, and the droplets of rain were like bits of steel biting into his face and hands.

He opened the door of her car for her.

"Take care, Pastor George," he said. He could hear the tremor in his voice, but hoped that she could not. "And please stay in touch. Please write me when you can. And send me news of Susie."

"I'll do that, Mr. Golding." This time her smile was bright and easy. "I'll keep you always in my prayers."

He stood watching as she drove down the hill to the gates.

It was an hour later that he told all this to Felix and Margon.

They were sitting in the kitchen, having their afternoon tea. They liked tea much more than coffee, it seemed, and every afternoon at four, of late, they had their afternoon tea.

They were surprisingly unconcerned, and each commended Reuben on how he had handled it.

"You did the very best thing that you could," said Felix.

"It doesn't really matter, does it?" asked Reuben. "She'll keep it to herself. She has to. Nobody will believe her if . . ."

Neither of them answered and then Margon said,

"She'll keep it to herself until somebody she knows and loves suffers some unspeakable violence, some terrible evil. And then you will hear from her. She will come to you for justice. She will call you and tell you about what's happened to her friend or her relative or someone in her flock, and she'll tell you who has done the terrible violence if she knows; and she won't ask you to do anything. She'll simply tell you the story, and leave it at that. And that's how it begins, the calls here and there from those who know and who want us to help. Nobody will ever explain why they are telling you their tale of woe. But they will call or come and they will tell you. She will be the first perhaps; or Susie Blakely may be the first. Who knows? Maybe Galton will be the first, or the sheriff of the county, or someone you can't recall ever meeting. Again, who knows? But it will start to happen, and when it does, you must handle it just the way you handled her this afternoon. Admit nothing. Volunteer nothing. Offer nothing. Simply take the information and bring it to us. And we will decide, together, you and Felix and I, what should be done."

"This is inevitable," said Felix calmly. "Do not worry. The more we do what they ask of us the more loyal they become."

26

It was New Year's Eve. A great storm had hit the coast, flooding out roads from one end of the county to another; the winds shook the rafters of Nideck Point, and wailed in the chimneys. On all sides, a blinding rain washed against the windows.

Phil had been brought up early that afternoon to spend the night in the house, in a fine bedroom on the east side, where he'd slept before, and where everything had been done for his comfort.

Sparks flew in the oak forest before the lights went out. The emergency generator kicked on to fuel the bare minimum of household circuits. And in the kitchen the supper was cooked by the light of oil lamps, with all that had been laid in ahead of time against the weather.

Once again the company was in black tie, at Felix's buoyant suggestion, and even Phil had given in, but not without quoting Emerson to the extent that one must be aware of all enterprises that require new clothes.

Laura had come downstairs in a long dress of cobalt blue, with jeweled straps over her bare shoulders. And all the servants were dressed to join the company, as was the custom, at the table.

Lisa had renounced her customary black for a striking long sleeve gown made entirely of intricate ivory lace, studded with pearls and tiny diamonds. And Henrietta, so silent, so shy, wore a youthful dress of pink taffeta. Even Heddy, the eldest of them all, and always so quiet and unobtrusive, had put on a festive green velvet dress that revealed for the first time her well-proportioned figure.

Berenice had not left yet to join the other pack, and indeed her leaving was now not certain at all. And when she appeared in black chiffon, Frank was appropriately delighted, showering her with kisses.

Margon surrendered the head of the table to Felix, taking Felix's old chair beside Stuart.

And as soon as the table was laid with the pheasant, the chicken roasted with honey, and the thick broiled steaks seasoned in butter and garlic, the servants came in and took their places for the blessing said in a quiet voice by Felix.

"Maker of the Universe, we thank you as this year comes to an end," said Felix, "that we are again under this roof, and with our very dearest friends, and we thank you too that the *Geliebten Lakaien* are once again here with us. Lisa, Heddy, Henrietta, Peter, and Jean Pierre, we give thanks for each and every one of you."

"The *Geliebten Lakaien*," Margon repeated, "and for those of you who don't share our German tongue, this is the old and legendary name for these 'beloved servants' who have for so long protected us and kept our home fires burning. All the world knows them by that name, and they are much sought after and cherished. We're grateful, truly grateful, to have their trust and loyalty."

All the company repeated the salute, and a blush came to Lisa's cheeks. If this is a man, thought Reuben, well, it's the best-disguised man I've ever seen. But in truth he now thought of Lisa exclusively as feminine. And he savored the title for these mysterious Ageless Ones, and welcomed this new bit of interesting intelligence.

"And to you, good masters, young and old," said Lisa with her glass raised. "Never for a moment do we forget the value of your love and protection."

"Amen," cried Margon. "And no more speeches now while the food is hot. The grandfather clock is chiming ten p.m. and I am starving." He sat down immediately and reached for a platter of meat, giving everyone else permission to start serving.

Frank saw to it that a spirited Vivaldi concerto was pouring out of the little speakers of the Bose player on the hunter's board, and then joined the rest of the company.

Laughter and lively conversation had returned to Nideck Point. And the pounding storm only made the whole party all the more convivial and stimulating. Conversation rolled easily round the table, often sweeping up the entire group, and other times breaking naturally into pockets of animated voices and eager faces.

"But what do the Forest Gentry do on a night like this?" asked Phil. They could hear the shifting and groaning of the old oaks. Far off somewhere in the darkness there came a violent cracking sound as of a branch broken from a trunk.

"Ah, well, I invited them to the feast," said Margon, "at least Elthram and Mara and whomever they might want to bring, but they told me in the gentlest terms that they had other centennials to attend in the far north, so I would suppose they are not here. But insofar as they have no real bodies, and exist as elements in the air, I can't imagine that a storm does anything more than excite them."

"But they'll be coming back, won't they?" asked Stuart.

"Oh, most certainly," said Felix. "But when only they know, and never believe that the woods are without spirits. There are others out there, others we don't know by name and who do not know us by name, but they might manifest if ever they feel the need to do it."

"Are they guarding this house?" asked Laura in a small voice.

"Yes, they are," said Felix. "They are guarding it. And no one under this roof should ever feel the slightest fear of them. As for anyone who tries to hurt this house . . ."

"But this is not the night to talk of such threats or such worries or such routine and petty annoyances," said Margon. "Come, let's drink again. Let's drink to each and every one of this rare and priceless company."

And so it went on, toast after toast, as the fowl and the meat were devoured, and at last the table was cleared by all hands as naturally as it had always been done here, and the fresh fruits and the cheeses were laid out with the more egregious and stunning chocolate desserts and German pastries.

It was eleven thirty before Felix rose to his feet again, and this time the gathering was subdued and perhaps ready for his more sober reflections. The music had long ago been turned off. Fresh logs had been thrown on the fire. All were comfortably settled with their coffee or brandy. And Felix's face was philosophical but the familiar smile played at the edges of his mouth as it always did when he was in a good humor.

"And so another year dies," he said, looking off, "and we have lost Marrok, and Fiona, and Helena."

Clearly he was not finished, but Margon spoke up quietly.

"I wouldn't for all the goodwill in the world," he said, "speak the names tonight of those who brought death to our Modranicht. But I will speak their names for you, Felix, if that is what you require, and for anyone else here who wants to mourn for them."

Felix's smile was sad but thoughtful.

"Well, for the last time," said Margon, "let us say their names, and pray that they have gone to a place of rest and understanding."

"Hear, hear," said Thibault and Sergei right after him. "And you forgive us for this, Philip, please," said Frank.

"Forgive you?" asked Phil. "What is there to forgive?" He lifted his glass. "To the mothers of my Modranicht and the life I have now inside me. I bear you no ill will and won't insult you with my thanks for this new chapter in my story."

There was a quick soft round of applause.

Phil drank.

"And to this coming year and all its blessings," said Felix. "To Reuben's son, and to all the bright futures of those gathered here. To fate and fortune, that they be kind, and to our hearts that they not forget the lessons learned from all we've witnessed in this Yuletide, our first Yuletide, with our new kindred."

Sergei gave the usual roar, and swung the bottle of brandy over his head, and Frank beat on the table and declared that solemnity had worn out its welcome.

"The clock's ticking towards midnight," said Frank, "and another year is dying whether we are any older or not, and the same damned challenges as always lie before us."

"Well, that's pretty damned solemn," said Berenice with a soft laugh. In fact, laughter was breaking out spontaneously on all sides for no apparent reason except the comfortable and drunken spirits of the group.

"So many thoughts are running through my mind," said Felix, "as to what this new year holds for us."

"Too much thinking!" cried Sergei. "Drink, don't think!"

"Ah, but seriously," Felix pressed on. "One thing that we must do in the next year is share the stories of our lives with our new brothers and sister."

"Now, I'll drink to that," said Stuart. "The truth and nothing but the whole truth."

"Who said anything about the truth?" asked Berenice.

"As long as I don't have to hear one single word of it tonight," said Sergei. "And you young ones just wait until the *Geliebten Lakaien* start weaving their tales of origins and histories."

"What do you mean? What are you saying?" Stuart said. "I wanna know the truth, damn it, about everything."

"I'm game to hear all of it," said Reuben. Phil nodded to that and raised his glass.

The laughter was rolling back and forth as if it were speech.

And Felix had all but given up on bringing any final serious note to the evening, settling for toasts and teasing Stuart and fending off Margon's light jabs.

Reuben drank his coffee, loving the sharpness of the taste and the jolt of the caffeine, and pushed his wineglass away from him. He gazed lovingly and sentimentally at Laura, her blue eyes so vivid with her blue dress, and the emotions welled dangerously inside him. Seven minutes to go, he thought, his watch right in time with the grand-father clock in the main room, and then you take her in your arms and crush her with all your might and main as she crushes you, and you never forget this night, this Yuletide, this Modranicht, this year, this season in which your new life was born, and your deepest loves and understandings with it.

Suddenly a loud booming sounded from the front door.

And for a moment no one moved. Again came the sound, someone out there in the downpour, pounding on the front door.

"But who in the wide world!" declared Frank. He rose like the sentry on duty and marched across the dining room and into the main room.

A fierce draft swept through the house as the door was opened, lifting the fragile flames from the candles, and then came the crack of the door being slammed hard and bolted once more, and the sounds of two voices in argument.

Felix stood quietly at the head of the table, glass in hand, listening as if he had a presentiment or realization of who it was that had come knocking. The others were listening, trying to catch the identity of the new voice, and Berenice gave a soft little sound of misery.

Frank appeared, flushed and annoyed.

"You want him in this house?"

Felix didn't immediately respond. He was looking past Frank into the alcove between the dining room and the living room.

And then as Frank moved away and returned to his chair, Felix beckoned to the newcomer.

A soaked and bedraggled Hockan appeared, his face and hands white and trembling.

"Good Lord, you're drenched," said Felix. "Lisa, one of my sweaters upstairs. Heddy, towels."

The rest of the company sat silent around the table, and Reuben found himself watching in fascination.

"Come, take off this coat," said Felix, unbuttoning the coat himself and slipping it from Hockan's shoulders.

Heddy came behind him, blotting at Hockan's wet hair, and then offering him the towel to wipe his face, but he just stared at the towel as if he didn't know the significance of it.

"Step out of your wet shoes, master," she said.

Hockan stood there in a daze.

He stood before Felix looking into Felix's eyes, his face quivering and unreadable.

A small sound came out of him, something like a strangled word or a groan, and quite suddenly, Hockan broke down, his hand up to cover his eyes as his body shook with dry sobs.

"They're gone, they're all gone!" he said in a deep agonized voice, sobs erupting like coughs. "They're gone, Helena and Fiona, and all the others."

"Oh, come," said Felix gently. He put his arms around Hockan and brought him to the table. "I know," he said. "But you have us. You will always have us. We're here for you."

Hockan clung to Felix, weeping on his shoulder.

Margon rolled his eyes, and Thibault shook his head. Out of Sergei there came the inevitable deep growl of disapproval.

And Frank said in a hard low voice, "My God, Felix, you are past all patience, my friend."

"Felix," said Sergei ominously. "Is there no person under the sun— fairy, elf, demon, troll, or perfect scoundrel—whom you will not try to love and live at peace with!"

Thibault uttered a short bitter laugh.

But Hockan seemed to hear none of this. His soft helpless choking sobs continued.

Felix held him in a gentle embrace but he still managed to turn his head and look at the others.

"Yuletide, gentlemen," said Felix, his eyes glazed. "Yuletide," he said again. "And he's our brother."

No one answered. Reuben stole a glance at Phil, whose face was almost heartbreakingly sad as he gazed down the table at the two men. But there was a serene and wondering quality to his expression, too.

Hockan seemed as shattered as a man can be, his soul emptying in his private sobs, utterly oblivious to everyone and everything except Felix. "I don't know where to go," came Hockan's muffled voice. "I don't know what to do."

"Yuletide," said Margon finally. He stood up and placed his right hand on Hockan's shoulder. "All right, brother. You're with us now."

Lisa had returned with the sweater over her arm, but it was not the time for it. And she waited in the shadows.

The muted, helpless weeping poured from Hockan.

"Yuletide," said Berenice. The tears were sliding down her cheeks.

"Yuletide," said Frank with an exasperated sigh and lifted his glass.

"Yuletide," said Sergei.

And the same word came now from Laura and Phil and from Lisa and the other *Geliebten Lakaien*.

Laura had tears in her eyes, and Berenice continued to cry, nodding as she looked gratefully to the others.

Reuben rose to his feet. He stood beside Felix.

"Thank you," said Felix in a small confidential whisper.

"Midnight," said Reuben. "The clock's chiming." And he put his arms around Felix and Hockan together before he turned to embrace his beloved Laura.

27

GRACE CALLED ON SUNDAY, January 6. Reuben was hard at work on an essay for Billie, this one on the tiny town of Nideck and its ongoing renaissance with new businesses and new home construction.

"Your brother needs you," Grace said. "And he needs his father, too, if you can get the old man to come down here with you."

"What's happened? What do you mean?"

"Reuben, it's his parish. It's that neighborhood. It's the Tenderloin. A couple of thugs attacked a young priest who was visiting Jim yesterday afternoon. Reuben, they beat the hell out of him, and castrated him. He died on the operating table last night, and maybe it was a blessing, I honestly don't know. But your brother's out of his mind."

Reuben was aghast. "I can see why. Look, we're coming. I'll be there as quickly as I can."

"Jim called the police, and they came here to the hospital. Jim knows who's behind this, some drug dealer, some contemptible piece of filth! But they said there was nothing they could do without the dead priest's testimony. Some other witness had been murdered too. I couldn't understand what they were talking about. Reuben, Jim just about went crazy when the priest died. And Jim's been missing since last night."

"What do you mean, Jim's missing?" Reuben asked. He was on his feet, pulling his suitcase off the top shelf of the closet.

"Just what I said. I begged him to come home, to stay at home, to clear out of that apartment and come back home. But your brother just doesn't listen to me. Now he's not answering his phone and the parish office doesn't know where he is either. He didn't say Mass this morning, Reuben, can you imagine? They called *me*.

"Reuben, persuade Phil to come down here. Jim listens to your father. Jim listens to you. But Jim simply never listens to me."

Reuben was throwing things into the suitcase. "I'll find him. He's out of his mind over this, and we'll be there as soon as we can."

Phil was in the oak forest when Reuben found him, walking and talking with Hockan Crost. Hockan excused himself to give them privacy and Phil heard the story before he said a word.

"How can I go down there, Reuben?" he asked. "Look, the change came over me last night. Oh, don't worry about it. I was with Lisa and she called Margon immediately. It was past midnight. Wow. Have I got a story to tell you—."

"Then you can't go," said Reuben.

"Exactly. The change will come again tonight and nobody knows at what time. But that's just part of the problem, and you know it. Look at me, son. What do you see?"

Phil was right. His hair was fuller, thicker, and the strawberry blond streaks in it were most lustrous and prominent and he had the physique of a man in his prime. His face still bore the stamp of his age, but his eyes, his expression, his movements—all had been beautifully altered, and Jim would see this at once. Grace would see it at once.

"You're right," said Reuben. "Jim's crazed, obviously, and seeing you like this, well—."

"Might just drive him right out of his mind," said Phil. "You've got to go in without me. Try to get him to move back home. Or get him someplace decent, Reuben, where he can recover from all this. A nice hotel suite. Jim hasn't taken a vacation in five years, and now this."

After a quick call to Laura, who was in the town of Nideck working with Felix and several of the new merchants—and three unanswered calls to Jim's cell—Reuben was on the road by noon.

He was almost to Marin County before he heard from Grace again.

"I've reported him missing," said Grace, "but the police won't do anything about it. It hasn't been twenty-four hours yet. Reuben, I have never seen Jim like he was. You should have seen him when we told him this priest was dead. I mean he was silently coming unglued. He just walked out of the hospital without speaking to anyone and disappeared. Reuben, we've found his car is in the parking lot. He's on foot."

"Mom, he might have taken a cab somewhere. I'll find him. I'll be there in an hour and a half."

He pulled off the road long enough to call Jim's rectory, with no success, to ring the apartment where he got no answer, and to leave another message on Jim's cell. "I'm practically to the Golden Gate Bridge. Please, please call me as soon as you can."

He was in San Francisco, on his way up Lombard Street, not certain whether to go home first or to the hospital, when a text from Jim appeared in his phone.

"Huntington Park, Nob Hill. Tell no one."

"Minutes away," Reuben texted and immediately turned right. This was not the worst place to be meeting his brother by any means. There were three hotels on top of Nob Hill right on the park.

It was raining lightly but the traffic wasn't bad. He reached the summit of the hill in five minutes and pulled at once into the Taylor Street public parking garage. Grabbing his suitcase, he sprinted across Taylor and into the park.

Jim was sitting alone on a bench with a briefcase on his lap. He was in full Roman collar and black clerics, and staring ahead of him as if he was in a trance. A light rain gave a sheen to the pathways and had speckled Jim's clothes and hair with silver, but he did not seem to feel the rain or the sharp cold wind.

Reuben reached out and put a firm hand on his shoulder. Still Jim didn't lift his head.

"Look, it's effing freezing here," Reuben said. "What about we get some coffee in the Fairmont?"

Jim looked up slowly as if waking from a dream. He didn't say anything.

"Come on," said Reuben, taking him firmly by the arm. "It will be warm in there. It will be nice."

He was still mumbling platitudes and inanities as he guided Jim into the big, bustling, and always glamorous Fairmont lobby. All the elaborate Christmas decorations were gone, but the lobby was in a way always dressed for a holiday with its shining marble floor, gilt-framed mirrors, gold columns, and gold-etched ceiling.

"Tell you what," Reuben said, moving towards the desk. "I'm going to get us a suite. Mom won't let you go back to your old apartment, not without turning the town upside down—."

"Don't use your real name," said Jim in a dull voice, without meeting Reuben's eyes.

"What are you talking about? I have to. I have to show my ID."

"Tell them not to reveal your real name," said Jim in a half murmur. "And don't tell anyone that we're here."

The desk was entirely cooperative. They had a fine two-bedroom suite with a beautiful view of the park and Grace Cathedral opposite. And they would not give Reuben's real name to anyone. Of course they recognized him. They knew he was the famous reporter. They would be absolutely discreet. They registered him under the pseudonym Creighton Chaney, which he offered on the spot.

Jim was in a daze as they entered the parlor of the suite, eyes passing over the ornate fireplace and sumptuous furnishings as if nothing was penetrating, as if he were engaged in some deep inner contemplation from which he couldn't quite wake. He sat down on the blue velvet sofa and stared at the gold-framed mirror above the mantel and then at Reuben as if he couldn't make much sense of what was going on around him.

"I'll call Mom," said Reuben, "but I won't tell her where we are."

Jim didn't answer.

"Mom, listen to me," Reuben said into the phone. "I'm with Jim and I'll call you as soon as I can." He cut the call off at once.

Jim sat there, holding the briefcase, as he had on the park bench, staring at the gilded fireplace screen as if there were a fire in the grate when there was not.

Reuben settled into a gold velvet armchair to his left.

"I can't imagine what you're feeling," he said, "to have something like this happen to a friend. Mom said you told the police everything you know, that they said they can't do a thing."

Jim didn't respond.

"Do you have any idea who's responsible? Mom said something about a drug dealer that you knew."

Jim didn't answer.

"Look, I know you don't want to tell me. You don't want me rushing in and making a meal out of the culprit. I get that. I'm here as your brother. Will it help to talk about what happened to your friend?"

"He wasn't a friend," said Jim in that same dull expressionless voice. "I didn't even like him."

Reuben didn't know what to say. Then, "Well, I figure that's confusing at a time like this, too."

No response.

"I want to call Dad and tell him I'm with you," Reuben said and he went into the bedroom on the right. It was as lavish as the parlor with an elaborately dressed king-size bed and a curved couch beneath the window. Surely Jim would be comfortable in these digs if he could persuade him to stay.

As soon as Phil answered, Reuben brought him up to speed. This was bad. He would go get Jim's things from the apartment and stay with him tonight, if only Jim would allow. "He's in shock," said Reuben. "It's like he doesn't know what he's doing. I'm not leaving him."

"I talked to your mother. She's in a rage that I'm not coming down there, and I'm giving her ridiculous excuses just like I've done all my life for not doing what she wants. Call me back later, no matter what."

Reuben found Jim seated on the couch still, but he'd laid the briefcase beside him on the sofa.

When he asked about getting Jim's things, Jim looked up again as if waking from a dream. "I don't want you to go over there," he said.

"Fine," he said. "I've got a suitcase with me. I always overpack. I've got everything you need." He went on talking, because he felt somehow this was better than not talking, reflecting on what this shock might have meant to Jim, this happening in his parish. And he said from his heart that he was so sorry, so very sorry about what happened to the young priest.

When the doorbell rang, it was room service with a tray of fruit and cheese—the usual fare in such suites—from the manager of the hotel. And yes, they'd bring him a pot of coffee, too, right away.

Reuben set the food down on the coffee table.

"Is it a long time since you've eaten?"

No response.

Finally, Reuben fell silent, as much from not knowing what to do as respect for the fact that this was what Jim might want.

When the coffee came, Jim did accept a cup of it and drank it though it was very hot.

Then slowly Jim's eyes moved to Reuben and he stared at Reuben for a very long time, looking him over in a slow, casual way, almost the way children look people over, without self-consciousness or apology.

"You know," said Reuben, "if you do have any idea who did this . . ." He let the words trail off.

"I know exactly who did it," said Jim. His voice was low and a little stronger than before. "I was the intended victim. And by now they know they failed."

The hair stood up on Reuben's neck. The old pringling began, and that inevitable heat in his face.

"They called him Father Golding the entire time they were beating him and carving him up," said Jim, his voice darker with the first hint of rage. "He told me that as they put him in the ambulance. He never told them they had the wrong man."

Reuben waited. "I'm listening," he said.

"Are you?" asked Jim, his voice stronger and more clear. "I'm glad."

Reuben was stunned, but he concealed it as he concealed the heat crawling under his skin.

Jim opened the briefcase and slipped out his laptop, and opened it on his knees, hitting a few keys, and apparently watching it connect with the Wi-Fi network of the hotel.

He set it down on the coffee table and turned it so that Reuben could see the screen.

A bright-colored photo of a young blond-haired man with sunglasses covering his eyes, and a *San Francisco Chronicle* headline: NEW PATRON OF THE ARTS IN TOWN.

Reuben swallowed, forcing the prickling to stop, to wait. "This is the guy," he said.

"Fulton Blankenship," said Jim. He slipped a folded piece of paper out of his jacket and gave it to Reuben. "This is his address. You know the area, Alamo Square." He turned the computer, hit a couple of keys, and then turned it so Reuben could see it again. Big Victorian house, spectacularly painted, very impressive, something of a landmark, one of the witches' cap Victorians they use in films whenever they can.

"Yeah, I know that house," said Reuben. "I know exactly where it is."

"This is what went down," said Jim. "He's a dealer, and his product is what they call Super Bo on the street, a mixture of cough syrup laced with every kind of junk drugs imaginable, selling for nothing at first and now for more than just about any other drug the kids can get. Highly concentrated. A test tube of it doctors a sixteen-ounce bottle of soda, sending kids to the moon after a mouthful. Perfect rape drug in larger doses, too. They're coming in from the suburbs to buy it on Leavenworth and he's signing up dealers just as fast as he can. About fifteen percent of those who OD on it die from it, and another five percent end up in a coma. Not a single one of those has ever woken up."

He paused but Reuben knew better than to say a word.

"About two months ago," Jim went on, "I started working hard on these local distributers, trying to get anybody to cop to who he was and what he was doing. Kids were dying!" Jim stopped because his voice had broken, and it took him a second or two to go on. "I was up and down Leavenworth every night. Last week, one of the boys comes to me, Blankenship's lover, he says, sixteen, a runaway, a hustler, a junkie, who'd been living with Blankenship in that Victorian house. I stashed the kid in a suite in the Hilton, oh, nothing as fancy as this, but I charged it to Mom, Mom pays for my extras, and he was on the twenty-third floor and I thought he was safe."

Again, Jim stopped, clearly on the edge of tears. His lips were working overtime and then he began again.

"The kid's name was Jeff. He was on e-pills and Super Bo but he wanted to get clean. And I was all over the police and the DEA trying to get them to work with him, get him some protection, take his statements, put a cop on the hotel room door. But he was too druggy, too unreliable for them. 'Get him clean,' they said, 'and then we'll have enough for a warrant. Right now the kid's a mess.' Well, the boss's men got to him yesterday afternoon. He was stabbed some twenty-two times. I *told* him not to call anybody—." Jim's voice broke again. "I told him!"

He stopped, and put his curled fingers against his mouth for a second, and then started again.

"When I got the call from the hotel, I went out the door immediately. And that's when they came for me, and they got the priest staying in my apartment, a know-nothing innocent guy from Minneapolis on a layover on his way to Hawaii. A young innocent guy who wanted to see my parish, my ministry! A priest I hardly knew."

"I see," said Reuben. The heat in his face was unbearable and the pringling had become a fact of life. But he held the change at bay as he waited, marveling quietly that sheer rage and anticipation could bring it on as was happening now. He was marveling too at what was happening, at what this had done to his brother. His brother's face, his brother's tears were breaking his heart.

"There's more," said Jim, gesturing with one finger. "I've met the son of a bitch. I've been to that house. Right after the kid came to me, Blankenship's lackeys forced me into a car and brought me there to meet with the man himself. They took me to the fourth floor of that house. That's where he lives, this, this little tinhorn Scarface, this latter-day Pablo Escobar, this little rat-faced Al Capone with his big dreams. He's so paranoid he's backed himself into a fourth-floor apartment up there with one entrance and only a handful of lackeys admitted to the house. He sits there pouring cognac for me and offering me Cuban cigars. He offers me a million-dollar donation for my church, a million dollars, he has it right there in a suitcase, and he says we can be partners, him and me, just tell him where Jeff is. He wants to talk to Jeff, make up with him, bring Jeff back, get Jeff clean." He broke off again, eyes dancing back and forth as he looked around the room, obviously struggling for calm.

"I didn't challenge the little monster. I sat there listening, breathing that revolting cigar smoke as he talks about *Boardwalk Empire* and *Breaking Bad* and how he's the new Nucky Thompson, and San Francisco is becoming again the Barbary Coast. San Francisco's much more beautiful than Atlantic City ever was, he says. He's wearing wingtip shoes like Nucky Thompson. He has a closet full of beautiful colored shirts with white collars. He gives twenty-five cents out of every dollar to charity, he says, right off the top. We have a future together, he says, him and me. He'd finance a rehab clinic and shelter at the church and I can run it any way I like. This million dollars is only the beginning. His heart goes out to his customers, he says. Someday soon they'll make a movie about us, him and me, and this Delancey Street–style shelter that I'm opening with his money. If he didn't sell to the rabble, somebody else would, he says. I know that, don't I? he asks me. He doesn't want anybody to be hurt, least of all Jeff. Where was Jeff? He wants to get Jeff clean, send him to an Eastern school. Jeff's got artistic talent, I might not know. I got up and left."

"I hear you."

"I walked out of there and I walked all the way back home. And the next morning they tell me about an anonymous million-dollar donation to St. Francis at Gubbio earmarked for the rehab and shelter. It's in the damned bank!"

He shook his head. The tears were thick in his eyes, a glaze.

"I didn't dare go see Jeff after that. I called him, every day, twice a day. Lie low. Do not call anybody. Do not go out. And he verified just what I thought. There aren't five people allowed in that Victorian house. Paranoia trumps greed and the desire for personal service. Three hardbitten henchmen do everything, and then there's Fulton—except for the lab work in the basement. The Super Bo concentrate is thrown together down there by a team that works by day without a master formula; it's whatever GHB, oxycontin, scopolamine they've got coming in. It's poison! And they're producing staggering quantities, everything going out on dollies to 'perfume' trucks. That's the cover. A perfume company. The street distributers mix it with soda pop and sell out the same day they're supplied."

"I'm getting the picture," said Reuben.

"You realize what might happen?" Jim asked. "If I were to go home? You realize what these monsters might do to anybody they found in the way if they came looking for me?"

"I realize," said Reuben.

"And I can't get a cop car to sit outside the house!"

Reuben nodded. "I'm getting the whole picture, as I said."

"I warned Mom. I told her to hire a private security guard. I don't know whether she listened to me or not."

"I'm getting it, all right."

"They're crazy, suicidal, Blankenship and this bunch. They're as dangerous as rabid dogs."

"So it seems," said Reuben under his breath.

Once more Jim gestured for attention with his finger.

"I Google-mapped the place," said Jim. "There's no vehicle access, not in front and not in back. The perfume trucks have to stop in the street. There's a tiny backyard."

Reuben nodded. "I understand."

"I'm glad you do," said Jim with a bitter smile. "But how can you do it, how can you get him without bringing the whole world out to hunt for the Man Wolf again?"

"Easily," said Reuben. "But you leave that to me."

"I don't see how——?"

"Leave it to me," said Reuben again, a little more firmly, yet quietly. "You don't have to think about any of it a moment longer. I have others to help me think about it. Go in there and take a shower. I'll order us some dinner. By the time you get out the food will be here, and we'll have figured it out to the last detail."

Jim sat there quietly reflecting for a moment and then he nodded. His eyes were like glass with their tears, flashing in the light. He looked at Reuben and he smiled bitterly, his mouth quivering just for an instant, and then he rose and left the room.

Reuben went to the windows.

The rain was coming down a little heavier now, but the view of the park below and the great pale mass of Grace Cathedral opposite was impressive as always, though something about the neo-Gothic façade of the church deeply disturbed Reuben and caused a pain in his heart. It stirred memories in him unexpectedly, not memories of this church so much as so many others that were like it, churches in which he'd prayed all over the world. A deep sense of grief was taking hold of him. He swallowed it down as he'd swallowed the change that had so wanted to break loose.

When Felix answered the phone, Reuben discovered for a split second that he couldn't talk. That pain deepened and then he heard his own voice, low, and unnatural to him, slowly unfolding the whole story to Felix, his eyes fixed firmly on the distant towers of the cathedral, so reminiscent of Reims, Noyon, Nantes.

"I was thinking I'd get you a couple of suites here," said Reuben, "that is, if you're willing . . ."

"You let me book them," said Felix. "And of course we are willing. Don't you realize this is Twelfth Night? This is the Carnival season now until Lent. It will be our Twelfth Night feast."

"But secrecy, the question of secrecy."

"Dear boy, there are ten of us," said Felix. "And Phil and Laura have never tasted human flesh. There won't be a morsel left."

Reuben smiled in spite of himself, in spite of the pain in his heart, in spite of the great dark outline of the cathedral against the western sky. It was dusk now, and quite suddenly, unexpectedly, the decorative lights of the huge cathedral were switched on, gloriously illuminating the entire façade. It was startling, the ghost of the church now solid and wondrously alive with its twin towers and softly glowing rose window.

"Are you there?" asked Felix.

"Yes, I'm here," said Reuben. "And that's what I was thinking," said Reuben. "Eat every last bite and lick the plates clean."

Silence.

The room was dark. He ought to turn on a few lights, he thought. But he didn't move. Distantly, he could hear a terrible sound, the sound of his brother Jim weeping.

The door of the bedroom was open.

There came the scent of innocence, the scent of innocent suffering.

He moved soundlessly to the door.

Jim, dressed in the soft white hotel terry-cloth robe, knelt beside the bed, his head bowed, his hands clasped in prayer, his shoulders shaking with his sobs.

Reuben moved away, and back to the window and the comforting sight of the beautifully illuminated cathedral.

28

It was planned in advance. They dressed in black sweatshirts and sweatpants, carrying the black ski masks in their pockets. Easy enough to slip out of the three vehicles and approach the Victorian house through the back alleys. Margon reminded the younger ones before it began: "You're stronger in human form now than you ever were; climbing fences, breaking down doors, you'll find that easy even before the change." Who knew what the getaway might entail?

Frank, the ever impressive Frank, with his movie star looks and voice, was chosen to knock on the front door and charm his way in. Hurling aside a confused and protesting lackey, he'd gone straight to open the back door, and the wolves were inside within seconds.

Phil had morphed as soon as the others began morphing, emerging a powerful brown Man Wolf as eager to kill as Laura. The place reeked of evil. The stench had soaked into the very beams and boards. The horrified lackeys raved, snarled like animals themselves, the hatred lusciously seductive and finally irresistible.

Margon gave Laura and Phil each a desperate protesting victim—to dispatch on their own. A third inhabitant, a sleeper on the second floor, leapt from his bed with knife in hand. He slashed over and over at Stuart, who embraced him before crushing his skull.

Merciful kills these, swift. But the feasting had been slow, scrumptious. The flesh had been so warm, so salty, so delicious, with a playful jockeying for the choicest "cuts." Reuben's body felt like an engine, his paws and temples throbbing, his tongue lapping, of its own accord it seemed, at gushing blood.

There were only four in all, and the first three were devoured almost completely, with bloody garments and shoes pushed into garbage sacks while the unsuspecting leader paced and ranted and sang along with his deafening music in the attic above.

Up the stairs they went to take the kingpin all together. "Man Wolves! And so many of you!" he screamed in frenzied delight.

He begged, pleaded, tried to buy his life. He raved about what he might do for this world if only they'd spare him. Out of a hole in the wall he produced bundles and bundles of cash. "Take it!" he cried. "And there's more where that came from. Listen, I know you defend the innocent. I know who you are. I am innocent. You are looking at innocence! You are listening to innocence! We can work together, you and me! I'm no enemy of the innocent!" It was Phil who tore out his throat.

Reuben watched in silence as Phil and Laura fed on the remains. He felt a subtle pride in their perfect instincts, their easy power. A subtle peace descended on them.

He didn't fear for them any longer as he had feared for them when they were human. It penetrated to him slowly and sweetly that Laura was now unassailable against the mortal enemies that lurked in the shadows for every female human. And Phil, Phil was no longer dying, no longer neglected, no longer alone. Morphenkinder. Newborn. And how harmless was the night around them, the foggy night pressing up against the glass; how transparent, how easily fathomed, how positively sweet. He was elated and curiously calm. Is this the calm the dog feels when he gives that rattling sigh and lies down by the fire?

What would it be like to remain in this body forever, to enjoy this brain which never hesitated, never doubted, never feared? He thought of Jim weeping alone in the bedroom at the Fairmont; he could not conceive of the agony Jim had been enduring. He knew what he knew, but he didn't feel it now. He felt the singular instincts of the beast.

The entire pack enjoyed an easy equality. At one point—as they went back to consume every last bit of bone and flesh—Frank and Berenice had tangled together, obviously making love. What did it matter now? The others looked away respectfully or simply didn't notice, Reuben couldn't quite tell. But a powerful surge of passion consumed Reuben. He wanted to take Laura but could not bear to do this in front of others. In a dark corner he embraced her roughly and tightly. The soft fleecy fur of her neck drove him half mad.

He watched Phil prowling the house by scent afterwards, finding even more money hidden in old armoires and in the plaster walls. His fur was brown but there were streaks of white in his mane. His eyes were large and pale and shining. How easy it was to recognize each Morphenkind, though to the crazed victims they had no doubt looked indistinguishable. Had the world ever registered particular descriptions? Probably not.

His mind ran to rampant humor suddenly, to the thought of a picture album of the pack. He felt himself laughing and he felt a little dizzy, yet certain of every step he took.

Surely Phil was feeling the sublime strength of the wolf body, so securely clothed in fur, and the bare pads of his feet moving over carpet or floorboard indifferently. Surely he was feeling the subtle warmth moving divinely through his veins.

A fortune was packed eventually into another garbage sack. Like pirates' treasure, Reuben was thinking, all this filthy drug money—it's like the chests of pearls and diamonds and gold in the Technicolor pirate movies—and these filthy drug dealers, are they not the pirates of our time? Who is likely to take it, this treasure, without asking a single question? St. Francis at Gubbio Church, of course.

Never before had Reuben seen victims devoured like these. Never had he known such a protracted feast. Easy to swallow hair and gristle. There had been time enough to suck marrow from bones. Never before had he tasted the soft mush of brains, the thick muscle of hearts. Consuming a human head was a bit like tackling a large and thick-skinned piece of fruit.

In luxurious silence, he had lain back on the bare boards of the living room floor finally, the music from the attic pulsing in his temples, letting his body continue to turn the flesh and blood of others into his own. Laura lay down beside him. As he turned his head, he saw the tall shaggy figure of his father staring out of the long narrow front window as if at the distant stars. Maybe he'll write the poetry of it, Reuben thought, which so far I haven't been able to do.

And we are all kindred now, he thought. *Morphenkindred.*

A short growl from Margon told them finally that it was time to move.

For a quarter of an hour they roamed the house, gathering up more random stashes of money. It had been hidden behind books in the bookcases; and in the kitchen stove; and in the bathrooms in plastic sacks in toilet tanks, and even slipped in bundles under claw-foot tubs.

Giant plasma television screens smiled and talked to no one. Cell phones rang unanswered.

Again, they lapped up the blood spilled here and there as best they could. Not a knucklebone left. Not a hank of hair. Down the back steps they crept to enter the cellar laboratory, where they smashed everything in sight.

Then away they went as they had come, human once more, dressed in their dark garments, slipping through the dark alleyways with their big sacks, back to the waiting cars. The houses were asleep around them. Their preternatural ears could still hear that rock music pounding in the distant attic. But the big Victorian was a lifeless shell, its front door wide open to the street. How long would it be before someone wandered up those granite steps?

29

IN THE EARLY HOURS of Monday, Jim had left the hotel. The bell-man remembered: about four o'clock.

Reuben had no chance to talk to him, tell him things had gone splendidly, that he had no worries now.

Better he be left in peace, Reuben thought. He went to sleep alone in the king-sized bed of the Fairmont suite.

The raid was all over the local news when he awoke.

Before noon, alerted by two different deliverymen to the matter of open doors and bloodstains in the hallway, police searched the man-sion, quickly discovering the smashed drug lab on the lowest floor. Caches of cell phones and computers were removed by law enforce-ment, along with numerous papers and a small arsenal of weapons, including semiautomatic guns and knives. The television reporters were speculating that Fulton Blankenship and his felonious associates may have been kidnapped and murdered in an ongoing drug turf war.

Meanwhile, Jim had called Grace and Phil to let them know he was going down to Carmel for a day and night to try to clear his head. He needed a time of retreat and meditation, and had to be left entirely alone. Grace was relieved to hear it and called Reuben at once.

"Jim always goes to Carmel when he's upset," said Grace. "I don't know why. He checks into some little media-free bed-and-breakfast down there and goes walking on the beach. That's what he did before he decided to join the priesthood. He went down there for a week, and came back determined to give his life to the church." There was something sad in Grace's voice. "But the police are telling me there's nothing more for him to be worried about. What do you think?"

"I think I better stay here for a while," said Reuben. He confessed he was at the Fairmont. He wanted to wait until Jim came home.

"Thank God," said Grace.

And thank God she didn't insist he come the Russian Hill house.

By Tuesday, the police had publicly connected Blankenship to the murder of the young priest in the Tenderloin, based on "abundant computer evidence" and blood-spattered shoes and weapons found in Blankenship's house. Father Jim Golding had been the intended target. There was no doubt. There was no doubt either now that the basement lab on Alamo Square had been producing the killer Super Bo which was flooding San Francisco and its upscale suburbs and accounting for so many overdoses and deaths. Meanwhile a preliminary study of the bloodstains in the mansion indicated that numerous victims had perhaps died on the premises though all bodies had been removed.

Reuben didn't want to wait for Jim any longer. He was too worried. He drove south to Carmel. Laura would have come down from the north to go with him, but he said no, that he had to find Jim and talk to him on his own.

That afternoon and evening Reuben walked up and down Ocean Avenue, in and out of shops and restaurants, looking for his brother in vain. He visited every inn and bed-and-breakfast. He visited the Catholic church and the Mission church. No Jim. He walked up and down the cold windswept beach until dark.

As the lights of the town came on, a great white fog moved in over the white sand. Reuben felt small and cold and miserable. When he closed his eyes, he didn't hear the wind, or the sounds of passing traffic, or the roar of the waves banging the shore. He heard only the sound of Jim crying miserably in that suite at the Fairmont before the massacre, before the Twelfth Night feast.

"Dear God, please don't let him suffer for this, for any of it," Reuben prayed. "Please don't let this hurt him, his conscience, or his will to go on."

Wednesday morning, Grace called to say no one had heard a word from Jim, and this included the parish office and the archdiocese.

Everyone was being very understanding. But she was near out of her head with worry. Reuben continued his search.

Billie called that night to tell him about all the rumors that Father Jim Golding of St. Francis at Gubbio was starting a Delancey Street–style hospice and rehab program for teens. "Now you listen to me, Reuben Golding," she said. "You may be the most brilliant informal essayist since Charles Lamb, but I want an exclusive on this. This is your brother. You get to him and find out if this is going down. I hear he's got a million-dollar donation for this rehab center. We need a long in-depth article on the entire program."

"Well, I'll do that, Billie, when I find him," said Reuben. "Right now nobody knows where Jim is. Oh, my God. Listen, I have to get off the phone."

"What's the matter with you?"

"Nothing," he said. "I'll get back to you." He couldn't very well tell her that he'd just remembered the drug money in the green plastic garbage bag in the trunk of his Porsche.

And all this time it had been parked here and there on the streets all over Carmel!

On Thursday morning, well before sunrise, he headed back up to San Francisco. He was at the St. Francis at Gubbio parish office when it opened. He plunked the heavy garbage bag down on the receptionist's desk. "Miss Mollie," he said to the elderly woman, "this is an anonymous donation for the rehab center. I wish I could tell you more, but that's all I can say."

"And that's all you have to say, Reuben," she replied, not even looking up as she reached for the phone. "I'll call the bank."

Hell, I'm a reporter, Reuben thought as he walked out, hoping and praying he'd find Jim in the church. They can't make me divulge my sources. Jim was nowhere to be found. And a call to Grace soon confirmed that no one had heard from Jim. She was relieved to hear that Reuben would stay at the Fairmont for now.

Sometime after noon, he was awakened in the Fairmont suite by a call from Felix.

"Listen, I know your brother's missing, and I know how concerned you are," Felix said. "But is it at all possible for you to come home now?"

"Why? What's happened?"

"There's a little girl here, Reuben. She says she's run away from home, that she wants to see you. And she won't talk to anyone but you."

"Oh, my God, this is Susie Blakely!" said Reuben.

"No, it's not Susie," said Felix. "This little girl is about twelve. She's English. She has a beautiful English accent, as a matter of fact. It's just a joy to listen to this child talk. Her name is Christine. She's quite the little lady, though she's been crying since she arrived. She was wet through as an abandoned kitten! She took something like four buses to get to Nideck and then the Forest Gentry found her walking along the road in the rain with her backpack. And in patent leather slippers. Elthram carried her up here. We've been doing our best to comfort her. She was at the Winterfest, I mean the Christmas party, Reuben, and I do remember seeing her there with a schoolteacher, but this little girl will not tell us her last name."

"Wait a minute. I know who this is. The schoolteacher, her mother—she was wearing a beautiful old-fashioned hat in the village. She's blond, with long hair."

"Yes, that's the woman. Exactly. She came with a whole class of schoolchildren from San Rafael. But I don't know the name of the school. And she was wearing the most charming vintage Chanel suit. Quite an unforgettable woman. Very pretty. Who is this girl, Reuben?"

"You tell her not to worry, you keep her there, please, Felix, take care of her, don't let her leave. And tell her that I'm coming, and I'll get there as soon as I can."

30

It was the longest journey between San Francisco and Nideck Point Reuben had ever made. And all the way there, he prayed that this was the gift from God to Jim that it seemed.

It was dark by the time the Porsche pulled up to the front door, and he ran up the steps.

Christine was in the library, sitting very primly on the Chesterfield in front of the fire. She'd had her supper, though Lisa said at once, the child had scarcely touched it. And Christine was crying again, with a damp knotted handkerchief twisted in her hands.

She was small-boned, dainty, with straight blond hair that hung down her back, trimmed only with a black grosgrain headband. And she wore a pretty A-line navy blue dress trimmed with white cuffs and collar. Her stockings were white and she wore black patent leather pumps. She was quite dry, of course, Lisa explaining that all her clothes had been washed and pressed. "She is the tenderest creature," said Lisa. "I have a bedroom ready for her upstairs, but she can come sleep in the back with us if you want."

The girl didn't look up when Reuben came in. He sat down quietly on the Chesterfield beside her.

"Christine Maitland?" Reuben whispered.

"Yes!" she said, staring up at him. "You know who I am?"

"I think I do," he said. "But why don't you tell me more about who you are?"

She sat very still for a moment and then she crumpled into soft, violent crying. And for a long time he just held her in his arms. She turned and rested against him, sobbing, and then after a long while, as he stroked her hair, he began to speak.

He told her gently that he thought he knew her mother, that if he remembered correctly her mother's name was Lorraine.

She said yes to that in a small, broken voice.

"You can tell me anything, Christine," he said. "I'm on your side, honey. You understand?"

"My mom says we can never talk to my father, never tell him about us, about me and my brother, but I know my father wants to know!"

He didn't ask the obvious question—which was, Who is your father? He let her go on.

And suddenly it all came pouring out of her, how she wanted to see her father, how she'd run away from her house in San Rafael to see her father. Her twin brother, Jamie, didn't care about their father. Jamie was so "independent." Jamie had always been "independent." Jamie didn't need a father. But she did. She did with all her heart. She had seen her father at the Christmas gala and she knew he was a priest, but he was still her father, and she just had to see him, really, really had to see him. And on the news they said terrible things about her father, that someone had tried to kill him. What if her father died without her ever talking to him, without ever knowing he had a daughter and a son? Couldn't she stay here until her father was found? "I am praying and praying for them to find him."

In a quaking voice she laid out her dreams. She'd live at Nideck Point. Surely there was a little room where they could put her, and she wouldn't be any trouble. She'd walk to school. She would do chores to earn her food. She'd live here in this house, if there was just the smallest place for her, and her father would see her, and he would be happy to see her, to know he had twins, a daughter and a son. She knew he would. And she could live here and see him in secret and nobody would ever have to know that he was a priest with two children. She would never tell another soul. If there was just the smallest room, the smallest room in the attic or in the basement, or in the servants' wing out back. They'd taken a little tour at the party, and they'd seen the servants' wing. Maybe there was a really, really small room out there that nobody else wanted. She wouldn't be any trouble at all. She didn't expect anyone to help. If only Reuben would tell her father, just let him know.

Reuben thought for a long moment in silence, holding her tightly, still stroking her hair.

"Of course you can live here, you can live here forever," he said. "And I will tell your father right away that you're here. Your father is my brother, as you know. I'll tell him just as soon as I can. I'll tell him all about you. And you're right. He'll be happy, oh, happier than you can imagine to know you're here. And he'll be happy to see your brother, Jamie. Don't you worry about this."

She sat still staring at him as if she were out of breath. She didn't move. She didn't speak. She was amazed. She was a lovely little girl as far as he was concerned, and he was once again fighting back tears. She was precious, adorable . . . all that. She embodied those endearing words and more. She was sad, however, terribly sad. He couldn't remember if her mother was half as pretty. If she was, then she was a beautiful woman.

"You really think he'll be happy," she said in a timid voice. "My mother said he's a priest and it would be terrible for him if people knew."

"I don't think that's true at all," he said. "You and your brother were born before he ever became a priest, isn't that right?"

"My grandmother wants us to go back to England," she said, "without us ever talking to my father."

"I see," Reuben said.

"She calls my mother every week, telling her to bring us back to England. And if we go back to England, I'll never see my father again."

"Well, you're going to see him," Reuben said. "And you have grandparents here, your father's parents, who will be happy too."

Reuben and Christine sat there alone for a long time in silence. Then Reuben stood up and prodded the oak fire. There was a wild explosion of sparks up the chimney and then a steady leaping orange flame.

He knelt down in front of Christine, looking up into her eyes. "But honey," he said, "you have to let me call your mother. You have to let me tell her that you're safe."

She nodded. She opened her little black patent leather purse and took out an iPhone. She punched in the call to her mother and gave Reuben the phone.

As it turned out, Lorraine was already on her way to Nideck Point. She had been hoping and praying she'd find Christine there. "This is all my fault, Mr. Golding," she said in a lovely British accent, quite as lilting and fluid as her daughter's. "I am so sorry. I'm coming to get her now. I'll take care of everything."

"It's Reuben, Mrs. Maitland," he said, "and we'll have supper for you when you arrive."

Meanwhile, the situation with Jim grew worse.

Grace called to say that the archdiocese was becoming alarmed. They admitted to Grace that they didn't know where Jim was. Father Jim Golding had never disappeared like this. They'd called the police. Jim's picture had been on the six o'clock news.

Reuben's heart was breaking.

He had gone into the darkened conservatory to take the call, sitting down with Elthram and Phil at the marble table.

There was the usual fire in the white enameled Franklin stove, and scattered candles flickered here and there.

Elthram rose without a word and slipped away, obviously to give Phil and Reuben privacy.

Reuben tried again to reach Jim, ready to blurt out everything, if the phone would just go to voice mail. But it did not. It had never gone to voice mail, not since Jim had disappeared.

Phil wanted to tell Grace all about Lorraine and the children now.

But that didn't seem fair to Reuben. Jim had to know first.

"If only he's all right, if only—."

"Now look," said Phil. "You're doing everything that you can. You went down to Carmel. You couldn't find him. If we haven't heard from him by tomorrow, we'll tell your mother. And for now, just leave this in God's hands."

Reuben shook his head.

"And what if he hurts himself, Dad? What if he's there in Carmel, in some little B&B, and he's stocked up on booze, and he's gone on a bender? Dad, lots of the people who commit suicide do it while they're drunk. You know that. Don't you understand what's happened? He asked me to get rid of that damned Blankenship. He asked me because he didn't have anyone else to turn to! And now he's dying of guilt from it, I know he is. And these kids . . . why, he thought he killed Lorraine's baby! With Jim, it's guilt and guilt on top of guilt. He's got to know about these kids, he has to."

"Reuben, I've never believed the old clichés about things happening for the best," said Phil. "Or that this or that coincidence is a miracle. But if ever there was a situation that seemed to be designed by God, it's this one. He's at his lowest ebb and now these children appear—."

"But Dad, this is only going to work if he finds out about the children before he does harm to himself."

Finally, Reuben asked to be alone. He just had to be alone to think about all this. Phil understood of course. He'd go see how little Christine was doing. And he would leave the decision on all these things to Reuben.

Reuben folded his arms on the marble table and rested his forehead against them. He prayed. He prayed to God with all his heart to take care of Jim. He prayed aloud. "Lord, please don't let him take his life because of what I've done. Please. Please don't let him be destroyed by all this. Please restore him to us and to his children."

He sat back, his eyes closed. He whispered his prayers aloud, in a desperate attempt to have faith in them.

"I don't know who You are, I don't know what You are," he whispered. "I don't know if You want prayers or listen to prayers. I don't know if Marchent's with You, and whether she or any other power between heaven and earth can intercede with You. I am so scared for my brother." He tried to think, to think and pray and think it all through. But his thoughts ended in confusion.

Finally, he opened his eyes. In the light of the flickering candles, in the light of the flickering fire, he saw the purple blossoms of the orchid trees dripping down from the airy shadows. A sudden sense of peace came over him, just as if someone was telling him that things would be all right. And it seemed for a moment he wasn't alone, but he couldn't figure why he had that feeling. Surely he was the only one in the vast shadowy conservatory with its black glass and dim candlelight. Or was he?

It was about seven o'clock when Lorraine and Jamie came in the front door. By then, bedrooms had been prepared for all of the Maitlands on the front and the east side of the house.

Lorraine was extremely attractive, a tall very delicate woman, perhaps too thin, with a narrow very sweet face. It was one of those faces that seems incapable of guile or malice of any kind. Great vitality to her eyes, and a generous mouth. She wore what was obviously a fine vintage suit of some sort of ivory-colored grosgrain material trimmed at the pockets with black velvet. Her long straight blond hair was free over her shoulders, and girlish. She didn't have a hat.

Christine flew into her mother's arms at once.

Beside them stood Jamie, about five foot four inches tall, and very much the man of twelve in his blue blazer and gray wool pants. He was blond like his mother, with a short neat Princeton haircut, but the resemblance to Jim was striking. He had Jim's clear, almost fierce gaze, and he had at once extended his hand to Reuben.

"I'm delighted to meet you, sir," he said gravely. "I've followed your articles in the *Observer* for some time."

"The pleasure's mine, Jamie," said Reuben. "You can't imagine. And welcome to the house, both of you."

Immediately Lisa and Phil encouraged the children to come with them, and to let Reuben have a few words alone with Lorraine.

"Yes, darlings, now both of you go with Mr. Golding, please," Lorraine said. "You don't remember me, Professor Golding, but we did meet once in Berkeley—."

"Oh, I do remember," Phil said at once. "I remember it perfectly. Garden party at the dean's house. And we talked, you and I, about the poet William Carlos Williams, and that he'd been a doctor as well as a poet. I remember that well."

This surprised and delighted Lorraine and put her at ease immediately. "And you actually remember that very afternoon!"

"Of course I do. You were the prettiest woman there," said Phil. "And you had on the most beautiful hat. I never forgot that hat. You looked so very British in that big brimmed hat. So like the queen and the queen mother."

Lorraine blushed as she laughed. "And you, sir, are such a gentleman," she said.

"But come," said Lisa, "let's get this young man some supper, and Christine, dear, you come with us too; we have hot cocoa in the breakfast room, and let Master Reuben and Mrs. Maitland talk alone."

At once, Reuben led Lorraine into the library, to the inevitable Chesterfield couch before the fire that all the household preferred to the couches and hearth of the cavernous front room.

He took the club chair as always, as if Felix were sitting in the wing chair when in fact no one was sitting there.

"This is all my fault, as I told you," Lorraine said. "I've handled this badly."

"Lorraine, these are Jim's children, are they not? Please let me assure you, we are not shocked and we are not disapproving. We are happy, happy for Jim, happy ourselves. And Jim will be happy as well when he knows. My father and I want you to understand this immediately."

"Oh, you are so very kind," she said, her voice darkening slightly with feeling. "You are so like your brother. But Reuben, Jamie, I mean Jim, does not know about these children. He must never know."

"But why in the world do you say that?"

She broke off for a moment, as if to collect herself and her thoughts, and then, in a rush of lilting and silvery British speech she gently explained.

The children had known that Jim was their father since they were ten years old. Professor Maitland, their stepfather, had made Lorraine promise before he died that she would tell them when the right time came. They had the right to know the identity of their true father. But they knew their father was a Catholic priest, and for that reason they could never approach him until they were fully grown. "They understand," she said, "that any talk of children would be the complete ruin of their father."

"Oh, but Lorraine, it's the opposite," said Reuben immediately. "He must know. He would want to know. He will acknowledge these kids privately and immediately. Lorraine, he's never forgotten you—."

"Reuben," she said in a soft voice, laying her hand gently on Reuben's hand. "You don't understand. Your brother could be forced out of the priesthood if this becomes known to him. He would have to tell his archbishop. And the archbishop could simply remove Jim from his ministry. It could destroy him, don't you see? It could destroy the man he's become." Her voice was low, urgent and sincere. "Believe me, I have investigated this. I've been to your brother's church. He doesn't know this, of course. But I've heard him preach. I know what his life means to him now, and Reuben, I knew him very well before he ever became a priest."

"But Lorraine, he can secretly acknowledge—."

"No," she said. "Believe me. He cannot. My own lawyers have investigated. The climate in the Church today would never allow it. There's been too much scandal, too much controversy over the priesthood in recent years, too many famous priests compromised by the revelations of affairs, secret families, children and such . . ."

"But this is different—."

"I wish it were different," she said. "But it's not. Reuben, your brother wrote to me when he decided to become a priest. I knew at the time that if I told him about these children he would not be accepted in the seminary. I knew he thought he'd somehow caused the death of my pregnancy. I realized all that, and I thought it through. I consulted my own Anglican priest in England on the matter. I talked it over with Professor Maitland. I made the decision then to let Jim go on thinking that I had lost the pregnancy. It wasn't a perfect decision, not by any means. But it was the best decision I could make for Jim. When these children are older, when they are adults—."

"But Lorraine, he *needs* to know. They need him and he needs them."

"If you love your brother," she said softly, "surely you must not tell him about these children. I know Jim. I don't mean to offend you when I say that I know him intimately. I know Jim better than I've known almost anyone in my life. I know the battles he has fought with himself. I know the price of his victories. If he is forced out of his ministry, it will destroy his life."

"Listen to me. I understand why you're saying this," Reuben said. "Jim's told me what happened at Berkeley. He told me what he did—."

"Reuben, you cannot know the whole story," she gently insisted. "Jamie himself doesn't know the whole story. When I met Jamie, my life was in tatters. In a very real way, your brother saved my life. I was married to a sick man, an older man, and that man brought Jamie—I mean Jim—into our home to save my life. I don't think your brother ever knew the full extent to which he was manipulated by my husband. My husband was a good man but he would have done anything to keep me happy and keep me with him, and he brought Jim into our little world so that Jim would love me, and Jim did."

"Lorraine, I do know this."

"But you can't know what it meant to *me*. You can't know the suicidal depression I suffered before I met Jamie. Reuben, your brother is one of the kindest people I've ever known. We had such happiness together, you simply cannot imagine. Your brother is the only man I've ever loved."

Reuben was quietly astonished.

"Oh, he had his demons," she said, "but he's vanquished them all and found himself in the priesthood—that's the whole point—and I cannot repay the love he gave me by destroying his life now, not when the children are happy, well cared for, well provided for. And not when I chose not to tell him about the children before. I must bear the consequences of letting him believe that our baby died. No, Jim cannot know."

"There has to be some solution to this," said Reuben. He knew in his heart of hearts he had no intention whatsoever of keeping this from Jim.

"I should never never have let the children come to the Christmas gala here," Lorraine said, shaking her head. "Never. But you see, the academy in San Rafael had three invitations to the party, and I was expected to bring the eighth grade; and Jamie and Christine were simply beside themselves with excitement. Everybody was talking about the festival at Nideck Point and the Christmas banquet, the Man Wolf mystery, all of it. They begged, promised, cried. They knew all about you from the news, of course, and they knew you were Jim's brother. They so wanted to come, just to see their father in the flesh, one time, and they promised to behave."

"Believe me, Lorraine, I understand completely," Reuben said. "Of course they wanted to come to the party. I would have wanted to come, too."

"But I shouldn't have brought them," she said, her voice dropping to a whisper. "Someday when they are no longer children, when they're adults, yes, they can meet their father. But not now. He's far too vulnerable for us to approach him now."

"Lorraine, I can't believe this! I want to tell my mother about this. Look, I don't mean to be crass, believe me, but the Golding family and the Spangler family—my mother's people—are huge supporters of the archdiocese of San Francisco."

"Reuben, I am aware of that. I'm sure your family's influence paved the way for Jim to be ordained. He told me in his letter that he'd been completely honest and contrite with his superiors about his past. And I don't doubt that. They approved his sincerity, his repentance; and no doubt there were the donations to smooth the way." Her voice was so softly eloquent and persuasive. She made it seem all very logical and fine.

"Well, they can smooth the way now for him to see his children in private, damn it!" said Reuben. "I'm sorry. I apologize. I mean I have to call my mother. My mother will be ecstatic. And I have to find Jim. The problem right now is nobody knows where Jim is."

"I know," said Lorraine. "I've been following the news. So have the children. I am worried sick about Jim. I had no idea Jim's life involved such danger. Oh, I wish we had not brought this problem to your very doorstep at this time."

"But, Lorraine, this is the best time. Jim's miserable right now over the death of this young priest in the Tenderloin." How he wished he could tell her more, but he could never tell her—or anyone else—more. "Look, these children are going to help bring him back to himself."

She was not convinced. She looked at him searchingly, her soft eyes full of compassion and concern. What a gentle person she was. She was exactly as Jim had described her. She sighed and sat with her hands composed in her lap, working at the clasp of her purse much the way Christine's hands had worked obsessively with her handkerchief.

"I don't know what to do then," she said. "I simply don't know. It's all so remarkable. They were resigned. They only asked to see their father from a distance. They wanted to know what he really looked like. And I didn't think it would do the slightest harm. We came to the festival in the village and then on to the banquet here at the house. Jim looked right at us and didn't recognize me, didn't notice them. I had prepared the children for this. There were plenty of children at the party. There were children everywhere. I tried to stay out of Jim's way entirely. The last thing I wanted was for Jim to see me—."

"That's why you didn't wear a hat, why you took off your hat before the party."

"Excuse me?"

"Never mind. It's nothing. Go on. What happened?"

"Well, Christine was so upset. She is so easily upset! She's always fantasized about her father, dreamed about him, written stories about him. She started drawing pictures of him as soon as she heard about him, though she hadn't the faintest idea what he looked like. I should have known how actually seeing him in the flesh would affect her. She started to cry. I should have taken them home then. But I didn't. And then towards the end of the party, this very small thing happened, such a small thing." She shook her head. Her voice was filled with sadness. "Christine saw Jim walking out to the pavilion with a little girl. He had the little girl's hand in his. He was talking with the little girl and with an older woman, a grandmother perhaps. And when Christine saw him with that little girl, you see, smiling at that little girl, and talking to that little girl—."

Susie Blakely, of course.

"Oh, yes, I can imagine," said Reuben. "I know that little girl. Yes.

And I can see why this happened, what Christine felt. I understand everything. Lorraine, will you stay here tonight, please? Please stay here while I talk to Phil and Grace, my mom and dad, about this. Please. We have everything prepared upstairs, everything—pajamas, night-gowns, toothbrushes, everything you might need—three bedrooms have been prepared. Just stay here with us while we take this into con-sideration, please."

She was clearly not persuaded. Her eyes were watering.

"You know, Reuben, you are very like your brother. You are kind the way he is kind. Your parents must be marvelous people. But I turned out to be poison for Jim."

"No, that's not how it was, not according to him, you were not poison!"

Reuben left the chair and sat beside her on the couch.

"I promise you this is going to work out! I give you my word," he said. He slipped his arm around her. "Please stay with us tonight. And will you trust me to handle this with Jim? Please?"

After a long moment, she nodded.

"Very well," she whispered. She opened her purse and withdrew a little packet of folded papers. "This is the DNA of the children," she said. "Your mother's a doctor. She'll be able to check it against Jim's DNA quietly."

"Lorraine, may I ask you something?"

"Of course," she said.

"Was the pregnancy ever in jeopardy? Did you have to go into the hospital—I mean after the last time you saw Jim?"

"No. Not really. There was a fight. It was ugly. Jamie . . . well, Jamie was drunk and he did slap me repeatedly. But he didn't mean it. He would have never done it sober. He cut my face in a number of places. It bled something fierce. And I hit Jamie and things went from bad to worse. At one point I hit my head on something. I fell down. But no, the pregnancy was never really in danger. But it was a dreadful quarrel, that I confess."

"Amazing," Reuben whispered.

"My lips were cut. My right eye was cut." Her hand fluttered over her right eye for a moment. "I had a gash on my head. And I was bruised all over. I had terrible swelling afterwards, but no, the pregnancy was never in danger. Clearly Jamie thought later he had terminated it. I could read that plainly in his letters. I must confess I was still angry perhaps when I first received his letters. I never answered those first letters. . . ."

"Of course you were angry," said Reuben.

"Jamie didn't remember what any doctor knows. Cuts to the face and scalp bleed."

Reuben sighed. "Amazing, simply amazing," he whispered. "Thank you for confiding in me. Thank you for telling me that."

"Reuben, I know what you're thinking. Why did I let Jamie believe that he'd killed our child? But as I've tried to explain—to tell him that he hadn't, well, it would have meant he couldn't become a priest."

"I do understand that."

"And the children were happy. Keep that in mind when you judge me. And then there was Professor Maitland. He didn't want me to tell Jamie about the children. The children saved me and Professor Maitland. They gave us our happiest years together. I couldn't have remained with Professor Maitland if it hadn't been for the children. And I couldn't divorce him. I could never have divorced him. I would quite literally have taken my own life before doing that."

31

GRACE DID NOT DISAPPOINT Reuben. As he poured out the story on the phone, his mother was quiet for far longer than he had ever known her to be in any conversation. He was on the landline when he told her, and with his iPhone he texted pictures of Christine, of Jamie, and of Lorraine that he'd only just taken in the breakfast room.

He could hear his mother crying, he could hear her struggling to say they were beautiful, he could hear her struggling to say, "Please, please, Jim, come home."

There was no way Grace could come up to Nideck Point. She wanted to come with all her heart. "You tell my grandchildren that," she said. But she was on call for the entire weekend, and she had two cases in ICU she couldn't leave under any circumstances. But she insisted Reuben put Lorraine on the phone.

They talked for perhaps a half hour.

By that time young Jamie was in a fierce argument with Phil about "violent" varsity sports and whether it was fair to pressure children to play soccer or football. Jamie himself refused to engage in such sports, and while Phil thought they served a purpose and tried to explain the history of sports, Jamie was adamant that a boy his age had a right to sue the school authorities to remain out of sports in which he could break his neck or his back, or fracture his skull. Jamie had researched this question quite fully.

It was amazing, the rapid young British voice, so crisp, so unfailingly polite, firing back with such speed at Phil. And Phil was trying hard to keep a straight face as he punched the opposing view. "What is the school board to do with a young male population pumped with

testosterone at an early age and absolutely unable to work it off or—."
Phil was clearly crazy about Jamie.

"Well, certainly, they have no right to deplete our numbers through
violent death and injury," Jamie retorted. "Look, Mr. Golding, certainly you know as well as I do that the state and all its subordinate
institutions face the same problem with the young males of any society.
The armed services exist to siphon off the dangerous exuberance of
young males. . . ."

"Well, it's good to see you know the background of all this," said
Phil. "You have an astonishing grasp of the big picture."

Christine dozed against the back of the breakfast room chair. Phil
tried to bring her into the conversation, but she said sleepily, "Jamie
gets all worked up about these things."

"You have no idea," said Jamie in a low confidential voice to Phil
and Reuben, "what it is like to be the twin of a girl!"

The next morning, Lisa drove south to collect clothes and personal
items for the Maitland family, and Phil took Lorraine and Christine
and Jamie for a walk in the woods as soon as the sun came out from
behind the clouds.

Reuben spent the morning calling guesthouses and hotels throughout the little city of Carmel with no luck in finding Jim. Grace found out
Jim hadn't used his credit cards or ATM cards since his disappearance.

Felix and Sergei asked Reuben if he wanted them to join in the
search. They could easily fly down to the Monterey Peninsula and
start looking for Jim. "If I was certain he was there, I'd say yes," said
Reuben. "But I'm not certain." He had a hunch. He started looking
for monasteries—isolated monastic communities that had guesthouses
anywhere within a hundred miles of San Francisco. It was frustrating making the calls. Jim might not have checked in under his own
name. And he was reaching out to remote rural places that obviously
knew nothing of the San Francisco daily news or that Jim was missing.
Sometimes he couldn't understand the thick accent of the person who
answered. Sometimes no one answered the phone at all.

By afternoon, Lorraine seemed to be completely in love with Phil, laughing irresistibly at his little jokes and catching his most obscure witticisms and literary quotes.

Jamie was so drawn to Phil, so eager to argue a million questions, that Lorraine tried gently to separate them now and then, but it didn't work, and Phil was clearly impressed with Jamie, and holding forth on everything from the superiority of baroque to the current state of San Francisco politics. Laura and Felix took Christine throughout the whole conservatory, explaining all the various tropical plants to her. Christine loved the orchid trees, and the exotic lobster claw palms. She asked what Father Jim Golding thought about these plants. Did he have a favorite? Did Father Jim Golding like music? She loved to play the piano. She was getting better at it, she hoped, all the time.

Jamie not only looked like Jim, he sounded like Jim. Reuben thought he could see Jim in Christine as well. She was the shy one, the quiet one, the sad one, and Reuben knew it was going to be that way until Jim appeared and took her in his arms. But she was a very clever little girl. Her favorite novel was *Les Misérables*.

"Because she's seen the musical!" said Jamie scornfully.

Christine just smiled. Who was her father's favorite author? she wondered. Did he read the poems of Edgar Allan Poe? What about Emily Dickinson?

Lisa cooked a huge dinner in the guesthouse, and Reuben tried to put on a brave face when he assured them they'd hear some good news from Jim soon. He went out into the night to call Grace, only to confirm there was nothing new. The police had confirmed Jim was on foot when he left the Fairmont Hotel. His apartment had been searched, and the little cashbox under the bed was empty.

"That means he probably has a couple of thousand with him," said Grace over the phone, "and no need to touch his credit cards. Your brother always kept that much, just to be able to help people. If only he knew what was going on. The new rehab fund is up to two million! People are making donations in his name, Reuben! And this is Jim's dream, this rehab shelter right by the church, where he can offer decent rooms to recovering addicts!"

"All right, Mom. I'm going back down to Carmel tomorrow morning, and I'm going to cover the entire area if I have to seek out every single little guesthouse or bed-and-breakfast in existence from Monterey to Carmel Valley."

He texted the last four or five pictures he'd taken of Lorraine and the kids, being most careful not to include the robust and radiant Phil in any of them.

For a long time, he stood outside in the cold darkness looking through the multipaned windows of the guesthouse. Phil was sitting by the fire reading aloud to Jamie and Christine. Lorraine was lying, with a pillow under her head, on the carpet in front of the fire. He heard a footstep in the shadows behind him, and then he caught the scent of Laura, of Laura's hair and Laura's perfume.

"Whatever happens," said Laura, "they're going to be all right."

"That part I know," said Reuben in a thick voice. "They're part of our family." He turned and took her in his arms. "I wish we could be alone tonight in the forest," he said. "I wish we could go off up there into the treetops, and just be us alone."

"Soon," she said. "Soon."

Inside the warm cozy house, Lisa brought in steaming mugs on a tray. Reuben could smell the chocolate. He nuzzled his face into Laura's warm neck.

"You've never told me," she whispered.

"Told you what?"

"How did I do during the Twelfth Night Feast?"

He laughed. "Are you joking?" he said. "Your instincts were perfect." He was thinking, remembering, and he could not bring his human attitudes now really to bear on what had happened. He could recall every second of it; but he could not feel what he'd felt when the Twelfth Night Feast had been in full swing. *These are the monsters, these are the reeking killers who slaughtered a boy and a priest, who poisoned children, who sought to maim and murder Jim.* "You were one of us," he said to Laura. "And there was no male or female, really, or young or old, or lover and lover, or father and son—we were kindred. Just kindred. And you were part of it, as were we all."

She nodded.

"And how was it for you?" he asked. "The first taste of human flesh."

"Natural," she said. "Completely natural. I think I thought too much about it beforehand. And it was simple. That's the word. No conflict involved at all."

It was his turn to nod. He smiled. But it was a slow and sober smile.

The little gathering broke up about eight.

"We turn in early in the country," Phil explained. Lorraine was obviously exhausted. But Jamie wanted to know if he could stay up to watch the eleven o'clock news.

They climbed the hill to the house, and found Felix in his robe and pajamas in the library. He gave Reuben a knowing glance. Phil would change sometime close to midnight. That was the way with new Morphenkinder. And Felix would not let Phil go out into the woods alone.

The next day, the house was in a pleasant little uproar. Felix unveiled his plans to build, with Reuben's approval of course, "a great enclosed swimming pool" off the north side of the conservatory, stretching along the western wall of the house. The architectural plans had already been drawn up. Jamie obviously thought it was the most exciting thing ever, and he stood gazing down over the intricate drawings with wonder, asking if people had done these on a computer or by hand. Of course the enclosure would be a dramatic and harmonious extension of the existing conservatory with lots of white iron, gingerbread, and beautifully shaped windows. And more tropical plants. And Felix was looking into the matter of geothermal heat. Jamie knew about geothermal heat. He'd been reading about it online.

Margon was watching all this with amusement, and Sergei came in with Frank for breakfast and expressed his usual friendly but cynical dismissal of Felix, who was "always building something, always making plans, making plans."

"And Sergei will be the first one," said Berenice to Laura in a polite voice, "to swim the length of that swimming pool fifty times each morning, once it's built."

"Did I say I wouldn't swim in the pool?" asked Sergei. "But what about a heliport out back or a jet runway? Or better yet a harbor down there where we can dock a hundred-foot yacht."

"I never thought of that," said Felix with genuine exuberance. "Reuben. What do you think? Imagine it, a harbor. We could dredge a small harbor, a slip for a yacht."

"I think these are marvelous ideas," said Reuben. "The luxury of an indoor pool, totally connected to the house, is something unimaginably wonderful. Yes, go ahead. Let me get my checkbook."

"Nonsense, dear boy," said Felix. "I'll take care of it, of course. But this is the question. Do we make the northern end of this new enclosure connect with the old household office off the kitchen? Does that room go, so to speak, and do we replace it with a bright dining area at the northern end of the pool?"

A sword pierced Reuben. Marchent had been in that office, working, when her brothers, her murderers, had broken into the house. From there she'd run into the kitchen, where they had viciously and brutally stabbed her to death.

"Yes, let's take that room away," said Reuben. "I mean, let's open that space up into the new enclosure."

Hockan drifted in, distant, but smiling agreeably enough, and deeply polite to Lorraine and the children as he had been all along. He gazed at the blueprints with respectful awe, murmuring something under his breath like "Felix and his dreams."

"We all need dreams," Frank muttered. He had been on the fringes, drinking his coffee in silence.

Hockan and Sergei pulled Reuben aside at the first chance. "When do you want us to start looking for your brother?" Hockan asked with obvious sincerity. "Sergei, Frank, the rest of us. We have ways of finding people that others don't have."

"I know, but where do we look?" asked Reuben. "We could go back down to Carmel and start there." But he had his doubts.

"Say the word," said Sergei.

"If we haven't heard anything by tomorrow, I'm going back down there, with anyone who's willing to help."

That night was Saturday night, and the house was filled with a celebratory atmosphere, with a huge dinner in the main dining room and plenty of extraordinary wines. Everyone was present, and the little Maitland family seemed dazzled by the candlelight, the display of china and silver, the rapid-fire conversation flying back and forth, and the soft piano music floating from the living room where Frank and Berenice traded off playing Mozart.

For the first time since his spectacular arrival, Hockan was genuinely talkative, chatting about beauties of the British Isles with Lorraine and Thibault. He was so attentive and so unfailingly polite that Reuben worried about it a little, that there was a note of sadness and humiliation in it. He couldn't be sure.

Stuart was in awe of Hockan but he didn't trust him. That Reuben could tell.

Hockan is trying very hard, Reuben thought, to be part of all this. For others it's natural. Felix makes it all natural. And Hockan is truly trying to fit in. But he couldn't help notice the suspicion in Berenice's eyes when she studied Hockan. Lisa watched him rather coldly also. Who knew what stories these two had to tell?

Each and every one of the Distinguished Gentlemen and the Distinguished Ladies made it a point to engage the newcomers in conversation, to ask polite yet slightly unusual questions, and to invite them into enduring threads of discussion. Phil and Jamie had called a truce as to certain irreconcilable differences over politics, art, music, literature, and the fate of Western civilization. Christine rolled her eyes when Jamie held forth and Jamie rolled his whenever she shrieked with laughter at one of Sergei's jokes or Felix's playful teasing. But Reuben detected a deep anxiety behind Lorraine's unfailingly pleasant speech and expression. And he himself was both happy and miserable, happier perhaps than ever in his life, as if his life now was a staircase of ever-escalating happinesses, while at the same time he was so frightened for Jim, he could scarcely bear it.

Felix rose to make a final toast.

"Tonight, dear ladies and gentlemen, and beloved children," he said, his glass raised. "This is the very end of the Christmas season.

Tomorrow, Sunday, will be the official end with the Church of Rome celebrating the Feast of the Baptism of Jesus Christ. Then the church calendar will begin on Monday what has always been called so solemnly and beautifully 'Ordinary Time.' And we must reflect tonight on what Christmas has meant to us."

"Hear, hear," said Sergei, "and we shall all reflect on this as deeply and briefly and concisely as possible."

"Oh, let Felix go on," said Hockan. "If Felix finishes by tomorrow night at midnight when 'Ordinary Time' begins, we should count ourselves lucky."

"Or are we going to get another toast tomorrow night," asked Thibault, "as the last few hours of the Christmas season slip through our fingers!"

"Maybe what this house needs is a public address system," Sergei suggested. "And Felix could broadcast at regular intervals."

"And anyone turning off his PA system would be arrested," said Stuart, "and confined to the dungeons beneath us."

"And we should print out the entire liturgical calendar," said Sergei, "and post it on the kitchen wall."

Felix laughed good-naturedly. He was absolutely undeterred.

"And I must say," he went on, raising his glass once more, "that this, our first Christmas season at Nideck Point, has been exceptional. We have given gifts and received gifts that we could not possibly have anticipated. Our old and dear friend Hockan is once again with us. And Jamie, Christine, and Lorraine, you come to us as gifts—and you too, Berenice—gifts to our beloved Reuben and his beloved father Philip, and to our entire household. We salute you. We welcome you."

Clapping, cheering, with embraces and kisses for Lorraine and Jamie and Christine.

"And a prayer for James," said Felix lastly. "That James will come home safely very very soon."

And then the company broke up for dessert and coffee buffet style in the great front room.

An hour or so later, just about everyone had gone off to sleep, read, watch TV, who knows what? And the house suddenly seemed dark and empty, though its fires roared as always. Felix came to find Reuben in the library, where Reuben was at the desk computer searching for the numerous motels and guesthouses he meant to visit personally tomorrow.

"Don't worry about your brother," said Felix with an easy smile.

"And what in the world makes you say that?" Reuben asked gently. "For you—of all my beloved friends—never say anything that doesn't mean something."

"I know he will be all right," said Felix. There was a light in his dark eyes. "I simply know. I have a feeling." He drank the last of his wine and put the glass on the edge of the desk. "I have a feeling," he said again. "I can't say more, but I know your brother is all right now. And whatever happens when he knows about the children, well, he will be all right. And they are infinitely better off just now than they ever were before, without the loving knowledge and support of your family."

Reuben only smiled. He couldn't quite bring himself to answer.

"Well good night, dear boy," said Felix. "And I should take this glass to the kitchen, shouldn't I? I am so annoyed when people litter this house with cups and glasses!"

"And things go well with my father in the woods?"

"Splendidly," said Felix. "But it's good he had the Twelfth Night Feast. Morphenkinder by instinct want to hunt humans. I don't think the forest is appreciated until that innate desire has seen some fulfillment."

"Thank you, Felix," Reuben said. "Thank you for everything."

"Not at all. Don't say another word," said Felix. "I think I'll walk down the hill and visit with your father."

For a very long time, Reuben sat there, thinking, reflecting. Then he brought up a new blank page in his word processing program, and began to type.

"I died at the age of 23, in the season of the year which the church calls 'Ordinary Time,'" he wrote. "And as we come once again to 'Ordinary Time,' I want to write the story of my life since that moment."

And for another hour he wrote, stopping only now and then for a moment or two, until finally he had filled some fifteen double-spaced pages. "And so I went from being ordinary, terribly ordinary, shamefully ordinary—out of 'Ordinary Time'—into a world of exceptional expectations and revelations where miracles abound. And though my place has been given me in this new realm, my future is in my hands, and must be shaped by me with infinitely more care and thought than I ever gave before to my actions."

He broke off finally, and stared at the distant window with its inevitable silver spatters of rain. And he thought with a sigh, Well, that didn't take my mind off anything. And if he's dead somewhere on a motel room floor, well, I know I killed him. I killed him. I killed his soul before I killed his body. And he's the first casualty among my family of what I have become. And if I ever breathe this secret to another living being who is not one of us, well, I will probably become the murderer of that one too. And that cannot ever happen.

If he didn't stop thinking about it he'd go crazy. Better to go upstairs and pack a bag for tomorrow.

Three a.m.

Something had awakened him.

He turned over and reached for his iPhone.

E-mail from Jim.

He sat up, quickly scrolling through the writing.

"Back at my apartment. Just got in. Can I see you tomorrow after nine a.m. Mass at St. Francis? And thank you for sending Elthram. God only knows how he found me, but until he tapped on my window, I had no idea anybody was looking for me!"

32

Mass was well under way when Reuben slid into the third pew.

He'd dropped off Lorraine and the children with his mother, doing his best to fend off interrogation as to why Phil had not come down with them, and promising to bring Jim to the house on Russian Hill just as soon as he possibly could.

He was so relieved as he watched Jim on the altar that he almost started to cry.

Jim wore his splendid white and gold vestments for the special Feast of the Baptism of Our Lord, and he seemed utterly calm as he went through the liturgy, coming at last to the sermon, and stepping down to walk back and forth before the pews as he spoke. His small clip-on mike amplified his voice perfectly, as always, in the vast crowded church. Only a deep redness in his eyes and a distinct paleness to his face revealed that the past few days might have been a trial.

At once he took up the very theme that Felix had mentioned the night before.

This was, though many did not know it, the last day of the Christmas season and tomorrow would be the first day of what the church so poetically called "Ordinary Time."

"What is a baptism?" he asked the congregation. "What was baptism for Our Blessed Lord? He was sinless, was He not, so He didn't need to be baptized. But He did it for us, didn't He? To set an example, just as His entire life on earth was an example—from His birth amongst us as a baby, through boyhood and manhood amongst us, until He died as each and every one of us dies, to His resurrection from the dead. No, He didn't need to be baptized. But it was a turning point for Him, a rebirth, the end of His private life and the beginning of His ministry, and He went out into the wilderness to confront the temptation of Satan as a 'new' being. Okay, so what is a turning point? What is the meaning of rebirth or renewal? How many times do we experience this in our own lives?"

At once he went into the theme of Christmas, of Midwinter, and of all the age-old ways in which the Church and people of all nations in the West celebrate the Feast of Christmas.

"You know, for centuries, we've been criticized for grafting our sacred feast on a pagan holiday," Jim said. "I'm sure you've heard the charges. Nobody knows the actual day on which Christ was born. But December twenty-fifth was a great feast to the pagans of the ancient world, the day when the sun was at its lowest ebb and people would gather in the fields, in the villages, and in the depths of the forest to beg for the sun to come back to us at full strength, for the days to lengthen once more. And for warmth to return to the world, melting the deadly snows of winter, and gently nourishing the crops of the field once again.

"Well, I think it was a stroke of genius to put these two feasts together," said Jim. "Christ, born into this world, is a magnificent sign of transformation—of complete renewal, renewal of the physical world and the renewal of our souls."

It was remarkably—though not surprisingly—like what Felix had said about Christmas and Midwinter, and Reuben loved it. He was lulled by Jim's voice as with ease and authority his brother went on talking about the capacity for renewal being the very greatest gift we have been given in this life.

"Think about it for a minute," Jim insisted. He stopped with his arms slightly raised, hands gently appealing to the congregation. "Think about what it means to renew, to repent, to start all over again. We human beings always have that capacity. No matter how badly we stumble, we can get up and try again. No matter how miserably we fail ourselves and God and those around us, we can get up and start all over again.

"There is no midwinter so cold and so dark that we can't reach for the shining light with both hands."

He paused for a moment as if he had to check his own emotions, and then he resumed slowly. walking up and down and speaking again.

"That's the meaning of all the candles of Christmas," he said, "the bright electric lights on our Christmas trees. It's the meaning of all the celebrations throughout the season, that we have the hope always and forever of being better than we are, of triumphing over the darkness that might have defeated us in the past, and realizing a brilliance never imagined before."

He paused again, his eyes moving over the congregation, and when he saw Reuben sitting there looking at him, there was a faint flicker in his eyes of recognition, but then he went on.

"Well, I'm not going to hold you here in the pews with a long exhortation to repentance. We all need to reflect every day of our lives on what we are, what we're doing, what we ought to do. We need to make that part of the fabric of our lives. And that's why I want to talk now about the curious phrase in the church calendar, 'Ordinary Time.' There is a simplicity and brilliance to that title. When I was a boy and I first heard it, I loved it: 'This is the first day of "Ordinary Time."' But the reason I love it is that every season, every celebration, every defeat, and every hope and aspiration that we have is rooted in time, dependent on time, revealed to us in time.

"We don't think about that enough. We spend too much time cursing time—time waits for no man, time will tell, oh, the ravages of time, time flies! We don't think about the gift of time. Time gives us the chance to make mistakes and correct them, to regenerate, to grow. Time gives us the chance to forgive, to restore, to do better than we have ever done in the past. Time gives us the chance to be sorry when we fail and the chance to try to discover in ourselves a new heart."

His voice had grown soft with emotion, and pausing again, he faced the congregation and said, "And so with the Christmas cribs dismantled, and all the Christmas trees taken down and the lights packed again in the attic, we find ourselves, at the end of this Christmas season and once again in the glorious miracle—I mean the pure and glorious miracle—of 'Ordinary Time.' How we use this time means everything. Will we take the opportunity to transform ourselves, to admit our hideous blunders, and to become, against all odds, the people of our dreams? That's what it's about, right?—becoming the people of our dreams."

Now when he stopped, he appeared to be reflecting, and slightly undecided, and then he went on.

"There was a point in my life when I wasn't the man I wanted to be. I did something unspeakably cruel to another human being. And very recently I found myself in the grip of a temptation to be cruel once again. I succumbed to that temptation. I lost my battle with anger, and with rage. I lost my battle with love, with the solemn and inescapable commandment: *Thou shalt love!*

"But this morning, as I stand here, I'm grateful with all my heart that time is once more stretching out before me, providing me again with the chance to somehow—*somehow*—make amends for the things I've done. God puts in our path so many opportunities for that, doesn't He?—so many people out there who need so much from each and every one of us. He gives us people to help, people to serve, people to embrace, people to comfort, people to love. As long as I live and breathe, I am surrounded by these limitless opportunities, blessed by them on all sides. So I come away from Christmas—and that great shining banquet of riches—thankful once more for the absolute miracle of 'Ordinary Time.' "

The sermon was over; the service moved on. Reuben sat there with his eyes closed, offering his prayers of thanks. He's whole again, he's here again, he's my brother, he thought. And opening his eyes, he let the intense colors of the church with its grand Tuscan murals and painted saints penetrate him and warm his soul. I don't know what the hell I believe, he thought. But I am grateful, grateful that he is on that altar again.

When Communion time came, he slipped out of the pew and went outside to the fresh cold air of the courtyard to wait for Jim.

Very soon the congregation began streaming out, and finally his brother appeared in his long white and gold chasuble, to clasp hands, and give greetings and to accept thanks.

Clearly Jim saw Reuben waiting patiently for him, but he did not rush. And it was a good twenty minutes or more before they were finally alone. The courtyard was cold and wet but Reuben didn't care.

Jim was smiling radiantly when Reuben embraced him.

"I'm so glad you could come," he said. "You know when I e-mailed you, well, I forget it takes a full four hours for you to get down here. I forget you can't hop on a monorail and doze till you arrive."

"Are you kidding?" said Reuben. "We were so worried about you!"

"But tell me, how in the world did Elthram find me?" Jim asked. "I was in the middle of the woods outside Carmel Valley. I was in a little Buddhist retreat place that doesn't even have a phone."

"Well, someday I'll fill you in on Elthram," said Reuben. "Right now, I'm just so glad you're back I can't tell you. And if you think Mom was out of her mind, well, what do you think was going on in my head?"

"That's what Elthram said. You were so worried. I should have figured. But Reuben, I needed that time to think."

"I know you did, and I know you're all right. The minute I sat down in the pew in there, I knew you were all right. That's all anybody wanted to know, that you're all right."

"I'm all right, Reuben," he said. "But I'm going to be leaving the priesthood." He said it simply, without emotion or drama. "That is inevitable now."

"No—."

"Wait. Hear me out before you begin objecting. Nobody will ever know the full reason why, but you know why, and I want you to keep that secret for me as I've kept yours."

"Jim—."

"Reuben, a man cannot be a murderer and a priest," he said. His tone was patient and resigned. "That is simply not possible. Now years ago, I was accepted in spite of what I did to Lorraine, as I told you. But I was a drunkard when I beat Lorraine. I had that excuse. Not a very good excuse, mind you, in fact, it was an appalling excuse, but still a form of excuse. It hadn't been cold-blooded murder, what I did to that child. It was another kind of sin, but not cold-blooded killing, no." He paused. He lowered his voice as he leaned closer to Reuben. "But this time I had no excuse, Reuben. I asked you to kill Fulton Blankenship and his cohorts; I told you where to find him; I provided you with a map."

"Jim, you are not a killer, and these men——."

"Stop. Now look. We have to go see Mom. And I have to somehow endure all her questions about where I've been. Now you must promise me: don't say a word to her about this ever as long as you live. I keep your secret as I'm bound to do, sworn to do, and you must keep mine."

"Of course," Reuben said. "This goes without saying!"

"I'm going to see the archbishop this week and explain why I'm asking to leave. And when the time comes the official announcement will be made. I cannot tell him the full story of how Blankenship and company departed this world, but I don't have to. I only have to tell him what I myself willed to happen and that I asked others to make it happen. And beyond that, I will say nothing more. I can tell him that I sent people to murder Fulton Blankenship and they weren't officers of the law. And when I do, I'll tell him this in Confession, binding him to keep the circumstances secret, but to act upon the information as he sees fit."

Reuben sighed. "Jim, they had marked you for death. They might have killed your family!"

"I know that, Reuben," he said. "I'm not as hard on myself as you might think. I saw that wounded priest being carried out of my apartment on a stretcher. And I'd just seen the corpse of the boy they'd killed. I'm no saint, Reuben, I told you that. But I'm not a liar either."

"And what if the archbishop gets carried away, thinks you hired some mercenaries or something and he calls the police?"

"He won't do that," Jim said. "I'll handle it. I'll tell the truth. But never the whole truth. I know what I have to do." He smiled. In fact, his entire manner was almost cheerful and certainly resigned. "But if by some miracle he allows me to stay, well, then, I'll stay. That's what I want, to stay, to work right here as I've been doing for years, to make amends here. But I don't think that's going to happen, Reuben. And I don't think it should."

Suddenly he stopped and reached beneath his chasuble for his phone. "That's Mom calling. Listen, come into the sacristy with me while I change. We've got to get over there. And let me tell you what I plan to do."

They hurried back into the church and up through the nave and into the back sacristy, where Jim quickly peeled off his vestments, and put on a fresh clean white shirt. Then came the Roman collar with the black clerical shirtfront and his always impeccably pressed black coat.

"I'll tell you what I'm thinking, Reuben," he was saying. "I'm thinking that perhaps I can somehow quietly run this rehab center here as a layman. I don't know if you know about the rehab center."

"Everybody knows about it, Jim," said Reuben. "Two million dollars in donations so far, probably more."

"Yes, well, if I can't be the steward of this project, there are others. After all, I don't deserve to be the steward of it and if the archbishop sends me away from this parish, well, that's what I deserve. So what I'm thinking is, I'm thinking that maybe with some donations from you perhaps, little brother, and from Mom and Dad, who knows, and maybe from Felix too perhaps, maybe I can start a Delancey Street–type of operation of my own."

"Absolutely," said Reuben. "That's entirely possible. Jim, that might be better than anything."

Jim paused, looking into Reuben's eyes. And only then did Reuben sense the pain there, just the faintest glimpse of the pain Jim was feeling at leaving the priesthood.

"I'm sorry," Reuben whispered. "I didn't mean to make it sound so simple."

Jim swallowed, and forced a little accepting smile. He put his hand on Reuben's hand as if to say, It is all right.

"I want to keep working with addicts and alcoholics, you know that," Jim said.

As they walked back through the church, he went on talking about it, about the months he'd spent working at Delancey Street, studying their famous program, and about what he would do if he did get to be captain of his own little ship. They walked through the courtyard and out the gate.

"But you know, Mom and Dad are going to take it hard if you leave the priesthood," said Reuben.

"You think so? When have Mom and Dad ever been proud of me for becoming a priest?"

"Maybe you're right about that," Reuben mumbled. "But I've always been proud of you and so was Grandfather Spangler. And I'll be proud of you no matter what you do."

"Look, I'm thinking I can volunteer for a while at Delancey Street again, or somewhere. There is so much opportunity, and this is all going to take time—."

They were almost to Reuben's car, when Reuben put his hands up and demanded to be heard.

"Now just wait a minute!" he said. "You're telling me that after all these years, you're just going to be shoveled out of the priesthood because you told me about that scum, that unspeakable scum, that scum that murdered that young priest, that scum that murdered the kid at the Hilton, that scum that targeted you for death . . ."

"Oh, come on, Reuben," he said. "You know what I did. I'm not you. I don't have some secret biological metamorphosis to blame for what I am! I suborned murder as the man that I am."

Reuben went silent. Frustrated. Angry.

"And what if I do it again?" Jim whispered.

Reuben shook his head.

"What about the next time that some unspeakable scum stalks these streets killing kids and threatening me for interfering?"

"Well, what was all that in there about repentance, renewal, the miracle of time?"

"Reuben, repentance begins with acceptance of what one has done. And for a priest it begins with Confession. I have already done that part with my confessor, but now the archbishop must know what I have done."

"Yes, but what if nobody . . . oh, hell, I don't know what I'm saying, for God's sake. Jim, did you talk to Mom this morning?"

"No, and I'm not looking forward to it now. She's furious with me for disappearing. That's why I'm counting on you to come with me and somehow steer the conversation to Celeste and the baby and anything else you can think of, please."

Reuben was silent for a moment. Then he unlocked the Porsche and walked around to the driver's side.

Jim piled in beside him. He went on again with that same easy energy talking about how he was resigned. "It's like any failure, Reuben. It's an opportunity—all failures are opportunities—and I have to see it that way."

"Well, you are going to be facing a slightly more complex and interesting future than you realize," said Reuben.

"And why is that?" he asked. "Hey, slow down, will you? You drive this thing like a race car driver."

Reuben let up on the gas, but it was Sunday morning, and the usually crowded streets were relatively clear.

"Well, what do you mean?" asked Jim. "Mom and Dad aren't getting a divorce, are they? Speak!"

Reuben was thinking, thinking just how to play it, just which way he should go. He could feel his iPhone throbbing in his coat pocket, but he ignored it. He was thinking about Christine, about those precious moments to come when she would lay eyes on Jim and Jim would lay eyes on her. She would be so vulnerable in those moments, but this man was not going to let her down. And Jamie, Jamie would walk up to his father just as he walked up to Reuben and extend his hand. Reuben sighed.

"Are we speaking to each other?" asked Jim. "What are you not telling me!"

The car was now speeding up Russian Hill.

"You didn't kill Lorraine's pregnancy," Reuben said.

"What are you talking about?" And then, "How do you know!"

"She was at the Christmas gala," said Reuben.

"Damn it, I *thought* I saw her!" Jim said. "I thought I did, and I looked everywhere for her and I couldn't find her again. You mean you've spoken to her? How long have you known she was here?"

"She's at Mom's waiting for you now."

Reuben resolved not to say another word.

"Are you telling me that she's there and that I have a child?" Jim demanded. He flushed red. "Is that what you're saying? Reuben, talk to me. You mean I didn't kill the baby! Are you saying I have a child?"

He hit Reuben with another twenty questions, but Reuben said not a word. At last he slid into the narrow driveway of the Russian Hill house and cut the ignition.

He looked at Jim.

"I'm not going in with you," he said. "This is your moment. And I don't have to tell you that there are people depending on you in there, people eagerly waiting for you—and that they'll be watching you, observing your most subtle facial expressions, your voice, whether you put your arms out—or not."

Jim was speechless.

"I know you can handle it," said Reuben. "And I know this too. This is the best gift Christmas could have given you. And all the rest can be worked out, somehow—all worked out . . . in 'Ordinary Time.' "

Jim was in shock.

"Go on," said Reuben. "Get out and go in."

Jim didn't move.

"And let me tell you one last thing," said Reuben. "You're no killer, Jim. You're no murderer. Blankenship was a killer, and so were his lackeys. You know they were. I'm a killer, Jim. You know that. And you know those bloody bastards were after you. And who knows better than you the full extent of what they did and what they intended to do? And you made the best choice that you could. But go on now. You've given hostages to fortune, and they will definitely be part of however you work this out."

Reuben reached over and unlatched the door for him.

"Get out and go in," he said.

Grace appeared at the top of the front steps. She was in her green scrubs, and her red hair was loose over her shoulders, and her face was shining with irrepressible happiness. She waved enthusiastically as if she were welcoming a homecoming ship.

Jim finally climbed out of the car. He stared at Reuben and then at his mother.

Reuben sat there for a moment watching Jim slowly climb the steps towards Grace. How straight and poised he looked, his short brown hair as always perfectly combed, his black clerical attire so sober and formal.

Reuben wanted with all his heart to go up there with him, to be with Jim when he laid eyes on Lorraine and Jamie and Christine, but he couldn't. This was truly Jim's moment, as he had said. It would do no good for Reuben to be standing there, a dark inescapable reminder to Jim of all that they shared that no one else could ever share.

He fired up the Porsche and drove away, heading home to Nideck Point.

33

ELEVEN P.M. at Nideck Point. The house was quiet, the fires out. Laura had long ago gone into the forest with Berenice. Felix and Phil had come back from the forest early and Felix had gone up to bed.

Reuben walked down the hill alone in the soft soundless rain. He approached the dimly lighted guesthouse, hoping, praying his father might be awake, that they might sit and talk.

He felt restless, slightly hungry, with a little ache in his heart.

He knew all was well in San Francisco. He'd never doubted that it would be well. Lorraine and the children were staying with Grace until the end of the week. Grace had not been able to put into words how well things had gone. But the many pictures told the story, coming in over the late afternoon. The whole family at lunch, including the ecstatic father flanked by his children and a happy Lorraine beside a cheerful and relaxed Celeste. Then there was little Christine sitting beside her beaming father by the fireplace. Grace with both her grandchildren. And Jamie in front of the same fireplace, standing straight and tall for the inevitable record beside his proud dad.

No one ventured to speculate as to where Jim's future would take him. But Reuben had every confidence that Jim was in possession of a rare and priceless treasure that would smooth his path no matter which way he had to go.

And Reuben was restless, and alone.

As he drew closer to the little guesthouse, he realized there were two figures inside, only dimly illuminated by the dying fire. One was his father, naked and barefoot, and the other was Lisa in one of her characteristic dark dresses with lace at the throat.

His father was embracing Lisa, kissing her, kissing her as passionately as Reuben had ever seen a man kiss a woman. Reuben waited,
fascinated, knowing he should not remain there, that he should look
away but he did not. How healthy, how strong was this man who was
his father, and how pliant and yielding seemed the figure of Lisa, as
Phil pulled down her long hair.

As Reuben watched, the two left the dying light of the fire and
moved towards the spiral stairs to the attic above. A gust of rain hit the
large multipaned windows. The icy wind from the sea stole through
the rattling branches and the newly fallen leaves that littered the terrace and the path.

Reuben felt suddenly crestfallen and strangely disturbed. He was
happy for Phil. He knew his father's time with his mother was over.
He had realized that quite some time ago. Yet it still saddened him to
realize it with such sharpness, and he felt suddenly extremely alone.
He knew in his heart of hearts that Lisa was a male, not a female, no
matter how elaborate her accoutrements, and that faintly amused him
and fascinated him—how little difference it seemed to make. *There is
no normal life. There is only life.*

He stood very still in the darkness, realizing he was cold and wet
and his shoes were wet through, and that he ought to go back up the
hill. He looked up at the dark trees around him, at the pines soaring above the scrub oaks, at the dark tortured shapes of the Monterey cypress forever grasping in desperation for what they would never
reach, and he felt a strange longing to shed his clothes and to move off
into the forest alone—to break out of the shell of this all too human
discomfort into a different and savage realm.

Quite suddenly, he heard a rush of sounds near him, faint, crackling, rustling, and then the touch of hot breath on his neck. He knew
the claws that were clutching his shoulders, and the teeth pulling at his
shirt collar.

"Yes," he whispered, "darling dear. Rip it off."

In a moment he'd turned and given himself up to her, feeling her
fur sealed against him as she pulled away the shirt and jacket like so

much wrapping paper on a gift. He kicked off his shoes as she ripped his trousers away. His shredded underwear fell away as her paws moved over his naked chest and legs.

He held off the change, even though he was chilled to the bone, his hands running through her mane and fur roughly, and loving the feel of her tongue against his naked face. He could hear her laughing, a deep vibrant laugh.

She lifted him off his feet with her left arm, and sprang off down the hill, and into the thick of the uncleared forest and then she started up into the trees. He had to hold on to her with both arms as she used both of hers. He was laughing like a kid. He locked his legs around her, loving the feel of her easy power as she climbed higher and higher into the redwoods, into the pines. From tree to tree, she ventured on. He didn't dare to look down, but he couldn't see well in the darkness anyway, not till he changed, and he was holding it off with all his strength.

"And the beast saw beauty," she growled against his ear, "and carried him away with all her might and main."

He'd never laughed this hard in his life. He kissed the soft silky fur of her face. "Wicked beast," he said. The pringling would not stop. He couldn't fight the change now; the change was rampant. And she was laughing, lapping him with her tongue as if this would hasten the metamorphosis. And maybe it did.

She leapt down, down through the groaning and snapping branches and they fell together softly on the damp leafy earth. He was in full wolf coat now and they wrestled with one another, finally embracing side by side, face to face, and his organ battered against her as she teased him until finally she let him in.

This was who he was; this was what he wanted; this was what he'd longed for, and he did not know now why he had denied himself this for so long. All the victories and defeats of the human world were far away.

They lay together silently for a long while, and then he leapt up, urging her to follow him and they took to the trees again. Rapidly they moved through the wet foliage towards the sleeping town of Nideck.

Now and then they fed on the wild things, the tiny scurrying abundant life of the treetops, and now and then they dropped to lap the water from shimmering pools. But mostly they traveled the canopy until they had come to the edge of the sleeping town.

Far down below were the gleaming rooftops, the bright yellow sparkle of occasional streetlamps, the lingering smell of oak fires in the air. Reuben could easily make out the dark rectangle of the old cemetery, and even the glint of light on the wet headstones. He could see the small shimmering roof of the Nideck crypt there, and beyond the slumbering Victorian houses, some with the softest lights burning still within.

He and Laura embraced one another, a great heavy branch easily supporting them. He felt fearless, as if nothing in the world could hurt them, and the town below with its faint streak of twinkling lights along the main street seemed at peace.

O little town of Bethlehem, how still we see thee lie. Above thy deep and dreamless sleep the silent stars go by.

"Maybe they're all safe somewhere," Laura said against his chest, "all the lost children of the world, loved, unloved, young and old. Maybe they are safe, or they will be safe, somehow, somewhere—even my children somewhere, safe and not alone."

"Yes, I do believe that," he said softly, "with all my heart."

He was content for them to remain there forever as the rain fell gently around them.

"Listen, do you hear that?" she said.

Below, in the little town, a clock was solemnly chiming the hour of twelve.

"Yes," he said at once picturing a polished hallway, a quiet parlor, a carpeted stair. "And Christmas is indeed complete upon the midnight," he whispered to her, "and 'Ordinary Time' has begun."

All the houses looked to him like toy houses, and he heard the chorus of the woods rise around him, his eyes closed, his hearing sharpening, probing over greater and greater distances until it seemed to him all the world sang. All the world was filled with falling rain.

"Listen to it," he said in her ear. "It's as if the forest is praying, as if the earth is praying, as if prayers are rising to heaven off every shimmering leaf and branch."

"Why are we so sad?" she asked. How tender her voice sounded, even deepened and roughened as it was.

"Because we're moving away from them down there," he said. "And we know it. And my son when he comes into this world isn't going to change that. And there is nothing we can do to change it. Can a Morphenkind shed tears?"

"Yes, we can shed tears," she answered. "I know we can, because I have. And you're right. We're moving away from them, all of them, and we're moving ever deeper into our own story and maybe that is as it should be. Felix has done all he can to help us, but we're moving so rapidly away from them, what can we do?"

He thought about his little boy, that tiny slumbering creature in Celeste's womb, that tender hostage to fortune that was his very own. Would he grow up in that cheerful house on Russian Hill with Jamie and Christine? Would he know the wholesome safety and happiness there that Reuben had long ago trusted so completely? It seemed so very distant suddenly, so bound up with sadness, with grief.

His mother was young yet, vital, a woman in her prime. And when Celeste entrusted the newborn infant to her, would Lorraine be there to also take it in her arms? He saw his brother vividly in the picture that began to glow ever more brightly, yet distantly, in his mind. He heard Jim's words from the sermon at the altar steps: *So I come away from Christmas—and that great shining banquet of riches—thankful once more for the absolute miracle of "Ordinary Time."*

"I love you, darling dear," he said to Laura.

"And I love you, my beautiful one," she answered. "What would the Wolf Gift be to me without you?"

THE END

June 22, 2012
February 4, 2013
Palm Desert, California